QUICKSILVER

Elise Noble

Published by Undercover Publishing Limited

ISBN: 978-1-910954-94-2

Edited by Nikki Menges, NAM Editorial

Cover design by Abigail Sins

www.undercover-publishing.com

www.elise-noble.com

Who wants to live forever?
- *Freddie Mercury*

CHAPTER 1 - CORA

HELP ME.

TWO little words spoken in a breathless whisper before the line went dead.

Two little words from beyond the grave.

Two little words that would lead me to hell.

If only I'd known how things would turn out, perhaps I'd have acted differently. Walked a little slower from the kitchen to the living room so I missed the call. Chalked it up to a wrong number. Convinced myself that I'd misheard.

But I didn't. I knew who'd called, not so much from the words themselves but from the tiny squeak that came afterwards, right before she hung up.

Isabella.

I'd heard her make that sound a hundred times before, every time she got caught doing something she shouldn't. Taking *mecatos* from the kitchen as a seven-year-old. Borrowing my make-up when she hit her teens. And later, in her difficult phase, stealing from her mama's purse.

The problem now?

I'd attended Isabella's funeral three weeks ago.

And now her mama walked into the living room.

"Cora, are you okay? You look as if you've seen a ghost."

Not seen one; heard one. But I couldn't tell Dores Morales that. No way. She'd always been nervy, highly strung, much like Izzy herself, and it only got worse after Izzy's father died. After losing Izzy as well, Dores had barely kept herself together, and the last thing I wanted to do was give her false hope that her daughter was still alive. Or worse, send her further into the pit of despair by suggesting Izzy was in trouble.

"I'm fine. Is it five o'clock already? I'll be late for work."

"What time will you be back?"

She never used to ask, not when Izzy was alive. But now she called, worried, if I was more than five minutes late.

"My lesson ends at eight, so maybe half past? I'll message you when I leave; I promise."

"You're coming straight home? Your grandma's making bandeja paisa."

Grandma always made bandeja paisa. A huge platter of food with beans, rice, pork, chorizo, fried egg, avocado, arepa... The list went on. Usually, I ran every day, or went to the gym at least, but since Izzy died, I'd spent all my spare time at home and now half of my clothes didn't fit anymore.

I gave Dores a quick hug. "Yes, I'm coming straight home."

In my bedroom, I pulled on a pair of jeans and a pale pink top. Pumps or ballet flats? Flats were more comfortable, but after dating a guy who spent six months complaining I was too tall, I'd bought three new pairs of high heels when we split up. I'd bumped into him on the odd occasion since, and each time, I'd looked down on him from four inches above. *Screw you.* I picked the pumps.

As usual, traffic in Medellín was at a standstill, and I choked on the thick cloud of exhaust fumes that hung in the air as I hurried along the street towards the Metro. And as I walked, I began to second-guess myself. What if I *had* been mistaken? Or could one of the neighbourhood kids have been playing a sick joke?

I quickly discounted that idea. The call had come on the house phone, and it was only by luck that I'd picked up rather than my grandma. The local children loved Marisol da Silva. She'd babysat most of them over the years, and none of them would want to hurt her.

Could it really be possible? Was Izzy still alive? All they'd found of her was a single hand, too decomposed for fingerprints, but Izzy's favourite ring had been on the middle finger. I'd identified it myself. A created white sapphire I'd given her on her eighteenth birthday —diamonds were a little out of my price range—flanked by amethysts and inscribed on the inside with two joined hands and our initials to show we'd always be friends, no matter how much she tested me. And back then, she *had* tested me. Isabella Morales had gone wild between the ages of sixteen and nineteen, but over the last year, she'd settled down and followed in her mother's footsteps by going to nursing school.

I'd never given up on her then, and with a sinking feeling, I realised I couldn't give up on her now. Not if there was the slightest chance she was still alive, no matter how crazy that may seem.

But first, I needed to earn some money. Izzy had worked part-time as a waitress, so we were already one income down in our little household, and although my brother would send cash if we needed it, I hated to ask.

Rafael had his own life, one he didn't share with us anymore, and he was as reliable as a politician's promise when it came to visiting.

Did I sound bitter? Perhaps that's because I was. When my brother split aged sixteen, I lost a quarter of my tiny family, and although I knew that deep down he still cared, pesos made a poor substitute for his presence.

You're probably wondering about my strange living arrangements, aren't you? What slammed the da Silva and Morales families together eleven years ago? Tragedy. It was tragedy. None of us had anybody else left, so together, we'd moved from the wilds of the Amazonian region to Medellín for a fresh start in the tiny three-room home we were able to afford at the time.

Which was another reason I had to get to the bottom of what happened to Izzy. My grandma may have always been the strong, level-headed one, but when we came to the city, she was already in her sixties and confined to a wheelchair. Dores had worked like an ox to feed us all. If Izzy was out there, I owed it to Dores to find her daughter.

With that daunting thought, I boarded the Metro. I'd worked as an English tutor for five years now, with some translation work on the side. More and more US ex-pats were moving to Medellín, attracted by the good weather and low cost of living, and not all of them spoke Spanish. My boss, Juan, had started his language school to take advantage of the influx of US dollars, and I'd been one of his first recruits.

Occasionally, I ended up with a client who mistakenly thought he could buy my affections as well as my linguistic expertise, but Juan was always quick to reassign me when that happened. He passed those assholes to Rodrigo, who weighed two hundred pounds and spent his spare time wrestling. Other than those rare cases, I enjoyed my job.

Take this evening's clients, for example. Stefan and Esther. I'd been teaching them for over a year, starting off with an intensive six-week course when they first arrived in the city, and although they still insisted on paying me, our sessions had turned into more of a social event than work. Esther made snacks or occasionally dinner, something else that didn't help my expanding waistline one little bit. Now that Izzy was gone, Stefan and Esther were the closest thing to friends I had.

"Hey! Come on in."

Esther gave me a hug before I could walk through the door. Stefan followed up with a kiss on each cheek, and I trailed them into the dining room, where Esther had already set out banana bread and sweet-potato cake. She loved to cook dishes from Haiti, where she was born, and she'd even started teaching me basic French Creole. Stefan, on the other hand, preferred Key lime pie and sweet tea from his home state of Florida, although Esther had once confided that his favourite recipe for pie took ages to make, so he had to earn it.

"How have you been?" Esther asked in Spanish.

Terrible. Awful. And things had only gotten worse with that phone call. But I didn't want to cast a shadow over tonight's lesson. As Juan always said, happy clients were repeat clients.

"Things have been okay. How was your vacation?"

They'd just got back from a month-long tour of

Europe, a trip they'd been looking forward to for as long as I'd known them. A late honeymoon, Esther said. Two years late.

"Amazing! We saw Buckingham Palace and climbed the Eiffel Tower and visited the Colosseum and drank far too much schnapps in Germany." She held out a shiny paper bag. "Here, we got you a gift."

I unwrapped the layers of pink tissue paper and found a hair clip, silver studded with colourful gems. I'd always worn my hair long, so it was a perfect choice, and one that necessitated another hug.

"Thank you so much. Is there anything in particular you want to work on today?"

"When we were in Spain, I picked up a pile of brochures, but I'm not sure of some of the words. Can we look through them?"

"Tell her about the movie," Stefan said.

"We watched *El Secreto de sus Ojos* while we were in Seville. Have you seen it?"

"I loved that movie!"

And so did Izzy. We'd watched it together a few years ago, complete with a giant platter of empanadas and Grandma's sweet corn arepas.

"There were some parts I didn't understand. Could we watch them together so you can help translate?"

"Of course."

But as with so many things in life, our plans got derailed, and it was entirely my fault.

"Are you sure you're okay?" Esther asked as I sniffled for the tenth time. "Do you want a tissue?"

"I'm f-f-fine."

What was wrong with me? I didn't cry at movies. I barely cried at all. Even at Izzy's funeral, I'd stayed dry-eyed while Dores wept.

Stefan looked away while Esther squashed next to me on the couch and handed me a wad of tissues.

"I'm so sorry," I mumbled. "It's a sad movie."

"But we've barely started watching it." She leaned back to study me for a moment. "Cora, did something happen while we were away? Man trouble? Is your grandma okay?"

"Isabella. Izzy...died."

Now the tears came thick and fast, and I'd never been so embarrassed in my life. *Get a grip, Corazon.*

"*The* Isabella? The girl who's practically your sister?"

I managed to nod. They'd met Izzy when she threw me a twenty-second birthday party six months ago, and since it was a surprise, she'd just scrolled through my phone and invited everyone in my contacts list. All forty-seven people. About half turned up, although the plumber I'd hired to replace the kitchen tap last year looked kind of confused to be there.

"Ohmigosh. We only bumped into her a week before we left, didn't we, Stefan?"

He nodded.

"What happened? I mean, sorry, you don't have to talk about it, but sometimes it's good to get things off your chest. When my brother died, I bottled my feelings up for ages, and looking back, it poisoned me inside."

"If you want to talk, we're here to listen," Stefan said. "I think we need a bottle of wine."

"But your lesson..."

Esther threw her arms around me. "Forget the lesson. You're more important."

Who else could I talk to? Not Dores, that was for sure, and I didn't want to upset Grandma either. My brother? No way. I might have known him my whole life, but I still didn't understand the man. Rafael was a black hole.

"She drowned," I said. "Izzy drowned. Or so the police said."

Today's phone call had turned everything I thought I knew on its head.

"Where? In the Medellín River? Or a swimming pool?"

"No, in the sea. She went swimming in the sea in Puerto Velero, near Barranquilla. I don't even know why she did that—Izzy always hated swimming because it messed with her hair and make-up."

"People sometimes do crazy things on vacation. I hate heights, but I still climbed the Eiffel Tower."

"But what was she even doing there? She told me she was visiting a friend in Cali, and the next thing I knew, the police were on the phone saying she was missing. A man called 123 to say he'd seen a woman in trouble in the water, and they found her clothes and purse on the beach..."

"She left her purse on the beach? What girl does that?"

"Exactly what I asked, but that's where they found it. One of the investigators said she might have been suicidal, that it wasn't the first time a girl had done that, but I don't believe it. She'd been so happy during those last few weeks."

Depression had plagued Izzy for years, a shadow that crept over her in the dark times, usually triggered by the anniversary of her father's death or a reminder of his life. I'd encouraged—no, begged—her to get help, but as a medical professional, she always insisted she knew better and refused. I'd breathed a quiet sigh of relief this year when the anniversary passed without her sinking into her usual murky depths, only for the true horror to hit weeks later.

"She looked happy when we saw her too," Esther said. "I figured it was down to her new boyfriend."

"Boyfriend? What boyfriend?"

Esther and Stefan looked at each other. "The guy we saw her with. She didn't tell you?"

No, she didn't tell me. Not a word, and hurt pinched at my insides because Izzy had always said she could tell me anything. Last year, she'd been dating a law student from Universidad EAFIT who, let's be honest, was a bit of a dick. She'd talked about him endlessly, and although we'd had the occasional disagreement over my assessment of his character, she'd come around to my way of thinking in the end. After she finally got sick of his shit, we'd spent an evening and a bottle of wine cutting every gift he'd ever given her into little pieces, then installed the whole lot in the tailpipe of his car late one evening. The blown exhaust valve served him right. He needed to learn that kissing girls who weren't your girlfriend had consequences.

And after that episode, Izzy had sworn off men for life, which was why news of a mystery boyfriend surprised me even more.

"She never mentioned him. Are you sure he was her boyfriend?"

"That's what she introduced him as. What was his name, Stefan? Can you remember?"

"Robert? Roger? Something like that. He was American."

My tears receded, replaced by curiosity and confusion.

"Are you sure?" Usually, I heard about every date Izzy went on in excruciating detail.

They both nodded.

"He was definitely foreign," Esther said. "How many Colombians have blond hair?"

"Maybe they went to Barranquilla together?" Stefan suggested. "If she didn't want to tell you about the man for whatever reason, perhaps that's why she said she was visiting an old friend instead?"

"I guess, but where was he when she walked into the sea?" The phone call replayed in my head again. "*If* she walked into the sea."

"You don't think she did?"

"Truthfully? I don't know what to believe anymore." I took a deep breath. "I swear she called me earlier."

"Izzy?"

"Sounds crazy, doesn't it?"

The more time passed since the phone call, the more I began to doubt myself. Right afterwards, I'd been so sure it was Izzy, but now...

"Did they find her body?"

"Part of it. Just a hand. They said..." Dammit, the tears were back. "They said it had been bitten off by something."

"Did they take fingerprints? Do a DNA test?"

I shook my head.

"Then maybe it wasn't her hand."

"Her ring was definitely on one of the fingers."

"What did she say on the phone?"

"She said 'help me.'"

Esther's eyes sparkled as she shifted to look at me properly. "Then isn't it obvious?"

"Uh, no?"

"The mystery man kidnapped Isabella and killed another girl in her place."

Stefan held up both hands. "Wait, wait, wait. Baby, I love you, you know I do, but you've got a bad habit of putting two and two together and making seventeen."

"No, I—"

"Remember what happened with old Mr. Bellingham when we lived in the Keys?"

Esther deflated a bit and chewed her bottom lip. "That was an innocent mistake."

"What happened with Mr. Bellingham?" I asked.

"Esther here hadn't seen Mrs. Bellingham for a week or two, so when Mr. Bellingham walked into the house carrying a spade, a saw, and a roll of garbage bags, she thought he'd murdered his wife."

"What happened? Did you call the police?"

"If only. My darling Esther waited until Mr. B went out, then convinced her friend Jessica to go check out his basement with her."

"Hey, there were some really strange noises coming out of it."

"You and your friend broke into his house? Alone?"

"Of course not. He left a window open, so we didn't break a thing."

Oh, because that made it so much better. "And did you find a body?"

Stefan shook his head. "No, they found a bookcase. Mr. B thought he'd surprise his wife with a reading nook and a new peach tree when she got back from visiting her sister in Wisconsin, except he nearly died from a heart attack first when he bumped into Sherlock and Watson coming up the stairs."

"The EMTs said it was just angina."

"You're lucky you didn't get arrested."

"Okay, okay, so I made a slight misjudgement in that instance. But that doesn't mean I'm wrong about Isabella."

If Stefan had looked any more incredulous, his eyes would have rolled through a portal to another realm.

"The police must have looked into the case, though." He focused on me. "Right?"

"So they said."

His gaze softened. "Cora, I'm so sorry to hear what happened to your friend. But there could be any number of reasons why she didn't tell you about the man we saw her with. Maybe they decided to joke with us for some reason when we saw them, and they weren't really dating? Or if they were, perhaps she was afraid to jinx it?"

I hated to admit it, but Stefan was probably right. And if Izzy *had* been having a relationship with Roger/Robert, and it turned sour in Barranquilla, a broken heart might have pushed her over the edge.

"But what about the phone call?" Esther prodded.

"As I said, I don't know what to think anymore."

"If it truly was her and she managed to call once, the chances are she'll call again," Stefan said. "And if she does, then you can take action."

"I guess, but what if she's in trouble?"

Esther folded her arms and stared at Stefan. "Exactly. What if she's still alive and in trouble?"

"Honey, you need to cut back on the thriller

novels."

"Well? What if? Cora, we should look for this guy."

Stefan cut in before I could answer. "No, you shouldn't. Say you're right and something sinister happened—that Isabella's boyfriend was involved in her death. That would make him a killer. And if you start digging around, he could come after you too. Both of you."

"We can't just ignore this."

"Cora knows far more about what happened than we do, and if she thinks it's necessary, she can go to the police. They're professionals, Esther. You're a yoga instructor." He turned to me. "Don't you agree?"

"Don't knock yoga," Esther said.

I needed to process all this. My head had been spinning since I left the house, and now it had turned into a centrifuge with my thoughts stuck uselessly to the sides. Something wasn't right in Izzy's disappearance, and for the last few weeks, I'd been too blinded by grief to think properly. Sometimes, I envied my brother and his ability to act like a cyborg. He'd come to the funeral and said the right things, but his eyes were the same two chips of granite they'd always been. People say the eyes are the window to the soul, and Rafael's soul was dark.

"It sounds a little farfetched," I said.

"But what—"

"Esther..." Stefan warned. "Cora, we'll always be here for you. If you need to talk, or cry, or you just want company, come over any time. But you need to take Esther's conspiracy theories with a pinch of salt."

"They're not—"

I didn't want to cause an argument. "Stefan, you

have no idea how grateful I am, and I promise we won't do anything risky. Perhaps we should just finish the lesson?"

Esther huffed, but when I leaned forward and pressed play on *El Secreto de sus Ojos*, she grudgingly concentrated on the Spanish, and this time, I managed not to turn into a crybaby. And when she ate half a loaf of banana bread and started planning which movie to watch next, I thought she'd forgotten her hare-brained idea as quickly as she'd thought of it.

I should have known better.

Esther leaned in close as she showed me out the door at the end of the evening.

"I'll call you tomorrow, okay?"

"But we already have a lesson scheduled for next week."

"I mean about Roger or Roberto or whatever his name is."

"Huh?"

"We're gonna find him." She gripped my hands. "You didn't get brainwashed by Stefan, did you? I mean, he doesn't even believe in extraterrestrials."

"We don't actually have any evidence that they exist."

"Pffft. Seven hundred million trillion planets, and you think we're alone? That's even crazier than the idea of faking a suicide. Are you working tomorrow night?"

"Until seven."

"Perfect. We can go out after."

"Go out where?"

"To the bar where we saw Isabella, of course. A tall blond gringo in Medellín? Someone must have seen him. And I didn't want to say it in front of Stefan, but the guy was hot."

Hot, and potentially a murderer if Esther was to be trusted. Stefan was right—Esther needed to cut back on the thrillers.

And now he walked up behind her. Dammit.

"I'll speak to you tomorrow," I said, leaning down to kiss Esther on the cheek.

She winked. "Don't forget your dancing shoes."

CHAPTER 2 - CORA

I'D HOPED GETTING out of the apartment would give me clarity, but talking to Esther and Stefan left me more confused than ever. Particularly Esther. Could there be any merit in her crazy idea, the conspiracy theory as Stefan called it?

Because how else could Izzy be alive?

If it *had* been her who called me, she must be hurt, or lost, or being held against her will. And why hadn't she told me she was seeing someone? The answer was all too obvious—she thought I'd disapprove if I knew, which meant her so-called boyfriend was bad news.

Izzy hadn't always had the best taste in men. As well as the mistake with the law student, she'd lost six kilos when she dated a guy who only ate fruit, put all the weight back on again when she got involved with Steroid Santino from the gym, then accidentally gone out with a drug addict. He'd hidden it well for a month or so, then a baggie of coke fell out of his pocket as he climbed into his car, and my brother put him in the hospital.

So was it possible she'd hooked up with a man who wanted to wear her damn skin? Unfortunately, yes.

I thought I'd sleep on the problem, but that plan didn't work out so well. I tossed and turned for most of the night until eventually, I shoved the sweaty sheets away and stared out the window at the street outside. When we first came to Medellín, we'd lived in little more than a shack on the outskirts of the city, nestled into the mountainside in Comuna 13. District 13. Some people didn't believe the number thirteen was unlucky, but for me, the name was no coincidence.

In Colombia, neighbourhoods—barrios—were divided according to the estrato system and given a number between one and six. Estrato—estate—six was the best, and you paid accordingly with higher rates for gas, electric, water, and phone services, which helped to subsidise the lower rates in the lower estratos. Comuna 13 scored a solid zero. We didn't even have a phone.

Although our current apartment in Belén was small, it was clean and comfortable and a vast improvement on what we'd once had. Izzy's abstract paintings adorned the walls, and Grandma played the old upright piano in the living room every evening. To me, it wasn't just a cheap apartment in an okay part of town with a view over the street outside. It was home.

A car drove past in the early hours, an old sedan, and I wondered where the driver had been. Where he was going. Work? Pleasure? Did his life have more direction than mine?

When I was a little girl, I'd read countless books, and I couldn't decide whether I wanted to be a warrior princess or a world-famous explorer. Then my world fell apart, and my sole goal became survival. And now? I came to the realisation that I'd spent the last few years coasting along, relief at being alive and relatively comfortable quashing any ambitions I might once have had. And if Izzy hadn't died—or disappeared—I'd probably have kept on doing the same thing until I died of old age or boredom, whichever came first.

But with yesterday's phone call, everything had changed. I wasn't the same girl anymore, and I couldn't live with myself if I didn't at least try to find the man Esther and Stefan had seen, if for no other reason than to understand Izzy's state of mind when she travelled to Barranquilla.

Which was why, when Esther messaged me after breakfast with the name of a bar and the news that Stefan would be at a seminar on global energy production all evening, I immediately began planning what to wear.

Me: Meet you at 8?

Esther: Te esperaré afuera.

She'd wait for me outside. Good. A little of the tension that had built up inside me since yesterday receded, not because I thought finding Robert/Roger would be easy, but because at least I'd be doing *something*.

"Do you have a full day today?" Grandma asked as I walked into the kitchen.

"Private lessons from ten until two, then a group from three until seven."

"So you'll be back for dinner?"

"Actually, no. I'm going out with the students afterwards. It's the end of their course, and I promised I'd celebrate with them."

Why didn't I just tell Grandma the truth? Well, because Grandma's friend Rufina's son worked with Stefan, and Grandma loved to talk—it was how I'd gotten Stefan and Esther as clients in the first place. And I certainly didn't want news of tonight's little excursion to get back to Esther's husband after I'd promised we wouldn't do anything risky.

"Be careful if you're walking home alone," Grandma said.

"I always am. Have you got a busy day?"

"Rufina and Dulce are coming over for lunch, and I promised Dores I'd do some mending."

Rufina? Yes, I'd made the right decision with my fib. The only thing that worried me was Grandma being home all day, because what if Izzy called back? Part of me wanted to spill the whole story, to get Grandma's advice because she'd always been my sounding board, but I also knew Stefan was right. The kidnapping theory was just that—a theory—and I didn't want to burden Grandma if we'd got it totally wrong.

So instead, I stuffed a sparkly necklace into my purse, then smiled and waved as I left the house in my uniform of jeans and a camisole. And pumps. I'd need every ounce of confidence I could muster tonight.

"You're sure this is the right place?" I asked Esther as we headed into Café Bourbon.

Izzy usually went somewhere cheaper, but if her new beau was paying...

"Definitely. Stefan wanted to eat American-style food that night, and they do the best ribs here. As long as you've got a good appetite, that is—the portions are enormous."

I saw what she meant when a waiter glided past, carrying two burgers with cheese dripping down the sides that had to be six inches high. My mouth watered, although I felt slightly sick at the same time.

Downstairs, the room was split in half, with tables on one side and a dance floor on the other. Stairs led to a balcony with bar-height tables and a few stools, but that space seemed to be filled with couples doing things I'd never done in private, let alone in public.

Esther didn't seem bothered as she led me towards the bar, leaving me to wonder whether my life until this point had been a tiny bit sheltered. She'd dressed flashier than me as well, in a sparkly black dress and pumps, although I still stood six inches taller.

"What do you want to drink?" she asked me.

"Limonada de coco."

"But that's non-alcoholic."

"I think we need to stay sober tonight, don't you?"

"We also need to blend in, and nobody at Café Bourbon drinks coconut limeade."

"Fine. One drink and no more."

Esther waved at the bartender, and he came over almost immediately. *"Dos besos al atardecer, por favor."*

I dreaded to think what was in a "sunset kiss," but I wasn't surprised when I saw him reach for a bottle of aguardiente, otherwise known as the local firewater. Perhaps I should have worn flats tonight, although that would have put my chest level with the bartender's eyes, not that he seemed to need an excuse to stare at my boobs.

Drink in hand, I backed away, searching the room for a blond-haired man who fitted Esther's vague description, but it was almost dark and I tripped over a guy's foot.

"Lo siento," I muttered in apology, but of course he

didn't hear me. The music was loud enough to pop my eardrums.

"Do you see him?" Esther shouted.

"You're the one who knows what he looks like."

"Yeah, but you're taller."

I accidentally made eye contact with a greasy-looking guy six feet away and quickly averted my gaze in case he thought I was interested. Even if I *had* gotten sick of the single life, I certainly wouldn't come to a place like this to find a date.

A flash of light-coloured hair on the far side of the dance floor caught my attention, and I poured half of my drink down my throat so I wouldn't spill it all over myself or someone else as we tried to squeeze through the crush. Damn, that burned.

By the time we reached our target, I'd had my ass pinched three times, my toes trodden on twice, and been elbowed in the side once, only for Esther to shake her head.

"His face is too round."

"Are you sure?"

"Yes. Hey, look, there's another blond guy."

And another... And another... We even ventured upstairs, where we didn't find Robert/Roger, but we did get invited to a threesome by a man who gave us a mouthful of abuse when we turned him down. What a charmer.

"This is hopeless," I said to Esther when we regrouped in the ladies' bathroom. "He's not here, and we can't do this every night."

"It's busier than it was last time. Maybe we could ask people if they've seen him? The bartender... We should ask the bartender."

"I can't even hear myself think out there."

"He has to go home sometime."

"So you're basically suggesting we stalk him?"

Esther shrugged. "Yes?"

"No!"

"Do you have a better idea?"

"Not exactly."

A girl in a strapless red dress tapped me on the shoulder. "Excuse me, are you waiting in line?"

"You go ahead."

I wasn't cut out to be a detective. Sometimes, I was barely cut out for putting my pants on the right way around in the mornings. The last decade with all its battles and setbacks had left me tired. So tired.

"Okay, how about this..." Esther started, and I knew I wouldn't like her suggestion. "You order another drink and flirt with the bartender a bit, get his number, and you can call him tomorrow."

"Are you crazy?"

"He likes you."

"He likes my cleavage."

"Then we're back to the stalking thing."

"You're impossible." But the alternative was to give up, and I'd never been a quitter. A quitter would have died in the rainforest near Leticia eleven years ago. "Fine. I'll try for his number."

Esther straightened my necklace and handed me her lipstick. "That's the spirit."

Except when we got back out to the bar, I saw the barman we spoke to earlier disappearing out the fire exit.

I grabbed Esther's hand. "Quick, follow me."

"I can't run in these shoes."

We caught up to the guy as he lit a cigarette in the dingy alley behind the club, and after regarding us through lazy eyes for a second, he held out a packet of Marlboros.

"Smoke?"

"No, uh, thank you. We just came outside for some air."

Esther nudged me, and I stumbled sideways.

"Air," she said, "and we're looking for a friend of ours. His name's Robert. Or maybe Roger. Blond guy. American."

The bartender raised one bushy eyebrow. "You don't know your friend's name?"

Busted. "He's not a close friend, more of a..."

"A hook-up," Esther blurted. "A one-night stand."

"With you?"

"Hell, no." She flashed her wedding ring. "I'm married."

Now he looked more closely at me. Great. I tried for a giggle and choked on my own tongue instead. Dammit, I could hardly back out now.

"Uh, yes, a one-night thing. And he wrote his number down after, but I lost it, and then I realised he left a...uh...a sock behind in my apartment."

What was I even saying?

"A sock? You're trying to return a sock?"

When the world seems like it's falling apart, smile —that's what my mama always used to say. It didn't usually work, but I'd been blessed with good teeth, so I figured I had nothing to lose.

"That's right."

A girl to the barman's left had been watching the whole exchange with interest. Or possibly incredulity.

She tapped the ash off the glowing end of her cigarette before speaking.

"Roscoe. You're looking for Roscoe."

"Roscoe?"

"Yeah, but I haven't seen him for weeks. Usually, he hangs out at El Bajo Tierra."

El bajo tierra? The underground?

"The club in Laureles?" Esther asked.

Thank goodness one of us was up to speed on Medellín's nightlife.

"That's it. Let me give you a piece of advice, chica." She gave her head a shake, and I knew inside she was laughing at me. "Roscoe's an asshole. Just burn the damn sock."

She followed the bartender back inside. The door slammed behind them, leaving me with Esther and a barely controllable urge to murder my friend.

"A hook-up? A one-night freaking stand?"

"A *sock*?"

"I panicked, okay?"

"At least we got Roscoe's name, and it's still only nine o'clock. Ready to go underground?"

Esther wiggled her hips, and I groaned out loud. The further I got down this rabbit hole, the more uncomfortable I felt.

"No. No, I'm not. We really haven't thought this through. I mean, what happens if we find this man? Do we just ask him about Izzy?"

"Girl, have you lost your mind? If he *is* holding her hostage, he might..."

She made a slashing motion across her neck, and I feared she was enjoying this escapade a little too much.

"This isn't fun, you know."

"Oh, I totally get that. Sorry." She looked at her feet, contrite. "But it's more exciting than yoga."

The whole thing was a bad, bad idea.

"So we don't tip our hand to Roscoe... Then what? We go to the police?"

In Esther's eyes, the student-teacher role had clearly been reversed, and I realised I was about to get a lecture.

"Corazon da Silva, use that brain of yours for just one minute. The police confirmed Isabella's death, didn't they? If they made a mistake, they won't want to admit it, and what if it's worse? What if they're involved?"

"Now you think the *police* are involved?"

"There could have been a cover-up. Colombia's almost as bad as Haiti when it comes to government corruption."

"Colombia's come a long way in the last decade."

Her tone softened. "I know that, but..."

Yeah, corruption was still rife. We both understood that.

"So what can we do?"

Her eyes sparkled in the flickering light from the exit sign. "Take a look for ourselves."

Break into Roscoe's home?

"No way. Last time you tried that, you got caught."

"Only because Mr. Bellingham forgot his grocery coupons and came back home early. A fluke, that was all."

"If Roscoe *is* holding Izzy prisoner, he might lock us up too."

Esther pondered that for a moment.

"You're right. What we need is a lookout."

Drag a poor, innocent third party into this scheme?

"A lookout. Brilliant. Do you have anyone in mind?"

She totally ignored my sarcasm. "Let's cross that bridge when we come to it. First, we need to find Roscoe."

"You're serious? Tonight?"

"There's no time like the present."

Chapter 3 - Cora

AS ITS NAME suggested, El Bajo Tierra was located in a basement, not that the earth did much to muffle the heavy base throbbing from the sound system. The *thump-thump-thump* clashed with my rapidly beating heart and gave me palpitations.

A gaggle of girls hanging around outside all wore skirts shorter than their heels and left me feeling decidedly underdressed. For a moment, I worried we wouldn't be allowed in, but the bouncer waved us to the front of the line and gave me a slow, sleazy appraisal, held out his hand for the sixty-thousand-peso cover charge, and lifted the velvet rope.

"Rumour has it a drug lord owns this place," Esther told me as we picked our way down the stairs in near darkness.

"Dare I ask which one?"

"El Gato."

The Cat, also known as Eduardo Garcia. And rumour also said Garcia once dissolved a man in acid while the poor sod was still alive.

"Perhaps we should go home."

"Oh, don't be such a chicken. He's not gonna kill us for visiting his nightclub."

Logic said that was true, but for me, logic went out the window when it came to the drugs trade, replaced by fear, hatred, and terrible memories. Still, now wasn't the time to rake over my past.

"You might even enjoy yourself," Esther added as we walked into the club proper.

Unlikely.

Café Bourbon had been colourful in its own way—neon signs, bright cocktails, a rainbow of outfits—but El Bajo Tierra was just dark, dark, dark. From the strangely haunting music to the ebony bar to the black clothes worn by almost every patron, the atmosphere sent a tingle of fear up my spine. The only respite from the gloom came from the waitresses gliding past, whose catsuits glowed under the ultraviolet lights. And when I said catsuits, I really meant skintight kitty costumes. Tails, whiskers, and silver freaking claws.

Guess the rumours were true.

I was edging towards the bar, parched from the heat, when Esther elbowed me in the side.

"I see him!"

"Who? Roscoe?"

"No, freaking Yoda."

With Esther's penchant for conspiracy theories, that was entirely possible.

"Where is he?"

"There, by that platform thing."

Ah yes, the one with the half-naked girls dancing on it. Their tiny skirts and halter-neck tops left almost nothing to the imagination, and I felt weirdly self-conscious in my jeans. But then I spotted Roscoe. Tousled blond hair, a straight, slender nose that turned up slightly at the end, and a shirt that stretched tight over his chest. He'd opened enough buttons to let a smattering of hair show. Preppy meets pimp.

"Now what?" Esther asked. "Should we go over?"

No need. I'd spent too long staring, which meant he caught me looking, and now he was headed in our direction. Oh, shit. I frantically searched for the bathroom, but I'd have had to walk past him to reach it.

Normally, I liked confidence in a man, mainly because it made up for my lack of it. But tonight, as Roscoe stopped a foot away and looked me in the eye, I kind of wished he'd kept watching from afar.

"*Pareces periódico*," he said.

"I look...newspaper?"

Confusion crossed his face for a second before his cocky grin came back. "*Perdido. I meant perdido*. You look lost. And it seems your English is better than my Spanish."

"Then shall we speak English?"

He nodded. "That'd stop me from making any more stupid mistakes. First time at El Bajo Tierra?"

"How did you guess? Me and my friend wanted a change of scene, and someone suggested this place."

"Your friend?"

"Yes, my..." I looked to my left, but Esther had vanished. "She was right here."

"Don't worry, I'm sure she's having a good time. Let me buy you a drink."

"But I don't know you."

My phone buzzed with a thumbs-up emoticon from Esther. Dammit, she was supposed to be my wingwoman, and now I'd have to kill her later. I conjured up a smile for Roscoe. He couldn't do anything criminal in a public place, could he? El Gato probably had heavily armed foot soldiers hidden away in closets, just waiting for an excuse to prove the size of their *cojones*. Unless Roscoe was somehow connected with Eduardo Garcia... No, that didn't bear thinking about.

Roscoe leaned in closer, and for a moment, I thought he was going to kiss my cheek. But he only smiled, thank goodness.

"I'm Roscoe."

"Is that your first name or your last name?"

A shrug. "Just Roscoe."

He raised an eyebrow expectantly.

"I'm C—" *Mierda*. What if Izzy had mentioned my name to him? "Catalina. I'm Catalina."

"That's a pretty name."

"Most people just call me Lina. And thank you, I'd love a drink."

I *needed* a drink. My mouth was drier than the Atacama Desert.

"What do you want?"

"Diet cola."

He stared at me.

"With, uh, aguardiente."

He ordered himself a beer, then put his hand on the small of my back as he led me over to an empty table. *Don't shudder, Cora.* At least El Bajo Tierra was emptier than Café Bourbon. If I'd been this close to Roscoe there, I wouldn't have been able to breathe. As it was, I had to stop myself from hyperventilating.

"So, Lina-Catalina... Why did you want a change of scene?"

I really hadn't thought this through, had I?

"My ex-boyfriend used to take me out to expensive restaurants all the time, and now when I see a fancy menu, it brings back horrible memories."

"Bad break-up?"

"I found out he was only dating me to get back at his wife for cheating on him."

Hopefully, Roscoe hadn't watched that particular telenovela episode the night before last.

"Ouch. Well, you've come to the right place. El Bajo Tierra doesn't even serve food."

"Why do you come here?"

"The music. The people. The atmosphere."

The cocaine? I hadn't seen anyone openly taking drugs, but it would make sense for El Gato to use the club as a sales outlet.

"It's not as busy as I thought it would be."

"They're picky about who they let in."

"Really? I didn't even have to wait in line."

"Like I said... Have you lived in Medellín your whole life, Lina?"

"Why do you ask?"

"Because you speak English with a British accent. That's not something you hear often around here."

But he'd have heard it from Izzy. My great-grandparents, Marisol's parents, had been British missionaries, and their way of speaking had been passed down through our family. Izzy's too, because my grandma and her mother before her had taught English to anyone in our village who wanted to learn. How much of that had Izzy told Roscoe?

"I studied in England. Have you been there?"

Please say no, because I've never once set foot out of Colombia.

"Not yet. It's on my bucket list. I've always wanted to travel around Europe."

Phew. I started breathing again.

"What brought you to Medellín? You're American, right?"

He nodded. "Walnut Creek, California. I moved here a few years ago for work."

"What do you do?"

"Exports. My fellow countrymen pay top dollar for Colombian handicrafts."

"Handicrafts?"

That wasn't what I'd expected.

"Jewellery, purses, clothing, furniture. You know what this month's bestseller is?"

"What?"

"Hammocks. My online store got featured in a lifestyle magazine, and I can't get enough of them. Women in three villages are working around the clock." He reached out to touch my necklace. "Where did you get this?"

"From El Pulguero."

I named the big market in Llanogrande, when in actual fact, the piece of jewellery was Izzy's handiwork. Making jewellery was something she'd always done, even through the difficult years. She had an artist's soul. Perhaps that was why she'd got involved with Roscoe? Because she thought he could sell some of her pieces?

"That's only on four times a year?"

I nodded.

"Too bad. I'll have to make sure I visit next time. I could clean them out of trinkets like those."

The whole conversation left me off balance. Roscoe was friendly, charming even, and if I hadn't suspected him of doing something really, really awful to Izzy, I'd probably have liked him. Was this how she felt when they first met? Flattered? Intrigued? As if she were the centre of Roscoe's world?

Another guy stopped beside us, a Colombian by the look of him.

"*Quiubo, parce*?" What's up, bro? "You have a new friend?"

"This is Catalina." Roscoe tapped his head near the corner of his eye. "And her face is up here."

The newcomer slowly raised his gaze. A smile tugged at the corner of his lips, and I got a hint of dimples. He was too cute to be scary but too confident for me to relax.

"Your first time in El Bajo Tierra?"

"Yes."

"What do you think of the club so far?"

I held up my glass. "First drink. But okay, I guess."

"What did he buy you? Aguardiente? *Parcero*, this is a five-star girl. You buy her a five-star drink." He clicked his fingers, and one of the cat-women appeared instantly. "Maria, bring a glass of champagne for the lady."

"There's no need—"

He acted as if I hadn't spoken. "We have a large selection of European drinks. Six different kinds of gin. I'd recommend the Bombay Sapphire."

"But no food?"

"You're hungry? I'll make a reservation for you at the restaurant next door."

"No! I mean, no thank you. I'm not hungry—it was just an observation."

Another faint smile. "In that case, enjoy the dancing."

He melted back into the crowd, leaving me alone

with Roscoe and a glass of chilled champagne. I wasn't sure what to make of the encounter.

"Do you know that guy?" I asked Roscoe. "Is he a friend?"

"Marco. His father owns this place, and the restaurant next door too. He likes to keep track of who's in here, especially if they're as pretty as you."

Great. Now I'd caught the attention of a drug lord's son, and Roscoe had carefully dodged my question about whether they were friends. The air conditioner in the club was working overtime, but still a bead of sweat rolled down my spine. This undercover thing was hard.

"Do you live near here?" I asked.

"Not so far away. La Florida."

No, not Florida in the USA. La Florida was a barrio in the El Poblado neighbourhood, and if Roscoe could afford to live there, then his export business must have been doing very well indeed. The place was full of ex-pats and luxury high-rise apartments, and ranked firmly as an estrato six.

I took a sip of my champagne, stalling for time because I didn't know what to say to men at the best of times, let alone men I suspected of kidnapping my best friend.

"And your office? Is that nearby?"

"In Campo Amor, near the airport. But enough about me—I'd rather hear about you, Lina-Catalina. Where do you live?"

"Conquistadores." Esther had got me into this mess, so the least she could do was lend me her address. "Near the Unicentro mall."

"You live with your family?"

"No, it's just me. I'm an only child, and my parents

died in a car crash."

He reached across the table and squeezed my hand —a gesture of sympathy rather than anything creepy.

"I'm sorry."

"It happened a long time ago. As long as I keep busy, I'm okay."

"Do you work?"

"Of course. I'm an English...administrative assistant. I mean, I'm an administrative assistant for an English company. They sell, uh..." *Think, Cora. Think.* "Speakers. They sell speakers."

How did people do this undercover thing for a living?

"Speakers?"

"For music."

Luckily, the music came to my rescue. The song changed to something more upbeat, and Roscoe held out a hand.

"Dance?"

"What about our drinks?"

"In here? They'll be fine."

"Really?" I'd heard enough horror stories about date-rape drugs.

"Trust me."

Trust him? I choked back a laugh. How could I possibly trust him knowing what I knew? But I took his hand and let him lead me to the dance floor, following —quite literally—in Izzy's footsteps. Where would they take me?

CHAPTER 4 - CORA

MIERDA, MY HEAD hurt. Not just from last night's alcohol consumption and the music and the lack of sleep, but because I was confused as hell. I'd danced with Roscoe for almost an hour, and when I twisted my ankle, he'd half carried me outside and helped me into a cab. Sweet. He'd even offered to see me home, but that would have been super awkward since Esther was still hiding in the ladies' bathroom. As it was, I had to get the driver to wait around the corner until she could escape and join us.

"This is going so well," she squealed as she climbed into the back seat beside me. "Don't you think?"

"No! You abandoned me."

"Only because I thought Roscoe might recognise me from last time in Café Bourbon. I panicked, and I'm so sorry."

I suppose she did have a point. "My ankle's swelling up already."

"Here, take a painkiller." She fumbled in her purse and handed me a packet. "But that wasn't what I meant. Roscoe likes you. I saw you dancing."

"I'm not sure if that's a good thing or a bad thing. He wanted my phone number."

"Did you give it to him?"

"No, but I took his."

"What about his address? Did you get that?"

"I only know he lives in El Poblado."

"Then you'd better call him and set up a second date."

Now, alone in my bedroom, I had space to think, but my trip to El Bajo Tierra had left me with more questions than answers. And it wasn't a first date, for goodness' sake, no matter what Esther might say.

What to do...

If I'd met Roscoe in any other situation, I'd absolutely have called him. He'd acted like a complete gentleman, and I struggled to imagine him kidnapping Izzy. Why would he even have needed to? If he treated her the way he'd treated me yesterday evening, surely she'd have spent time with him willingly? Any red-blooded woman would. What if Esther's theory was totally wrong?

If only Izzy had talked to me. Not just during the mysterious phone call, if indeed that had been her, but before she went to Barranquilla. Why had she shut me out? Was it because Roscoe was older? He hadn't told me his age, but he was definitely in his late twenties. Did she think I'd disapprove? I'd never felt so alone in my life, and the pressure to make the right decision weighed heavily on my shoulders.

And that load didn't lighten when I walked into the kitchen and found my brother sitting at the table, tucking into Grandma's huevos pericos—scrambled eggs with tomatoes and scallions.

"What are you doing here?"

"Eating breakfast."

"Exactly. You never eat breakfast here anymore."

And rarely lunch or dinner either. Grandma said

Rafael stopped by in the afternoons to visit sometimes, but I didn't see him. In the eight years that had passed since he moved out, my brother had become a virtual stranger.

"I came to see you."

Grandma wheeled past me in her chair. "You were back late last night, Cora."

"I lost track of time, that's all."

"How was dinner?"

Non-existent. "Really good."

"How many arepas do you want with your eggs? And do you want coffee or hot chocolate?"

"Hot chocolate." My answer was automatic even though the butterflies in my stomach weren't hungry in the slightest. "And just one arepa."

Rafe, as I'd nicknamed him when I was a toddler because I couldn't pronounce his name properly, was drinking coffee, the same as he always did. Black, and so strong you could stand the spoon up in it.

And now he locked his gaze on me, the same dark eyes that my father once had. I'd inherited them too, but while I tried to lessen their intensity with smiles and eye make-up, Rafe had been cultivating his death glare since childhood.

He just didn't usually turn it on me.

"What have I done?"

"Why were you talking to Marco Garcia yesterday?"

"You followed me to a freaking nightclub?"

"I was already there."

Where? I'd been at El Bajo Tierra for two hours, and I hadn't seen him. My brother was a damn ghost.

"I spoke to Marco Garcia for about two minutes, and I'd never met him before. Happy? He just wanted to know if I liked the club."

"You need to steer clear of him, Cora. And El Bajo Tierra."

"How dare you give me a lecture?" Especially with Grandma listening. "Until today, you've never taken the slightest interest in my life. You don't have a clue who my friends are, and you've got no idea what I do in my spare time. Do you even know where I work?"

"You work at La Escuela de Idiomas Gomez. Juan Gomez is forty-five years old, married, and has no criminal record. You currently have sixteen regular students." My brother ticked off the points on his fingers. "Herman Krantz was convicted of manslaughter in his early twenties, but he doesn't appear to have reoffended, and since you teach him at the language school rather than in his own home, it's probably safe. You don't have many friends, but you've been spending time with Esther and Stefan Corbin. Esther moved to the United States as a refugee at thirteen years old and met Stefan in Orlando, Florida. Stefan got a DUI five years ago, so I'd avoid getting in a car with him. Your hobbies? You watch too many telenovelas, you go to the gym, and you occasionally made jewellery out of beads with Izzy." He reached out to touch today's necklace the same way Roscoe had done last night. "This is one of hers, isn't it?"

I ignored the question as my jaw dropped. "You've been background-checking my clients? My friends? You... You..."

"You're my little sister. I care."

"I'm twenty-two years old."

"You'll always be my little sister. And that other guy you were with last night? Roscoe? He's only going to hurt you."

"How do you know that?"

"Because he never keeps the same girl around for long."

"You know him?"

"Never saw him before yesterday, but I asked around."

I was torn between being mad at Rafael for invading my privacy and curious because he seemed to be a lot better at finding out information than I was. In the end, the need to help Izzy won out.

"What else did people say about Roscoe?"

"Not much. That he showed up three years ago and spends more time partying than working. That he's never short of pretty girls. You're too good for him, Corazon."

"You don't run my life."

"Why were you in El Bajo Tierra, anyway? It's not your kind of place."

I was about to retort that he wouldn't have a clue what my kind of place was when I realised he'd probably reel off a list of everywhere I'd visited for the last six months. My brother was a freak. I'd always figured he was into some messed-up stuff from the bruises he came home with as a teenager and the way he cut me off whenever I asked what he'd been doing. And now? He'd become smoother, more polished, with an expensive watch that didn't match his cheap clothes, but he hadn't changed. Rafael would always be my brother, and I loved him, but I didn't know him anymore.

"Life should be an adventure," I told him.

"No, Cora. Your life should be safe and easy."

Then why did it feel so damn difficult?

"Okay, so how about we do a deal? You check into Roscoe's background more thoroughly, and if you find anything concerning, I'll stop seeing him."

Not only would my brother be happy because I'd listened to his concerns, he'd also do my dirty work for me. And if it turned out Esther's suspicions about Roscoe were unfounded, I might even enjoy seeing him again. I smiled to myself, pleased with my idea. What do you know? I *did* have a devious side lurking under the surface.

Rafe didn't look quite so thrilled, but he nodded once.

"Fine. But stay away from El Bajo Tierra, okay?"

"Why?"

"Because there are plenty of other clubs in Medellín that aren't owned by criminals. Pick one of those instead."

"Okay." I managed to relax a little. "And Rafe? I'm glad you visited. I've missed you."

Finally, I got a smile.

"Missed you too, Cora."

CHAPTER 5 - CORA

WHILE RAFAEL DUG into Roscoe's history, I took a bus ride to El Centro and bought a cheap prepaid cell phone. I'd watched enough TV to know that bad guys could track you through your phone signal, and I didn't want Roscoe finding out that I lived in Belén and not Conquistadores as I'd claimed.

Then I sent him a message.

Me: Nice meeting you last night. Lina.

Wouldn't it be a joke if he'd given me a fake number?

But he hadn't. Right after my first lesson, ironically with Herman Krantz, where I spent the whole hour and a half wondering exactly who he'd killed, and how, and why—thanks, Rafe—Roscoe replied to my message.

Roscoe: Me too. I was worried you wouldn't contact me. You made quite an impression, Lina-Catalina.

What kind of impression had Izzy made?

Me: You're not an easy man to forget.

Roscoe: How about I give you something else to remember? Dinner?

No way was I agreeing to meet him again until I heard back from my brother. How much time would a background check take? I could avoid replying until this evening, then put off dinner for a few days after that, but any longer and I risked Roscoe losing interest. And I didn't want to chase Rafe too hard in case he grew suspicious.

Esther called in the afternoon for an update, and I could tell she was disappointed about the delay.

"What if he's got Isabella chained up in his bedroom?"

"That's not helping."

"Just saying."

"We need to do this slowly, okay? No big risks."

And when I got home in the evening, Grandma only had more awkward questions.

"Cora, did you give out our home number to anyone new?"

"No, why?"

"I had a strange call today. Two, actually."

My heart stuttered. Had Roscoe somehow found out where I lived? Was he checking up on me like I was checking up on him?

"What kind of calls? Was it a man or a woman?"

Grandma fussed around making herself a drink before she answered, and I forced my hands to relax. They'd curled up into fists at my sides all of their own accord.

"The first one, I'm not sure. Nobody spoke, and then somebody screamed but the line went dead halfway. I thought it was a prank until the second call came."

"And somebody spoke that time?"

"A man. He asked who I was, and when I said I wouldn't answer that question until he told me who *he* was, he hung up."

"Did you recognise his voice?"

"No, I didn't."

"He spoke Spanish?"

"Yes. But I don't think he was from around here."

"Why not? His accent?"

"Partly. And partly because when he hung up on me, I called my friend Consuela who works at the phone company, and it turns out the number was registered to an American cell phone. One of those prepaid SIM cards. And the call came via an American network."

America? My knees went weak, and I collapsed into the chair opposite Grandma.

"Really? An American phone?"

"And when I called the number back half an hour later, it was out of service. Don't you think that's strange?"

"Yes, I do."

"And do you know what else is strange?"

"What?"

"That same number called the day before yesterday."

Not for the first time, I'd forgotten how smart my grandma was. Her legs may have withered away, but there was nothing wrong with her mind. She'd proven that time and time again. Soon after we moved to Medellín, I'd been bullied by a girl at school. I never told a soul, but Grandma found out somehow and invited her over for dinner one baking-hot Thursday evening. I'd nearly died of fear. Fernanda Moreno sat in the very chair I was sitting in now, swinging her legs while Grandma dished up her famous bandeja paisa and explained what it was like to live life in a wheelchair. Every so often, one of Fernanda's feet connected with my shins, but I didn't dare to say a word.

And at the end of the meal, Grandma had leaned forward, elbows on the table as she smiled sweetly, and I still remembered every word she said.

"Fernanda, if you ever call my granddaughter another nasty name, or kick her once more with those little pink tennis shoes your mama worked so hard to buy, you'll be the one in a wheelchair. Do you understand?"

Fernanda's eyes had bugged right out of her squirrelly face.

"Do you understand?"

"Y-y-yes."

"Good." A knock sounded at the door. "Your mama's here to pick you up now."

Fernanda had never spoken to me again, and her horrible friends had given me a wide berth too. No, it didn't pay to underestimate my grandma, and now she watched me over the rim of her brightly coloured mug as she sipped her coffee.

"I...I might have taken the call."

She nodded. "And?"

"It was a woman. She asked for help. And..."

"Go on."

"And I thought it might have been Izzy. Which is crazy, I know, because she's dead, and the police found her hand, with the ring, but...I still think it was Izzy."

I screwed my eyes shut for five seconds. Ten. Opened them again. Did I mention that my brother and my father inherited their eyes from Grandma? She'd fixed me with that same dark gaze.

"Does your visit to El Bajo Tierra have something to

do with this?"

"Grandma, I don't want to burden you."

She leaned across the table and took both my hands in hers. "Corazon da Silva, I may be seventy-two years old, but I'm not a porcelain doll. And if I've learned one thing in my lifetime, it's that a problem is better shared. Look at what happened when we all came to Medellín—we worked together and achieved more than any one of us could have done alone."

"But—"

"Just tell me, Cora."

"A friend of mine saw Izzy with Roscoe before she died."

"Died, or disappeared?"

"I'm not sure."

"Don't dismiss your gut feelings, chiquita. I also had my doubts, but until now, we couldn't find any evidence to suggest Isabella hadn't just lost her mind."

"'We'?"

"Your brother and me. He travelled to Barranquilla."

"Really?"

"Yes. And we never did find the witness who claimed to have seen Isabella in trouble in the sea. The idea that she would take off her clothes and leave them on the beach with her purse while she went for a swim in semi-darkness? That girl did some silly things in her life, but nothing so utterly stupid as that."

"Why did you discuss this with Rafe and not me?"

"We didn't want to worry you."

"Well, it didn't freaking work, did it? And what did you just say about sharing problems?"

Grandma smiled, almost to herself it seemed.

"Looks as though you *do* have a hint of the da Silva fire, after all."

"What's that supposed to mean?"

"You were always the sweet one."

"Well, being bitter is like holding onto a snake and hoping it bites someone else."

"That's very true. But, Cora, you can't go running off after Roscoe by yourself. If he did have anything to do with Isabella's disappearance, he's a dangerous man."

"He was perfectly polite to me in the club."

"And Pablo Escobar could be very charming when he wanted to be, I know that from experience, but he still killed thousands of people in cold blood."

"You met him?"

My grandma baked polforosas and alfajores and taught local kids how to read. She didn't consort with drug lords.

"Several times. Did I trust him? Not one iota."

Wow. How many other secrets were being kept by people close to me? On second thoughts, did I really want to know?

"Promise you won't rush headlong into anything stupid," Grandma continued. "Let your brother look into Roscoe first."

"I planned to do that, but I've got no idea how long that'll take, and Roscoe wants to have dinner with me."

"Did you agree?"

"I haven't said yes or no yet. He only asked this afternoon."

"He called you?"

"Texted. I bought a second phone this morning, so he doesn't have my regular number."

Grandma nodded approvingly, and that worried me a little. Who the hell was Marisol da Silva?

"And does he know your real name?"

"I told him I was called Catalina, and when he asked about my accent, I said I studied in England."

"Good." She nodded once. "Your brother will be back for dinner. We can decide on the next step then. Would you prefer bandeja paisa or tamales?"

"I'm not sure I can eat anything at all."

"Tamales, then. Your brother would live on those given the choice. But I'll need some banana leaves."

Banana leaves? How could she think about banana leaves at a time like this? I had so many questions, about my past, her past, our future. But they stuck in my throat, and instead, I nodded in agreement.

"I'll go to the store."

It was nine o'clock by the time Rafe turned up, and the tamales were overcooked and drying out in the tamalera.

"Something smells good."

"Why are you so late? What did you find out?"

He bent to kiss me on the cheek. As always, he looked effortlessly stylish, even with a day's worth of stubble and wearing the battered boots he'd owned for at least three years.

"Good evening to you too."

"Well?"

"Why so impatient?"

"We had a talk earlier," Grandma told him. "Cora also has doubts over Isabella's death."

She explained about the phone calls and my messages with Roscoe, and my brother groaned.

"Izzy, what did you get yourself into?" he muttered at the floor, then straightened. "If you get any more strange calls, do me a favour and let me know sooner rather than later."

"Okay, fine, but what do we do now?"

"'We' don't do anything. You carry on going to work and eating lunch in those little cafés you like, and leave the questions to me."

"But what about Roscoe?"

"Forget you ever met him."

"No way. I can help with this. What should I tell him about dinner?"

"Cora, did you not hear a word I said? Tell him no."

"Don't you dare cut me out again. It seems like you've been doing that for my entire life, you and Grandma. Did you know she once met Pablo Escobar?"

"Yes. Look, I can't search for Izzy if I have to spend my time checking up on you."

Checking up? What an asshole! I was an adult and perfectly capable of taking care of myself.

"Then don't check up on me," I said through gritted teeth. "I'm not going to take any stupid risks."

"Then you'll stay away from Roscoe?"

"Did you find out something bad about him?"

"Not specifically, but he's dated at least six different women so far this year, and only one of them has been seen since."

"There are four other women missing besides Izzy?"

"I don't know for sure. I only know that I haven't been able to find any of them yet."

"Esther reckons he has Izzy stashed in his

basement, but five people?"

"Esther? Your student?"

"She went to El Bajo Tierra with me."

"Cora, you need to keep other people out of this. And Roscoe doesn't have a basement. He lives in a sixth-floor apartment."

"Perhaps a spare bedroom?"

Rafe just stared at me.

"Okay, I'll admit that sounds farfetched."

"Promise you won't go near him."

"But if I spend time with him, he might let something slip."

"Or he might bury you in a shallow fucking grave."

"No, he won't. We're doing this because we think Izzy's alive, remember?"

"She does have a point," Grandma said.

Good. I had backup. Us women needed to stick together.

"We're not using my sister as bait."

"If they're in public, the risk of him abducting Cora is low, and it could help us get to the bottom of this."

"What's he going to do?" I asked. "Carry me out of the restaurant and stuff me into the trunk of his car?"

"Maybe."

"With you spying on me the way you were last night?"

I had him. If Rafe forbade me to see Roscoe now, he'd be casting doubt on his own abilities, and my brother had a level of confidence that put any reality TV star to shame. No arrogance, just supreme self-assurance. And he'd always been fearless. Even as a child, he'd run through a hail of bullets to save Grandma's life while I trembled uncontrollably.

"Fine. Dinner. But it'll have to be tomorrow because after that, I need to go to Cali for a few days."

"I'll message Roscoe now."

Rafe sighed, long and resigned. "I should have become a security guard. Or a cleaner. Or a bus driver."

"What do you do for a living, anyway?"

My brother and my grandma exchanged a look.

"You don't want to know," they both said at the same time.

CHAPTER 6 - CORA

ESTHER DIDN'T WANT to get Stefan involved in our devious little charade, at least, not right now. The day before yesterday, he'd arrived home while she was wiping off her make-up from our trip to El Bajo Tierra, and she'd gotten another lecture on the dangers of amateur sleuthing.

Still, she buzzed me into their building, and I hid in the stairwell for fifteen minutes until Roscoe called to say he was waiting outside. Rafe had installed a tracking app on my phone, and he'd be following along behind.

"Where are we going?" I asked Roscoe.

"You'll find out soon."

He'd promised me a surprise, something that left me apprehensive after Izzy's experience. What had really happened that night in Barranquilla? *Surprise! We're going for a romantic stroll on the beach—hold still while I chop off your hand and toss it to the sharks.*

Even so, with my brother set to follow us, I climbed into Roscoe's Mercedes and we set off to our mysterious destination. The vehicle still had that new-car smell, something foreign to me since almost nobody drove new cars in Colombia. The import taxes were so high, only the super-rich could afford to. Roscoe made that much money selling trinkets? I was in the wrong line of work.

"Will you tell me where we're going now?" I asked as he paused at the end of the street.

"All in good time."

"But we're going to eat dinner, right? I'm starving."

"Not yet. We're going to make dinner first."

"Make dinner?" Like, manual labour? "Where? At your apartment?"

Because even if he wasn't a raving lunatic, inviting a girl to his apartment on a more-or-less first date was a bit forward.

He laughed at the suggestion. "No, at Sushi House. Have you ever made sushi before?"

"I haven't even eaten sushi before."

"You're serious?" He groaned. "Oh, no. You hate fish, don't you?"

"If you'd been more open with your plans, we could have discussed my dietary preferences."

"Shit. Hold on, I'll cancel the reservation." He slowed to pull over at the side of the road. "What do you want to eat? Pizza? Everyone likes pizza."

Now it was my turn to laugh. "Got you!"

"Huh?"

"I love fish, but your face when you thought I didn't..."

"I'm gonna get you back for that."

And he did. As we arranged sheets of nori and rice and fish and vegetables on bamboo rolling mats, he held out a tiny spoon with green paste on it.

"Here, try this."

"What is it?"

"Wasabi. It adds a sweet flavour to the dish."

I'd try anything once. Well, except bungee jumping, because I saw a slow-motion video where the person's eyes bulged when they got to the bottom and it totally freaked me out. I took the spoon and stuck it in my mouth.

There was a strange moment of calm before my eyes started watering, during which Roscoe's face morphed into one of those Edvard Munch paintings. *Joder*, my whole head was about to explode.

"What the hell was that?" I choked out.

"I didn't think you'd eat the whole lot!"

"Water! I need water!"

Roscoe ran—freaking ran—to the bar and grabbed a full pitcher. I didn't bother to wait for a glass before I poured half of the water down my throat. A decorative mirror hung on the wall, and I wouldn't have been surprised to see flames leaping from my mouth and smoke pouring from my ears, but all I got was smeared mascara and wet hair. Roscoe leaned forward and picked a slice of lemon off my shoulder.

"I'm sorry. I'm so, so sorry."

"You said it was sweet."

"I was kidding." He tucked the damp ends of my hair behind my ears. "You've really never had wasabi before?"

"Not once. My g—" Dammit, I nearly said my grandma didn't use it. "My girlfriends and I don't go out to fancy restaurants very often."

"If you'll forgive me, I'll rectify that."

Out of the corner of my eye, I saw my brother walk into the restaurant with one arm around a stunning brunette. When he took in the state of me, his free hand balled into a fist at his side. I quickly shook my head.

Don't kill Roscoe. Yes, the wasabi prank had been shitty, but it wasn't entirely Roscoe's fault I'd led such a boring life.

I narrowed my eyes at him. "You'll have to earn my forgiveness. And watch out, because I'm going to get my own back."

He grinned. "*Cariña*, I'd expect nothing less."

Conversation with Roscoe was easier than I expected. Over our slightly wonky handmade sushi, he told me tales of life in California with his two younger brothers, who'd played endless practical jokes on him as they grew up. At least I knew where he'd learned the wasabi trick. In turn, I made up a few stories about my own childhood, then felt guilty for lying, then felt guilty for feeling guilty about lying because I wasn't supposed to *like* Roscoe.

"So you learned to play the flute? Were you in an ensemble?" he asked.

"I wasn't that good."

In reality, I wasn't even sure which end to blow into. The only instrument I played was the piano—something else Grandma had taught me, although her musical tastes tended towards the melancholy nowadays. The music brought back memories for both of us, both good and bad.

"I bet you'd be good at anything you put your mind to, Lina-Catalina."

That's what my mama always used to say too. Oh, how I missed her.

"Do you play any instruments? The guitar? I picture you as a guitar guy."

"Is it the hair?"

He scrubbed at his sandy mop, and I laughed.

"No, not the hair. You just seem laid back. I can imagine you chilling out at a big music festival."

Which was more than could be said for my brother. Every so often, I snuck a glance over at his table, and he barely talked, let alone smiled. Still, that didn't seem to bother his date. She gazed at him adoringly, and if the table hadn't been in the way, I bet she'd have climbed into his lap and stuck her tongue down... Ick! No, I didn't even want to think about that. And what had he told her about me? Anything? Did she know she was being used as a cover story?

Truthfully, I felt as though I'd got the better end of the bargain. Roscoe was good company, and the more time I spent with him, the more difficult I found it to believe that he could have been involved in Izzy's disappearance. He acted like a gentleman to the end, paying the bill at the end of the meal then kissing me softly on the cheek as we sat in his car outside Esther's apartment.

"Can I see you again? I promise not to feed you any more wasabi."

"Okay."

"When are you free?"

"At the weekend. Sunday?"

On Saturdays, I always used to eat brunch with Grandma, Izzy, and Dores, and although that tradition had slipped since Izzy's disappearance, we needed to make the effort to spend time together again.

"I have to make a trip to La Gitana on Sunday. I'm meeting someone for lunch there. Saturday?"

"Saturday's good." Tradition would have to get put on hold again.

Another kiss. "I'll wait until you get inside."

Oh, great. I dragged my heels as I walked up the path, then pushed every intercom button until someone took pity on me and buzzed the door open.

"*Adiós,*" I mouthed as I waved goodbye.

Roscoe drove off, and I sagged against the wall inside. This evening hadn't gone at all how I'd expected, and apart from the wasabi joke, I'd actually enjoyed myself. And now that my mouth had stopped burning, I could even see the funny side of that. My brother had done far worse as a child, like the time he'd replaced my toothpaste with mayonnaise after I left my pet goat in his bedroom overnight. In my defence, I was only seven years old, and I didn't realise what a mess Humoso would make. At least I'd given my goat a sensible name—Smoky in English. My brother watched too much American TV, and his goat was called Butt-Head.

Those had been better days. When we moved to Medellín, Rafe had lost his sense of humour, and we'd no longer had our own bedrooms either. He slept on a couch in the kitchen-slash-living room while I shared the only bedroom with Grandma, Izzy, and Dores. Sure, things had gradually improved, but I still missed our true home in the south.

I'd only been inside Esther's apartment building for five minutes when my brother pulled up outside in his battered Honda. He'd owned the same car for years, and even though it looked boring, it went faster than usual because he'd modified the engine. Dores always said he'd kill himself driving it, but then he bought a motorcycle and now she crossed herself every time she saw him riding the thing.

"Who was the girl you were with?" I asked once I'd

put my seat belt on.

"Nobody important."

"Does she know that?"

Rafe shrugged, the master of eloquence.

"You shouldn't lead her on. That's not fair."

"And how was your date with Roscoe?"

My brother's tone reminded me that I was doing exactly what I'd just accused him of.

"That's different. There's a purpose."

Another shrug. Why did Rafael have to be so damn annoying?

"Did you find out anything else useful about Roscoe?" I asked.

"Difficult to talk to people when I'm babysitting you."

"I'm not a baby!"

"I wish you'd leave this to me. You looked as if you were enjoying yourself a little too much today. This isn't a game."

Busted.

"Maybe I'm just a good actress?"

"Right."

"Don't roll your eyes."

"So, Meryl Streep, what did you discover?"

"Not a lot," I admitted. "He grew up in California, he wanted to be a rock star until he realised he couldn't sing, and he doesn't like avocados."

Rafe snorted. "At least you didn't claim to be a good detective."

"Well, I'm going out with him again on Saturday. He couldn't do Sunday because he's going to La Gitana."

"La Gitana? What time?"

"He didn't exactly say, but he's meeting someone for lunch."

"That gives us five hours at least."

"Five hours to do what?"

My brother grinned for the first time in ages. "Break into his apartment."

"Break into his apartment? Are you crazy?"

"Fortunately for you, yes. You can play lookout."

This had to be a nightmare. In a few hours, I'd wake up, and Izzy would be making a mess with her paints at the kitchen table while Grandma tried to cook.

"How can you act so calmly about all this?"

"Practice. Where are you going on Saturday?"

"I don't know yet."

Even though it was only two days away.

"Wherever it is, you should wear a longer skirt."

"Your girlfriend's dress was shorter than mine."

"She's not my girlfriend, and I don't care how long *her* dress was."

I'd almost forgotten how impossible my brother could be when he put his mind to it. "Fine. I'll wear trousers."

"Good. Call me with the plan when you find out what it is. Guess I'm tagging along again."

CHAPTER 7 - CORA

LUCKILY, ROSCOE TEXTED me on Friday night telling me to wear jeans for our excursion on Saturday because we'd be spending time outdoors. That meant I didn't have to incur the wrath of my brother or risk twisting my ankle in pumps either.

Stefan had gone out to buy a new memory card for his computer—he was into gaming in a big way, which Esther said gave her peace to watch as much TV as she wanted—and so I waited in their apartment for Roscoe to arrive.

"Are you sure you don't want me to help with the breaking and entering tomorrow?" Esther asked once I'd updated her on our plans. "I'd make a great lookout. We could go in disguise. I've got a wig left over from Halloween last year, and a pair of coloured contact lenses. Oh, and you can borrow Stefan's glasses."

"He wears glasses?"

"Not really. He bought them to make himself look smarter."

When it came to Rafael versus Esther in the surveillance stakes, I knew who I wanted my partner in crime to be. "I'll pass, but thanks for the offer."

"Promise you'll tell me what happens?"

"You'll be the first person I call."

My phone *ping*ed with a message from my brother

—he was waiting outside. Before I could put it back in my purse, Roscoe phoned too.

"I'm downstairs. Shall I come up?"

"No! I mean, I'm on my way out the door right now."

"You're one of those rare women who's ready on time."

Nearly everyone I knew would disagree, but who was I to argue? "I'll be there in one minute."

Rafe was nowhere to be seen when I ran out the door, but I had to trust he was close. My phone was charged to a hundred percent, so at least he'd be able to track that if he lost sight of me.

Roscoe leaned across to kiss me on the cheek in a repeat of our parting on Thursday.

"*Hola, hermosa.*"

"*Hola, guapo.* Are you going to tell me where we're going yet?"

"Always so impatient, Lina-Catalina. Don't you like surprises?"

"Not really."

"Maybe you'll change your mind about that today." He reached across to turn the radio on. "Do you like rock?"

The guitar intro from Bryan Adams's "Summer of '69" blared out of the speakers and nearly deafened me. "It's a bit loud."

"Sorry." Roscoe dialled it down a few notches. "What do you think of the sound system?"

"Huh?"

"In your professional opinion?"

Oh, shit. Why hadn't I said I worked for a pet-food manufacturer or a company that sold olives?

Something innocuous that didn't require any actual expertise.

"Not bad. Good bass."

"I should hope so. They cost an extra two thousand bucks."

Or half a year's rent on our apartment. "You must be selling a lot of hammocks."

He smiled as he took a left onto Avenida 37, more to himself than me. "Yeah, a lot of hammocks."

A sign for Parque Explora came up on the right, and I pointed at it. "Are we going there?"

"Parque Explora? No. Why, do you like it?"

"I've never been."

"Me neither."

"It's one of those places I always wanted to go, but I've never quite got around to it."

"Not even as a little kid?"

No, because when I was a little kid, I'd lived as far south as it was possible to get, hundreds of kilometres away and almost in Peru.

"My parents were always busy working."

"Then how about we go next weekend?"

"You and me?"

"Unless you want to invite a few friends as well."

Little did he know... "It's a date."

We grinned at each other as he paused at a junction, and when he pulled away again, he reached over to twine his fingers through mine, resting our joined hands on his thigh as he wove through traffic. I got lost in the music as we headed out of the city, through Vereda Potrerito, and all the way up to San Felix.

The countryside was beautiful, and something I

rarely got to see, but what were we doing there? And where was my brother?

"Are we going hiking?"

"No, we're going paragliding."

"I'm sorry, for a moment, I thought you said we were going paragliding."

"I did."

All this time, I'd thought *I* was the crazy one. Now I knew it was Roscoe.

"You want us to jump off a cliff with a parachute?"

"Technically, it's called a wing. Come on, where's your sense of adventure?"

"Back in Medellín."

He got out of the car, walked around the back, and opened my door. "It's safe; trust me."

There he was, asking me to trust him again.

"Have you tried it before?"

"Once or twice." He held out a hand. "There's nothing like floating among the clouds with the birds flying past, and we'll be riding tandem with an instructor. There's nothing to worry about."

An instructor? Okay, that sounded better. And really, it was time to let go of the old, boring version of Corazon da Silva. The girl who spent all her spare time at home and never got out and *lived*.

"I'll have a go."

That earned me a smile. "You won't regret it."

What do you know? Roscoe was right. Talk about exhilarating. For twenty minutes, we floated above the valleys of Bello, and I even got a video of the flight. At first, I thought I'd need the footage to prove to Rafe that I'd actually done it, but as we turned back to land, he soared past us solo. When did my brother learn to paraglide?

I didn't get the chance to find out, because Roscoe settled the bill and led me back to his Mercedes.

"Dinner? We don't have to make it ourselves today."

"Nothing spicy?"

"Nothing spicy, I promise." He leaned in to kiss me softly, on the lips this time. "Do you trust me yet?"

"I'm starting to."

"Good." Once again, he opened my door. "I enjoy spending time with you, Lina-Catalina."

"The feeling's mutual."

That evening, we went to a small café hidden away in a village between Bello and Medellín. The bandeja paisa wasn't as good as Grandma's, but it was still delicious.

"How do you find Colombian food?" I asked Roscoe.

"At first, I thought it was kinda weird. Rice and beans for breakfast? But now I've gotten used to it, and it's healthier than what we have back home. Sure, there's still KFC and Burger King, but there are so many other options, and everywhere delivers. It's too easy for kids to live on burgers and fries in the US, and more and more people have a weight problem. Do you cook?"

"When I have time." And when Grandma would let me use the kitchen. "I make a mean pandebono."

"That's cheese bread, right?"

"Right."

"Maybe we could try cooking together one day. I'll be your kitchen bitch."

I burst out laughing. "You can do the washing up."

"No need. I have a dishwasher."

"You want me to cook in your apartment?"

"Unless you'd rather we went to yours?"

"No, no. Yours is fine."

I half expected my brother to appear with another supermodel, but he didn't show up, and the café stayed almost empty the whole time we were there. Another couple talked quietly in one corner, and an old man sipped from a cup of aguapanela. I'd always found that drink too sweet, but Izzy loved it.

Roscoe wrapped his arm around me for the short walk back to the car. Truthfully, although this was supposed to be work, I'd enjoyed the trip to Bello more than any of the dates my ex had taken me on, and I found myself hoping more and more that Roscoe wasn't wrapped up in Izzy's disappearance. He drove slowly on the journey back to Medellín, and when he parked outside Esther's apartment, I was in no hurry to get out.

"Thank you for today," I said. "And thank you for pushing me outside my comfort zone."

"Right now, you're pushing me outside of mine."

He leaned towards me, and our lips met across the centre console. My first proper kiss in over a year, and although it wasn't a tear-each-other's-clothes-off sort of a kiss, it left me breathless. And yes, there were tongues.

Roscoe cupped my face in his hands and leaned his forehead against mine. "Can I take you out one evening next week?"

"Yes."

"I'll call you. And I'll miss you."

"I'll miss you too."

As I walked up the path to Esther's front door, texting her with an update as I went, I found myself wishing I was wrong. Wrong about Izzy, wrong about the phone call, wrong about the big conspiracy. Usually, I hated being wrong, but I wanted Roscoe to be one of the good guys. I wanted to go on more dinner dates and unexpected trips to the countryside. I wanted to find a little of the happiness that had eluded me for the last eleven years.

But first, I had to help my brother break into Roscoe's apartment.

CHAPTER 8 - CORA

"JUST SIT ON the bench opposite and call me if Roscoe comes back. That's all you have to do. Pretend to be on the phone or something."

So far, my brother had been worryingly vague on his plans.

"But what are *you* going to do? How will you get into Roscoe's apartment?"

A secret smile flickered across his face for a second, and then it was gone. Why did the bad stuff make him happy?

"Leave that to me, patata."

"Stop calling me a potato!"

Okay, so I'd been chubby as a child, but I'd lost all the puppy fat. Fifteen years on, my brother's old nickname for me didn't really fit anymore.

He pinched my cheeks, then leapt back before I managed to kick him. I'd missed this side of Rafe. The silly, playful side that had faded away with our parents' lives. Perhaps when this was over, we could spend more time together. Right now, I didn't even know where he lived.

Grandma wheeled herself through from the living room. "What's going on?"

"Rafe called me a potato again."

"Rafael, apologise to your sister."

"*Lo siento.* I guess you're more of a porcupine now, anyway. A bit prickly."

"Shut up! Are we going to do this or aren't we?"

Grandma's mouth twitched, and she showed us towards the door. "Be careful today, Cora. Listen to your brother."

"He's barely told me a thing."

"He's told you everything you need to know at this stage. Just don't panic if Roscoe returns early."

Deep breaths, Cora. I followed my brother out to his car, and half an hour later, he dropped me off two streets from Roscoe's apartment building, a huge glass edifice that probably cost him more rent in a month than I paid in a year. As Rafe had said, there was a bench opposite nestled under a shady tree on the edge of a small park, and I settled at one end with my phone in my hand. I should have bought a drink on the way. Or a snack. Dammit, I wasn't cut out for this job.

Five minutes passed before my brother reappeared, and I did a double take when I saw him. Instead of his usual jeans, well-worn boots, and henley, he'd changed into a scruffy pair of cargo pants paired with a grubby white T-shirt, a cap pulled low over his eyes, and a hi-vis vest with *JD Aire Acondicionado* emblazoned across the back. He carried his toolbox with all the enthusiasm of a man walking to his own death. Wow. I'd never realised my brother was quite such an actor, and he didn't turn a single female head as he shuffled up the front steps and disappeared into the apartment building.

Now came the difficult part. Watching and waiting. It was surprisingly hard to keep a close eye on the street while looking as if you were doing anything but.

In the end, I sent Roscoe a text message, telling him I missed him and asking how he was getting on in La Gitana, and when he replied saying he was just about to eat lunch and sent me a picture of a pizza, I relaxed infinitesimally. Of course, he could be lying, but he'd seemed genuine so far.

Thirty minutes passed, forty, and I thanked my lucky stars I'd worn a dark shirt because the back and underarms were soaked with sweat. How long did it take to search an apartment? And how much practice had Rafe had at this? In all honesty, I didn't want to know the answer to that second question.

Then the sirens started. Quiet at first, but as my fingers twitched over the screen of my phone, the wails grew louder. Closer. What if they were coming for Rafe? Had somebody reported a break-in? My heart pounded as I willed my nerves to hold out.

Finally, I could take it no longer.

Me: The police are near.

Nothing.

The first police car appeared around the corner, and although I willed it to drive past, it slewed to a halt outside Roscoe's apartment building. *Mierda!*

Me: Rafe, you need to leave NOW!

No answer. Should I create some sort of diversion? How? I was seriously considering throwing myself under a passing car when Rafe ambled down the steps, as cool as the air conditioner he'd pretended to fix. *Thank goodness.*

My phone buzzed in my hand.

Rafe: Pick you up outside the supermarket in 5.

When I slid into the passenger seat of the Honda, he'd lost the cap and the vest and looked more like my brother again.

"What the hell happened? Why didn't you answer my messages?"

"Because I was busy putting everything back into Roscoe's closet."

"I thought the police were coming to arrest you."

"They weren't."

"Then why were they there?"

"Probably because a couple on the first floor were having a screaming match, and the guy threatened to kill her. I bet a neighbour called the cops." Rafe reached across and squeezed my hand. "Next time, don't worry, patata *pequeña*."

"Are you crazy? How can I not worry? Wait. What next time?"

"Just a figure of speech."

How could Rafe act so nonchalant? I was still shaking.

"Did you find something in the closet?"

"Have patience, Corazon."

"I've been patient for an hour."

He didn't answer, just signalled and pulled out into traffic. Rafe's poker face was strong, and I had no idea what he was thinking.

"Will you tell me what you found? Please? Anything of Izzy's?"

"I didn't find anything that looked like it belonged to a woman at all, and nothing to suggest she'd ever been there."

"So we wasted our time?"

"I'm not sure. I don't think so."

"Then what *did* you find?"

"Let's talk when we get home."

I was fizzing with impatience by the time we walked into the kitchen, but Grandma merely looked up from her spot at the kitchen table and raised one eyebrow.

Rafe shrugged. "Maybe." Why did I get the feeling the pair of them spoke a language I didn't understand? "I got through everywhere but the kitchen, then the cops turned up due to an unconnected problem, so I figured I'd better leave. Glad I don't live in that building. Drama fucking central."

"And?"

"Bank statements." Rafe took a seat opposite Grandma. "I found offshore bank statements in a shoebox in the closet. In the last year, Roscoe Ward has deposited $280,000."

"US dollars?" Grandma asked.

"Yes."

I paced out of habit. "Why is that strange? He runs a successful business."

"His 'export company'?" Rafe used air quotes around the words. "It's a warehouse barely bigger than this apartment filled with more dust than goods. The guy who sits at the desk out front has no idea what he does to earn his salary every month, but like he told me, he doesn't get paid to ask questions."

Oh. Then how...?

"Eight deposits of thirty thousand each, then one of forty thousand the day after Izzy went missing."

Grandma's hands balled into fists. "That *cabrón* is selling the girls?"

Roscoe was *what*? Oh, no. No way. Where the hell could he sell them? Women weren't merchandise, and who would want to buy them anyway?

Rafe just nodded. "It would explain why most of his

so-called girlfriends have never been seen again."

"You can't honestly believe this?"

Grandma's theory was even more farfetched than Esther's.

"Why would he go to the trouble of staging Izzy's murder?" Grandma asked, seemingly unphased by developments. "When he didn't do the same for the others?"

"Probably because Izzy had a family who cared about her."

I stopped and put my hands on my hips. "Why would he take her at all if he knew people would search for her?"

Grandma looked at me sadly. "An extra ten thousand dollars."

"You're crazy. You're both crazy." My legs didn't want to hold me up anymore, and I sat down with a bump.

"I only wish we were, Corazon." Grandma reached out to smooth my hair back the way she'd done since I was a little girl. "I only wish we were."

"Everything fits, but how do we prove it?" Rafe asked. "And how do we find out who bought Izzy?"

"Proving it's simple, unfortunately. Sooner or later, Roscoe's going to invite Cora to Barranquilla. And you, Rafael, have to go with them."

Rafe shook his head before she finished the sentence. "No way. Sending Cora out for dinner is one thing, but she's not going to Barranquilla. What if he gets away and we can't find her?"

"Have faith in yourself. How often have you let men get away?"

Rafe hardened. Every part of him hardened—his

face, his body, his eyes, his voice.

"Never."

This was insane.

"Wait. Wait! Don't I get a say in this? What if I don't want to be a worm on a hook for a demented kidnapper?"

"Of course you get a say," Grandma said. "But this is the fastest path to Izzy. If we delay, it might be too late."

"What do you think they're doing to her?" I whispered.

"Don't dwell on that. Concentrate on what we can do to find her and bring her back home."

But I did dwell on it. All night long, when I didn't sleep a wink. Rafe was next door, in Izzy's bedroom, and I heard him tossing and turning as well. If he and Grandma were right, it didn't take a genius to work out what had happened to Isabella Morales. What might be happening to her at this very moment. I once watched a documentary on girls trafficked into the sex trade, forced to work in brothels with no hope of escape, and it made me cry. Now, tears rolled down my cheeks and soaked the pillow once again.

Could I really follow the same path as Izzy and risk my own life, or worse? What if Rafe lost track of me and I ended up in the same boat? And I meant "boat" quite literally—if Izzy had phoned for help from the United States, she must have crossed the Caribbean Sea.

But the alternative was to stay in Medellín, drifting through my safe and boring life while my best friend went through hell thousands of miles away. Could I live with myself if I did that?

Of course not.

I was in.

Whatever I had to do, I'd do it.

I just had to have faith that my brother would hold up his end of the bargain.

Monday morning came, and I was still cycling between fear and anger and denial when Roscoe called me. Rafael had left at just after dawn, driving down to Cali to work for two weeks, although he didn't elaborate on the particulars. Before he went, he told me to keep my dates with Roscoe to avoid arousing suspicion and promised he'd have a friend keep an eye on me.

"What friend?"

"It doesn't matter. Just know that he'll be there."

"But what if something happens?"

"It won't. Not yet. Roscoe's MO is to charm the girl first, not take her by brute force and stuff her into his trunk for a fourteen-hour drive to the coast."

"But—"

"Trust me."

Funny. That was exactly what Roscoe said, and look how that turned out. Although a part of me still struggled to believe he was a people trafficker. He'd been so happy on our trip to San Felix, and nothing about the kiss we'd shared had felt fake.

When he invited me out to the Delaire Sky Lounge, Medellín's most beautiful restaurant with views over the city from the outside roof terrace, I wasn't sure whether to yell at him or gratefully accept. In the end, I agreed to meet him there on Tuesday evening after work, which at least meant I didn't need to go to Esther's place first.

"I wish Rafe was here," I said to Grandma as I touched up my make-up.

"So do I, Corazon. But these are difficult times, and we have to do the best we can with them."

"Do you truly suspect Roscoe took Izzy?"

"If not him, then somebody else. At the moment, I can't think of a better explanation for her disappearance." She wheeled herself a little closer. "This is a brave thing you're doing, Cora. And I know it's difficult to believe that things will turn out well, but if anyone can find Isabella, it's your brother."

"I keep wondering if we should go to the police."

She shook her head vehemently. "The police are not to be trusted. And even if they were, do you really think they'd launch an investigation with so little evidence?"

"I guess not."

"Just stay out in public tonight, and if you feel uncomfortable at any time, make an excuse and leave."

"Rafe said somebody will be watching."

"Then somebody will be watching." Grandma took my arms and pulled me towards her for a hug. "I'm so proud of you for helping Izzy."

Proud? I wasn't proud. I was terrified.

I'd always wanted to eat at the Delaire Sky Lounge, but now I was there, sitting on a comfortable couch and gazing out across the skyline, I longed to be somewhere else.

Roscoe sat across from me, tucking into a piping-hot pizza, freshly cooked in the wood-fired oven. He'd gone for mozzarella, ham, and caramelised pineapple. Ugh. Pineapple? That was the first obvious chink in Roscoe's perfect exterior, because who did that?

"You seem quiet today, Lina."

"I've been busy. Lessons from nine until six."

"Is your pasta okay? Hot enough?"

"Delicious. It's just a big portion, that's all."

I looked surreptitiously around the restaurant, trying to work out who my brother had sent to watch over me. The couple in the corner in their mid-twenties? No, they were almost finished with their meal. The group in the far corner were all far too drunk. I thought it might be the smart man in the suit, but then his girlfriend arrived and they only had eyes for each other. One of the waiters? Could Rafe have resorted to bribery?

Then I spotted him. The old man in the corner, wearing a linen suit and reading the paper as though he didn't have a care in the world. I'd never have guessed if I hadn't seen that same man in the café in Bello, although he was wearing glasses now.

That was him? That was my brother's partner in crime? He looked older than Grandma. Last time, I'd barely given him a second glance, but now I realised he was my babysitter, I studied him a little harder. Had I seen him somewhere before? Besides in the café, I mean.

"Do you want to come over later in the week?" Roscoe asked. "We could cook dinner together."

No, I absolutely didn't want to. Not until we worked out whether he was a bad guy or merely a bystander who'd got caught up in this mess. I wished I could ask him outright what was going on, but if he was guilty, that would tip him off and we might never find out the truth. No, that wasn't an option, so I had to stay saccharine instead.

"Sorry, I can't. I have late lessons every evening this week, but I can still go to Parque Explora at the weekend."

He cut another piece of pizza and popped it into his mouth, chewing slowly, then reached over to take my hand.

"Saturday?"

"Perfect."

"I look forward to it. And I'm glad you came tonight. What do you think of the restaurant?"

"The view's amazing."

He broke into a smile and gazed in my direction. "Yeah, it is."

Cheesy, but if I hadn't been having doubts about Roscoe's character, I'd have found it kind of cute. This double-agent thing was so freaking difficult, and I had to keep remembering to focus on my goal: find Izzy and rescue her from whatever trouble she'd gotten into.

"You know what I meant—the view over the city."

"I do, but you're beautiful, Lina-Catalina. I'm a lucky man."

Lucky in what way? How much money would I fetch on the black market? Thirty thousand dollars? Forty? I forced a smile.

"I'm the lucky one. I've never met anyone quite like you, Roscoe."

He leaned forward to kiss me, chastely since we were in public, and it felt better than it should have.

"Do you want dessert?"

I shook my head. "No, thank you."

Because my insides were in turmoil. My heart wanted to believe Roscoe was innocent. My head told me to wait and see. And a niggle in my gut told me he was too good to be true, that no bona fide gentleman would pluck a girl like me from a place like El Bajo Tierra and make her dreams come true.

Did that twinkle in his eye hide darkness in his soul?

When we locked lips again at the end of the evening, I felt sick inside. I was lying, and maybe Roscoe was lying too. Everything between us was built on a foundation of quicksand, and I was getting sucked further and further into the mire.

"Where do you want to go?" Roscoe asked as we stood in line outside Parque Explora.

"The Mind exhibition. And the planetarium. How about you?"

"The reptile house and the aquarium. Did you know they have a replica of the Amazon basin? Have you ever been to the Amazon? One day, I want to see it for myself, but I've never gotten that far south."

"No, I never have."

Not in the last eleven years, anyway. In truth, I didn't want to visit the aquarium because of the memories it would bring back, but I could hardly explain that to Roscoe.

First, the planetarium lulled me into a false sense of security. Roscoe held my hand as we learned the secrets of the universe, and I almost forgot why I'd come to Parque Explora in the first place.

Izzy. It was all about Izzy.

Predictably, he left it until we reached the aquarium to drop his bombshell on me. Right beside the piranhas, in fact, and either he was oblivious to the symbolism or he had a sick sense of humour.

"I realise this might seem a bit forward, and feel free to say no, but I've got to take a trip to Barranquilla next weekend to talk to a business associate, and I thought you might want to come for the ride. Nothing heavy..." He carried on, oblivious to the fact that my guts were trying to heave themselves up. "We can get separate hotel rooms if you prefer. But it's an interesting city. Great nightlife, there's a good beach nearby at Puerto Velero. Do you like salsa?"

He wiggled his hips, and I swallowed down bile.

"You're a much better dancer than me," he carried on, not bothered by my silence. "And the modern art museum is worth a visit."

Across the tank of fish, my septuagenarian shadow caught my eye. He understood I was in trouble, but his face stayed impassive as he ambled closer.

"So, what do you think?" Roscoe asked.

I thought I wanted to run right out of the aquarium and carry on going until I found either my brother or a gun. Years had passed since I wished harm on anyone, but at that moment, I knew all our suspicions about Roscoe were correct and I wanted to strangle him with my bare hands. But only after I beat the information we needed out of him. What had he done with Izzy?

But I couldn't do any of that, of course. No, I blinked once, slowly, in an attempt to hide the emotions simmering beneath the surface.

"Next weekend? I'll have to check." Rafe had suspected this would happen, just not so soon. And he was supposed to be in Cali for at least another week. "I promised a friend I'd go shopping with her. What about the weekend after instead?"

"Sorry. This guy's only in town for a couple of days, and he won't be back for months. We can fly there on Friday after you've finished work and head back on Sunday evening. No need to take any time off."

Deep breaths, Cora.

"Let me make a call? I'll see if I can rearrange."

"Sure. Hey, did you see this eel?"

"I need to use the bathroom."

I backed away, heart hammering against my ribcage. Roscoe was a monster in Ralph Lauren clothing. The last thing I wanted to do was go to Barranquilla with him, but I had no choice if we wanted to find Izzy quickly.

Outside, my hands shook as I dialled my brother. *Please answer.*

"Rafe?"

"What's wrong?"

"He wants to go this weekend, on Friday evening. Roscoe. To Barranquilla."

"Shit. That's soon."

"I know, and I tried to delay until next weekend, but he said that wasn't possible."

"He's probably got a boat coming in."

A tear leaked out. *Mierda*, I'd been so emotional these last few weeks. I felt a tap on my shoulder, and the old man handed me a handkerchief before melting back into the crowd.

"What should I say?"

There was a long pause, so long I thought the line had gone dead. But then Rafe spoke.

"Tell him yes. I'll be back by Friday."

"Are you sure?"

"Patata pequeña, I'm always sure."

I smiled in spite of the tears. "I'm not a potato."

"Cora, you'll always be my potato."

CHAPTER 9 - CORA

"WHERE THE HELL is Rafael?"

I paced the kitchen, only I didn't look where I was going and stubbed my toe on the mini-suitcase waiting by the door.

"Ouch!"

Grandma sat calmly at the table, a cup of coffee in her hands.

"If he said he'd be here, then he'll be here."

"But I need to leave in an hour!"

Roscoe was picking me up from Esther's building at six, and my nerves were bad enough already without my safety net going AWOL. All week, Roscoe had been messaging me sweet comments and more ideas for things we could do in Barranquilla. Did I want to go to San Nicolás de Tolentino church? Not unless it was for Roscoe's funeral.

I tried calling Rafe again, but it went straight to voicemail. If he hadn't answered my other ten messages, why bother leaving one more? I was just about to unleash another string of curses aimed at my brother when the front door crashed open.

What the...?

Rafe staggered in, clutching his arm, followed by the old man who'd been tailing me for the last two weeks. Grandma got halfway out of her chair, supporting herself on the table with her arms. She could just about stand in an emergency, and this sure looked like one if the blood dripping from my brother's arm was any indication.

"It's just a nick," he said through gritted teeth. "It opened up again when I got out of the car."

"You drove like that?" I gasped.

"No, Vicente drove."

Vicente. So that was his name. But who was he and what was he doing with my injured brother? I took a closer look, and a vague memory flitted back of a similar-looking man talking to my father one night. Was Vicente from our old village?

I didn't get the chance to ask before Grandma took over.

"Cora, call Dores. She's at the supermarket."

"And tell her what?" I shrieked.

My brother tried to protest. "I'll be fine."

Grandma was having none of it. "Rafael da Silva, you're supposed to be going to Barranquilla in one hour, and we need you in the best shape possible to look after your sister." She turned back to me. "Call Dores. Tell her she needs to do some sewing."

My hands shook as I relayed the message. Dores didn't say much, just that she'd be back in ten minutes. She sounded almost resigned. Why? What did she know that I didn't?

Meanwhile, Rafe had taken off his leather jacket, and my knees went weak when I saw the huge red stain spread out over his white T-shirt.

"What happened?" I whispered.

"Did you finish the job?" Grandma asked.

"I don't know. I hit him, but then someone shot at

me, and I had to run." Rafe screwed his eyes shut. "Fuck. I thought I'd accounted for all the guards. There must have been an extra one."

"The bullet missed the bone," Vicente added.

Grandma closed her eyes, breathing softly. No stress. She never got flustered.

Not like me.

"What the hell is going on?" I yelled.

Rafe and Vicente looked at each other, and I swear my stupid brother rolled his eyes. Grandma merely patted the chair next to her and beckoned me closer.

"Just tell me!"

"Cora, come and sit down."

My legs didn't want to hold me up anyway, so I collapsed onto the seat. "I don't understand. What's happening?"

"It's time for you to have a little lesson in our family history." She shook her head sadly. "I'd hoped to avoid this, but I should have realised it was inevitable."

"*What* was inevitable?"

"That the past would come back to haunt us. Eight years ago, your brother followed in your father's footsteps and joined the family business."

Family business? "He's a builder?"

My papa used to leave us for weeks at a time to work in the nearby city, building houses and shopping malls and warehouses. He built our house too, and basic though life was in our remote little village, I'd loved the peace and the closeness of nature. Every night, I fell asleep listening to the sounds of the jungle, whereas now the traffic kept me awake.

"Your father wasn't a builder, Corazon. He was a sicario."

"A *what*?" A hitman? No, no, no. She had to be kidding. This was a cruel, cruel joke.

"No. No way. My father was gentle. He was your son! How can you say that about him?"

"Because it's true. Your grandfather was also a sicario, and so was I when I had legs instead of wheels."

I couldn't take any more of this. I ran to the bathroom and threw up, once, twice, three times, until there wasn't anything left inside me. It was Vicente who passed me a handful of wadded-up tissue. He seemed to be making a habit of this.

"I know this must be a shock, child," he said.

"I'm not a freaking child!"

"Until today, you still had that innocence. I'm sorry you've lost it."

"Who are you?"

"A friend of your grandfather's. I trained Rafael."

"Then you're... You're also..."

I couldn't even say the word.

"A sicario? Yes."

"I want to wake up now."

"We all wish for the nightmare to end."

"But Grandma... Tell me she wasn't serious. Is she suffering from delusions? Dementia?"

"Your grandma's mind is as sharp as it's always been. La Leona, they called her. The lioness. She was as fierce as they came. Even now, I don't want to get on her bad side."

"What about my mother? Was she involved in this... this business?"

"She was a fixer. Your grandma fulfils that role now."

Once again, my whole world had been flipped on its

head. Grandma played the piano and crocheted and made an excellent bandeja paisa. She didn't freaking kill people. Right?

I staggered into the kitchen in time to see her wipe a vicious-looking knife on the remains of my brother's shirt—now cut into tatters on the table—fold the blade up, and tuck it down the side of her wheelchair. Oh. My. Gosh.

"Why didn't anyone tell me?" I asked hollowly.

Grandma sighed. "Because I wanted one person— just one person—in this family to turn out normal."

A key rattled in the lock.

"Does Dores know?"

"Some of it. Vicente, would you mind fetching the first aid kit?"

Dores was silent, stoic, as she pulled a bullet out of my brother's arm and stitched up the wound. If she was surprised at tonight's events, she didn't show it. Me? I paced the tiles like a woman possessed. My entire family were criminals. What was I meant to do? I could hardly turn them in.

"Corazon knows now?" Dores asked Grandma.

"We just told her."

"Who did Rafe shoot?" I asked. "He shot someone, didn't he?"

"Another drug lord," Grandma told me. "Those are the only jobs we take now. Cocaine has been a scourge on this country and a scourge on our family for as long as I can remember. We lost our home because of it. The police, those that haven't been bribed into turning a blind eye, only chip away at the edges of the industry, but we can make big holes right in the middle if we dig in the right place."

"I can't believe this."

"I appreciate this is bad timing."

"You think? In twenty minutes, I'm supposed to fly to Barranquilla and get sold into freaking slavery. What about him?" I pointed at my brother. "Will he be in a fit state to come with me, or am I on my own?"

"What's this about Barranquilla?" Dores asked.

"Perhaps you could explain, Grandma, since you seem to be in such a talkative mood tonight."

"You shouldn't be fighting among yourselves," Vicente told us. "Not today. Put your differences aside and get the job done."

"Like Rafe did?"

"That was the first time he's made a mistake, and it only happened because he was rushing to come back and help you."

"So him getting shot is my fault?"

"I didn't say that."

"But you insinuated it."

"Enough!" Grandma said. "Rafe, are you able to continue?"

"I'm fine." He sounded subdued, sulky almost, a far cry from his usual assured self. "Just give me some painkillers."

"And, Cora, can you cope? Or should we call the whole thing off?"

I glanced at Dores, and she'd gone a few shades paler. No, I couldn't back out now, not when Dores and Izzy needed me.

"I'm going."

"Good. However much we might have sheltered you, in your heart, you're a da Silva. You were born to do this."

"You can't honestly believe that."

"I do believe it. You're like your brother in more ways than you would imagine."

"What ways? I've certainly never freaking shot anyone."

"You have the same inner strength. You're smart. Those instincts that you try so hard to ignore? You should listen to them more often. Cultivate them. Trust your gut. It'll get you out of trouble."

"I thought Rafe was supposed to get me out of trouble."

"He will. I have faith in him. I have faith in both of you." She looked me up and down, and I swear her eyes had gone a shade darker. "You need to change your shirt. That one's got blood on it."

"*Mierda.*"

"And then it's time for you to leave. Your brother will follow with Vicente."

"How? How will they get to Barranquilla?"

"In Vicente's plane."

Of course. How stupid of me.

"And how will they find me once they get there?"

"I'll track your phone," Rafe said.

Vicente stepped forward, digging around in his pocket. "I also have this for you." He drew out a bracelet made from chunky multicoloured plastic beads, each one decorated with an abstract pattern. "It has a tracker concealed inside. See, here." He pointed at the only purple bead. "There's a tiny switch in this groove you can press with a fingernail. One click to turn it on, another to turn it off."

"How do I tell whether it's on or off?"

"The button will be raised when it's off."

I tested it, and Vicente nodded approvingly.

"What happens if someone takes the bracelet?"

"It doesn't look expensive, so we're hoping that doesn't happen. But as long as it isn't destroyed, we can track it to the thief and make him talk."

Oh hell. This was real, wasn't it?

"Or you can break that bead off and swallow it," Vicente continued.

The mere thought of that made me want to puke again.

"And here's your passport. Rafael said you were using the name Catalina?"

"Yes."

It came out as a croak. Needing new identity documents hadn't even occurred to me, but here I was, Catalina Perez, almost twenty-three years old and with a photo more akin to a mugshot. When I flicked through the dog-eared pages, they'd even included stamps for England. These people, my family who I barely knew, operated on a whole different level to me.

It took me three tries to get a fresh shirt buttoned up, and Vicente had to fasten the bracelet on for me because my fingers were trembling so much. Rafe's bleeding had stopped now, and Dores's neat row of stitches stuck out from his arm like a spiky black caterpillar.

"That's better," Grandma said. "We've suffered a small setback today, but we'll win. We always do." She took both of my hands in hers the way she had so many times in the past, except this evening, my brother's blood speckled her tanned skin. "Come back safely, Corazon. I've already lost my husband and all three of my sons. You, Rafe, Dores, Isabella, and Vicente are all

I have left. I can't lose another three."

No pressure, then.

"I have to go."

As I walked out the door, I heard Grandma speaking in that eerily calm voice of hers.

"Sit down, Dores. We need to have a talk."

CHAPTER 10 - CORA

THE LIGHTS OF Soledad twinkled up at us as we descended towards Ernesto Cortissoz International Airport. Barranquilla was a short drive away, and Roscoe promised we'd get dinner right after we found our hotel. In the rental car, he chatted about his previous trips to the city and how the energetic vibe made up for the fact that the buildings were a bit ugly. Oddly enough, he neglected to mention any former travel companions.

He'd chosen to stay in the Sonesta, which made sense when I pondered it. The place was huge—a hundred rooms at least—so who would notice when he checked out alone? Any other girl would have been impressed by the opulent decor, but I only grew more twitchy as we rode up to our floor in the elevator. Two rooms, side by side. At least he'd kept his promise on that, because I'd be damned if I was gonna sleep with the asshole.

"I thought we'd have sushi for dinner," he said as he fumbled with his key card. "There's a great restaurant downstairs."

"Sushi's good."

"Meet you in the lobby in twenty minutes?"

"Sure."

"Are you okay? You seem quiet."

Finally, he'd noticed. "Flying always makes me tired. The pressure changes, I think."

In reality, today's trip had been my first time on an aeroplane, and I'd have enjoyed it if not for the company. The exhilaration of the takeoff, the way everything below looked so tiny. At twenty-two, I'd seen a whole different side to my country, and it made me want to get out and explore the world. Just not from the inside of a shipping container or wherever Roscoe planned to stash me before the weekend was over.

He reached out and twirled my hair between his fingers. "Me too. Perhaps we can have an early night?"

Surely he wasn't suggesting... He was. That lazy little smile confirmed it. The sly *cabrón* actually planned on trying to get me into bed before he sold me like a side of meat. Well, he'd be spending some quality time with his hand this evening, because I was playing the game by my own rules.

And now I yawned for effect. "An early night sounds like a great idea. I'll be asleep as soon as my head hits the pillow."

His smile faded, but mine grew as I turned away and walked into my own room. Did he have an expense account for this sort of thing? Did he treat my room rental as tax deductible? I slipped my shoes off and flopped back on the bed, drained. This afternoon's events had rocked me to my core. Grandma's revelations, my brother getting shot... Four inches to the left, and the bullet would have gone through his heart. And now I had to pretend to be someone else when I barely knew myself anymore.

Twenty minutes passed all too quickly. I hadn't

bothered to unpack, because what was the point when I'd never see any of my stuff again? I'd deliberately left anything I cared about at home. Roscoe was already waiting when I got to the lobby, and in the restaurant, I found myself looking around for Rafe. There was no sign of him, but I breathed a little easier when I spotted Vicente in a corner, sipping on a glass of wine. Who'd have thought I'd ever be happy to see a sicario?

"What would you prefer to do tomorrow?" Roscoe asked. "Go to a museum? The beach? Shopping? An art gallery?"

"Why don't you tell me about your favourite places?" Because then I wouldn't have to talk.

He rambled on for a full fifteen minutes while I nodded in the appropriate places and forced some food down. I wasn't hungry in the slightest, but common sense told me I needed to keep up my strength for the ordeal ahead. After this, I'd never eat sushi again.

We narrowed it down to two places—the Caribbean museum or the beach, which was a short drive out of the city but apparently worth the trip—and Roscoe popped California rolls in his mouth without a care in the world.

"What's it to be, Lina-Catalina? Where do you want to go?"

I asked the obvious question. "Can't we do both? One tomorrow, and one on Sunday? After all, we're here for two days."

Roscoe's smile faded for a second before it ratcheted back into place, and then I knew. *I* wouldn't be here on Sunday. Whatever he had planned for me, it would happen tomorrow.

But the asshole just nodded. "Of course, of course.

So, which place do you want to visit first?"

"The beach. Can we watch the sunrise?"

"We'd have to get up at some crazy hour."

"That's okay. We can have an early night tomorrow instead." I smiled as I reached across the table for his hand and squeezed it. "Good things are worth waiting for, right?"

Roscoe didn't look quite so happy with that plan, but he could hardly say no. "Right."

The next morning, we drove through the city in near darkness. Roscoe was right—Barranquilla wasn't the prettiest. It suddenly struck me that if everything went wrong, this could be the last time I saw my country. Colombia. For two decades, the place had torn at my soul then mended the holes. The lows had left dark smudges on my heart that I'd never erase, but with each year had come new highs and hope for the future.

I didn't want to die young.

The sun rose over the land rather than the sea, so not quite a picture-postcard view, but I still relished being outside in the fresh air without the pollution that hung over Medellín. If it weren't for Roscoe at my side, I would have felt free. If only he could just stop *breathing*.

Then I caught a shadow in my peripheral vision, and the spell was broken. My brother had come along for the ride too.

Thank goodness.

I'd messaged him last night to tell him today was the day, but all I'd got back was a one-word reply. *Ready.*

Well, I was glad somebody was.

I thought when Roscoe encouraged me to swim in the sea with him, that would be the moment, because wasn't that how Izzy had disappeared? In the sea? But all that happened was that my skin went wrinkly, and after an hour in the water, Roscoe led me back to the beach and rented a couple of sun loungers. A waiter from a nearby restaurant brought cocktails and seafood for lunch. The sun rose higher in the sky, and the wait was grating on my last nerve.

Couldn't he just hurry up and kidnap me already?

No, it seemed.

"Hey, your back's burning," he said. "Let me put more sunblock on for you."

Always the gentleman, he'd brought everything we needed for a day out—sunblock, a blanket, a cooler with drinks, towels, sunglasses for both of us. And now he dribbled cool liquid over my back and rubbed it in with his slimy little hands.

Get a move on. Adrenaline had been simmering inside me since daybreak, and lying still wasn't easy when I wanted to punch something, preferably Roscoe's perfectly straight nose. But he rolled back onto his own sun lounger, totally relaxed, and there he stayed until the sun dropped low over the horizon.

"Guess we should head back," he said when I'd almost reached the end of my tether.

"Great idea."

I had my sundress on before he got to his feet, and it only took a few minutes for us to pack everything up and carry it back to the car. Where was my brother? He'd been on the beach half an hour earlier, but after the fourth group of women approached him, he'd rolled up his towel and disappeared again.

"Do you need to use the bathroom before we go?" Roscoe asked.

"No, but I'm thirsty. Could you pass a bottle of water?"

"Sure."

I nearly missed it. The tiny black dot on the corner of the label, and the slightly bitter taste of the water itself. But there was no mistaking the wave of tiredness that crashed over me as Roscoe started the engine and pulled away from the beach.

"What's happening?" I mumbled.

He reached over and squeezed my hand, almost regretfully it seemed.

"I'm sorry, Lina-Catalina. Really I am."

"What do you...?"

The road ahead faded, and my eyelids began to close.

"You're special, Lina-Catalina. You're the only one I've ever wanted to keep."

He kept talking, but the words made no sense. Half a minute later, Roscoe disappeared completely, and I didn't know whether to be relieved or upset about that.

Then...darkness.

CHAPTER 11 - BLACK

BLACK GROANED AS he took in the scene on the third floor at the headquarters of Blackwood Security.

A large, open-plan office.

Fifteen bemused employees.

And his wife standing on a desk at the far end, hands on hips.

"I'll ask one more time," she said. "Where the hell are Bob and Stewart?"

He skirted around the people gawping at Emmy and ducked into their shared office. Sure enough, her fish tank contained one goldfish—Kevin, presumably, although he had no idea how she told them apart—and two carrot sticks. Bradley, their shared personal assistant, had bought her the trio a month ago after watching a documentary on the Discovery Channel that said keeping fish helped people to de-stress, but looking at Emmy outside, it wasn't fucking working, was it?

One of the clowns working in her Special Projects department had undoubtedly taken them, but none of the people outside looked particularly guilty. Well, apart from Nate, one of their business partners, but he always looked guilty. Black dropped his briefcase beside his desk and went to retrieve his darling wife.

"Diamond, get off the table."

"Someone's taken my fish." She stared daggers around the room again. "You'd better be feeding them, you asshole."

"They'll bring them back."

"But Kevin's getting lonely."

Black secretly doubted Kevin had even noticed his two companions were missing, but he kept that opinion to himself.

"I'll find the fish, but we've got a meeting in fifteen minutes and I need to speak with you first."

When Emmy didn't move, he plucked her off the desk and set her on the floor. Now he got the benefit of her annoyance before she turned on her heel and stomped back to her own seat.

After three days in Albuquerque, a week in Belize, and another two days in Chicago, Black had hoped for more than a dirty glare when he arrived home. If only his wife looked at him the same way she looked at her remaining goldfish.

"The carrot sticks were a nice touch," he said.

"Fuck you."

Now, that was the answer he'd been hoping for. Before she could come up with any more piscatory complaints, he bundled her into the private bathroom that opened off their office and locked the door.

"On your knees, Diamond."

"Asshole," she muttered, but she stood on tiptoe and crushed her lips against his anyway.

"That can be arranged."

"Prick."

"That too."

Black grabbed a towel from the heated rail and dropped it onto the floor. Really, they should get a cushion in here. Bradley left enough of them all over the fucking house. Emmy already had Black's belt undone, and a low groan escaped his lips as her hand closed over his cock.

"Why are you still standing?" he asked.

That earned him another glare, which he ignored as he fisted one hand in her long blonde hair and forced her to her knees. Emmy pretended to hate being ordered around, but secretly, she liked it as much as Black did, in the bedroom at least. Outside? All bets were off.

Now she tugged his pants down, then his boxer briefs, and the instant his cock sprang free, she sucked it into her mouth. Well, not quite all of it. For a moment, he wished it were smaller so it would fit, because Emmy with a bigger mouth would be unbearable.

Then she scraped her teeth along the sensitive underside and swirled her tongue around the head, and rational thought became impossible.

Emmy was bent over the sink with her pants around her ankles when Nate shouted from outside in the office.

"Get out of the bathroom, you asshole."

"Two minutes."

Emmy raised her head an inch. "Five minutes."

"We're all waiting," Nate told them, and Black knew his old friend would be shaking his head. But fuck him, because if he'd just got back from a job, he'd be doing exactly the same thing with his wife, Carmen.

So Black ignored Nate's grumbling and thrust into Emmy once more, reaching around to play with her clit because yeah, they were kind of late.

"You won't last five minutes," he murmured.

"Yes, I— Fuck."

She clenched around him, and he came too, holding himself deep as he peppered kisses down the side of her neck.

"Love you, Emerson Black."

"Love you too, Chuck. Why the hell did you schedule a meeting for fifteen minutes after you got back?"

"Because I wanted to get it over with so I can take you out for dinner this evening."

"Okay, you're forgiven. But I still want my fucking fish back."

"Would you like your swear jar back as well?"

"It's full."

The pair got a round of applause as they walked into the conference room, five minutes late for their ten a.m. meeting, and one joker threw a condom at them. But Black didn't care. As the boss, he had to prioritise getting the job done, but as long as Blackwood kept running smoothly, he did whatever else he pleased. His wife, mainly.

She took a seat next to him and gave her friend Daniela some serious side-eye. No prizes for guessing where the condom came from. Their office assistant, Sloane, brought in coffee and a fruit platter, Nate dimmed the lights, and the first item on the agenda flashed onto the screen.

They needed a new executive-protection lead in the Texas office. Black had a preferred appointee, but as always, they'd discuss the options and take a vote on it. Eight people sat in on these management meetings, and Blackwood was bigger than any one man. Or woman.

Nick Goldman, the firm's head of executive protection, leaned forward to speak.

"We have three men in the running for the job. First up, Joe Arlint. He's been with us for seven years, and before that, he worked for the secret service under..."

Emmy's phone vibrated on the table. Not her normal, everyday phone—she'd left that on her desk— but the one designated as her "red" emergency phone that she always had to answer.

Sebastien calling.

But why? Sebastien Garcia was the son of a man Emmy considered a surrogate father. She had two of those—Jimmy James, an ex-boxer from England, and Eduardo Garcia, a borderline-insane drug lord who lived in Colombia. Sebastien rarely called Emmy, not on this phone. He Skyped her in the evenings or sent emails. If he was phoning now, that meant there was a problem, and that problem was most probably to do with Eduardo since Sebastien was calling rather than the old man.

Emmy slid out of her seat, and Black watched her legs through the glass window of the conference room. A frosted panel obscured her face, but she was pacing, and that wasn't a good thing. He took out his own phone, still half listening as Nick outlined the pros and cons of each shortlisted candidate.

Black: Bradley, pack bags for Emmy and me. Colombia. Enough for 2 weeks. Thx.

And another message to his pilot.

Black: Brett, be on standby with the Global 8000. File a flight plan for Cali, Colombia. Thx.

Very little fazed Emmy, so one look at her ashen

face when she walked back into the conference room, and Black knew he'd guessed right. Something had happened to Eduardo, and they needed to fly to Cali.

Nick trailed off as Emmy gripped the back of her seat, and all heads turned in her direction.

"What happened?" Black asked.

"Someone shot Eduardo."

"Is he still alive?"

"At the moment. The bullet lodged in his lung and it collapsed. Seb sealed the entrance hole, which let him breathe, but he hit his head when he fell down the stairs, and now he's in a coma. Shit. I need to go to Colombia."

"*We* need to go to Colombia."

"Are you sure? Your last trip there wasn't so great."

Wasn't that the understatement of the century? Black had spent eight and a half months imprisoned underground by a drug lord following a case of mistaken identity, and no, he didn't really want to go back. But Eduardo had been instrumental in the operation that ultimately freed him, so he owed the crazy old coot, and there was no chance he was letting Emmy go alone. Because Black knew his wife too well. While she undoubtedly wanted to spend time with Eduardo, she'd also want retribution.

"I'm coming. What happened to the shooter?"

"He got away. Floriana emptied a magazine at him, and there was blood, but he escaped."

Floriana was Eduardo's wife, a tiny woman in her late thirties who came across as more deferential than deadly. But some people stepped up in unexpected ways when the people they loved were threatened. Black nodded once. They'd need weapons. Eduardo had an arrangement at the local airport, so flying into the country with anything from a Beretta Nano to a full-on missile wouldn't be a problem.

"Do you want company?" Nate asked.

While Black would have liked nothing better than a helping hand from his old Navy SEAL swim buddy, Blackwood wouldn't run itself, and it made sense to get to Cali and find out what was going on before throwing endless manpower at the task.

"Not right now. Maybe in a few days. If you've got any capacity, talk to Sloane and get her to move some shit from my schedule to yours."

"Will do."

"We'll all share the load," Nick chipped in. "Won't we?"

Everyone around the table murmured their agreement, and Black wrapped an arm around Emmy's waist. Nobody asked further questions; they didn't need to. They'd all been involved in the last Colombian operation, so they understood what Eduardo meant to Emmy.

"Just do me a favour and get those damn goldfish back in their tank," Black said over one shoulder as they left the room.

Back at the Riverley estate, he abandoned his Porsche Cayenne outside the main house. Emmy leapt out of the vehicle before he turned the engine off, then strode towards the front door with a sense of purpose that made him both proud and slightly nervous. He'd spent over a decade training her to compartmentalise her feelings and get the job done, and now she wanted blood.

Bradley was waiting in the hallway, two bags beside

him—Black's leather duffel and a dark purple suitcase for Emmy.

"I wasn't sure whether you needed beachwear, so I just packed one bikini for Emmy and a pair of swim shorts for you. And flip-flops. Everybody needs flip-flops."

"We're not going to the beach."

"I don't need a bikini. I need a fucking bullet," Emmy said.

"Why? What happened?"

"Someone shot Eduardo."

Bradley's hands flew to his mouth. "Ohmigosh! Is he dead?"

"No, but the asshole who pulled the trigger soon will be."

A chill fell over the cavernous room. Okay, so Black might have been imagining that, but Ana was eternal fucking winter with a black bob and bright red lipstick. Carmen stood behind her with a sniper rifle cradled in her arms.

"You need to kill someone?" Ana asked.

"Somebody shot Eduardo," Bradley told her. "I have a whole selection of sympathy cards upstairs. Should we send flowers? Lilies? Roses?"

"Flowers? Pshhht. You should send a message instead."

"Duh. That's what you write in the card."

Ana rolled her eyes, and Black swallowed a snort. Ana wasn't talking about a note, she was talking about finding the son of a bitch who put Eduardo in the hospital and slitting his throat from ear to ear. Knowing Ana, she'd probably tie the guy spread-eagle over the hood of his car and insert his gun barrel up his rectum too. Thank goodness she wasn't coming to join the party, or things could get messy.

"I'm gonna rip his fucking guts out," Emmy said.

"Sounds fun. Give me five minutes; I'll pack a bag."

Oh, shit. "*I'm* going with Emmy," Black told her.

"And I'll come too."

"What about your daughter?"

"Sam's taken her to visit her grandparents for a week."

"Haven't you ever heard the phrase 'two's company, three's a crowd'?"

Ana was a fearsome assassin, but somewhat of an unknown quantity. Black still hadn't quite fathomed her out, and he wasn't sure anyone else had either. Ana's loyalties lay with Emmy, the two of them bound by blood, and the prospect of Ana ricocheting around Colombia like a loose cannon with Emmy, who was driven by anger at the moment, didn't exactly fill him with glee.

But Eduardo had helped Ana out in the past too, and now she fixed her violet eyes on Black's. She was one of the few people who didn't back down from his stare.

"*Berís' drúzhno, ne búdet grúzno.*"

Loosely translated as "take hold of it together, it won't feel heavy." Many hands make light work.

Fuck.

Black ticked the points off on his fingers. "No grenades, no rocket launchers, no high explosives."

Ana had a knife in her hand before he could blink, a wicked-looking Emerson CQC-7B with a matt black tanto blade, perfect for slicing through a man's chest.

"This will be enough."

Heaven help him.

CHAPTER 12 - EMMY

EMMY PACED THE aisle of Black's jet as it flew south over Virginia. She'd managed to stay in her seat for takeoff, but now her stress leaked out around the edges. What if Eduardo didn't make it? She hadn't even seen him in three months, and soon guilt crept in too. She should have made more time to visit because Skype was no substitute for a hug.

Black snagged her hand as she walked past and pulled her into his lap. Without the help Eduardo had given, her husband would be either dead or festering in a hole in Colombia's Amazonian region, and Emmy would still be piecing together the remains of her shattered life. They both owed Eduardo everything.

Yes, he was a drug lord, and yes, he'd done some pretty fucked-up shit in the past, but over the last few years, he'd changed. He'd seen the damage drugs did, and the final straw had been the raid at the Ramos compound that freed Black. Since then, he'd made a concerted effort to diversify his investments so his sons wouldn't have to sell coke for a living. Now the Garcia family owned a string of nightclubs, bars, and restaurants, four coffee plantations, an airline, a shopping mall, a handful of hotels, and a portfolio of rental properties among other things.

And Eduardo had a heart. If you were a friend, his

loyalty was unquestionable.

"Diamond, they call Eduardo 'The Cat' for a reason. He's got nine lives. He's survived the drug war for fifty-eight years so far, and there's every chance he'll pull through this."

"What if he doesn't?"

"The hospital said he's stable right now."

"Stable but critical."

"Quit with the negativity. Sometimes you're your own worst enemy."

Dammit, Black was right, just like always. Emmy had totally lost the plot when she thought he'd died a couple of years back, and if she wasn't careful, she'd do the same again. No, she needed to focus on something else. Like finding whoever did this and carving the skin off his body in tiny flakes. But according to Seb, he was a fucking *fantasma*. A ghost. A wraith. A shadow. The bloody bogeyman. He'd got into Eduardo's compound unnoticed before evading a dozen bodyguards and all the other household staff on his way out. Then he'd vanished.

But they'd find him.

No question, they'd find him.

See? Emmy could do positivity.

One of Eduardo's men picked the trio up at the airport —Ramiro, a guy Emmy recognised from previous visits. He barely fitted behind the wheel of the SUV, and although he wasn't taller than Black, he was significantly wider.

"Is there any more news?" she asked.

"No change. We will go straight to the hospital. Sebastien and Marco are waiting there."

Usually, Emmy stayed at Eduardo's estate in the country, but today, they drove towards the concrete jungle. Still, this was Colombia, so the sun was shining and colourful birds flitted from tree to scrawny tree at the side of the road. Cali was a mix of beauty and poverty, good and bad, but apart from the odd sicario, the people were invariably friendly, and if Emmy had learned one thing on her previous visits, it was that they were fiercely proud of their country.

The hospital loomed ahead, and Ana squeezed Emmy's hand. Although they'd only met recently, Ana was the puzzle piece that had been missing for the whole of Emmy's life, and now she couldn't imagine them being apart.

And Black was her rock. Her soulmate as well as her husband. She couldn't have asked for two better people to be with her today.

"Where is he?" Emmy asked Ramiro.

The big man pointed towards the elevator, not with his finger, but with his lips in that funny way they did in Colombia, almost a pout. "On the second floor."

Upstairs, Emmy spotted Seb right away, sitting on a plastic chair in the corridor, flanked by two bodyguards. His defeated posture—slumped forward with his elbows on his knees—told her there was no good news.

But she asked the question anyway. "How is he?"

Seb stood to hug her, and if she thought of Eduardo as a father, then Seb and Marco were her brothers.

"Still in a coma. The doctors are worried about his head. If the swelling on his brain doesn't go down today, they'll have to operate."

"Are they good? Competent?"

"We have the two best neurosurgeons in the country on standby."

"Can I see him?"

"Of course."

Eduardo lay deathly still. He'd always been larger than life, but now he looked older than his years, his tanned skin papery under the fluorescent lights. Floriana sat in a chair beside him, and by the looks of her puffy eyes, she hadn't stopped crying since the incident happened.

"Thank you for coming," she whispered, standing to give Emmy a hug.

She'd always been a quiet woman, deferential around Eduardo, and some of his frailty had transferred to her.

"Eduardo means a lot to me."

"I just can't..." More tears came. "I just can't believe this is happening."

"I heard you shot the guy."

"Not well enough."

"Don't worry, we'll finish it. Have you had any sleep?"

"How can I sleep when my husband is like this?" She waved her arm towards the bed. "I'm staying here until he wakes up, or...or..."

"Don't think that way. He'll wake up."

Why was it always easier to be optimistic with other people than with yourself? Emmy perched on the edge of the bed and took one of Eduardo's hands in hers.

"Hey, old man. You'd better wake the fuck up because who else is gonna shoot pizza with me?"

Emmy's dislike of pineapple on pizza was well known, but only Eduardo joined in enthusiastically when she lined up the slices out back and introduced them to her Walther P88. "And the holidays wouldn't be complete without you sending me a whole bunch of shiny stuff I have no idea what to do with."

Nothing. Just the wheeze and hiss of the ventilator and the steady beep of the heart monitor. The guy was a mess. The hole in his chest would have been bad enough on its own without the head injury. Brains were funny things, and who knew what went on in Eduardo's.

"Where's Marco?" Black asked Seb.

"He's out looking for the motherfucker who did this."

Figured. Over the last two years, Seb had aligned himself with the Garcias' more legitimate enterprises, while Marco dealt mainly with what was left of the coke business. His connections on the street were better than Seb's, although the younger brother's methods sometimes lacked a little finesse.

"We're here to assist. Whatever you need."

"And we appreciate that," Seb said. "The men back at the house are going through the security camera footage, but there are no fingerprints. He wore gloves."

"You have his blood. What about DNA?"

"Our country's database is still in its infancy."

"We should still cover all bases. Our lab can help with the testing. But the most important thing right now is to protect Eduardo. The guy's still loose, and you need a man in this room."

"We have men in the hallway outside."

"You also have a window."

"We're on the second floor."

"Trust me, that isn't a problem."

Sebastien stared at Black for a beat, then nodded. "We'll put a man in the room."

A nurse tried to walk in, but Ana blocked her with an arm.

"I need to see an ID badge."

The nurse stared blankly, and Emmy helped them out. "*Ella necesita ver una insignia de identidad.*"

The poor woman fumbled in her pocket, never taking her eyes off Ana. "*Aquí está.*"

"*Gracias.*"

Good thing Ana's shooting was better than her Spanish.

The nurse fussed around Eduardo, checking his vital signs and rearranging his pillows. If she minded treating a known drug dealer, she didn't show it. Mind you, Eduardo had always been good to the ordinary citizens of Cali, and he'd donated a lot of money to the hospital. Yes, he sometimes killed people, but only bad guys, and Emmy could hardly judge him for that seeing as she did exactly the same thing herself.

Black crouched beside Emmy and rested a hand on her leg. "Do you want to stay while I lend a hand at the estate?"

"I'll come with you. There's more I can do there than here. Seb, will you call me if anything changes?"

"Right away."

"I'll come back in the evening."

"Can you bring a bag for Floriana? One of the maids will pack."

"Sure." Emmy gave him a hug. "Wish us luck."

Seb sucked in a breath. "It's not you who will need

the luck. The man who did this to my father... *He* will need the luck."

CHAPTER 13 - BLACK

BLACK MIGHT HAVE told Emmy to stay positive, but shit... The old man didn't look good.

This time, it was Ramiro who asked the question when they got into the SUV. "Any change to the boss?"

Emmy shook her head. "Still asleep."

At least she hadn't wanted to stay at the hospital. It would be easier to keep her mind on track at the estate, and Black needed her help if they were going to find the man responsible. He barely knew Sebastien and Marco, Ana spoke about five words of Spanish, plus there was the small matter of the Colombian authorities thinking he was the son of a drug lord himself. Long story.

Anyhow, he'd spent more time locked up in Colombia than walking the streets there, which was going to make this investigation a little...challenging. Let's say challenging. It was better than "fucked."

Eduardo's sprawling hacienda wrapped around three sides of a courtyard and opened up into a wide terrace at the rear. Emmy had a bedroom on the second floor with a view over the back lawn, and Black followed her as she headed for the stairs, shoulders slumped.

"Want me to take your bag?"

"I've got it."

Of course she did, and usually, the offer would have

earned him a sarcastic comment about her being perfectly capable, but today, Emmy was subdued. Black hated seeing her like that. Call him a masochist, but he preferred the snark. Ana stalked along behind them and shoved her backpack into the room next door, then went back outside, presumably to fetch more guns from the car.

"I'm glad you came," Marco said from behind before stepping forward to hug Emmy.

Usually, Black wanted to kill anyone who put their hands on his wife, but today the urge didn't arise. Strange times indeed.

"I'm so, so sorry about your father."

"He always said his lifestyle would catch up with him, but now, when he is getting ready to quit? And in his own home? That was a line that should not have been crossed."

"Agreed. What do you have so far?"

"Not much. Some blurry camera footage, but the *cabrón* kept his head down most of the time."

"A coincidence?" Black asked. "Or did he know where the cameras were?"

Silence fell over the room, and Black gave Marco room to think. An uncomfortable gap often encouraged people to tell the truth.

"I'd say he knew where the cameras were."

"Then he had somebody on the inside."

"We can't discount that possibility. But I have no idea who it is. Who do I trust?"

"No one. You don't trust anybody except your brother, Emmy, and me." Emmy trod on his foot. "And Ana," he added.

Marco snorted a laugh. "You're asking me to trust

you above my own men? I barely know you." True. "Following your theory, how can I be sure *you* didn't try to kill my father?"

"Simple. If one of us three had hit Eduardo, you'd be picking out his casket right now."

The bluster went out of Marco, and he sagged against the wall. "I'm sorry."

"It's been a tough twenty-four hours, but we're here to help. You may not know me or Ana, but you know Emmy."

"I wasn't ready for this," he whispered. "I knew my father lived dangerously and that my brother and I would have to take over the business one day, but not yet. It shouldn't have happened yet."

"And it may not happen at all. Your father's still alive, and he's more likely to stay that way if we can find whoever's trying to kill him and stop the bastard from coming back for another go." Because if the wannabe assassin was working under contract, which Black very much suspected he was, he'd have to finish the job to get his money. "Or since he failed the first time, whoever hired him may simply sever ties and employ somebody else."

They were in a race, and the clock was ticking.

"Will you take a look at the video with us? See if there's anything we've missed?"

"That's what we're here for. And if any of the footage needs enhancing, we can send it to our tech people. They're ready and waiting."

Emmy was already fidgeting by the door, impatient, and Black realised he'd have to keep an eye on her. She could be impulsive sometimes, and she wanted blood. If he didn't keep her under control, things had the potential to get messy.

"Roll back a bit. More." Black squinted at the screen. "Dammit. You're right—he always turns away."

Whoever the guy was, he was good, Black had to grudgingly admit that. He seemed to have ridden in on the roof of the truck that delivered Floriana's weekly order of flowers—the woman bought enough bouquets to cause a hay fever epidemic—too high up for any of the guards or the camera on the gatepost to see. One of the cameras on the outside of the house captured a blur as he dropped down and disappeared into the foliage beside the delivery entrance. He'd reappeared in the sunroom at the back of the house before skirting two pairs of guards and making his way upstairs, then caught Eduardo coming out of his study. The old man had made a run for the stairs before being shot in the back. The assassin was on his way forward to finish what he started when Floriana ran out of the bedroom with one of Eduardo's gold-plated semi-automatics, but by the looks of things, she'd only winged him. They had blood, and they had DNA, but what they didn't have was a face.

Unless...

"There. Stop. Zoom in."

"What? He's looking away from us."

"Yes, but he's facing a glass cabinet." Full of china shit. What was the point of plates if you didn't eat off them? "See there? It's his reflection."

Marco enlarged that portion of the image, and sure enough, a blurry, dark-eyed ghoul looked back at them, his mouth fixed in a hard line.

"Our techs can enhance that." Nate or Mack, another of their tech gurus, could clean up the image in minutes. "Someone has to know who he is."

"I think... Hmm..." Marco leaned forward. "I think I've seen him before."

"You recognise him?"

"I don't know his name, but I'm sure he was in one of our nightclubs last week. El Bajo Tierra in Medellín. I kept an eye on him because he was watching a particular girl, but then she left."

"What girl? You think he knew her?"

"No, more like he wanted to know her. She was with another guy, and they left together."

"Did our suspect follow?"

"No, he picked out another girl and went with her instead."

"Then that's who we need to find. How quickly can we get to Medellín?"

"An hour by plane from the airport or two and a quarter by helicopter from here. The Eurocopter you liberated last time you were here is parked on the back lawn."

Technically, it had been Emmy who stole the helicopter, but Black wasn't about to quibble over the details. Its former owner was dead, anyhow.

"Or we could take the helicopter to the airport, then the plane to Medellín and shave off half an hour."

Marco nodded his agreement. Good.

"Warm up the turbine while I get some equipment."

Within fifteen minutes, they were in the air. Emmy had wanted to come too, but when Black gave a subtle shake of his head, Ana had reminded her of Eduardo's potential surgery and also the possibility of a traitor amongst Eduardo's men and suggested they both stay near Cali.

Black had to be grateful for that and so, it seemed, was Marco.

"Does Ana worry you?" he asked.

"In what way?"

"In an if-I-get-too-close-she-might-suck-the-life-out-of-me way."

Yes. "She's not that bad once you get to know her."

"Right."

Marco was at the controls of the helicopter, and the trees shrank quickly as they gained altitude. Black hated small talk, but thankfully Marco seemed content just to fly. Which gave Black some thinking time. Why would someone try to kill Eduardo now? An old vendetta? Because Sebastien and Marco were the men in charge of the money, and the Garcia empire would keep running without their father. Or were they next? Was that why the would-be hitman had been skulking around Marco's club in Medellín? Black checked his gun, more out of habit than anything else. Today, he'd brought a Colt Rail Gun as his main piece with a Sig Sauer P290RS as his backup. Unlike Emmy and her Walther, he didn't have a lifelong affinity for one gun; he often tried out new toys and swapped if he found a different model he preferred.

Would he need his gun tonight? Black would rather talk first, but despite the initial failure of the assassin who got into the Garcia compound, the man wasn't an amateur, and negotiation didn't appear to be his strong point. He was a little rough around the edges, perhaps, but Black was careful not to underestimate him.

Black had also brought an evidence collection kit, because who knew what they might find in Medellín? Since leaving the CIA and starting Blackwood, he'd discovered he liked investigating crimes almost as much as committing them, and modern forensics fascinated him.

At the airport in Cali, they switched to the Garcia family's Learjet, which came complete with a leggy brunette to serve drinks and snacks.

"Champagne, sir?"

Black gave her a bored once-over. No, she wasn't a patch on Emmy. "Just water."

A car met them at the small domestic airport in the centre of Medellín, and a quarter of an hour later, they pulled up outside El Bajo Tierra. The Underground. Black should have brought a pair of fucking earplugs.

"How do people have a conversation in here?" he shouted at Marco.

"Huh?"

Exactly. Thankfully, the volume dropped a bit towards the back of the bar, and Marco led him past a bouncer and into the security office. The man with his feet up on the desk struggled to stand and brush white powder off the polished surface at the same time.

"Boss? We weren't expecting you tonight."

"I see that."

"I can explain..."

"Not now. We need the camera footage from three weeks ago."

"What are you looking for?"

Marco passed over the picture of the suspect on his phone. "Him. I saw him in here last time I visited."

"A Wednesday, right?" The manager scrolled through files until he found the right ones and turned his screen towards Marco. "Which camera do you want to see first?"

"The tables to the left of the bar."

Sure enough, it played out like Marco described. The guy had a good eye for faces. The whole family did, in fact, which was the only reason Black was here now and not rotting in the ground.

"Do you know any of these people?" Marco asked his man.

"Never saw the dark-haired guy or the girl sitting down before. But the blond man talking to her is Roscoe."

"Roscoe—is that a first name or a last name?"

"Not sure. People only ever call him Roscoe."

"Find out. And the other girl?"

"She's in here most weeks, usually hooks up with somebody. Laura? Lola? Something like that."

"I talked to the first girl briefly," Marco said. "She's Catalina. So we have three names, and now we need to find them. I don't care who you call or how you do it, but I want full names and addresses within an hour."

CHAPTER 14 - BLACK

TWO OUT OF four. They got two out of four.

Laura was easy. They found her in a bar along the street, dancing with an Eastern European guy who probably felt like a king in Colombia because back home, pretty girls wouldn't give him a second glance. Black just stared at him until he backed away.

"What do you want?" Laura asked, focusing first on his chest then craning her neck back to look him in the eye. She soon averted her gaze.

"We want to talk to you."

"What would you like to drink?" Marco asked.

Now she smiled. "Rum and Coke."

"Easy on the rum," Black muttered to Marco. The woman was already tipsy despite it only being eight o'clock in the evening. Black guided Laura over to a table, and the guy occupying one of the seats soon got up and left.

Marco followed with her drink, and as he slid it in her direction, her eyes lit up in recognition.

"I know you! From El Bajo Tierra, right?"

"Right. One of our patrons stole something from the back office there a few weeks ago, and we think you talked to him." Marco passed over a printout of the suspect. The manager at the club had run off a whole sheaf of them. "Do you remember his name?"

Laura's eyes widened in shock. She had expressive eyes, and they would have been a nice feature if she hadn't caked them in make-up.

"Uh, uh..."

"You *did* talk to him, didn't you?"

She'd done more than talk to him. Black could tell from the way she paled under the sickly neon lights.

"Yes, we talked."

"His name?"

"Lorenzo. What did he steal? He seemed nice. Kind of intense, you know? But...but..." Now she blushed. "Really hot."

"Where did you and Lorenzo go after you left the club, Laura?" Black asked. "Your apartment? A hotel?"

She shook her head, and a chunk of mascara flaked off and landed on the table. "His apartment."

Black glanced at Marco. Now they were getting somewhere.

"Can you remember where his apartment was?"

"I don't want him to get hurt. He was kind, you know? Made me breakfast in the morning."

"Nobody's going to get hurt," Marco said. "I just want my money back. And he shouldn't go around stealing. Did he take anything from your purse? Any cash?"

"No. At least, I don't think so." Her voice dropped. "Maybe. I didn't check."

"Can you show us where he lives?"

A quick nod. "Promise you won't hurt him?"

"We promise."

Lorenzo's apartment was in the Los Pinos neighbourhood, a small walk-up on the third floor of a shabby block. Laura pointed it out, then Marco gave her a few thousand pesos and sent her home in a cab.

"What do you think?" he asked Black.

"No lights on. Too early for him to be asleep, so I'd say he's out."

"Are we going in?"

"Damn right we're going in."

Up on the third floor, Marco was about to kick the door down when Black grabbed him.

"What the hell are you doing?"

"Going in."

"For fuck's sake." Black put on a pair of thin leather gloves, produced his set of lock picks, and opened the door in under a minute. "This is how we go in."

Inside, the air was still. Stale. Black turned on the lights and took a good look.

"Stay by the door," he told Marco. "And don't touch anything."

The apartment was furnished, but with the kind of soulless shit that came out of a catalogue. Like someone had visited IKEA and ordered everything from the first set of mock rooms they saw. The bed was neatly made, and a thin layer of dust covered everything in the lounge. Black flipped open the bathroom bin. Empty. Same in the kitchen. The fridge contained two bottles of beer, a bottle of white wine, and a can of cola. The only food in the kitchen cupboards was a solitary bag of pretzels.

This wasn't a home. It was a bolthole. A fuckpad. How did Black know that? Because he'd once owned one himself.

A more thorough check revealed nothing more personal than a bottle of shampoo, but Black did have one hope left.

"Marco, would you get the big black case from the car?"

Fingerprints. Lorenzo had to have left a print somewhere, and a quick dusting of magnetic powder with a fibreglass brush revealed a veritable treasure trove. If the guy was in a database anywhere, Mack would find him. Half an hour later, Black carefully wiped down all the surfaces and packed up his toys.

"Ready to go?" he asked. "Did any more information come through?"

He'd heard Marco talking softly on the phone a moment ago.

"Roscoe Ward isn't home. He runs an export company, but according to my guys, it's literally an empty warehouse near the airport, so that has to be a front. One employee, and when they visited him at home, he said Roscoe took off on vacation a couple of days ago. Mentioned something about a windfall."

"When's he coming back?"

"Didn't say."

"Keep a man on his house."

"Already done."

"Nothing on Catalina?"

"Nobody's seen her before or since."

Black's phone buzzed with a message at the same time as Marco's.

Emmy: Eduardo needs to have the surgery. If you find the fucker, save him for me.

Shit.

Judging by Marco's face, he'd received a similar communication.

"Do you want to go back to Cali?" Black asked.

The younger man closed his eyes for a moment and

took a long inhale. "I should. Yes. A day, and then we will continue the hunt."

"I'll come with you." Emmy needed moral support. "Meanwhile, my team in the US can process these prints and start work on the blood sample."

Mack could also go through flight records and look for Roscoe. A vacation? No. The timing was too convenient.

"I hate having to abandon the search. It feels as if we're giving up."

"Not giving up. Just putting things on hold for a few hours because your family needs you. Family's important."

At least, Black assumed it was. He didn't have any family left, not blood relatives. His parents, who he now knew weren't his real parents at all, had died in a car accident right before his sixteenth birthday, and his twin brother had been the victim of an assassination plot meant for him before they ever got the chance to meet. Last year, he'd made an attempt to find his birth parents, but every trace of his history had been wiped out.

But he had Emmy and the family he'd created for himself in Virginia—Nate, Nick, Dan, Mack, and all the others—and that was enough for him.

At the airport, he opened up his laptop and set about sending the information to Richmond before the pilot even closed the door. Photos, names, fingerprints. The blood samples would have to go by courier, but thanks to Nate, Black had a tiny high-resolution scanner for the prints.

The brunette was back.

"Sir, can I get you a drink or any..." She trailed off,

and Black turned to look at her.

"Is there a problem?"

She'd gone white.

"Not really." She pointed at the picture of Lorenzo. "Uh, why are you looking at that man?"

"You know him?"

"Not exactly." A giggle. "Sort of."

For fuck's sake. Had Casanova claimed another victim?

"You had a little fun with him?"

"Shh!" She glanced past Black to Marco. "We're not supposed to get distracted on duty."

Black waved Marco away. For a moment, junior looked as if he might argue, but then he took the hint and backed off.

"On duty? You slept with him on duty?"

"I don't want to lose my job."

"I promise you won't lose your job. What happened?"

"Sometimes we have to wait around for hours. Whole days, even."

"And you get bored?"

"Totally." Now her eyes cut towards the cockpit. "Pablo never wants to talk. He just drinks coffee and reads."

"So you talk to other people, and Lorenzo was one of them?"

Her brow crinkled. "Lorenzo?"

Black tapped the picture. "Him."

"Oh, he's not called Lorenzo. His name's Alonso."

Great. So it was a sure bet the suspect was called neither Lorenzo nor Alonso. "Okay, Alonso. Where did you meet him?"

"At a drink stall in the terminal."

"And?"

"We'd talk sometimes."

"Sometimes? You saw him more than once?"

"Every few weeks. And then one day... I don't know what came over me. Alonso's got this way of talking to you, like at that moment, you're the only thing that matters. So we snuck out to a hangar, and in the bathroom...you know." Her eyes went dreamy. "He was amazing."

"How did you get into the hangar? Didn't anyone try to stop you?"

"The door was unlocked, and we walked straight in. The only person we saw was the old man Alonso flies with, and he just laughed on his way out."

"Wait. What old man?"

"Ernesto, I think his name is. He works at one of the flight schools."

"Which one?"

"I'm not sure of the name, but I could probably find the hangar."

"Then let's go."

Black grabbed his case again and beckoned to Marco.

"What's going on?" he asked.

"Flight's delayed."

At the EJC Escuela de Aviación, Black again worked his magic with the lock picks and once inside, pointed the brunette to a spot beside the door.

"Wait there."

"Can somebody tell me what's going on?" Marco asked.

"Yeah. Our suspect can't keep it in his pants," Black

told him under his breath. "Miss Champagne and Snacks over there reckons she saw him in here."

"And when you say saw him..."

"I mean fucked him."

"*Mierda*. I hope she used protection."

"Don't tell me you..."

Marco shrugged. "She sucks like a vacuum cleaner."

A four-seat Cessna 172 took up most of the space, but at the back, there was a small office and, sure enough, the bathroom. Black pushed the door open out of curiosity. Hmm. Miss C&S must be flexible as a garden hose too.

For a business, the office yielded remarkably little in the way of paperwork. A maintenance log for the plane. A few invoices for fuel, coffee filters, and ink cartridges for a printer that didn't seem to exist. A handwritten planner on the desk had all the entries from two weeks ago onwards crossed out. What had happened to cause the cancellations? Preparation for Eduardo's execution? Nothing new had been written in, and as with the soulless apartment, dust had begun settling. Black took pictures of everything, then set about hunting for fingerprints. A quick examination showed two recurring sets—on the desk, the coffee machine, and the plane. Ernesto and his mysterious amigo?

On the way back to the jet, they stopped off at the office where Marco spoke to an acquaintance behind the desk. Ernesto was last seen two days ago. He'd filed a flight plan for Barranquilla and taken off with one passenger. Their suspect.

He returned alone.

Back in Cali, Black and Marco headed straight to the hospital. Emmy paced the hallway outside the operating theatre while Ana sat cross-legged in a chair, watching her. Sebastien was chewing on a fingernail, but he stopped when Black arrived.

"Hey." He caught Emmy's hand and pulled her close. "What's happening?"

"He's been in there for two hours. Nobody's telling us a thing."

"Right now, that's probably good news."

She sagged in his arms. "I know. But I still want to strangle someone with my bare hands. Did you find anything?"

"A lot, considering the time we've spent so far. We have a suspect and a possible acquaintance."

"Who's the suspect?"

"No name so far, but we've got prints. I've sent them to Mack. The acquaintance is Ernesto Castillo. He runs a flight school out of Olaya Herrera Airport, but he doesn't seem to give many lessons."

Seb, who'd leaned closer to listen, shook his head. "Never heard of him."

"It could be innocent. Our suspect might just be a pupil, but from the booking calendar, those seem to be so rare they're practically an endangered species."

"And your gut says no?" Emmy asked.

"My gut says no."

Lorenzo/Alonso knew Ernesto well enough to screw around with a girl in his hangar, and he'd been seen with him after all the lessons were cancelled, right after the attempt on Eduardo's life. That wasn't a casual friendship.

Emmy nodded once and wriggled free of Black's grip to resume her pacing, and by the time a doctor appeared three hours later, she must have traversed the waiting area a thousand times. But the old man lived to fight another day. Emmy sank onto Black's lap, and he made a silent wish that the only funeral they'd have to attend was for the man who'd flown to Barranquilla.

"He's not called Ernesto Castillo," Mack informed everyone over a video link on Blackwood's internal messaging program the following morning.

Emmy hadn't slept well, which meant Black had been awake for most of the night too, and now he sat in the dining room at Hacienda Garcia with two mugs of coffee in front of him. Emmy and Ana were also there, as were Seb and Marco.

"That's not a huge surprise," Black said. "Who is he?"

"Vicente Ochoa. Sixty-nine years old, whereabouts unknown." Mack brought up a rather sparse file that looked as if it came from a government agency. "This is all I've found so far, buried in police records."

Vicente Ochoa

Sicario

Nickname: La Parca

Area of operations: Nationwide, concentrated in the Amazonian region.

Kills: Thirty-six confirmed. Forty-three possible.

Black read through the notes underneath. Vicente

Ochoa had been active for three decades until being captured and imprisoned. He'd escaped a year later and hadn't been heard from since. Under "preferred methods," the file listed an A-Z of assassination, everything from a simple bullet to the head to an elaborate car bomb. That seemed appropriate for a man nicknamed The Reaper. Fuck.

Known associates:
La Araña (deceased)
La Ostra (deceased)
La Leona (missing, presumed deceased)

The Spider, the Oyster, the Lioness. A woman? Black glanced at Emmy sitting beside him. That little fact really shouldn't have surprised him and yet it did, mainly because the dates involved suggested she was the same age as Vicente. Back in those days, assassination had been thought of as a man's job. Emmy and Ana were somewhat pioneers in their field.

"Can you find out more about the associates?" Black asked.

"I'm trying, but there's nothing in the system. If they died years ago, those records are probably on a piece of paper somewhere."

"Any word on the second set of prints?"

"Not yet."

Black almost asked if Mack had tried Interpol, but that was a stupid question because of course she had. Mack knew how to do her job, and the best thing he could do was leave her to get on with it.

"Keep looking."

"Did you find anything more?"

Other than the fact that Lorenzo/Alonso fucked like a stallion and could elude a small army, no.

"I'll fly back to Medellín later today as long as Eduardo stays stable. We're going to the hospital in a few minutes, so email me if anything new comes up."

Mack gave him a salute. "Yes, boss."

CHAPTER 15 - CORA

WELCOME TO HELL, part two.

Six days ago, I'd woken on a yacht. A large yacht, by the feel of it, but I still got seasick as it hammered through the waves. My spartan cabin contained only a bed with a blanket, plus a tiny bathroom with a single roll of toilet paper and a bar of soap. Spray blew against the porthole as we cruised towards a destination unknown. America?

Once a day, two bolts thunked back and the door opened to reveal an ape of a man with a tray of food and bottles of water. He never spoke, no matter how many questions I asked, and his expressions ranged from mild displeasure to an outright scowl.

On day two, I began to feel woozy, and by day three, I realised they were putting something in the bottled water. The stuff in the bathroom tap tasted nasty, but at least I didn't fall asleep when I drank it.

Yesterday, we docked at a marina in the dead of night. Since I was supposed to be drugged, I acted unsteady as two men hauled me out of the cabin and onto a walkway.

"Scream and you'll regret it," the larger of the two warned me.

I kept quiet even though the blood was rushing in my ears. I couldn't have screamed if I'd wanted to, because if I didn't reach my ultimate destination, I'd never find Izzy. Luckily, they'd left me fully clothed, and I'd activated the tracker for short bursts at a time, hoping beyond measure that my brother was following, that his bullet wound hadn't turned septic and left him incapacitated.

They bundled me into the back seat of an SUV, and as I watched out the window, another girl was marched off the boat by two more apes and stuffed into an identical vehicle. Were the men clones? They all shared the same sullen looks and the same bad attitude.

As we drove, I glanced out the window whenever I could, although ape number one's chest blocked the view most of the time. Florida. We were in Florida, according to the road signs. Miami, heading for Fort Lauderdale. I'd guess we travelled for half an hour before the SUV drove into a dilapidated warehouse through a huge roller door.

Ours wasn't the only vehicle in there. The other car pulled in behind us, and we parked beside a red sports car, a white panel truck, and a third SUV with tinted windows.

Metal racks filled most of the vast building, stacked high with boxes of all shapes and sizes. Drugs? Stolen goods? Surely nothing legitimate. A series of wooden rooms had been erected to one side, made out of plywood that I'd later find out was sturdier than it looked. It was into one of these that I was unceremoniously deposited like an unwanted pet. At least on the boat, I'd had a window and a bathroom. Here, I only got the bed and the bottled water I absolutely didn't want to drink.

Last night, soon after I arrived, I'd heard a girl

sobbing on the other side of the wall.

"Hello? Are you okay?"

She didn't answer, but moments later, one of the apes wrenched my door open and glared at me.

"No talking."

Great. Was Izzy here? How could I check if I was confined to a box?

The apes visited more often than they had on the boat. Every two or three hours, they grunted their orders. If I needed to use the bathroom, they walked me over to a dingy toilet stall in the far corner, waited while I peed, then watched while I washed my hands in the basin outside which meant I couldn't drink from the tap anymore. But on my third visit, I realised I could move the lid of the cistern and drink directly from the tank as long as I was quiet, which was disgusting but better than being sedated all the time. Then I emptied the water bottles under my bed.

After a day or two, one guard held me down while another stripped me naked, and I began to fear the worst until a doctor arrived. An actual doctor, with a black bag and a stethoscope. He poked and prodded me and drew a vial of blood, but when I asked him what part of the Hippocratic Oath this fell under, he ignored me.

"Healthy pending the results of the blood work," he declared, sick freak that he was, then jabbed another needle in me.

"What the hell was that?"

"Contraceptive injection."

Joder.

Every time one of the men came, I asked the same questions. Where was I? Who were they? Why was I here? What was going to happen to me?

It wasn't until this morning that one of them had answered.

At first, I thought he wasn't going to speak, but as I sipped water from my cupped hands, a soft voice came through the door of the toilet stall.

"This is a halfway house. You'll be here for a week, maybe two, and then they'll take you somewhere else."

"Where? Where will they take me?"

"I'm not sure. It varies."

Mierda. So I might not end up in the same place as Izzy? Where was she? If we *all* got moved on after a week or two, then she'd probably left already.

"What will they do to me?"

"Honestly? You don't want to know."

No, I didn't. "How many other girls are there?"

"You need to hurry up and finish."

He seemed nicer than the others. Rather than manhandling me to and from my cell, he let me walk by myself, and he held the door open rather than shoving me through it. Trust my gut, Grandma had told me. My gut told me that if anyone in this place could make my life a little more bearable, it would be that guy. Could I connect with him? He seemed human rather than primate.

Then at lunch, one of the apes came back, and my hopes were dashed.

The biggest question on my mind during the whole ordeal, though, was about Rafe. Where was my brother? And had he followed me here? I still turned the tracker on in bursts, but should I leave it on the whole time? Why hadn't I thought to ask how long the battery would last?

With every hour that passed, I grew more and more worried. The revelation that there was more than one ultimate destination left me scared for both my future and Izzy's, and also sick to my stomach because this ordeal might all be for nothing.

There was little to do in my prison but think, and that depressed me so much I almost turned to the bottled water. What did they put in that anyway? Prescription drugs? Illegal substances? Something to get the girls hooked and compliant and willing to do anything as long as the sweet oblivion kept coming?

No, I couldn't touch it.

I'd resigned myself to a long wait, a slow journey through all nine circles of hell, but I plunged into the fiery depths faster than anticipated.

That very afternoon, in fact.

The first hint I got that anything was wrong came after a lunch of dry cheese sandwiches, when a particularly greasy ape led me to the bathroom. Halfway through the warehouse, he turned as if he'd seen something, paused, and shrugged.

Another ape ambled past.

"Where's Luigi? I can't find him."

A grunt suggested he didn't know, and we carried on walking.

Then all hell let loose.

A muffled *boom* shook the walls, and a jagged hole appeared in the roller shutter. Black-clad men with guns swarmed everywhere as light flooded the warehouse, and it wasn't long before the first sounds of gunfire deafened me. My heart went from the trippy, fluttery beat I'd experienced for the last week to an all-out sprint.

Should I run? Hide? Throw myself on the floor and hope the bullets missed?

Movement above caught my eye, and I looked up in time to see my brother leap from one giant stack of shelves to the next, high above my head.

Thank goodness.

Rafe had found me, but my relief was short lived as someone yelled, "Grenade!"

A flash of light blinded me, and something knocked me to the ground. A shock wave? A person? Smoke began to fill the air. Hands grabbed me under my armpits and dragged me deeper into the warehouse, and then we burst through a hidden door into daylight, the first daylight I'd seen in days.

I scrambled upright and turned, expecting to see my brother, but it wasn't Rafe.

The guard who'd talked to me this morning stood there, his mouth set in a thin line.

Now what?

We locked eyes for what felt like hours, although in reality, it couldn't have been more than a few seconds.

"Go," he said.

Like an idiot, I stood there. Was he letting me leave?

"Get out of here."

He turned on his heel and disappeared inside, back into the chaos. For a moment, I froze, my brain telling me to run but my feet refusing to comply. And *what about Izzy*?

"Cora?"

I almost collapsed with relief. But before I got a chance to hug my brother or even speak, a scream came from inside the building. A female scream. Probably not Izzy, but what if it was? What if she'd been delayed in leaving somehow? And even if it wasn't Izzy, another girl was trapped inside and the place was full of freaking ninjas with guns and that could have been me and...

"We have to help her," I whispered.

"No, we have to leave."

"There's a woman trapped." My voice rose in pitch, bordering on hysterical. "What if she can't get out? She might die!"

"Cora, we have to leave *now*."

I ran for the door, not that I had a clue what I was doing, but I couldn't stand outside and listen to a girl die. I got it halfway open, wide enough to glimpse the flames, then Rafe grabbed me around the waist and yanked me back.

"No."

"Let me go!"

"You're crazy."

"I'm a da Silva. Of course I'm crazy."

"*Joder.*" He cursed under his breath. "Wait here. Hide behind that truck. I'll be back."

Rafe pointed towards a dilapidated panel van rusting in the corner of the lot, its tyres flat and the driver's door hanging lopsided on its hinges. I stumbled towards it as my brother slipped back into the warehouse, but before I even got halfway, bile rose in my throat.

What had I done?

I'd sent my brother into an urban war zone, and if something happened to him, it would be my fault. I half turned around to run after him, but if he got out and I was missing, he'd waste more time looking for me.

What should I do?

My hesitation was a mistake. A big mistake. Huge.

A strong hand wrapped around my wrist, and one of the apes dragged me away from the warehouse.

"Get off me!"

His other hand clamped over my mouth, and he plucked me off the ground and carried me to another black SUV, or perhaps it was the same vehicle from earlier. Who could tell? Thirty seconds later, I found myself squashed in the back between him and the vaguely human guard, the one who'd tried to help me escape earlier. His stony expression told me exactly what he thought of my presence.

Mierda.

Behind us, a series of bangs erupted, but when I tried to turn and look, the ape shoved my head down.

For the third time that week, we took off for a destination unknown, and the worst part? When I went to rub some feeling back into my wrists, I realised my bracelet was missing.

CHAPTER 16 - CORA

WHENEVER YOU WATCH the movies, undercover work seems so glamorous. Think James Bond, Ethan Hunt, Jason Bourne, La Femme Nikita. Well, let me tell you, the reality couldn't be more different.

Although my previous lodgings weren't five star, it turned out the rooms on the boat and in the warehouse were a vacation compared to what awaited me at the luxury mansion in... Truthfully? I had no idea where we were. After I got recaptured outside the warehouse, we'd driven around for what seemed like hours before the ape behind the wheel got a phone call and we came to this place.

From the outside, the house was beautiful. Acres of manicured lawns, tall white columns framing the front door, pale pink stucco on the walls. An ornate fountain in the centre of the drive. I couldn't see the ocean, but I heard it washing against the shore not too far away.

But inside, the place was filled with vermin. Vermin who walked around laughing and joking, wearing well-cut suits, fancy watches, and expensive leather shoes. In the ballroom, they sipped champagne poured from one of the bottles in the ice bucket, helped themselves to food from the buffet, picked whichever girl they wanted from the line-up, and then they raped her.

Last night, it had been my turn.

When I first arrived, an ape shoved me into a prison cell on the third floor. A comfortably appointed cell, but a prison cell nonetheless. Behind the fancy drapes, bars covered the windows, and anything sharp or pointy or heavy had been either removed or bolted down.

"Take a shower and dress up," he told me. "I'll come back in an hour."

"Then what?"

"Then you perform."

"What if I don't want to?"

He gave me a malicious smile. "We'll make you. Some of the men like that." A shrug. "And if it doesn't work out? There are plenty more girls where you came from."

His words sent a chill through me. Every instinct told me to resist, to fight whatever they tried to make me do, but even if I managed to escape, I'd never find Izzy that way. After everything we'd gone through to get this far, I couldn't just give up. Where was Rafe? Had he made it out of the warehouse? With no answer to that question and no way for him to track me even if he was still alive, I had to assume I was on my own.

The room itself was reasonably spacious, decorated in pale pink with accents of purple. I wondered why they bothered. If we were basically slaves, why give us double beds and showers with three nozzles? I rapped on the mirror in front of the dressing table with my knuckles. Metal rather than glass, and the padded stool was screwed to the floor.

The closet held a variety of dresses, all of them designer, none of them comfortable. No underwear. And everything was too tight or too short or both. But with little choice other than to comply with the ape's orders, I blow-dried my hair, put on make-up from the box on the bathroom counter, squeezed myself into something stretchy and black, and waited.

And waited.

And waited.

In some ways, the waiting was the worst part. Sweat trickled down my spine as I imagined what might happen to me. I'd read *Fifty Shades of Grey*. Would there be whips? Ropes? Chains? Bile coated my throat, and with every minute that passed, I hated myself a little more. Hated that I had to give up my dignity and hated myself for being so far out of my depth in this situation. If Rafe were here, he'd know what to do, but he wasn't, and I didn't have a clue.

Finally, an ape came back and herded me towards the ballroom. Half a dozen girls stood by the floor-to-ceiling windows, whispering amongst themselves, and all heads turned when I walked in.

"They'll tell you what to do," the ape told me.

Their expressions ranged from fear to sympathy to nervous smiles, and when he shoved me in their direction, two of them stepped back so I could join their little group. Three blondes, two brunettes, and a redhead.

Well, didn't this feel like the first day at school all over again?

"Hi," the tallest blonde said. "I'm Hallie."

"Catalina."

"You just got here?"

"A few hours ago, I think. What time is it?"

"Maybe nine o'clock? None of us are allowed watches. I don't know what they think we'll do with them. But sometimes, you can sneak a look at one of the guards' wrists or a client will wear a watch."

"Always a Rolex," the redhead said. "As well as being total scum, they have no imagination."

"What happens now?"

"We eat dinner, and then guests start arriving. That's what they call them—guests. Not monsters or rapists or criminals or any of the hundred other things that would be more appropriate. And we're expected to entertain them."

Eat dinner? I was about to vomit.

"What if we refuse?"

The redhead deferred to Hallie.

"The first time, they beat you. Black and blue. I tried it, and I couldn't walk for a week. I'm ninety percent sure they broke my arm, but all I could do was keep it real still and hope it healed."

Freaking hell.

"And the second time?"

"Who knows? Nobody's ever balked more than once."

"Except for Jessie," the smallest brunette said. She had a Colombian accent too—another of Roscoe's victims?

"No, Jessie was different. The second time, she tried to escape."

"And what happened?" I asked.

"They dragged her back inside, and we never saw her again."

Oh, this got better and better.

"So, what? We just hang around in luxury, waiting to be raped each night for the rest of our lives?"

Now Hallie shifted uncomfortably. "Really, I'm not

sure. I've been here the longest, about fourteen months now, and girls get moved around. Some disappear forever, but occasionally one comes back. There are more houses—at least two."

"Three of these places?" And Izzy could be in any one of them. "That's...that's depraved. Do they realise that?"

"I'm sure Radcliffe does, but he doesn't care."

"Who's Radcliffe?"

"Garrett Radcliffe. He runs this place, although I think he works for somebody else."

"And it's basically a brothel?"

"More of a gentleman's club, or so they say. My theory is that the men all pay an outrageous membership fee so they can get their kicks without their wives finding out. Half of them don't even bother to take off their wedding rings."

She sounded so matter-of-fact about everything. Was that what happened after a few months in the pink palace? You became numb to the reality and the sheer indecency of it? In some ways, it reminded me of the drugs trade. Cocaine had been everywhere while I grew up. Growing coca and processing the leaves and smuggling the finished product was just a way of life, as was the violence that came with it.

"Sometimes they bring gifts," one of the brunettes said, moving her hair out of the way to show off a pair of sparkly earrings. "Like these. I'm Tasha, by the way. And some of them aren't that bad. I mean, they're no worse than the guys I met at frat parties. I only wish we could go out shopping or something."

"Stockholm syndrome," the other brunette mouthed from behind Tasha's head.

Great. Split loyalties. And that meant until I worked out who I could trust, I wouldn't be able to ask about Izzy, because if word that I'd come here on purpose got back to the mysterious Radcliffe, I'd probably become another of those girls who vanished.

The other girls nibbled on plates of food while I knocked back a glass of champagne and then another—I'd surely need it this evening. Classical music played quietly in the background, and I hated that most of all because it somehow made the whole affair seem legitimate when it was anything but.

Around half an hour later, a pair of men walked in, talking quietly between themselves. As always, the ape at the door stared impassively, and the guard who'd told me to leave back at the warehouse stood on the other side of the room. At times, I felt him watching me.

"How much do you think they get paid for this?" I whispered to Hallie.

"Who? The guards?"

"Yes."

"No idea, but it's not exactly a hard job, is it? All they have to do is wear a suit and make sure a bunch of women don't leave the grounds. And they get perks."

The way she said it, I wasn't sure I wanted to know the details.

"Perks?"

"Us. After hours." *Joder.* "They're not allowed to leave any marks, and everyone has to use a condom, guests included. If anyone tries without, tell Radcliffe and he'll fix it." Hallie jerked her head towards the door. "That one's not too bad—he just grunts a bit, shoots, and leaves. But watch out for Chad, the small guy with glasses. He likes to choke you, and I swear one day I almost passed out."

"What about him? By the window?" Warehouse guy.

"He keeps to himself. Tasha says he's gay, but I'm not sure. Yes, he dresses well, but it's more that he thinks he's too good for us. And he always nags us about tidying up."

"Do we ever get any sleep?" I tried to make a joke even though I felt like crying.

"Depends whether anyone picks you. Maybe half of the nights we get left alone."

I prayed nobody would choose me tonight, but my hopes faded when a newcomer, a fifty-something asshole with a paunch and a red nose who I christened the alcoholic, sidled over to talk to me. A cloud of cologne floated around him, strong, as if he were trying to cover up the stench of his rotten soul.

"You're new?"

"Yes."

"What's your name?"

"Catalina."

Thank goodness I hadn't used my own name. At least that was still sacred.

He held out a hand, and I ignored it.

"Alan. I see Radcliffe hasn't instilled any manners in you yet."

"Forgive me if I prefer not to shake the hand of a rapist."

"In time, you'll learn to enjoy being here, just like the other girls." He waved a hand at the opulent decor. "I mean, isn't this better than a shack in Mexico or wherever you came from?"

I'd never wanted to kill anybody before, but with what I now knew about my family, I guess I shouldn't have been surprised when I felt a little bloodlust. Then and there, I vowed that when—not if, *when*—I got out of that fucking mansion, I'd hunt Alan the alcoholic down and castrate him. And what was more, I'd take pleasure in doing it.

But this evening, I was a prisoner not only of walls, but of circumstances too.

"Mexico. Right. I sure miss those burritos."

He didn't pick up on the sarcasm. "Ask Radcliffe nicely, and I'm sure he can have the chef prepare one. Join me for a drink?"

"Do I have a choice?"

"Very good—you're learning."

Over canapés I didn't eat and a glass of white wine I didn't drink, Alan bragged about his prowess as a real-estate developer and his new investment in an ostrich farm. When I cut his dick off, I'd remove his pudgy little sausage lips too.

Then came the moment I'd been dreading. He patted his bulging stomach and glanced towards the door.

"I'm full. Would you accompany me upstairs?"

It wasn't a question but an order, and the ape at the door watched to ensure I followed. Panic got the better of me in the bedroom doorway, and I tried to back away, but an ape propelled me forward and sent me sprawling onto the bed. Not my bed, thankfully, but a king-sized four-poster in a luxurious room on the second floor that came complete with a rack of what looked like torture instruments and a view of the swimming pool we weren't allowed to use.

"So feisty," Alan said, eyes gleaming. "I like that. The new girls always give a better ride."

That fucker.

While he pounded into me, I screwed my eyes shut and refused to look at him, although he did let out a satisfying yelp when he tried to kiss me and I bit his lip. I picked a spot on the ceiling and stared at it, willing both my body and my mind to go numb while the horrible act took place.

Then it was over, and Alan dropped the used condom onto the floor on his way out the door.

"See you in a week or two, Catalina. It'll be interesting to see how you've changed."

Back in my own room, I sat in the shower until the water ran cold, and even after I turned it off, I couldn't stop crying. I'd *volunteered* for this. I thought I'd steeled myself mentally, but nothing could have prepared me for how dirty I felt. Dirty from the inside out. No amount of fancy toiletries could wash that away.

Then my bedroom door opened.

I flew out of the shower and grabbed the robe from the hook beside the sink. A *silk* robe, because every girl should feel special after she's been mauled by an animal. A filthy pig.

"Who's there?"

"Leandro."

Who the hell was Leandro?

I poked my head around the doorjamb and found the warehouse guy standing beside the dressing table.

"Don't you knock?"

"I did knock. You've been crying?"

"Well spotted. Have a gold star."

"Are you okay?"

"*Eres estúpido*?"

He *must* be stupid if he didn't know the answer to that question.

"Sorry. Wrong thing to say. I guess... I guess I just wanted to check you weren't injured. And also see if you wanted some food. I noticed you didn't eat anything earlier, and you need to keep your strength up."

"I wasn't hungry."

"Yeah. That's understandable."

We stared at each other for a few seconds, and a hint of worry crept into his eyes.

"Why didn't you leave?" he asked finally.

"I tried, but one of your colleagues caught me. Why did you tell me to leave?"

Now he shifted uncomfortably. "Because..." He paused, thinking. "Because you didn't belong there."

"None of the girls belonged there. Or here. Or anywhere else where they're held against their will to provide entertainment for men who are sick in the head."

"Yeah. Look, I shouldn't have done that at the warehouse. Said that."

I got it. This was a fishing expedition. If the boss found out he'd tried to set me free, Leandro would be in big trouble. Tempting though it was to drop him in it, he was the only man who'd treated me like a human being, and who would believe me anyway? The gut Grandma had told me to rely on decided that Leandro was the one person who might make my stay in this house of horrors a little more bearable.

"I won't tell anyone, if that's what you're worried

about."

His shoulders dropped. "Thanks."

"Can I get some sleep now?"

He backed out the door, and the electronic lock bleeped.

I kept the bathrobe on and crawled into bed with wet hair. Who cared about the pillow? The row of switches above the nightstand worked all the lights, and I turned off everything but the floor lamp in the corner and burrowed under the covers. I could still feel that man between my legs, and I hated myself. Hated what I'd become.

A while later, somebody unlocked the door, but I pretended to be asleep in the hope that it was just some sort of late-night check. China clinked on glass before my visitor left again, and when I sat up, I saw a plate of finger food on the dressing table. No cutlery, of course, because if I had a fork, I could stab someone in the eye.

Much as I hated to admit it, Leandro was right—I needed to keep my strength up. Still feeling sick, I padded across the room and forced down a couple of bite-sized soufflés and a mini quiche. He'd brought a bottle of water too, and I eyed it up suspiciously. None of the other girls had looked as if they were drugged. I sipped a mouthful cautiously. Tasted okay. In the end, I swallowed the rest because if it *was* spiked, at least it might help me to sleep.

CHAPTER 17 - BLACK

BLACK WAITED FOR ten seconds to see if Emmy would reload, then took his fingers out of his ears.

"Diamond, there's not much left of that target."

"Good."

Seven days had passed, a full fucking week, and he shared his wife's frustrations. After the initial flurry of activity, information had proven difficult to come by. Roscoe had taken a flight to France, landing at Charles de Gaulle Airport before he caught a train towards Lyon. He'd popped up briefly when he'd withdrawn five hundred euros from an ATM near Dijon, then promptly disappeared again. The man seemed to be backpacking around Europe, but Blackwood's people had so far been one step behind. Not that he was a particularly viable lead, more of a loose end.

Catalina, to all intents and purposes, didn't exist. They'd reviewed months' worth of camera footage from El Bajo Tierra, and she hadn't been to the club before. Lorenzo/Alonso had, though. One of Marco's men spotted him the month previous, although he'd arrived and left alone that time.

And as for Lorenzo/Alonso's current whereabouts... Sebastien said there was only one reason a man went to Barranquilla, and that was to leave. He could be anywhere, and so far, they hadn't had any luck in locating him. But they had a name. Well, sort of. One of the cops on the Garcias' payroll—yeah, Black had rolled his eyes at that—picked out a dozen other murders they'd attributed to him and said there were probably more. All drugs-related. All audacious in their planning and meticulous in their execution. The police had nicknamed the culprit Mercurio. Mercury. Quicksilver. Deadly as fuck and impossible to catch. Reading between the lines, it seemed the cops figured that since Mercurio was only killing criminals, they didn't want to get too involved, although they did send a bunch of flowers to the hospital for Eduardo.

The old man was still unconscious and barely responsive. The swelling on his brain had gone down, at least, and so far, Emmy had held it together although the anger was building. Ana was a strange oasis of calm in the household, gliding silently from room to room as Eduardo's men plotted their revenge on a ghost.

Black was about to pick up his Colt and blast a few rounds through a target himself when his phone vibrated. Mack was calling.

"Tell me you've got news."

"You're not gonna believe this."

"Try me."

"I set up an alert on those prints, and it turns out I'm not the only person who's been running them through the databases this week. Your number one suspect just got picked up."

"Picked up?" Black gripped the phone tighter. "Where?"

"Florida. Fort Lauderdale."

"Are you positive?"

"The prints match, and so does the mugshot."

"Send it through."

"On its way."

Pure, dumb luck. Good thing the jet was fuelled and ready.

"Emmy, we have to go."

"Go? Go where?"

"Florida."

"We've found something?"

"Maybe. Enough that I think we should head stateside to check it out."

If Mack said they'd got the man, then they'd got him, but Black deliberately downplayed the possibility. Why? Because if Sebastien and Marco found out, they'd be on their own jet before he could blink, and the Atlantic Ocean would turn red with blood.

Which meant when Sebastien saw them packing, Black had to lie. Fortunately, he was the master at that.

"You're leaving?"

"Just temporarily. Ana's daughter fell out of a tree house at her grandparents' home, and she's in the hospital."

"She's injured?"

"A fractured arm, but she wants her mom."

"Emmy's going with you?"

"There're a couple of leads I want to check out while we're home. Long shots, most likely. One of my colleagues thinks Vicente may have been spotted in North Carolina, and a Roscoe Ward flew into New York two days ago. Probably a different person, but it's an unusual name."

Sebastien nodded his agreement. "We appreciate your help on this."

"Eduardo means a lot to all of us. Make sure you

keep that security tight."

Two hours later, they were back on the plane. Ana sat up front, playing co-pilot with Brett again. Brett was a former USAF combat pilot who'd been with the team since Black bought his first jet, a quiet man who enjoyed travelling and didn't mind unexpected trips to foreign countries. He wrote historical war novels in his spare time, so he'd spent the last week working on his tan and his book by Eduardo's pool.

"So," Emmy said. "What's this lead? And don't give me some bullshit about Vicente or Roscoe. Tabby fell out of a tree house? She climbs like a bloody monkey."

"Mercurio's in custody."

Emmy was rarely left speechless, and Black quite enjoyed the sight. And the silence, brief though it was.

"*What*? Whose custody?"

"Fort Lauderdale PD. He got picked up in a drugs raid."

"Drugs? So he's part of a rival cartel?"

"Nobody knows yet. He's not talking." Black had spoken briefly to a contact in the police department while Emmy was packing. "Nothing. He won't even speak to an attorney to give his name."

"How do we know it's him?"

"Fingerprints, and a photo confirmed it."

A mugshot of a sullen, twenty-something man, eyes cast down at the floor and a little ragged around the edges, which was hardly surprising if he'd been on the run.

"Was he picked up alone?"

"No, they arrested four other men, two more died, and they estimate another half-dozen escaped."

"How did two die? Crossfire?"

"One died in an explosion, and the other was found with his throat slit."

Emmy raised an eyebrow. "That doesn't sound like your average drugs raid."

"No, it wasn't. The drugs were in a warehouse along with a whole bunch of other fucked-up stuff. Someone tossed a grenade in, which started a fire, and a crate of fireworks went off like the Fourth of July. One wise guy got hit in the throat by a rocket."

"A wise guy? La Cosa Nostra?"

"So they say."

"The American Mafia and a Colombian sicario working together?"

"Possibly not. They caught Mercurio carrying an unconscious girl out of the burning building, and they might even have written him off as a concerned passer-by if it weren't for the bloody knife they found in his pocket."

"He slit the mobster's throat?"

"More like sawed it in half. They're waiting for the DNA results to come back, but yes, it looks that way."

"So maybe he wasn't running from the Garcias at all? Maybe Mercurio was hired for another job, and he flew straight to Florida to do it."

"Busy man."

"And careless."

Very careless. Because now he had Blackwood, the Garcias, and La Cosa Nostra baying for his blood, and there were only so many places he could hide. He undoubtedly had some money stashed away, but did he have connections in the United States?

"Who was the girl?"

"The cops don't know yet. She's still unconscious.

According to my contact, there were a handful of women running around at the scene, but when the chaos died down, they only found one remaining."

"Will she make it?" Emmy asked.

"The doctors couldn't say. She suffered burns to twenty percent of her body, and Mercurio got treated for smoke inhalation."

Emmy's mouth set into a hard line. "We need to talk to him."

"And when you say 'we,' you mean me."

"No, I mean me."

"Diamond, you're not going near him."

"Yes, I am. He's obviously got a soft spot for women if he risked his own freedom to help one, and both of the girls he screwed around with in Medellín said he was a gentleman. I'm the obvious choice for this."

Black sighed, because he knew she was right. But he also knew how impetuous she could be when something knocked her off balance.

"You've been through too much lately."

"Eduardo got shot eight days ago. Yes, it upset me, but I've had over a week to get my head back in the game, okay? I'm not going to go off on some crazy, half-baked crusade. I just want the name of the man who hired Mercurio to kill Eduardo, and we're not going to get that unless Mercurio starts talking. And, dude, in the game of good-cop, bad-cop, you're always going to be the bad cop."

True. Black had spent years cultivating his bad-cop persona, and usually, it stood him in good stead. Emmy was right; he had a reputation to uphold.

"I'll speak to my contact. But if I get you inside that room, you're leaving all your weapons at the front desk, capisce?"

"No weapons. Got it."

Fuck. Everything about this screamed "bad idea." But with the clock ticking on Eduardo's life, they needed to find out who wanted him dead. And sometimes, just sometimes, bad ideas turned up good results.

CHAPTER 18 - BLACK

AFTER A HURRIED stop at a local strip mall, Emmy was dressed appropriately for the occasion in an ill-fitting suit, ugly shoes, and a name badge proclaiming her to be Quenby Broitzman, consultant psychologist. They were staying in Nate and Carmen's Miami condo, and this morning, they'd made the thirty-mile trip up to Fort Lauderdale in the Porsche Cayenne Bradley had rented for them. It didn't quite have all the bells and whistles that Black's Cayenne in Richmond had, but at least he felt at home behind the wheel.

And now Emmy was sitting in an interview room next to Detective Brent Shelton of the Fort Lauderdale PD, and opposite one pissed-off sicario with his hands cuffed in his lap and an attorney beside him. A public defender who was way out of his depth, judging by the nervous twitch of his mouth. Through the one-way glass that took up most of one wall of the observation room, Black had a better view of Emmy than of the suspect, and today, she wore her poker face. Still. Bland. Unthreatening. A relaxed mouth offset by a touch of ice in her eyes, the frostiness enhanced by a pair of blue contact lenses.

The only hint of her troubled thoughts was the Montblanc fountain pen she held in one hand. It had been a gift last Christmas from Oliver, their attorney, and when she got stressed, she'd also adopted his habit of twirling it around his fingers. *Flip. Flip. Flip.*

Shelton did the talking. "I'll ask one more time... What's your name?"

Silence.

"Where are you from? Are you American?"

Silence.

Black could have helped them out with that question, but he preferred to operate on a need-to-know basis, and right now, he was of the opinion that the cops didn't need to know. His Fort Lauderdale contact hadn't been too keen on letting Emmy into the interview room either, but Black had called in a favour with the FBI and they'd applied a little leverage. Thanks to Blackwood smashing the mother of all paedophile rings a few months back, the agency owed him a lifetime of favours, and Black intended to collect as and when required. As far as the cops were concerned, Mercurio was a person of interest in a burglary at one of the palatial beachfront mansions Blackwood had a monitoring contract for, and Blackwood's main interest was in recovering stolen property.

Secrets and lies... Black's biggest secret was that he enjoyed lying more than telling the truth. Sometimes, he made shit up just because he could. Call it a hobby of sorts. He found lie detector tests genuinely fun because he could beat them every time.

"Can you speak?" Shelton asked. "Because we can get a sign-language interpreter here if we need to."

Unsurprisingly...silence. Then the door to the observation room burst open, and all heads turned as a newcomer strode in.

"What the hell is going on?" he demanded.

From the captain's pissed-off expression, the man's arrival was an unexpected development. Interesting. None of the other cops standing with them seemed to know who he was either.

"And you are?" the captain asked.

"Special Agent in Charge Merrick Childs from the Miami Field Office."

"Well, Special Agent in Charge Childs, I'm Captain Walsh. Perhaps you'd like to explain why you've gatecrashed my interview suite."

"And perhaps you'd like to explain why you tried to sabotage a two-year investigation."

"I have no idea what you're talking about."

Wasn't this amusing? Black should have brought popcorn.

"That warehouse you managed to destroy two days ago was the subject of a surveillance operation."

"Nobody informed us of that. What kind of operation?"

"That's classified. You just blew months' worth of work."

"As I said, nobody told us. Are we meant to be psychic? The place was full of drugs, and kids in our neighbourhoods are dying."

"And this case is bigger than one warehouse. If you'd gone through the proper channels—"

"We filed all the paperwork we needed to. Maybe if you'd been open about your operations in our jurisdiction..."

Men arguing like boys. Black tuned them out and turned back to the interview. The classified operation piqued his curiosity, but he'd find out the details later.

"What were you doing in the warehouse?" Shelton asked Mercurio.

Silence.

"Right now, we've got enough to charge you with murder, and you won't get bail if we don't know who you are. Or maybe we're wrong? Maybe someone else killed Salvatore Favero and you just happened to pick up the knife. You have to help us out here."

Silence.

"What about the girl you saved? Do you know her? We need to contact her parents, and we can't do that without a name."

Shelton slid a small stack of photographs across the table, clipped together at the top. Jane Doe, still lying alone in the ICU. Mercurio picked them up and thumbed through them slowly. Deliberately. Put them down and didn't say a word.

What was going through his head? If Black had to guess, Mercurio would rather go to prison in the USA than risk extradition to Colombia, because with the number of enemies he'd made, he wouldn't last five minutes in jail over there. In Florida, he had the option of a life sentence or the death penalty, and if he got life, he'd be eligible for parole after twenty-five years. That would make him, what, fifty?

The cops could only hold him for seventy-two hours without charge, and Shelton was right; they weren't about to let him go free.

Tick, tick, tick.

"I understand you must be traumatised," Emmy said, injecting warmth into her voice. They'd been in there for an hour, and she'd played her part well so far. "Perhaps it was self-defence? Are you having trouble remembering what happened?"

Silence.

"We could bring a therapist in for you to talk to. Would that help, Mr... Mr... Well, have a think about it."

Silence.

"Let's take a break," Shelton said. "Mr. Doe here can consider his options while we get a coffee. Interview terminated at eleven twenty-nine."

"Maybe we *should* cut him loose," the captain muttered. SAC Childs had stormed out moments earlier. "He'd soon start talking if the mob got their hands on him."

The man was bullshitting. The cops would never do that because they played by the rules. If Blackwood had gotten to Mercurio first, they wouldn't be going through this fucking charade. Black sighed. Sometimes, a little pressure was necessary in these situations, but thanks to all the ambulance-chasing attorneys and pesky human-rights advocates, the bad guys often had the upper hand nowadays.

Shelton and Emmy stood, and a small smile played across Emmy's lips. A genuine smile, not the humourless mask she'd been wearing for the last week. What was she so pleased about?

Her gaze dropped to the table, just for a second, and Black followed it. Why had she left her pen behind? That thing cost hundreds of dollars, and she'd carried it with her for months. Mercurio started to get up, and too late, Black realised what was missing from the picture. The paper clip. The fucking paper clip that had been on the stack of photos earlier. Black knew exactly what was about to happen, but stuck on the other side of soundproof, bulletproof glass, he was powerless to stop it.

Mercurio moved fast, dropping the handcuffs and the paper clip on the floor then grabbing the pen. Before Shelton turned halfway, Mercurio had flipped the cap off and pressed the pointed tip to Emmy's carotid artery.

Fuck.

Put him down, Emmy. You can do that in your sleep.

But she didn't. Instead, she half whimpered, half screamed as Mercurio wrapped one arm around her throat and shoved her forward. Was Black nervous? No. Just slightly confused.

"Open the door," Mercurio ordered Shelton.

Those were the first words he'd spoken, and he did so with a strange accent. Mostly Spanish, but with a hint of British underneath. Who was this guy?

Black moved towards the door to find out, but the beefy captain blocked his way.

"Stay where you are. We'll handle this."

"Unlikely."

"Need I remind you that you're a civilian, and you're only here as a courtesy, as is your associate, who's now managed to get herself taken hostage."

Okay, so Black had neglected to mention that oh-so-forgetful Ms. Broitzman was actually his wife. Like he said, information on a need-to-know basis only.

Black shrugged. "It was your man who gave John Doe the paper clip he used to pick his cuffs."

Anger flashed across the captain's face, and Black resisted the urge to laugh. He understood what Emmy was doing now. The best way to convince Mercurio to talk was by getting him outside of the police precinct, and that was exactly where they were headed.

"Just get out of the way!" Emmy shrieked from the hallway.

Confusion reigned long enough for her and Mercurio to make it to the parking lot, and Black cursed under his breath when he recalled her offer to put the car keys in her purse when they arrived earlier. The little bitch had planned this all along, hadn't she? Mercurio pushed her in through the passenger door of the Porsche, then climbed in beside her as she wriggled into the driver's seat. The engine started with a roar, and she floored it out of the gates.

Poor bastard. Black almost felt sorry for Mercurio because the man clearly had no idea what sort of trouble he'd just gotten into.

For a moment, the gaggle of cops just stared at the disappearing car, incredulous. Seemed they'd never had a murder suspect escape from an interview room with a hostage before.

"Don't just stand there!" the captain yelled. "Go after them!"

The first police cruiser peeled out of the lot twenty seconds later, but Black just shook his head. Emmy in a Porsche Cayenne versus a dozen cop cars? He knew who his money was on.

Instead of panicking, he meandered back inside and poured himself a cup of coffee from the ever-present jug in the now-empty squad room. Checked his watch. Waited five minutes. Pulled out his phone and dialled.

Emmy's dulcet tones greeted him. "Leave a message or don't bother."

Hmm. She never turned her red phone off. Was she out of signal range? Black waited two more minutes then tried again, only to get the same result. Dammit. A vein began to throb in his temple as he called Nate. Now he was starting to get a bad, bad feeling about this.

CHAPTER 19 - BLACK

"WHERE'S EMMY?" BLACK asked Nate.

Half a minute passed, and he heard Nate tapping away at his computer in the background.

"Strange. She's turned her red phone off. Why would she do that?"

An excellent question, and one Black wasn't sure he wanted to know the answer to.

"Is there any way you can track it?"

"Not when she's taken the battery out."

"What about Ana?"

Another pause. "Her phone's turned off too. What's going on?"

Black tossed the remains of his coffee into the trash, cursed in his head, and lowered his voice.

"Would you believe Emmy's kidnapped a sicario?" He held the phone away from his ear until Nate had finished laughing. "It's not fucking funny."

"Buddy, it's hilarious. Are you serious? Hey, guys! Emmy's kidnapped a hitman."

"Just shut up and find her. Can you track my rental car instead?"

"Yeah, I can track the rental car. Give me ten minutes."

Black went outside to get some fresh air while he waited for Nate to work his magic. Dammit, he should have guessed Emmy planned to pull a stupid stunt after she insisted on going for a run along the beach with Ana this morning. Right now, he didn't know whether to be absolutely pissed or applaud her ingenuity. In the end, he settled for phoning Bradley and requesting he organise another vehicle, stat.

"You want it delivered to the precinct in Fort Lauderdale? That's gonna take half an hour at least," his assistant told him.

"I don't have half an hour."

"What happened to the first one?"

"Trust me, you don't want to know. Just get me a fucking car."

Bradley tsk-tsk-tsked at him. "And what happened to 'please'?"

"*Please* get me a fucking car."

"Fine, I'll sort something out. Take a chill pill."

Thankfully, Bradley hung up before Black cracked a tooth. Why did he do this shit? He was a fucking billionaire—he should have been cruising the Caribbean on a yacht or cavorting with half-naked models in a Jacuzzi filled with Veuve Clicquot.

But unfortunately, he'd made some poor choices in life.

Where the hell had Emmy gone with Mercurio? They had a condo in the Keys they never used, but no way would she have taken him there. Too busy. Black called the agent who managed his real estate and got a list of the empty properties they owned within a hundred-mile radius. There were six, but he ruled out the two apartments. Dragging a presumably unconscious murder suspect past a concierge and into an elevator might raise a few eyebrows.

That left four houses to check, but honestly, Black's instincts told him she'd avoid them all. Too obvious. She'd clearly thought this through, and since he'd spent the last sixteen years teaching her how to evade and escape, he'd be almost disappointed if she took such an easy option. Ana had few connections in the US, at least that Black knew of, so where else would Emmy turn? Not Dan or Mack—they were good friends of Emmy's, but also of Black's, and neither of them would split their loyalties like that. Ditto for Nick. Xavier was on vacation in Europe for three more days. Jed? Black called him, but he was at his desk in Langley. Next, he tried Sofia, but Leo, her boyfriend, picked up instead.

"Is Sofia there?"

"Sorry. She went away for a few days and left her phone behind. Didn't Emmy mention the trip? I thought they were going together."

"It must have slipped her mind."

"They've gone to Florida. Fia said something about water sports, which is great, isn't it? I mean, when you think she wouldn't even go in a pool a year and a half ago."

Water sports? Waterboarding, more like. "Fantastic. Emmy said they were planning a trip, but I didn't realise it was this weekend. Must have got my dates mixed up."

"Don't worry—those girls can look after themselves."

"Yes. Yes, they can."

An ancient Mercedes sedan drove into the parking lot and shuddered to a stop in front of him. The window wound down, and a dreadlock-crowned head popped out.

"Mr. Black?"

"Yes?"

"I'm Mahmoud, your Uber driver."

His *what*? Bradley had sent a fucking *Uber*? That was it—when Black got home, he was cancelling Bradley's credit cards, and his ridiculous Lamborghini could go in the crusher.

For a moment, Black contemplated borrowing one of the police cruisers parked nearby, but that would only cause more problems later. He was about to toss Mahmoud a hundred-dollar bill for his trouble and phone Bradley again when Nate called back.

"The Porsche is in a parking garage six miles from you. I'll send a map." He laughed again. "A fuckin' sicario."

Okay, six miles. He could take an Uber for six miles. And if Emmy hadn't left the damn key in the car, he really would kill her. Black sighed as he slid into the back seat. Why him? Was this some sort of cosmic revenge for all the dead bodies he'd left in his wake over the years?

"Where are we going, sir?"

Black read out the zip code.

"Very good. There are drinks in the cooler, and the TV on the back of the seat, and I also have the Wi-Fi."

He'd installed a motherfucking disco ball too.

"I'll give you two hundred dollars if you get me to that parking garage in ten minutes."

"No problem, sir."

Mahmoud burned rubber as he shot out of the parking lot, and Black slid across the seat and landed on a tasselled throw pillow. Had Bradley arranged that too? The engine screamed louder than the cacophony of horns that followed them through the streets of Fort Lauderdale, and Black bit his damn tongue when Mahmoud bumped the car up onto the sidewalk. Steam rose from the hood when they arrived, but the driver turned to him proudly.

"Nine minutes, sir."

Black handed over three hundred dollars and took Mahmoud's business card. Perhaps he could fly the man to Virginia on Dan's next birthday and have him chauffeur her to the restaurant? It was hard to find someone who drove worse than she did, but today, Black had finally managed it.

"Thanks."

"Have a good day, sir."

Oh, how he wished he shared Mahmoud's optimism.

The Porsche was parked in a dark corner on the third floor, and when Black patted the top of each tyre in turn, he found the key tucked under the rear wheel well on the driver's side. On the steering wheel, a bright orange Post-it note held a one-word message from his wife.

Sorry.

She would be when he caught up with her, but first, he had the not-insignificant task of tracking her down.

Where to start? He walked through the parking garage, relieved when the red light of a security camera blinked back at him over the exit ramp. How much cash did he have with him? Another eight hundred dollars. That was plenty to buy off a parking attendant.

He found the man in an office next to the stairwell, a grey-haired guy in a white vest with the figure of a sumo wrestler and a snore that rivalled a military jet taking off. Black knocked on the open door, and he nearly fell off his swivel chair.

"You got a problem?"

"Yes, I have a problem."

The man pointed to a sign next to the door, a long list of legalese that absolved management of responsibility for just about everything.

"Not that kind of problem. I think my wife's been seeing another man."

"Join the club, pal. Way I see it, I get me a little peace and quiet and some other dumb schmuck forks out for her dinner."

A quite unique way of looking at things.

"Between you and me, she's after my money, and I'd rather not give it to her. A friend said he saw her drive out of here with the asshole she's cheating with, and I want to find out if that's true. More ammo for my divorce attorney."

"I didn't see nothin'."

"No, but I bet your cameras did. I'll give you a hundred bucks if you let me review the tapes."

The lazy fucker pursed his lips.

"Two hundred."

"A hundred and fifty."

"Deal."

He held out his hand and Black ignored it, just looked pointedly at the door until the man got the message and levered himself up out of his chair.

"You've got an hour, pal. Any longer, and the boss'll start asking questions."

Black doubted that very much, but he nodded anyway. "One hour."

As it happened, he only needed fifteen minutes. At

a quarter past twelve, a black Suburban drove down the ramp with Ana in the passenger seat. The shadowy silhouette in the back was Emmy—Black would recognise her anywhere—and Mercurio was presumably in the trunk. But behind the wheel?

Alaric McLain.

Emmy's last serious boyfriend before she committed to Black, and a man who knew more about disappearing than Black himself. For a moment, he wondered if Alaric was helping Emmy in revenge, as payback for what Black did seven and a half years ago, but he quickly discounted that thought. Nobody but he knew what happened that night. He had an alibi only one man could break, and Pale would never talk.

CHAPTER 20 - EMMY

"I CAN'T WAIT to hear this tale." Alaric McLain passed Emmy a bottle of sparkling water and took a can of Sprite out of the fridge for himself. "Why do I have an angry man duct-taped to my weight bench?"

Emmy had been deliberately vague when she called Alaric on Ana's burner phone, but thankfully, he'd always had a sense of adventure. When she and Ana had stuffed the unconscious Mercurio into his car boot, he'd just rolled his eyes and sighed.

"It's a long story," she said.

"Pretty sure he's not going anywhere."

Emmy took a seat next to Ana, who was carving slivers off an apple with a combat knife. Why didn't she take a bite out of the bloody thing like a normal person?

"Okay, so last week, the dude downstairs shot my pseudo-father."

"Which pseudo-father? The boxer or the drug lord?" Alaric shook his head. "Now, there's a sentence I never thought I'd utter."

"The drug lord. But he's a hired gun, I'm sure of it, and I want to know who hired him. So far, he's been a little reluctant to talk."

In the Porsche, Mercurio had uttered a few directions about where to drive after leaving the precinct—not that he had a clue where he was going, that much was obvious—then he fell asleep. Well, not fell asleep, exactly. More like passed out. For Emmy's last birthday, Sofia had gifted her a one-of-a-kind poison ring, a work of art in white gold complete with a hidden compartment. Twist the top, and a tiny needle popped out, loaded with enough Fentanyl to knock out a grown man. Emmy had been dying to test it out for ages, but today was the first time a suitable victim had come along.

The intercom buzzed, and Alaric picked up the phone.

"Yes? ... Sure, come and join the party. Why not?" Then he turned back to Emmy. "Carry on."

"When Fia gets here. I'm not going through this twice."

"You didn't tell her the details either?"

"What, did you think you were special?"

In actual fact, Alaric *was* special. Not many men would have dropped everything to help with such a crackpot scheme, especially an ex-boyfriend. Those had been good times, her days with Alaric. The man had a gift. If Black was the king of the information game, then Alaric was a god, and he could talk his way into anywhere. On one date, he'd blagged tickets to a movie premiere by pretending to be a Hungarian porn star. Which he totally could have been because...

"What did I miss?"

"Hey..." Emmy got up and hugged Fia tightly. "Thanks for coming."

She and Fia had been friends for a decade. At one point, they'd even gone beyond friendship, but that was more of an experiment than anything else. Still, they'd remained close, and if there was another person crazy enough to go along with Emmy's plan, it was Sofia Darke.

"It's Florida. Girls' weekend, right? I've brought plenty of sunblock and bikinis for everyone."

"I won't complain if you wear them," Alaric said. "But I'm not sure it's that kind of trip."

Fia waved a hand. "Oh, the sicario? Yeah, Emmy mentioned him. But that won't take long, right? I mean, you're looking at the dream team right here. Shame Xav's on vacation. He would've *loved* this."

Cheerful Fia had come to visit, and Emmy was glad to see her smile. Fia had always been prone to massive mood swings, but since she met Leo, there'd been more of the good times. Today, she was the sunshine to Ana's perpetual darkness and Emmy's simmering-anger-tinged-with-a-hint-of-guilt.

And Mercurio unnerved Emmy. Not because he was smart and sneaky and deadly, yadda, yadda, yadda, because she was all those things too, but because of the way he looked at her. It was the eyes. They had an intensity she'd only seen on one man before.

"A sicario?" Alaric asked. "He's Spanish?"

"Colombian. Ever hear of a guy called Mercurio?"

Alaric's eyes widened. "Mercurio? That's who you've got in my basement?"

"I knew I should have called you sooner. What can you tell us?"

"In truth? Not a whole lot. He stays in Colombia, and I don't do much work out there. But I've heard the name, and everyone who's ever mentioned it lowered their voice and looked over their shoulder before they spoke. Rumour says he came out of Comuna 13 in

Medellín, and if you want to book him for a job, it's done through a fixer who vets you first. He's picky, but he's good."

"That's kind of what I wanted to hear."

"That he's deadly as fuck?"

"No, that he vets his clients. I want the client's name."

"Good thing my basement's soundproofed. The previous tenant used it as a recording studio. But if you're gonna make a mess, you'll have to put plastic sheeting down. Blood's hell to get out of concrete, and I'll be moving on in a few months."

Alaric never stayed in one place for long. Since Emmy met him, he'd lived everywhere from Italy to Barbados to Alaska, and his intelligence network covered the globe. That was his job—intelligence. He'd started with the FBI, specialising in tracking US citizens overseas, but when a sting operation went wrong and he lost his job, he'd turned freelance. At heart, Alaric was a nomad, and now the world was his playground.

He'd dropped off the face of the planet for a while, but soon after he reappeared, he'd started a new business venture—Sirius, a private intelligence agency selling research services to governments, corporations, and anyone else who could afford their prices. Emmy had passed a few pieces of work his way, quietly since there was no love lost between him and Black.

Emmy shuffled her stool a little closer and gave him a smile. "Honey, could you do me a favour and find us some plastic sheeting?"

"You women are crazy," he muttered, but he got up and fetched his keys. "There's a Home Depot down the road. I'll be back in twenty minutes."

With Alaric gone, Emmy turned to Sofia. "So this might sound crazy, but I want you to walk into the basement and look at this dude. Just look at him. Then tell me what you think."

"Huh?"

"I want to know if he reminds you of anyone."

Fia raised one eyebrow. "O-kaaaay."

"Now?"

"Pass me the water first. I'm parched."

After she'd drunk half the bottle, Fia followed Emmy to the basement with Ana bringing up the rear. Secretly, Emmy was more than glad to have Ana there because if the worst happened and Mercurio got loose, Ana would probably snap her fingers and turn him into a rat or something.

The three of them filed silently into the cavernous room, empty apart from Alaric's gym equipment and a securely locked strong-room at the far end. Mercurio was exactly where they'd left him—flat on the weight bench, unable to move an inch. Only his head was free, and Emmy tore the strip of duct tape off his mouth.

"Feeling talkative yet?"

Nothing.

They'd parked Mercurio under a fluorescent light, and Fia leaned over to take a closer look. The sicario glared back at her with cold, hate-filled eyes and a twisted sneer.

Finally, she stepped back, and the girls convened in the far corner.

"Well?" Emmy asked.

"Shit."

"I'm not wrong, am I?"

Ana folded her arms. "Stop talking in code."

"Mercurio looks like Black did ten years ago," Fia said. "Before he mellowed."

"Black is mellow? Psssht."

"No, seriously. Black used to be so uptight he could eat coal and shit diamonds. What we have now is more dark grey. Do you really think...?"

A while back, Emmy had clued both Fia and Ana in to Black's secret heritage. That he wasn't American as everyone believed, but had in fact been stolen as a baby from Colombia by a CIA agent and his wife who'd brought him up as their own. Last year, Emmy had travelled back to Colombia with him to see if they could find the village he came from, but there was little left of it. Valento, hidden away in the jungle on the banks of the Amazon, had been razed to the ground eleven years ago in a war between rival drug cartels. According to the stories circulating in Leticia, the nearest city, nobody had survived the massacre, and the rainforest was gradually reclaiming what was left of the village as its own.

They'd visited. Driven as far as they could, then trekked through the oppressive heat behind a guide and found the remains of Black's birthplace. The motley collection of houses, a church, a school, a small store, all charred by fire and riddled with bullet holes. For only the second time since Emmy had met her husband, he'd cried. They'd both wept over the life he'd never known. Over the drug war that had claimed his entire family including, three years ago, the twin brother he'd never met.

But now Emmy was on the run with an incapacitated hitman who had eyes that looked exactly

—*exactly*—like her husband's.

Until she walked into the interview room, her only goal had been to get the name of whoever paid for the hit on Eduardo then put the sicario out of his misery, but now she had more questions. Who was Mercurio? Where did he come from?

Le sigh. Why did nothing ever go according to plan?

Fia and Ana were still looking at her, and she nodded once. "Let's do this."

"How?" Ana asked.

"I'll start off by asking nicely. I mean, he's got to realise he's in a sticky situation."

Four rolls of duct tape would do that to a man.

"You think that'll work?"

"Probably not, but professional to professional, I feel I should give him the chance."

"And then?"

"We'll have to get creative, but I don't want him to die before he's answered my questions. Best to keep the bloodletting and internal injuries to a minimum, at least to start with."

Ana's turn to nod. "I'll go and find what we need."

"I brought sodium thiopental," Sofia said. "That might help."

The fabled "truth serum," otherwise known by its brand name, Sodium Pentothal. But it didn't work quite like it did in the movies. Sure, it made people talk, but they mostly told you what you wanted to hear, and sorting out fact from fiction wasn't always easy. And getting the dosage right was tricky. Even with Fia's expertise, people often ended up unconscious.

"Last resort, okay?" Emmy drew in a breath and walked over to Mercurio. Those eyes... "In the interest of transparency, I'll explain why you're here. Eight days ago, you shot Eduardo Garcia. I want the name of the person who hired you. I can get that the easy way or the hard way, so I'll start by asking you straight. Who's your client?"

Nothing.

"Dude, you're not helping yourself here. Congratulations on pissing the Mafia off, though. They'll be lining up after me to fuck you over."

Nothing.

"Okay, we'll do this your way."

When they'd stripped Mercurio and tied him to the bench, Emmy had noticed the half-healed bullet wound on his arm—the result of Floriana's efforts, no doubt. Now, she cut a patch of the tape away and waited to see what goodies Ana would bring back. A nice selection, as it turned out. Emmy chose a pair of pliers, and Mercurio closed his eyes and steeled himself, clearly understanding what was to come. He barely flinched when she yanked out the first stitch.

"Just the name, sweetheart, and I'll kill you quick."

Fuck. Emmy pulled out all the stitches, and it had to hurt when she poured half a bottle of vodka into the wound, but Mercurio still didn't speak. In fact, he was barely breathing hard, and worryingly, he reminded her more than ever of Black. Emmy had seen her husband behave exactly like this when Alex, their sadistic, ex-Spetsnaz personal trainer, poked needles under his fingernails. Black was serious about training for every eventuality.

"We could wire him up to the mains," Ana suggested.

"I don't have a defibrillator handy."

Perhaps they should try the needle trick? Ana had found one of those sewing kits you got in hotel rooms, as well as sandpaper, a mallet, a packet of habanero chillis, a bag of oranges, a dozen bamboo skewers, a lighter, a Taser, coat hangers, and a banana.

"What's the banana for? Not...?"

"No, I'm hungry. But I suppose we could..."

Ick. Emmy would take a pass on that. For now, at least.

Footsteps sounded at the top of the stairs, and Alaric appeared with a Home Depot bag.

"I got drop cloths, wire, a couple of screwdrivers, electrical tape, and..." He glanced at Ana's goodies, and his gaze alighted on the sewing kit. "You went through my bedside table?"

Ana shrugged.

"Hey, you brought donuts," Fia squealed, giving Alaric a hug. "We should get together more often."

Yup, she was definitely in one of her manic phases. As usual, she'd refuse to see a doctor, but she tended to self-medicate if she felt particularly high or low.

"Or not," Alaric said, turning to Emmy. "You'd better hurry up with this because it's only a matter of time before your dearly beloved catches up with us."

Because there were cameras, cameras everywhere. Emmy figured they had a few hours, maybe a day before Black and Nate dug their way through the shell companies Alaric had undoubtedly used to rent this place.

Better get going, then.

Emmy stuck a needle under Mercurio's thumbnail.

"Let's try a new question. Where were you born?"

The slightest crinkle appeared in the man's brow,

but it vanished just as quickly.

"And I don't mean Colombia. I want the name of the town. Or the village."

Nothing.

She tried with another needle, and he didn't even flinch. Did the asshole have some weird insensitivity to pain?

"Why is that such a difficult fucking question? And I know you can speak because you told me to drive the wrong way towards Miami."

A third needle had no effect either, so Ana removed the cartridge from the Taser, jabbed the prongs into his skin nice and wide apart, and *zzzzzzzapp*ed for five seconds. Ten. Fifteen. Mercurio pissed himself, but he still didn't speak.

What next? They could start sandpapering his skin off or rub cut chillis in his eyes, but Emmy had a horrible feeling that wouldn't make a difference. She checked his pulse. Right now, her heart was beating faster than his, and if she started on him with a knife, he'd probably bleed out. The man was inhuman, and she felt a grudging admiration for him. If only he hadn't shot Eduardo, she'd probably have invited him out for a beer.

"Alaric, could you be an angel and find a car battery and a soldering iron?"

"What the hell do you plan to do?"

Emmy tried a smile. "Look on the bright side—it won't make a big mess."

Alaric sighed and climbed the stairs, leaving Emmy to turn to Sofia.

"Go for the Sodium Pentothal."

What did they have to lose? If he lost

consciousness, they'd just have to wait for him to come round then try again.

"I thought you'd never ask. What's the car battery for?"

"My backup plan."

In truth, Emmy had just wanted Alaric out of the way. If Mercurio did start talking, Black's secrets were none of her ex's business.

Sofia started with a low dose of sodium thiopental, leaving the cannula in Mercurio's arm to increase the amount as necessary. Ana sat cross-legged on a folding chair, looking bored. At one point, she gazed longingly at the electrical socket.

"Where do you live?" Emmy asked.

"Cali."

The word came out reluctantly, whispered through lips that didn't want to let it go. And it was a lie, Emmy was sure of it. But Mercurio had spoken, which was a step in the right direction at least.

"Whereabouts do you live? Which neighbourhood?"

"Aguablanca."

"Who lives with you?"

"Alone."

"And what do you do for work in Cali?"

"Student. English language."

"What's your name?"

"Lorenzo."

"Lorenzo what?"

"Bonilla."

"That's the fucking airport, you prick. Where were you born?"

"Bogotá."

"For an English student, you don't seem to have

much of a grasp of the language."

Oh, they were back to glaring again. Fia depressed the plunger on the syringe, and Mercurio got another hit of the good stuff.

"Maybe we should just try a bottle of Patrón," Ana muttered. "Men never shut up after tequila shots."

"Do you want to feed him the lime, or should I?"

Mercurio's eyelids drooped slightly, and Emmy tried again.

"Where do you live?"

"Medellín."

"Be more specific."

"Sabaneta."

A quieter neighbourhood outside of the city centre. That sounded more plausible.

"Who lives with you?"

"Justicia. My dog."

A sicario with a dog named Justice? Oh, the irony.

"What do you do for a living?"

"I kill people."

Okay, it was safe to say they were getting to the truth now.

"What's your name?"

"Rafael da Silva."

Silver? Quicksilver. That was a nice touch.

"And where were you born, Rafael da Silva?"

"Valento." He began laughing. "But you'll never fucking find it, because it's gone. All gone. Everybody's dead."

His eyes slowly closed, and Mercurio fell silent once again.

"Oops," Sofia said.

Holy fuck.

Chapter 21 - Emmy

SHITTING HELL.

NOW Emmy had a problem. A big problem. About six feet six and two hundred and thirty pounds, to be precise. Stuffing him into Alaric's car boot hadn't been an easy task.

And much as Emmy wanted to put a bullet through Mercurio's head, she couldn't kill him because he was probably the only person on the planet who might be able to shed any light on her husband's past. Talk about an awkward situation.

"Now what?" Fia asked.

"I don't know, okay? I'm thinking."

"Genetics is a funny thing," Ana said. "You turned out like your father, and you barely even met him."

"I did not turn out like my father!" Emmy snapped.

"Psssht. You're standing over a man with a knife in your hand."

Okay, so perhaps now wasn't the best time to have that particular argument.

"And Rafael da Silva is exactly like Black," Ana continued. "Look at him."

Emmy did. They weren't identical in appearance—da Silva had a narrower face, a straighter nose, a sharper jaw, darker skin—but the eyes, the build, the mouth, those were all the same. And the attitude was identical.

"We could give him another dose of sodium thiopental when he wakes up," Fia suggested. "If you want, we can carry on all day. He'll feel like shit for the rest of the week, but it won't have any lasting effects."

They could, but everything had changed. If Emmy was to keep da Silva alive, she needed to change her tactics. Leaving him duct-taped to a weight bench for the foreseeable future wasn't a viable option. He'd need food, and water, and bathroom breaks, and... Yeah. Not happening.

The pain thing wasn't working so well anyway, and if the same blood pumped in his veins as in Black's, that wasn't entirely a surprise. Emmy needed to try a different tactic, one that involved negotiating with the man who'd tried to kill Eduardo, much as it pained her.

"No. No more drugs."

She paced the basement until da Silva started to stir, then fetched another of the folding chairs and set it next to his head, straddling it so she could lean on the back and look down at his face.

"Welcome back, Rafael da Silva."

He closed his eyes momentarily. "*Joder.*"

Well, at least they weren't back to the silent treatment.

"So, Valento, eh?" Emmy took a deep breath and crossed her fingers. "Did anyone ever tell you about the twins?"

Despite all the tape, da Silva visibly jolted, and Emmy felt like punching the air.

"What do you know about the twins?" he whispered.

"Possibly a little more than you."

"Tell me."

Emmy shook her head. "That's not how this works, sweetheart. Give and take. You have something I want, and I have something you want."

"You are also an assassin, yes?"

"Yes."

"Have you ever given up the name of a client?"

"No. But then again, I've never been duct-taped to a weight bench by three other assassins."

"Sicarias? All three of you? Fuck."

"I just want the name. There won't be any comeback on you, because I'll kill your client personally."

"Why do you care about Eduardo Garcia? He's a drug lord. They all deserve to die."

"Because Eduardo's the closest thing to a father I've ever known. When I was at the lowest point in my entire life, and I'd lost somebody very close, Eduardo went to war for me to make things right. No questions asked."

"But he's been responsible for the deaths of thousands of innocent people."

"Actually, he's pretty picky about who he kills."

"What about the drugs he sells?"

"People choose to take those of their own free will. It's supply and demand. Eduardo's one of the better guys in the coke trade, and he's getting out of the drugs game, in any case. Almost half of his business is legitimate now. But do you know how many guys are fighting to take his place? He can't just quit cold turkey because there'd be all-out carnage."

"You sound as though you've discussed this with him."

"I have. At length. Why do you hate him so much? Because what I'm getting from you is more than a simple cash-for-killing vibe."

"Comparing one drug lord to another is like comparing a cobra with a rattlesnake." Da Silva tried to shrug, but his shoulders barely moved. "It's nothing personal. Drug lords, drug dealers—they're all the same. Cogs in a machine that causes the deaths of millions. The world's better off without them, and my goal is to terminate as many as I can before I leave this earth feet first."

"That's a suicide mission."

"Nobody lives forever."

"Why are you so bitter?"

"Because my family was wiped out by the drug war. They stole my life, my parents' lives, my grandparents' lives, so now I kill them in return. Why should they get to live?"

"The twins?"

"They disappeared during the first invasion. Nobody ever found their bodies. My father spent years searching the forest for their remains, and my grandmother never got over the loss."

"Your grandmother?"

"Their mother."

Holy freaking hell. Emmy had been right! And that made da Silva Black's...nephew?

"And your father was their brother?"

"Yes."

"You said the first invasion. There was a second? Was that what happened eleven years ago?"

He nodded. "The first invasion took my grandfather, the twins, and half of the village. The second took my parents and almost everyone else."

"*Almost* everyone? Who was left?"

Now da Silva fell silent once more. Dammit, Emmy had been so close. Time to change tack again.

"What were the twins' names?"

"You don't know?"

"Not their birth names. Only their new names."

Da Silva sucked in a breath, no easy task given his bounds. A spark of hope lit in his eyes. "They're still alive?"

"One of them is. The other died three years ago. I'm sorry."

And Emmy genuinely was. Rafael da Silva may kill people for money, and he may have shot Eduardo, but she saw now that he was human. And she felt his pain.

"And the other?" he asked.

"First, their names."

Give and take, remember?

"Mathias and Emilio. The other?"

Emmy allowed herself a small smile. "I'm married to him."

Chapter 22 - Emmy

"YOU'RE MARRIED TO one of the da Silva twins? My uncles?"

"I'm pretty sure of it, yes. Except he's not called da Silva."

Now Mercurio's eyes narrowed. "Then how do you know this?"

"I didn't until today when I sat in the interview room and looked you in the eye. You have the same damn eyes. I'm not sure if my husband realised the similarity or not—I mean, how often do we study our own eyes? I look into his every day, so it was obvious, but—"

"He was there? Today? At the precinct?"

Emmy nodded. "Behind the glass."

"So close..." Those dark eyes closed again. "What must he think of me?"

"If you'd tried to kill anyone but Eduardo, he'd probably be pretty proud. He's in the same line of business as we are. But as it stands, I'd say it's a toss-up who he's more pissed off at—you or me."

"Me," da Silva said. "Since I held you hostage."

"No, sweetheart, you didn't. He knows that was my fault as much as yours. Why do you think I left my pen on the table?"

"You knew what I planned?"

"As soon as you took that paper clip. Don't worry; I've been at this a few years longer than you." Why was Emmy trying to make him feel better? Mercurio had nearly killed Eduardo, for fuck's sake. This was an interrogation, not a pity party. "And you still haven't answered my question. Who else from Valento is still alive?"

He ignored that. "How did you end up married to my uncle?"

"If I tell you that, will you answer?"

Silence reigned for a full minute, but finally, da Silva nodded. Yes, he could be lying, but in situations like this, Black was a man of his word, and Emmy had to trust that his nephew would be the same. She'd deal.

"The twins were taken separately, one by somebody in the drugs trade, and the other by a CIA agent who raised him in America as his son. That's the man I married. He didn't find any of this out until two and a half years ago, and when we visited Valento, there was nothing left."

"You went there?"

"Last summer."

"I haven't been for over a decade." Another pause. "Valento was a staging point for drugs to cross the Amazon between Colombia and Peru. A flashpoint. There was often fighting, and perhaps we should have left earlier, but it was our *home*." His eyes darkened, and memories swirled in the haunted depths. "Six of us survived that day. Mama was sick—malaria, we think—and Papa went back for her. We buried them both in what was left of the churchyard. Me and my sister carried our grandma into the forest, and three of our neighbours escaped too."

"Your grandma? From which side of the family?"

"Our father's mother." *Black's mother.* "The other side of the family got wiped out years before. Our mother grew up in an orphanage."

"Is your grandma still alive?"

"Yes."

"Where is she?"

"Now? In a safe house."

"And your sister? Is she with her?"

A new expression flickered across da Silva's face. A mixture of pain and, for the first time, fear.

"Rafael? Where's your sister?"

"I have no idea," he whispered. "Those men in the warehouse... They were really Mafia?"

"You didn't know?"

"No."

"I figured it was another drugs hit."

He shook his head. "I've never worked outside Colombia. Those men, they have my sister and one of the others from Valento."

Oh, shit. The dead man in the warehouse... The girl da Silva had gone back inside for... It had been a rescue operation, not a hit.

"And you were trying to find them?"

"Yes."

"The girl you carried out of the warehouse?"

"I'd never met her before."

"Why were you at the warehouse in the first place? How did you know where to go?"

"My sister was wearing a tracker in her bracelet. But she doesn't have it now. I saw it broken on the ground right before I got arrested."

"You're gonna have to start at the beginning with

this."

So he did. Over the next ten minutes, Rafael da Silva told the story of Isabella Morales and how Corazon had offered herself up as bait to rescue her. The girl was ballsy, Emmy had to give her that. And so was Rafael himself. He'd travelled to the US with no network and no backup and taken on the fucking Mafia. Maybe ballsy was the wrong word. Insane. Insane was a good word.

And he ended with a plea.

"I don't care what you do to me. Whatever you hand out, I can take it. But please, let me find my sister and Isabella first. You have my word that I'll come back afterwards and accept my fate."

"No deal."

Now Mercurio deflated. Before, he'd been tough, steely in his resolve, but Emmy had finally broken him. Victory didn't feel as sweet as she'd anticipated.

"Here's my offer. I've got the manpower and I've got the connections to help you, but in return, I want the name of the person who hired you to kill Eduardo."

Fury still burned in Emmy's gut, but deep down, she understood Mercurio was just a tool. She needed to redirect her anger, and she couldn't make Corazon da Silva suffer for her brother's mistake.

A full minute passed before he nodded. "Okay."

"And my husband's gonna want to meet his mother."

"Okay."

Thank goodness. Tempting though it was to do a victory dance, Emmy needed to move on with the new plan. How long had Corazon been in the wind? Two days now? A lot could happen in forty-eight hours, and for a girl in that situation, none of it was pleasant.

"I'm gonna cut you loose. You may be bigger than me, but it's three against one." Ana and Sofia had been standing silently, sentries by the door for the duration of Emmy's questioning, but now they stepped forward. "And I assure you I know how to use this knife."

"I believe you."

"I also have a billion-dollar private army at my disposal, and if you cross me, I'll hunt you to the ends of the fucking earth."

Emmy slit the tape along each side of the bench, and Rafael rose to his feet, a giant mummy covered in silver bindings. The faint smell of urine drifted on the air, and Emmy realised they had a new problem.

"Where are my clothes?" Rafael asked.

She pointed to a tattered pile in the corner, and Ana held up the hotel mending kit.

"I may have been a bit cross when we first arrived," Emmy said. "Sorry about the Taser. And the, uh, needles."

He stared down from a foot above her, managing to look somehow majestic despite the circumstances.

"In your position, I'd have done the same thing. And my mentor used wood splinters instead of metal needles. Those stick."

"Vicente? The dude with the plane? La Parca?"

"You *have* done your homework."

"He trained you?"

"Along with my grandma."

"Your grandma?"

Rafael smiled for the first time. Just a quick flash of teeth, but it was there. "She was a sicaria too. But I should probably mention that she relies on a wheelchair now. Her spinal cord was damaged in the first invasion. She can stand with sticks, but her muscles no longer work properly, so she can only manage a few steps."

"La Leona?" Emmy guessed, recalling the details from Mack's research.

"Get within two feet of her, and she'll still kill you." Rafael pulled at one end of the duct tape, grimacing when it tore out a clump of chest hair. "How am I supposed to get this off?"

"I'd suggest just yanking it quickly."

"*Joder.*"

"Don't be such a coward. Women wax all the time."

He took a deep breath and tugged. The tape peeled off to his waist, leaving mostly smooth skin behind, now covered in little red dots. Holy hell, the man had abs. Emmy totally shouldn't have been looking, but hey, she wasn't blind. Perhaps she needed a new nickname? *La asaltacunas*, maybe?

"How old are you?" she asked. "Twenty-five?"

"Twenty-four."

Mierda.

The situation deteriorated further when Emmy remembered she'd cut off his underwear too. At that point, she'd been more concerned about fastening him down securely than what he looked like naked, and besides, she hadn't expected him to get up again.

"Fia, can you see if Alaric has any stretchy shorts in his closet?"

Alaric wasn't small, not at all, but he was still six inches shorter than Rafael and quite a bit narrower. They'd need to find new clothes from somewhere. Black's would fit, but they were at Nate's condo in

Miami.

Rafael turned his back and carried on peeling. *That ass.* Emmy sucked in a breath. Pointing out that when Rafael pissed himself, the urine might have loosened the tape probably wasn't the kind of optimism he was looking for right now. Yeah, he'd need a shower too.

Emmy nudged Ana. "Where's the bathroom?"

"Huh?"

At least Emmy wasn't the only one staring. So Ana *was* human after all.

"The bathroom?"

"Upstairs, second door on the left."

"Silver, did you hear that?"

He turned back around, one massive hand covering most of the good bits.

"Got it."

He jogged up the basement stairs, footsteps light on the wood. Mercurio looked like Goliath and moved like a cat. Ten seconds later, Fia appeared, fanning herself.

"I gave him the shorts, but I'm not sure they'll fit. Shit. I feel like such a cougar."

"Join the club."

"I mean, holy fuck, that guy's built. And Black's gonna shit bricks."

"What do we do now?" Ana asked.

"I've got to call him. I mean, I can hardly keep this to myself. Fuck. I need a drink."

"We used up all the vodka."

"No, not alcohol. Water or juice or something. My mouth's drier than Black's sense of humour."

They climbed the stairs slowly, and Emmy opened a carton of pineapple juice. Pineapple was fine as long as it didn't come on a pizza. She needed to talk to people.

Blackwood's Miami office. Mack. Dan. Alaric. Her contacts at the FBI. The DEA, the ATF, the DOJ. But most of all, she needed to call Black and pray he didn't tie her to the bed for a month. Granted, that wouldn't normally be a bad thing, but this week...

Shit. Two missing girls.

"Have either of you had much involvement with the Mafia?" she asked the others.

"Only Bratva," Ana said. "Russian Mafia."

"I've killed five..." Fia counted up on her fingers. "No, six, but they were all from New York and Chicago. Plus there was Raul in Atlanta, but he was plain ol' organised crime."

And Emmy usually butted heads with terrorists rather than the mob. Well, Black had always told her to try new things.

Speaking of Black... She might as well get it over with. His phone rang once, twice, and then a shadow darkened the doorway.

"Trying to call me, Diamond?"

Alaric stood behind him, holding a bag from Ace Hardware. "Sorry," he mouthed.

"Uh, I can explain."

"You promised you wouldn't go off on a crazy, half-baked crusade."

"I didn't. This was a fully baked crusade, and you're not gonna believe the story we've got to tell you."

"Where's the sicario?" Alaric asked. "Tell me we don't have a body to dispose of? The 49ers are playing the Dolphins tonight, and I didn't buy a spade."

"Good news—there's no body. The bad news is that we've got more important things to do than watch football."

"What's this 'we' business? I agreed to play cab driver and turn a blind eye to whatever you're doing in my basement. That's it."

Black had finally had enough of waiting, and his voice rose. "Would somebody tell me what the hell is happening?"

Emmy opened her mouth to speak, but the silent appearance of Rafael behind her husband made her jaw drop all the way. Hot damn. He'd squeezed himself into the shorts, and they bulged at every seam. Droplets of water glistened on his chest, and damp hair curled over his forehead in a manner reminiscent of the man-totty in a perfume ad.

Black turned slowly, and for a rare moment, he looked adorably confused.

"What the...?"

"Rafael, meet Charles Black. Black, meet Rafael da Silva. Your nephew."

CHAPTER 23 - BLACK

"MY WHAT?"

WHY did Black get the feeling he'd walked through Alaric's front door and ended up on a whole other planet?

Alaric's business dealings were more tangled than a spiderweb in a hurricane, but while Mack sifted through various filings, Dan recalled Alaric phoning her a few weeks back. The phone was turned off now, and tracing historic calls was nothing like in the movies —in reality, they could narrow the location down to thirty square miles, not thirty square feet—but Nate had hacked into the phone company's network and traced a bunch of calls made around this area. Black had headed over to await further information, spotted Alaric driving away from a hardware store, and followed the man right to his home address. Business must have been good because it wasn't a bad house. Big lot, triple garage, a swimming pool to the side.

And a reasonably competent assassin wearing a pair of overly tight shorts in the kitchen. Blood seeped down his arm from what looked like a bullet wound. Floriana's handiwork?

"Your nephew," Emmy said. "I told you I'd get answers."

"What the hell are you talking about? Have you lost

your mind? Oh, my mistake. You did that when you practically kidnapped a suspected killer out of police custody. They're out there searching for your body, you know. I still haven't worked out what to tell them."

"Just say he dumped me at the side of the road and I can't remember anything."

Deep breaths. "Emmy, he killed a Mafia thug. Why is he standing half-naked in Alaric's kitchen?"

Sofia put down her glass of juice. "He's actually three-quarters naked."

"Seven-eighths," Ana countered.

"And he's bleeding everywhere," Alaric said. He didn't seem happy about Emmy's antics either. McLain actually agreeing with Black on something—that was a truly momentous occasion.

"Do you have a first aid kit?" Emmy asked. "Fia can stitch up that hole again."

"Diamond, what the fuck is going on?"

Emmy's gaze flicked towards Alaric. "It's a very interesting story."

And she was asking him if he wanted Alaric there to hear it. Good question. Black and Alaric had gotten on fine before Alaric started sleeping with Emmy, but afterwards? Messy. On the surface at least, Black had supported Alaric through the Office of Professional Responsibility's investigation, and in the years since, Alaric had kept Black's secrets and he'd reciprocated. Knowing Alaric, his interest had been piqued enough by Rafael's presence that he'd start digging for his own amusement, and Black wouldn't have been surprised if the entire house was wired for sound anyway.

"Better start telling it, then."

"Okay, it's also kind of long, but bear with me,

because there are some really good bits. It all started in Valento..."

Mercurio sat at the kitchen table, unflinching as Sofia stitched up the wound sustained when he broke into Eduardo's home. Black prided himself on his self-control, but as Emmy told her tale, occasionally interrupted by the man now revealed to be Rafael, Black's insides rode a roller coaster.

His mother was *alive*?

For over two decades, Black had believed his only relative was an aunt he hated; then, two and a half years ago, he found out he'd had a brother who died before they could meet. He'd processed that. Dealt with it. But now his world had been flipped on its head again with these new revelations—some tragic, some miraculous.

Yes, there would need to be DNA tests to confirm everything, but now he saw Mercurio up close, there were definite similarities between them. And every detail of his story fitted with what Black already knew.

He had a nephew. A mother. And a niece who was missing in the country he called home. And since one set of his grandparents had been missionaries from England, that made him half-British just like his wife. Once again, what he thought he knew about his heritage had been shifted on its axis.

Emotions battled inside his head, the desire to fly to Colombia and meet the woman he'd been stolen from forty-one years previously fighting against the need to find Corazon. In the end, logic prevailed. Marisol da Silva was safe in Medellín, whereas Corazon was very much in danger. She had to take priority.

From what Black had seen so far, Rafael was

talented but raw. There was no point in asking him what he needed in the way of help because he simply wouldn't know. Time to take charge.

"We have an empty property twenty miles from here, and we'll use that as a base of operations. I'll call our Florida office and get them to reassign staff. Sofia, you finish fixing Rafael's arm. Ana, try not to kill anyone—yet. Alaric..." Dammit. This could get awkward. "What do you know about an FBI agent named Merrick Childs?"

"He's a dick."

"Beyond that?"

"Thirty-seven years old. Ambitious. Determined to climb to the top, doesn't care who he tramples on the way there, but in terms of talent, he's mediocre at best. Got accused of harassment by a female agent five years ago, but he claimed he just misread the signals and got away with it."

"What does your schedule look like at the moment?"

"Free tomorrow, then I'm flying to Nevada for a job."

"Merrick Childs was running some kind of surveillance on the warehouse where Corazon was being held. He turned up in the observation room while Emmy was plotting her hare-brained scheme, and he got into an argument with the police captain."

"Sounds about right. And I suppose you want me to find out what he was doing?"

Much as Black hated to admit it, Alaric's FBI contacts in Florida were probably better than his. While many of Alaric's former colleagues had publicly disowned him, a select few believed his side of the sordid tale that cost him his job.

"We'll pay your day rate."

Alaric sighed. "Okay. The 49ers haven't been playing so well anyway."

"And Rafael…" Black walked towards the back door and beckoned for the younger man to follow. "While Sofia finds a dressing to go over the top of that wound, we need to talk."

Outside, Black leaned against one post of the pergola beside the pool. The sun was dropping, casting long shadows over the garden.

"So…" he started. What did a man say in this situation? "This wasn't how I'd expected today to turn out."

"No."

"Did the girls hurt you badly?"

"No offence, but your wife's a bitch."

Black had to laugh at that. "She'd take that as a compliment. Would you have talked otherwise?"

"To the police? No."

"In that case, she did the right thing."

"I guess she did. But she's angry at me for shooting Eduardo Garcia. Is he still alive?"

"Yes, but barely. He's in a coma and it could go either way. Ultimately, she wants the person who hired you, and you'll have to give her that name."

"Yes. But not now. Now, we focus on my sister and Isabella."

Black couldn't argue with that, because in Rafael's position, he'd say exactly the same.

"Tell me one thing. Are you still on the hook for the job? Or is your client likely to hire someone else?"

Rafael took a barely perceptible breath as he

considered his answer. "Garcia is still in danger. Keep security tight. Put somebody inside the room."

"We've already done that."

"Then we have some time."

"If Corazon manages to escape, does she have a way of contacting you?"

"She'll call Grandma. But I need to get a new phone so Grandma can call me."

Black pulled his own phone out of his pocket. "Give her my number for now. I'll have my assistant organise clothes and a phone and whatever else you need."

"I need a gun. I flew commercial."

"What do you want?"

"Anything."

"By preference?"

"A Sig Sauer P226."

"Good choice. I'd offer you mine, but you don't have anywhere to put it."

Rafael grinned for a second, then took the phone. Without being asked, he put it on speaker after he dialled, and a moment later, Black heard Marisol da Silva's voice for the first time.

"*Sí?*"

"It's me."

"What happened?"

"Cora was being held at a warehouse, but the police came while I was there looking for Isabella. Not for me, but because there were drugs."

"And?"

"I got arrested, but I'm free again now."

And alive, which was a bonus after an angry Emmy had gotten involved. Black had to be thankful for that.

"And Cora?"

"We'll find her. Isabella wasn't there. Did you tell Dores the full story?"

"I had to, and now she's more upset than when she thought her daughter was dead. Who's 'we'?"

"We?"

"You said 'we'll find her.'"

"Uh..."

Black interrupted the conversation. "My name is Charles Black. I run a security company here in Florida, and Rafael has hired us to help find the women in question."

The sound of a breath being sucked in came down the line. "Rafael, are you sure about this?"

"I needed help."

"Vicente can come and—"

"No, Vicente stays with you."

"You can't trust strangers."

"Grandma, you need to trust *me*. I'll call tomorrow with an update, I promise."

"But—"

"Take care of Dores."

Rafael hung up and passed the phone back to Black.

"*Mierda*. That could have gone better."

"She's smart."

"Yes, Marisol da Silva is smart. Too damn smart. Every time I got into trouble as a kid, she found out and had something to say about it."

"My parents just wrote cheques to cover the damage."

"You still think of them as your parents, even after what they did?"

"How can I not? They brought me up, and they gave me a good life, even if their actions in Valento were abhorrent. They didn't start what happened that day."

"No, but they ended it."

"We can't argue over this. We can agree not to see eye to eye, but quarrelling over the past is futile. We need to focus on the future instead."

"Agreed."

"All of our resources are at your disposal. We'll get Corazon back, and Isabella too."

"That's what I have to believe."

"But it could take time, and you need to look after yourself. We work as a team, and Emmy's lunacy notwithstanding, we prefer to avoid lone-wolf tactics. I know you're used to working on your own, but you'll need to learn to defer to others when their expertise in a particular area exceeds yours."

"But—"

"No buts. Do you have police contacts? An expert hacker on hand? Access to real-time satellite imagery? The ability to conduct twenty-four-hour surveillance?"

Rafael shook his head.

"And, like me, you'll find undercover work difficult because your size makes you stand out too much. Better to leave that to men like Alaric. No, your primary role in this operation will be at the end, if we have to mount a rescue operation, which means you need to stay fit, eat well, train hard, and get enough sleep. Understood?"

"Yes."

"Good. Let's go and find that bandage."

CHAPTER 24 - CORA

THE PINK PALACE was a strange mix between a prison, a psychiatric unit, and a hotel. Each morning at around the same time, an ape woke us up and took us downstairs for breakfast while somebody cleaned our rooms. After breakfast, we had the choice of going to the gym, being locked up again, or watching a movie in the lounge. Everyone except Jodie, the redhead, had picked the lounge today, but I heard her pounding away on the treadmill in the next room. Two guards hovered at all times, usually seated on chairs by the door, and a grey-haired cleaner dodged around us with a feather duster.

"If it weren't for Netflix, I'd go crazy," Hallie said on the morning of my fourth day in the mansion. "Even if I've watched all the good movies at least twice."

The other Colombian girl, Paloma, sat beside me. "I miss books. I asked for something to read, but all I got was three Jack Reacher novels and a copy of *Vogue*. The boredom's the worst thing about this place."

"Apart from the nightly abuse, you mean?"

Her cheeks coloured. "Well, of course. But you kind of get used to that."

Last night, a banker named Kyle shoved his finger up my ass at the end then laughed when I screamed, and the night before, Randall, whose daddy was apparently big in oil, had pushed his cock down my throat until I choked. No, I would *never* get used to that. In fact, my stomach still churned with an odd combination of nausea and anger that sapped my energy and left me weak.

One of the blondes, Kristen, painted her nails by the window, and Tasha—Miss Stockholm Syndrome—chatted with a guard. The other blonde, Kelsie, sat in an armchair on the far side of the room with her knees drawn up to her chest, rocking.

I realised everyone coped with being here in their own way. Tasha, and to a certain extent, Paloma, had normalised the ordeal, while Kristen and Jodie tried to block it out. Despite being here for so long, Hallie seemed the least institutionalised, but she was also scared of putting a foot wrong in case it brought consequences. And Kelsie? She just kept to herself.

Mid-morning, Jodie went to use the bathroom and came back grinning.

"What are you so happy about?" I asked.

"I got my period. Five days off."

I laughed. I had to, really. This had to be the only place on earth where a woman looked forward to bleeding for five days straight.

"Didn't they give you a shot?"

"Last time, I came out in hives, and they had to call the doctor."

Lucky her—I'd never had an allergic reaction in my life. But I couldn't dwell on my disadvantage because I needed to start digging.

"Do you get many Colombian girls here?" I asked Hallie and Paloma.

"A few," Hallie said. "One every month, one every

two months, something like that. I lose track of the days. On the outside, I used to be such a stickler for timekeeping, and now I barely know what year it is. Funny how the stuff that was so important doesn't seem to matter anymore, isn't it?"

No, it was funny how all the little stuff became even *more* important. Eating food with a knife and fork. Making a cup of coffee. Buying groceries. Opening the window to smell the world outside, even if it was the pollution-filled streets of Medellín.

"I really miss home. If Colombian girls come over regularly, why are there only two of us left?"

"They get moved to the other houses," Paloma said, rolling her eyes. "Apparently, we're exotic."

Just when I thought my queasiness had subsided, it came back with a vengeance.

"How come you're still here?"

Hallie answered for her. "Because Radcliffe likes her."

"Radcliffe? Seriously?"

I still hadn't met him, but from what I'd heard, he was a rather dull man who hated untidiness—hence all the cleaning—and insisted the fruit be organic. Because pesticides were totally the worst thing in our lives right now.

"Yeah, once a week or so," Paloma said. "Okay, sometimes more."

"What's he like?"

"Straight missionary, and he grunts a bit. Could be worse. He's easier to deal with than most of the clients."

"Whereabouts in Colombia are you from?"

"Cartagena. You?"

"Medellín."

"The last girl was from Medellín too."

My chest tightened. Izzy? I didn't dare to ask, and Paloma continued.

"Did you meet a guy named Roscoe?" she asked.

"Yes! How did you know?"

"Because so did I, and the last girl too. Isabella."

Whoosh. All the air left my body, along with the last little bit of fear that this whole nightmare had been a wild goose chase. Izzy *had* been here, and I bumped Roscoe up the list of men whose testicles I wanted to skewer with an ice pick, right to the very top.

But the cleaner was still dusting, and I wasn't sure where her loyalties lay, so I couldn't ask too many more questions.

"Do you know where she went?"

Paloma shook her head. "We just came downstairs one morning and she'd gone."

"That's how it always happens," Hallie said. "Nobody ever tells us anything."

"Roscoe's such an asshole. He took me out to all these fancy restaurants, and then he said a friend of his had a hotel in Barranquilla where we could get a discount for a dirty weekend, and like a fool, I went. I mean, I should have smelled a rat when he talked about sitting on the beach, because who would go to Barranquilla when they could go to Cartagena?"

"Or even La Guajira or Cabo San Juan."

"Exactly. Anyhow, he said another friend had a boat, only when we got to the marina, I felt really sleepy, and then I woke up in some nasty warehouse with a bunch of weird Italian men. Two weeks, I stayed there, and it didn't even have a shower."

"I was only there a few days. The police raided the place."

Both girls' jaws dropped.

"Are you serious?" Hallie asked.

"Yes, but I don't think they were there for the kidnap victims. They seemed more interested in all the boxes, but then the whole place exploded in flames and the guards brought me here."

"Freaking hell. I wonder what they'll do if any new girls arrive? Take them straight to the houses?"

"Garrett told me they like to assess each girl before they decide on the best place to take her," Paloma said. "And if they're trouble, they offload them to a pimp."

How could they do that to a living, breathing person? "That's crazy."

Hallie gave a lopsided smile. "It's like the TJ Maxx model, except for women."

An ape strode towards us, and our conversation fizzled out. Now what?

"You have to go to your rooms for a while. Someone's coming to measure for new drapes downstairs."

Paloma huffed at the inconvenience, and I almost smacked the wall in frustration. Just when I was getting some information, my plan got foiled. And who knew when I'd be able to steer the conversation back around to Izzy?

With nothing else to do, I shuffled back upstairs and buried myself under the covers. At least I could dream. Of home and family and happier times and freedom.

That evening, I thought I'd got a respite. The hours passed, and I nibbled on canapés while men came and girls went. According to Paloma, there was a booking system in place—clients reserved a slot for the evening, although the girls were first-come, first-served. None of us had more than one client in a day unless they wanted to share, something else that turned my stomach.

"Radcliffe says it's all about the quality," she told me. "Nobody wants sloppy seconds."

Except for the apes, it seemed. They weren't that bothered, but thanks to being the new girl and somewhat of a novelty among the clients, I'd got away without being chosen for after-hours action.

Until tonight.

Tonight, I ate fancy food and picked at my dress for two or three hours, plotting a way to find Izzy while I waited, then looked up to see Chad walking towards me.

Oh, *mierda*. He was the guy the others had warned me about, and the gleam in his eye made my stomach plummet. My mouth went dry, but then a voice came from behind me.

"Join me tonight."

Leandro.

I didn't want to go with him either, and apparently he hadn't touched any of the girls since he arrived, so I had no idea what he was like. But when it came to the choice between a guy who got off on violence and an unknown quantity, I'd take the latter option.

"Okay."

I stood on shaky legs and followed, averting my eyes from Chad's pissed-off gaze as we passed. Where were we going? The basement, it turned out.

"This is where you sleep?" I asked.

"Our rooms aren't as nice as yours."

Doors opened off both sides of the narrow hallway, five on each side, and Leandro led me right to the far end.

"Here."

He unlocked the door on the left, revealing a small space with a single bed, a narrow closet, and a desk covered in junk-food wrappers, used coffee mugs, and a stray pair of socks.

"Sorry about the mess."

He was about to rape me, and he was apologising for his cleaning habits?

A doorway with no actual door led to a minuscule bathroom, and his chair looked as if it moved across the concrete floor, which made me oddly envious. But overall, the tiny room was dark and oppressive, and I shuddered involuntarily as I hugged myself. Now what? Did he expect me to take off my clothes? Or did he want to go through the ridiculous charade some of the clients did, the one where they stroked our hair and told us we were pretty as they undressed us?

"Get some rest," he said, pointing at the bed.

Before his words sank in, he'd left, locking the door behind him.

Huh?

What just happened?

I kept an ear out for footsteps as I quickly searched his room, but as well as being untidy, Leandro was the most boring man on earth. The closet contained a spare pair of jeans, a suit, a couple of shirts, socks, and boxer shorts. The desk drawers yielded a single paperback—a memoir of someone I'd never heard of—and a family-size bag of Fritos. The only electronic thing in the room was his shaver.

Time passed, but the minutes distorted in my head so I wasn't sure how long, and the room didn't have a window. Did I want him to come back or not? Of course I didn't want to get molested by him, but being left alone like that freaked me out a little. Finally, when I got sick of pacing, I lay down on the bed, on top of the covers rather than underneath them because that would have been weird.

The *click* of the lock woke me up. How long had I been asleep? There was no way for me to tell, but I felt tired. Leandro closed the door behind him and sat on the edge of the bed.

"You can go back to your room now."

"What?" My brain was still fuzzy. "Aren't you going to...?"

He shook his head. "I saw Chad heading in your direction, and he's bad news."

Leandro had brought me to his room to *help* me?

"I don't understand."

"Chad's asleep now."

"What time is it?"

He glanced at his watch. "Three thirty. And I need my bed back because this floor doesn't look too comfortable."

"Sorry."

One of my shoes had fallen off, and he retrieved it from under the chair before sliding it back onto my foot.

"Here."

He offered me a hand, and I hesitated a moment before taking it. Leandro was the enemy, but I couldn't afford to alienate him, not if I wanted him to save me from Chad again. Besides, he let go as soon as I was on my feet and opened the door for me.

"I'll walk you up."

It wasn't a courtesy—we both knew I wasn't allowed to go anywhere by myself—but he still managed to make the gesture sound more kind than creepy. The occasional lamp lit our way as we crept through the silent house, and before long, I was back in my cell.

"Thank you," I whispered.

He didn't answer, just locked the door and left for the second time that night.

CHAPTER 25 - BLACK

BLACK STOOD ON the covered terrace outside the master bedroom of the Florida mansion they'd spent the last twenty-four hours turning into a temporary base of operations. Despite owning the place, he'd never visited before, though he vaguely recalled his real-estate manager talking him through the pros and cons of the purchase several years ago. Mostly cons. The estate had been neglected for years while two sets of half-siblings argued over who would inherit it. But Black had liked the location and the layout, and his team had done a great job with the renovations. The previous tenants—an elderly couple—had moved to be closer to their children, and right now, it was up for rental. But perhaps he should keep it for a while and take a vacation when this was done?

He laughed softly to himself. A vacation? He'd only taken one proper break in the last decade. But yes, he probably owed Emmy more than a few snatched days in the sun here and there.

Ana and Sofia were sharing the twin room next door, Rafael had claimed another, and Nate could bunk in with Cruz from the Miami office when he arrived. The other two bedrooms would undoubtedly fill up soon unless they got a lucky break on the case, so it made sense to double up now rather than move later.

So far, they hadn't found much. The aftermath of the warehouse fire had been chaotic, and Black had spent most of yesterday explaining how Quenby Broitzman, hapless psychologist, had been found wandering by the side of the road in Greenacres with absolutely no memory of how she got there, and another hour discussing how Blackwood's burglary case, which didn't even exist, might tie into the Fort Lauderdale PD's manhunt for a murder suspect. Black still had to come up with a way to clear Rafael of the crime he committed, but he'd do that later. The only good thing was that a lot of the evidence got burned.

For once in his life, Black was tired of lying. Perhaps he'd try telling the truth for a day and see how that went.

Emmy snuck up behind him and wrapped her arms around his waist.

"Still mad at me?"

"Not really."

"I'm sorry I stole Rafael."

"Much as I hate to admit it, that was a clever move. I just wish you hadn't cut me out of the loop."

"I was going for plausible deniability."

"No, you knew I'd try and stop you."

"That too."

Black kissed Emmy's hair and then her lips. Although she drove him crazy, he could never be angry at her for doing precisely what he'd taught her to do. Being a renegade. Thinking outside the box.

"Rafael's interesting," she said. "Don't you reckon?"

"At the moment, I'm not sure what to think. My priority is to find these missing girls, then I can stand back and take stock of everything."

"And meet your mother."

"Yes. And meet my mother. Fuck. I don't know what to do. For the first time ever, I don't know what to do."

"What do you mean?"

"How can I just walk into her life? She doesn't know me from Adam. What if she's disappointed?"

"Disappointed? Chuck, you're a billionaire."

Black had given up chastising her for calling him Chuck. At first, she'd done so because he hated it, but now it was more of an endearing habit. Though if anyone else tried giving him a nickname, they'd lose their teeth.

"Yes, but my life hasn't exactly been conventional."

"Neither has hers by all accounts. Besides, you've got a few weeks to think about what to say. Rafael said he wouldn't tell her for now, right?"

"Yes. He called her earlier and told her there's no news yet."

Emmy reached up to squeeze his shoulders. "Then relax. This'll all get sorted out. Just be patient—isn't that what you always say to me?"

"I hate being patient."

She dug in with her thumbs, and a little of Black's tension dissipated. But the relief was short lived when a voice called up the stairs.

"Honey, I'm home."

Nate.

"On my way."

"Alaric's here too, but Bradley stopped off at a mall on his way from the airport."

Bradley? Black had asked him to send clothes for Rafael, not bring them personally. A long groan escaped his lips.

"He only wants to help," Emmy said. "Plus we need groceries. Come on, I'll keep him under control."

Downstairs in the dining room, Nate already had his laptop open, and Alaric walked in a minute later with a cup of coffee. Rafael appeared and took a seat opposite Nate, half-interested and half-wary.

"Is the coffee pot on?" Emmy asked Alaric.

"Just filled it."

"Legend."

She disappeared in search of caffeine, but Black was more interested in Alaric's news.

"Well?"

"You haven't grown any more polite in your old age, have you?"

"Wasted words are wasted time. And you're only three years younger than me."

Alaric laughed, and then infuriatingly, he blew on his coffee and took a sip before speaking.

"Merrick Childs works out of the Florida field office, but as of a year ago, he was seconded to Task Force Atlantis."

"Which is what?"

"A multi-agency federal task force charged with tracking and disrupting the flows of dirty money. The proceeds of organised crime, terrorist funding, money laundering. They've got people from the FBI, ICE, the DEA, the IRS, the ATF, the DOJ, and the secret service."

"Sounds like a battle of the acronyms."

"Undoubtedly. And knowing Childs, it's a battle he's determined to win. Cooperation isn't in his vocabulary, and he doesn't understand the meaning of teamwork.

His MO is to say all the right things then stab you in the back so he can take the glory."

"You sound as though you're speaking from experience."

"We both started out in the New York office. When we went up for the same promotion, he arrested one of my informants on some bullshit charge and blew my biggest case."

Black smiled inside, because if Alaric had skin in this game, he'd put more effort into assisting.

"And what was Task Force Atlantis's interest in that warehouse?"

"I don't know yet, but I've got people looking into it. Word on the street says the warehouse belonged to La Cosa Nostra, but the girls weren't part of their operation."

"Then why were they there?"

"If I had to guess? LCN had the space, and they rented it out to an associate. Or maybe the other way around. LCN hasn't got a big foothold in Florida, but with the recent crackdowns on organised crime in New York and Chicago, they've started expanding into new territories. Survival of the fittest. They cooperate with other outfits in return for favours, much like you do."

"Does La Cosa Nostra often traffic girls like my sister?" Rafael asked.

"Historically, the Mafia always respected women, but lately, it's become all about the money. I've got one source who might be able to help, but she's not answering her messages."

"Is she still alive?" Black asked.

"Probably. She's never been the most reliable, but when she *does* provide information, it's usually good."

"Are you still planning to work elsewhere tomorrow?"

"I have to. It's a recurring undercover role, and one I actually quite enjoy. But I'll call you if I hear anything."

Speaking of calls, Black's phone rang, and his spine stiffened reflexively when he looked at the screen.

Marisol da Silva.

"It's for you." He held the phone out to Rafael.

It was kind of nice, the way she called her grandson. Audrey Black had liked to check up on Black too, especially after he blew up the summerhouse when he was thirteen.

But Rafael didn't look so happy.

"I told you, I don't need Vicente's help here. He should have stayed to take care of you and Dores. What if there's a problem in Medellín?" A pause. "What do you mean? Wait. You're *where*?"

Emmy came back in and handed Black a mug of coffee. "Everything okay?"

"I'm not sure."

Rafael had lost a few shades of colour, which according to Emmy, he hadn't done even under interrogation.

"Don't go anywhere. I'll sort something out."

He hung up and cursed the phone.

"What's wrong?" Black asked.

"Grandma. She's worried about—and I quote—leaving something so important as the search for Cora and Isabella to someone outside our Valento family."

"But you told her you were handling it. Right?"

"This is Marisol da Silva we're talking about. She's just landed in Fort Lauderdale with Vicente, Dores, and my fucking dog. Oh, and she wants to vet you."

Silence fell, broken only by the sound of Emmy's laughter.

"And I thought my family was dysfunctional."

"Diamond, shut up."

A door slammed, and Bradley jingled into the room. Yes, he'd tied bells onto his damn shoelaces.

"Hey, what did I miss?" He jerked his head towards Black. "Why does he look as if someone shit in his ice cream?"

"We'll explain later," Emmy said. "Could you be an angel and arrange transport from the airport for a lady in a wheelchair, two other people, and a dog? Rafael'll go along for the ride."

"Of course I can, but who are they?"

"We'll discuss that later."

"But—"

Emmy pushed him out of the room.

"Okay, okay. I'm going."

Panic. That feeling was panic, something Black hadn't felt since the first time his commanding officer pushed him into a swimming pool with his hands and feet tied together during BUD/S training. But that had passed after a second, and this too would pass.

"Maybe we could put them up in a hotel?" he suggested. "I own one near Orlando."

"You really think she'd stay there?" Rafael asked.

Good point.

"How about a house near Blackwood's Miami office? If we pretended they were running the investigation, we could carry on working from here."

"She'd see straight through that. I can lie to anyone except Grandma. She always knows when I'm not telling the truth."

"Guys, just bring her here," Emmy said. "Yes, this has all gone a bit pear-shaped, but she'll be more upset if you try to keep her in the dark." Emmy leaned forward to check the marks on Rafael's neck. "And if you could not tell her I made those bruises, I'd be very grateful. I don't want to die."

Black took a deep breath. Decision made.

"Yes, bring her here." He'd only ever have one first meeting with his mother, and he'd hoped it would be under better circumstances, but Emmy was right. They couldn't try to hide what was going on. "Let's get it over with."

The wait for Rafael and Marisol to arrive from the airport was the longest hour of Black's life, and considering some of the torture sessions he'd endured as part of his "education," that was saying something.

"You okay, buddy?" Nate asked.

"No."

Finally, the front door opened, and he heard voices.

"You said we were going to meet the investigator. This is just a house. What kind of outfit is this man running?"

Three figures appeared in the doorway. A wiry man with a salt-and-pepper goatee, a dark-haired woman who looked to be in her fifties, although Black knew Dores was no older than him, and Marisol da Silva. Even grey-haired and sitting in a wheelchair, she had a commanding presence. Her gaze locked straight onto his.

"Are you the man looking for Corazon?"

"Yes."

She didn't take her eyes off him and wheeled herself closer, closer, until she was two feet away. Now she didn't look quite so confident, and she glanced back at her grandson before closing her eyes for a second. When she opened them again, the hardness was back.

"My apologies. For a moment, you reminded me of somebody I lost."

Now Rafael stepped forward.

"Grandma, he *is* somebody you lost."

"What are you talking about? Ramiro died."

Ramiro. The other, older brother Black never got to meet.

"Not Ramiro. I don't even know where to start with this story. Neither of us does. We hadn't planned on telling you until we found Cora, but now you're here and—"

"Just spit it out."

"He's one of the twins. I don't know which."

Marisol looked back at Black, and if he'd thought her stare was intense before, now he wanted to wither like a seedling in the desert.

"How did…" Her words trailed off, and a tear rolled down her cheek.

Black did the only thing he could. He knelt before her and opened his arms, and then she was crying, he was crying, everyone in the whole fucking place was crying.

Only Emmy managed to speak.

"Reckon this breaks the record for the most assassins in one room?"

CHAPTER 26 - CORA

IF YESTERDAY WAS an unexpectedly good day, then today more than made up for it, like some weird form of karma.

Leandro had been kind last night, pleasant, even, but when I got downstairs for breakfast, he'd totally blanked me. Chad tracked my every move, though, with nasty little piggy eyes that matched his nasty little heart, and when he walked me to the bathroom, he rested his hand on my ass as if he owned me. I pushed it away, but it came right back, and this time he clamped his fingers onto one cheek.

"Didn't your mama ever teach you that it's rude to take without being asked?"

"Didn't anyone ever teach you that your job is to serve us, not to make stupid comments?"

"Serve *you*? No, *querido*, you're just a glorified babysitter."

That earned me a slap, but it was worth it. The irony was, I didn't even need to use the bathroom. Rather, I wanted to take every chance I got to look around the house, to memorise the layout and search for possible ways to escape. Finding out where Izzy went before I left would be a bonus, but now I knew for sure that she'd been here, I hoped my brother would be able to extract that information from Radcliffe if I could only let him know where I was.

But Radcliffe was careful. The windows were double-glazed and locked shut, and all the doors except for the guards' rooms locked with electronic pass cards. Even if I managed to get hold of one, someone could shut down my access remotely within seconds. The apes each carried some sort of weapon, fastened securely onto a belt or into a shoulder holster. Either a pistol, a Taser, or a stun gun. The walls around the garden were ten feet tall and topped with spikes, and Hallie said there were guards in a hut at the end of the driveway to monitor who came and went.

My brother could have found a way out, but not me. Not yet.

And so I had no choice but to do my business in the bathroom, then walk back to the lounge with Chad rubbing his grubby hands all over me.

Then things got worse. I got picked first in the evening, and I knew from the look on Hallie's face that the client was bad news. A big man in his thirties but already balding, he dragged me upstairs, tied me to a leather bench, and did unmentionable things while smacking me with what looked like a spatula. And when I cried out in pain, he just wound my hair around his fist and snapped my head back.

"Cry harder, little girl. I like that."

I refused to give him the satisfaction, and by the time he'd finished with me, my bottom lip was split from where I'd bitten it shut, and that wasn't the only part of me that was bleeding. *Mierda*. I could barely even walk.

And the evil bastard simply strolled out, grinning.

When Leandro heard me crying and rushed in, I

tried to cover myself up with my hands, but I don't suppose they hid much. He looked away then tugged the sheet off the bed, cursing under his breath.

"What the hell did he do to you?" he asked as he wrapped it around me.

"You don't want to know. But there's not a part of me that doesn't hurt."

"Shit. I didn't realise it was that bad here."

"We're kidnapped and sold into the sex trade. What the hell did you think was happening to us when you were working at that warehouse?"

"Well, I knew it wasn't good, but this..." He shook his head, biting his bottom lip much the way I had. "When I was here before, I never came upstairs."

"Just let me go back to my room, will you?"

Rather than helping me to my feet, he scooped me up in his arms and headed for the door. I was too tired to argue. All I wanted to do was take a shower in a vain attempt to wash the filth off myself, then crawl into bed.

"Tell Chad that if he stops by tonight, I'll bite his damn dick off," I said after Leandro had deposited me on my bed.

"I'll make sure he stays away. Did you eat?"

"Yeah, I chewed on a ball gag for a while."

"I'm sorry," he mumbled as he backed out of the room.

So was I.

Sorry for myself, sorry because my family must be going through hell, and sorry because I hadn't found Izzy. Had she gone through that experience too? Because it would have broken her.

The door beeped again as I was about to step into

the shower, and I froze.

"It's me," Leandro said from the bedroom. "I brought you some food and a packet of painkillers."

He was still sitting on the stool when I emerged clean on the outside, grimy on the inside, and wrapped in my silk bathrobe.

"You don't have to stay here. I'll survive."

"I promised I'd make sure Chad stayed clear. He was hanging around in the hallway when I brought your dinner."

Suddenly, I was grateful rather than annoyed.

"Thank you."

"Do you want anything else? A hot drink? Wine?"

"What I really want is to go home."

Now he shifted uncomfortably. "Can't help with that."

"Why are you here? The others, I get, but you don't seem like a bad guy."

He shrugged. "It's a job."

No, it was more than that, but I didn't want to push Leandro. Not now. He seemed to exhibit an odd protectiveness over me, and if there was one guard I might be able to exploit, it would be him, the weakest member of the pack. How could I turn that vulnerability to my advantage?

Tomorrow. I'd work that out tomorrow. Tonight, I just wanted to eat the snacks he'd brought me, then go to sleep.

My ass throbbed as I lay there in the darkness, listening to Leandro's steady breathing, but eventually, I drifted off. And I had a weird dream that in the early hours, Leandro brushed the hair out of my face, then softly kissed my forehead before he retreated back to his basement lair. Strange. And when I woke in the morning, he'd vanished, taking any evidence of his nocturnal visit with him.

Chapter 27 - Black

"DAMMIT."

BLACK COULDN'T help laughing as Emmy cursed. Yes, laughing. Despite the circumstances, he felt oddly happy.

He'd worried that meeting his mother would be an awkward affair, but after he got over the initial nerves, talking to her became as natural as breathing. They'd stayed up into the early hours with Emmy, Rafael, and Vicente, putting together the jigsaw puzzle of his childhood. And he had a name now.

Before he died, his twin brother had written him a letter with a few snippets of information. When Marisol read the scanned copy Black accessed on his phone, she'd welled up exactly as he did when he first received it.

"He said he was the one who smiled as a baby, which makes him Emilio."

"So I'm Mathias?"

"Yes. You liked to scowl a lot."

"No change there," Emmy said. "But thank goodness he's Mathias because one Emmy in the family is quite enough. Emerson and Emilio? Awkward."

Mathias da Silva. Yes, he preferred Mathias to Charles. It was a shame he'd never be able to use the name—people would ask too many questions that he didn't want to answer. And after a short discussion, they decided Marisol would remain as Marisol and not Mom. She said she was just thrilled to hear him call her anything after all these years.

When she got tired, he'd helped her upstairs—thankfully, his architect had included an elevator as part of the renovations—and lifted her into the king-sized bed in the master suite. Bradley had brought in an extra double for Dores, and Black and Emmy moved to a smaller bedroom on the other side of the house. Emmy didn't care where she slept, and he wanted Marisol to have the best.

Marisol reminded him a little of Emmy, in fact. She had the same steel core and the same irreverent attitude. Double the sneakiness and double the snark might drive him to distraction, but he wouldn't want it any other way.

Right now, Emmy was kneeling on the floor, pieces of duct tape clenched between her teeth, trying to stick a bunch of electrical cables to the tile so nobody would trip over them. But the tape wasn't behaving, hence her frustration.

"Diamond, did you just swallow a piece?"

"I think..." Cough. "So."

Fortunately, Marisol was on hand to help out.

"Here, try this." She lifted the arm of her wheelchair and pulled out a rather impressive ceramic knife. "It'll cut anything."

Good grief.

"Did you bring that on the plane?" he asked.

"Of course. Being an old lady in a wheelchair does have some advantages. I just smiled sweetly and they carried me on board."

"Chuck, I love your mom."

See? Double the trouble.

And because Black didn't have enough problems in his life today, Bradley bounced in with a sparkly pen and a clipboard covered in unicorn stickers.

"Okay. I've purchased clothing and toiletries for Rafael, Vicente, Dores, and Marisol."

"I already have plenty to wear," Marisol said, but he ignored her.

"Groceries are arriving in thirty minutes, and the restaurant down the road is delivering a sushi platter for lunch. Squeaky toys and dog food will be here at three, but the doggy bed won't arrive until tomorrow because the memory foam mattress was a special order. Anything else?" He took a step towards Marisol, then backed off when he saw the knife in her hand. "What about your hair? Your bangs are getting untidy."

"We're busy looking for my granddaughter right now."

"It won't take long, just—"

Black planted himself in front of Bradley. "I have a new task for you. By the time we're finished here, Riverley Hall has to be wheelchair accessible. Ask Marisol what she needs and fix it."

Bradley saluted. "Wheelchair accessible. Got it. We'll need to adapt a bedroom, and install handrails, and lower the bathroom fittings, and..."

He was still talking to himself as he wandered out of the room, but hopefully that little project would keep him busy for a few days. Black wanted everything to be perfect when his mom visited Virginia, and he'd have to go to Colombia too, which meant he needed a house in Medellín. He pulled out his phone and fired off a message to his property manager.

Black: Need to buy a place in Medellín. Wheelchair friendly.

Hmm. Where did Marisol even live? She'd mentioned an apartment, which sounded small, and like he said, he wanted her to have the best. Perhaps he could buy her somewhere bigger?

"How would you like a new house in Medellín?"

She rolled her eyes. "Mathias, work. Focus."

Fuck, he was losing his mind.

"Right. Of course."

Now it was Emmy's turn to laugh. "Yeah, dude. Focus."

By the time dusk fell, Black had talked with the team investigating the warehouse fire and learned that three men had been charged with possession of drugs with intent to supply—it was hard for them to mount a defence when their prints were found on twelve kilos of waterlogged coke—but they'd denied having any knowledge of why the girls were in the warehouse. The burns victim in the hospital was in an induced coma, but Black wasn't sure she'd be much help even if she did wake up. He wanted to know where the girls went after their stay at the warehouse, not where they came from.

And since he'd pretended from the beginning that Blackwood's interest was in Rafael and not the warehouse operation, it was difficult to dig deeper without arousing suspicion.

"One of our guys received a death threat," the police

captain told Black as they parted company. "Probably from the Mafia. So if this man you're after is La Cosa Nostra, watch your back."

Message understood.

Nate split his hacking efforts between the police and the Mafia, but so far, he hadn't found anything useful. The Florida operation was an offshoot of one of the New York families, but they seemed quite insular in their activity. Cruz and his Floridian colleagues hit the streets, and while the word was that nobody liked the newcomers much, nobody *knew* much either. Most of the members of the gang whose territory they'd taken over were in prison. Meanwhile, back in Richmond, Mack was trying to find out more information on Task Force Atlantis, but so far, she hadn't had any luck.

And sometimes luck was what they needed. A big break.

Cases like this were often slow to progress, but this time, Black's family was involved. Every hour, the cold anger building inside him ratcheted up a notch.

"You're tense," Emmy said at the end of the day. "Not just determined like you usually are. This is different."

"Everything's changed."

"But it's a good change. Last year, I saw how dejected you were after Valento, even if you tried to hide it. At least you have answers now."

"Corazon is still missing."

She stood on tiptoes to kiss him on the cheek. "We'll find her. And those fuckers who took her aren't gonna know what's hit them."

CHAPTER 28 - CORA

THE ONLY GOOD thing about being beaten black and blue was that when Radcliffe walked into the breakfast room and saw me—and I'd deliberately worn skimpy clothes so he couldn't miss the mess—his mouth went all thin and he stormed out, muttering something about last chances and revocation of membership. According to Hallie, the psycho asshole had done the same to at least two other girls, but when Radcliffe last tried to show him the door, he got overruled by someone higher up. Paloma had overheard that conversation.

Twenty minutes later, Radcliffe returned and peered at me as if I were a biological specimen floating in a jar.

"We can't let clients see you like that. You'll have to stay upstairs in the evenings until the bruises fade."

Oh, hallelujah! I thought I was onto a winner, at least until Chad slithered over to me like the slug he was.

"Radcliffe said clients couldn't see you, not staff."

"He meant everybody, you sick freak."

"I see your mouth still works. Good. I have a use for it later."

Mierda. Where was Leandro? I really needed him to get me out of this tight spot, but I hadn't seen him since this morning. And what should I say? How could I keep asking him to babysit me when it cost him his sleep? I had nothing to offer him. Nothing except myself, and I refused to go there. Leandro may have been kinder than the other apes, but he still willingly chose to work for a monster who imprisoned women and made them go through hell.

I wanted to use him, but I didn't want to be used myself.

Late morning, I saw him outside in the garden, lying on one of the sun loungers as he read a magazine. Did he have a day off? It sure looked that way, because a while later, he stood and dove into the pool, stroking lazily up and down while the sun shone overhead. Not a care in the world. It was enough to leave me nauseous.

But when it came to Leandro or Chad, there was no contest, and when Leandro walked past the window, I risked beckoning him. I wasn't sure whether he understood or not, but after lunch, my door lock bleeped. For a moment I stiffened, worried it might be Chad, but Leandro quickly slipped inside.

"Is something wrong?"

"Quite apart from the obvious? Yes." I sighed. "Chad. It seems he finds the bruises a turn-on."

"Shit."

"And I hate to ask, but can I come and sit in your room tonight? You could just sleep. I promise I wouldn't make a noise."

"You can't sit on the chair all night."

"Even for a couple of hours? Except then you'd have to get up to bring me back here, and... Forget it." I turned my back on him. "I shouldn't have asked."

"No, you should. Chad's an asshole, but I heard a

rumour he's related to Radcliffe. A nephew or something. So he gets a free pass on shit the rest of us would get fired over."

"What if you came up here?"

"And then when he comes looking for you, he'll walk right in and wonder why the hell I'm sleeping on the floor."

"I meant for you to have the bed. I can sleep on the floor."

"My point still stands."

Yes. Of course it did.

"I'll sort something out." Leandro pinched the bridge of his nose. "I'm working tonight, but so is Chad. I'll come and get you right after I finish."

"Thank you."

His turn to sigh. "Just be ready, okay?"

True to his word, Leandro arrived late in the evening, and I'd worn yoga pants, the loosest T-shirt I could find, and a pair of sport socks so I was ready to go.

"Quick. Chad went to take a leak."

I almost giggled as we ran down the stairs, and if not for the seriousness of the predicament I was in, I would have burst out laughing. Chad would undoubtedly be annoyed, and I feared his anger would only build each time we outfoxed him.

But this evening, we made it to Leandro's room without seeing a soul, and in the dark, I almost tripped over as soon as I got through the door.

"What the...?"

He flipped the light on, and I looked at the pile of

blankets I'd almost landed in.

Leandro gave me a lopsided smile.

"I told the housekeeper I was cold, and now she thinks I'm crazy."

"In this place, crazy is normal."

"You're not wrong there. Here, hold these."

He passed me the blankets, then stripped the quilt off the bed to form a makeshift mattress on the floor and tossed a pillow down at one end of it.

"You get the bed. Try not to snore."

Now I felt guilty, which was stupid considering I was a freaking prisoner. "I'll sleep on the floor."

"Catalina, you're having the bed. What sort of gentleman would I be if..." He caught himself. "Forget it. I'm obviously not a gentleman."

"Sometimes you're gentlemanly."

"It's late. Just go to sleep."

"What time is it?"

Knowing the time made me strangely happy now.

"Almost one o'clock, and you get up for breakfast at eight. My watch alarm's set for half past seven."

Leandro powered off his phone completely before he went to sleep and tucked it under the pillow right next to his hand. Not that it mattered. When I'd glimpsed the screen earlier, it didn't even have a signal down in the basement. No, I wouldn't be getting outside help tonight. But at least I wouldn't be getting Chad either, and I had to be grateful for that.

Screaming woke me. Not my own, although I felt like doing so most of the time. No, this was female, panicked, and getting closer.

"Leandro!"

I leaned over and nudged him awake. Seemed he slept like the dead, concrete floor or no concrete floor.

"What?"

"Listen."

Two seconds later, he sat bolt upright.

"What the hell...?" He hadn't changed out of his clothes last night, and now he pushed the blanket away. "Stay here."

"As if I have a choice."

He'd slipped out the door before I finished the sentence. The lock tumbled. Great. If the house burned to the ground or there was an axe murderer on the loose, I was a sitting duck. Unless... Could it be my brother? My heart skipped, then began racing. Had Rafe somehow tracked me to the pink palace? I pressed my ear to the door, listening for clues—gunfire, fists on flesh, the cries of dying men—but all I heard was the occasional sound of running feet.

My nerves were stretched to breaking point by the time Leandro returned.

"What? What happened? Are you okay?"

"Yeah." He slumped onto the bed, head down. "Shit. It was Kelsie. The housekeeper found her hanging from the shower rail."

"*Joder.*" The queasiness had subsided over the past few days, replaced with a heavy sense of resignation, but now it came back full force. "She killed herself? She always seemed troubled, but..."

Had she given up? Lost all hope? Kelsie had rarely spoken, but Hallie said she'd been there for seven or eight months. Why take her own life now?

Leandro's mouth set in a hard line. "So they say."

"But you don't think she did?"

"There was a lot of bruising around her neck. Some of the marks looked like fingers."

Oh, fuck. I recalled Hallie's comments about Chad's predilections. And I'd escaped him last night by hiding with Leandro, which left Kelsie to suffer what should have come to me.

"It was my fault," I whispered.

"How do you work that out?"

I explained, and Leandro's hands balled into fists.

"That sick little freak."

"If I hadn't come with you last night, Kelsie would still be alive." And I might be dead.

"You don't know that."

"What if I angered him by hiding?"

"He was choking women before you came along."

"But he never killed any of them."

The tears came again, but Leandro pulled my hands away from my face and gripped them tightly.

"Stop blaming yourself. Even my colleagues can see Chad's not right in the head, and..." He trailed off and shook his head.

"What? Tell me."

"I didn't want to worry you, but yesterday evening, I overheard one of the other guards telling Radcliffe that Chad seemed to be paying you a little too much attention. I've seen his type before—they always want what they can't have."

"And he'll keep going until he gets me."

"He won't get you."

"Why? What will you do? Hide me in here every night?"

"If it comes to that."

"Won't Radcliffe think that's weird?"

"Maybe. But firstly, he spends half of his nights with Paloma, and secondly, I think he realises Chad's a problem, but he doesn't want to confront him. Radcliffe's a coward at heart. I see it in his eyes."

"But—"

"And he probably doesn't want to admit there's an issue to the big boss either." Leandro suddenly seemed to realise he was still holding my hands and let them go. "I'll keep an eye on Chad, and I'll come and find you again tonight, okay?"

"Thank you." What else could I say? "What'll happen to Kelsie? To her body, I mean."

"Someone mentioned a spade."

Oh, *mierda*. I ran into the bathroom and vomited, although what came up was mostly bile. Leandro held my hair back while I heaved, an odd gesture from a man whose job it was to make my life hell.

"Hey, it'll—"

"Shut up. Don't you dare tell me it'll be all right. How can it be? What are you gonna do, smuggle me out?"

"I can't."

"Exactly."

His voice dropped so low it was barely audible. "Honestly? I don't want to be here either."

"Then why don't you just leave? They let you go in and out, right?"

"It's complicated."

"No, Leandro. A PhD in mathematics is complicated. Unravelling the human genome—that's complicated. Working here is vile."

He looked away, and at least he didn't try to justify himself, because I'd probably have slapped him.

"Time to go back to your room now, Catalina. I'll come for you later."

CHAPTER 29 - CORA

WHILE MY BRUISES healed, I settled into an odd routine with Leandro. Mornings in the lounge with the other girls, now one short. We'd discussed whether another victim would arrive to take Kelsie's place, but with the halfway house—the warehouse—unavailable, she'd have to come straight to the pink palace. According to Paloma, who got more inside information than the rest of us by virtue of her "relationship" with Radcliffe, Radcliffe's boss hated that. He was paranoid, not only about security but about health too, and while we were sitting in our little wooden prisons, we got screened for infectious diseases as well as temperament. Then he decided where we'd be sent—here, one of his other properties, or offloaded onto somebody else.

To the big boss, women were meat, and the girls here at the house of horrors were tenderloin.

After lunch, I'd go back to my room and read. What I wanted was Houdini's memoir, but Leandro had brought me a handful of paperbacks, thrillers mainly. They were tame compared to real life. Perhaps I should write my story if I ever escaped? On second thoughts, nobody would believe it.

In the evenings, Leandro came to fetch me, and we snuck downstairs to his room. At least, I thought we did.

"What do you think Radcliffe would say if he knew I was coming down here every night?"

"He already knows."

"What? How?"

"Cameras. They're well hidden, but they're everywhere."

My heart stuttered, and I froze. "Even in our rooms?"

"Not in the guards' rooms or the client rooms, but there's one in yours. In the light fixture."

"Why the hell didn't you tell me earlier?"

"What difference would it have made?"

"Well, I... I..." What difference *would* it have made? I suppose I could have got dressed in the bathroom, but most of the guards had already seen me naked when they retrieved me from the client rooms anyway. If I'd known the camera was there, I'd have felt even more uncomfortable, but... "I just like to see the full picture, that's all. Is that another reason you brought me down here instead of staying in my room?"

"Yes."

"Who watches the cameras? The guards?"

"No. I think only Radcliffe has access, but it wouldn't surprise me if they also stream off-site so the big boss can monitor things."

"Who's the big boss?"

"Nobody ever mentions his name."

"Every moment I'm here, I hate it more. I'm now at a level of hate I didn't even realise was possible. Did you see the way Chad's eyes kept following me around the room today?"

Like one of those creepy, old-fashioned paintings.

He'd stood on one side of the lounge and just *watched*.

"Yeah, I saw. I'm trying to come up with a solution."

"Maybe you could bury him next to Kelsie?"

"Tempting."

We also spoke about lighter subjects too, although rarely about ourselves. Neither of us wanted to rehash our pasts, and the most I gleaned was that Leandro grew up in Boston with his parents, his sister, and a dog named Bambi. His sister's choice, apparently, and she'd sulked for weeks because her parents wouldn't buy a pet deer instead.

That week, mostly spent bored in my room or hiding out with Leandro, was bearable. Like a lousy vacation with that one creep who always stared at you by the pool.

But on Friday, Radcliffe checked me over from head to toe and pronounced the bruises had faded enough for me to work again. I'd been bobbing around on the surface until then, but with his words, I sank back into the depths.

My greying client was another suit, a hedge fund manager, or so Hallie whispered before he took me upstairs.

"He's okay," she said. "Sometimes he takes a while, but that's because he also takes Viagra. The packet fell out of his pocket once when he dropped his jacket on the floor."

"At least it wasn't heart medication."

"No, that's Radcliffe. We live in hope."

Hope? I'd all but given up hope by the time the old guy finished pounding into me, rolled off, and headed into the bathroom. Great. Now I had to listen to him pee. Still, Hallie was right—it could have been worse. I found myself glancing over at the pile of clothes on the floor to see if I could spot a stray packet of pills, but my heart suddenly lurched when I realised what else had spilled out of the guy's jacket. His phone. His freaking phone!

How long did I have? A minute at least. He'd have to wash his hands, unless of course he was totally unhygienic, in which case, I'd surely get caught. Quick as a flash, I padded across the room on bare feet and snatched up the phone. I could still make an emergency call, even if it was locked, right?

But it wasn't locked. The man had a basic phone with buttons rather than a smartphone, and it was wide open. Seemed he could handle money, but technology gave him a problem.

My fingers shook as I typed out a message. I wasn't about to make Izzy's mistake and try a phone call. What if nobody answered? And even if they did, my "date" would probably hear me through the door.

Trapped. Florida I think. Pink mansion near ocean. High wall, metal gates, fountain in middle of drive.

The toilet flushed, and I almost dropped the phone. *Send, send, send.* Then *delete, delete, delete.*

Water ran, and I'd just tucked the phone back into Mr. Viagra's pocket and leapt back onto the bed when the bathroom door opened.

"Why are you still here?"

"I thought..."

"You can leave now."

With pleasure. I tugged my dress on and practically ran for the door, praying my plan had worked. I'd sent my text to Grandma since she seemed to be in this up to the hilt and I had no idea what had happened to my brother after the warehouse incident. If he'd been caught or worse, I had to believe she'd find a solution to my predicament. An anonymous tip to the police, maybe?

"Oh, *mierda*."

The small glimmer of hope I'd felt died in my chest when I found Chad waiting for me in the hallway. Where was Leandro? He'd promised to be there.

Chad smiled, not the hesitant, lopsided quirk I often got from Leandro, but a malicious grin.

"Finally, we get some time alone."

"Get the hell away from me."

His fingernails dug into my arm as he gripped me tight. "No, bitch. That's not how things work around here."

He may have been three inches shorter than me, but he was a whole lot stronger, and although I tried to resist, he propelled me forward towards the basement stairs. I screamed, but he cut the sound off with his other hand.

"Shut the fuck up."

"You can't do this."

"After hours, you belong to me."

"I don't belong to anyone!"

I tripped over my feet, and only Chad's hold kept me from pitching head first into the wall.

"Yeah, you do. The second you stepped onto the boat in your shitty fleapit of a country, you kissed your freedom goodbye."

When we reached the stairs, I tried to grip onto the bannister, but Chad put his full weight behind me. With little other option, I let go, and we both tumbled to the bottom.

"*Oof.*"

Chad was winded, but unfortunately, his stocky little neck didn't break. I barely got time to check myself for damage—twisted ankle, more bruises—before I scrambled away, but I didn't get very far before Chad grabbed my wrist.

"Let go!"

His grip only got stronger, but then footsteps thundered past me on the stairs and Chad went flying, blood streaming from his nose.

"Fuck." Leandro crouched beside me in an instant. "Are you okay?"

"Do I look like I'm okay?"

"Did you hit your head?"

"I don't think so."

Chad struggled to his knees, and I thought he might take a swing at one or both of us, but then he looked beyond us and deflated.

"That's enough," Radcliffe said.

Two of the other guards stood behind him, and neither made any move to help Chad.

"You..." He pointed at Leandro. "Get Catalina cleaned up. Chad, get into my office. Now."

Leandro scooped me up and carried me to his room. Only once I was lying on his bed did I realise how much I was shaking.

"Where does it hurt?" he asked.

"My ankle. My ass. Everywhere."

"I'll get you some ice once the heat's died down upstairs." He rummaged in his closet and passed me a T-shirt and a pair of gym shorts. "Put these on. You won't be comfortable sleeping in that dress."

"Can I stay here again tonight?"

"You're not going anywhere near Chad."

Thank goodness.

Leandro was right about the dress. It was a strapless number with a pencil skirt and a top so tight I could hardly breathe. I'd rather have slept naked, but I was glad I didn't have to. I paused before I slipped into the bathroom.

"Thank you."

"Chad had it coming. I might have enjoyed hitting him a little too much."

"Did you hurt yourself?"

Leandro flexed his fingers, and sure enough, his hand was swollen.

"It was worth it. Now go change, and when you come out, I've got some good news."

"Good news?" Of course, that was likely to be relative. The only truly good news would be that I was allowed to go home. "Can't you tell me now?"

Whatever it was, his wonky grin made me feel a smidgen lighter inside.

"In a minute. Change."

I gave him a mock salute. "Yes, sir."

CHAPTER 30 - BLACK

PURE DUMB LUCK, that's what the breaks sometimes came down to.

After a week of sifting through intelligence, hunting for informants, and chasing fruitless leads, Corazon da Silva was still missing and Black had developed a headache. Emmy passed him a bottle of Advil along with his coffee. Yes, it was nine in the evening, but he didn't intend to sleep anytime soon.

"I'm gonna head out with Fia," she said. "According to Cruz, one of our friendly neighbourhood drug dealers is back in town, and he sells information as well as coke."

"Forget the coke," Nate said from the other side of the room. "I've just got into one of Task Force Atlantis's files. Fuck, the security on those is tighter than a duck's ass."

What a great visual.

"And what's in it?"

"A briefing document. They're after information on some asshole called The Banker."

"Really? That surprises me," Alaric said.

He'd arrived at the Florida house from Las Vegas two days ago with a smile on his face and a hickey on his neck, apparently because Emmy had asked him to come, then he proceeded to sleep on the couch for twenty-four hours. If Black hadn't needed the man's brain, he'd have tossed Alaric outside on the sidewalk.

"You know of him?"

"Offhand, I recall he laundered money for a disgraced investment guru, at least four dictators, terrorist organisations on three continents, and the Mafia."

"The Mafia? A possible connection to the warehouse?"

"I'm not sure how. He died six years ago. A call girl shot him in the face, set his house on fire, then crashed her car into a tree fleeing the scene." He grimaced. "It was quite the scandal at the Bureau because the two agents assigned to surveillance duty were bumping uglies in a hotel down the road instead of watching what they were supposed to. The Banker's house was blazing by the time anyone noticed, both of the agents' wives were very upset, and so was the deputy director."

Understandable.

"So why is there a current task force investigating him?"

"Logically, there are only two reasons—either there's something in his old business dealings they're interested in, or they suspect that somehow he's still alive."

"Can you look into it?"

"I'll put some feelers out."

Apart from the mob associates the police still had in custody, the men from the warehouse had disappeared without a trace. Camera footage from a restaurant along the road showed a black SUV speeding off with five occupants, one of whom could have been Cora, but the tag on that was registered to a red minivan from

Orlando. The owner hadn't even noticed the licence plate was missing until Blackwood turned up at her door.

Rafael had been frustrated but calm as he trained with Emmy and Ana. Initial reports on his performance seemed promising—the only good news in an otherwise depressing week—and Black developed a new respect for Vicente. The old man had taught Black's nephew well.

Black worried about his mother, though, a new experience for him. Every time he asked, she said she was fine, but she looked so frail. At least Dores was there to keep an eye on her. He glanced in Marisol's direction again. She insisted on sitting in the operations room at all times, even eating her meals in there, much like Black himself.

"Why don't you go upstairs and get some rest?" he asked for the tenth time. "I'll wake you if anything happens."

"I'd rather stay down here."

"Shall I lift you onto the couch?"

"I can do that myself."

Black hated to watch her struggle, but Marisol da Silva was a proud woman. She parked her chair next to the couch, but she'd only gotten halfway out of the seat when her phone bleeped.

"It's a message from Cora," she half shouted as soon as she'd glanced at the screen.

He reached her side in an instant. "What does it say?"

She held the phone up so Black could see for himself.

"*Trapped,*" he read out. "*Florida I think. Pink*

mansion near ocean. High wall, metal gates, fountain in middle of drive. Nate, we need to find out who this number belongs to and where the message originated."

"On it."

Half an hour later, they had their answer. Theodore Symonds was a fifty-nine-year-old investment manager from Tampa, but the message had been sent within a twenty-mile radius of Naples. Currently, the phone—and presumably its owner—was on its way north on I-75.

"Where do you want to start?" Nate asked. "The house or Symonds?"

"The house. Get everyone still awake in the Richmond office on Google Earth, and we'll come up with a list of possibilities. Cruz, we'll need anybody local here ASAP to assist with checking out locations."

"I'll round them up."

"Emmy, forget the drug dealer and get some sleep. I've got a feeling we'll see action in the morning, and we need to be fresh."

"I'll get Mack and Dan to run the initial search," Nate said. "That should buy us a couple of hours' rest."

Black crouched by Marisol. "That goes for you too. Let me help you upstairs."

"Wait," Rafael said, staring at Nate's disappearing back. "Where are you going? What about Cora?"

That was the beauty of Blackwood. Black, Nate, Emmy, and Nick, the four co-owners and directors, had spent years building up a strong team, and Black trusted them implicitly to share the load.

"Some of this work can be done remotely, and we've got plenty of people available for that. The most important thing we can do right now is rest so we're ready in the morning. Nobody wants to screw up due to tiredness if we need to mount a rescue operation."

"I've only ever worked with Vicente before."

"Better get used to being part of a team." Because now Black had met his family, he wanted to keep them close. He hadn't had the conversation with Marisol and Rafael yet, but if they'd agree, he wanted to buy them a house in Virginia so they could spend at least part of the year nearby, as well as him visiting Medellín. "Get some sleep."

"I doubt I'll be able to."

"The ability to recharge is every bit as important as being able to shoot straight. It's a skill. Lie down, focus on your breathing, and empty your head. Tomorrow might get difficult, and we need you at full strength."

CHAPTER 31 - CORA

"OKAY, WHAT'S THE good news?"

I emerged from the bathroom in Leandro's baggy T-shirt and shorts. Thankfully, the shorts had a drawstring, so I'd been able to tie them tight instead of waiting for them to fall down. He'd changed too, from the suit he wore when clients were around into sweatpants and a T-shirt advertising a brand of beer I'd never heard of. And he'd brought ice too.

"Lie down and put this on your ankle."

Reason told me I should hate Leandro. He was part of the establishment, the group of monsters who kept me a prisoner in this nightmare and who'd stolen Izzy too, but on a personal level, he'd been kind. Sweet, even. If we'd met under any other circumstances, I'd have fluffed my hair, tidied my make-up, and flirted like crazy in the hope that he might suggest a date. And even now, with circumstances what they were, I couldn't help liking him a tiny bit.

"The good news?" I asked again.

"The good news is you're leaving."

Leaving? What did he mean, leaving? A chill ran through me as Leandro perched on the edge of the bed and carried on.

"Chad's caused too many problems. While you were with that client earlier, Radcliffe called me into his office and wanted to know why you kept sleeping in my room. So I straight-up told him that Chad seemed fixated and I'd been trying to keep you out of his way so we didn't end up with another Kelsie on our hands. After her death, Radcliffe could hardly deny that Chad has issues, and if he loses two girls in a couple of months, the big boss will ask questions. Fuck knows how he explained away the dead body. The cameras must have shown Chad walking into the bathroom with her, then coming out alone."

"Where am I going?"

"To one of the other properties."

"But... But..."

I couldn't leave. Not now. Not when there was the possibility of rescue. And here, I sort of had an ally in Leandro and the other girls were nice too. In a new place, I'd be starting again from scratch with nothing.

On the other hand, what if Izzy was there?

"But what?"

"I'm not sure I want to leave."

"Catalina, this is a good thing. Chad's escalating, and if you're not here, he can't hurt you."

"I'll miss you," I whispered. The words slipped out unbidden.

Now Leandro smiled, not just his usual flicker, but an actual smile.

"I'm coming too. After the crew from the warehouse ended up here, this place has too many guards. The other house lost a guy."

"But I'd rather stay."

"If you stay here, Chad won't give up." Leandro reached across to brush a few stray hairs out of my face. "Sorry I was late this evening. When Radcliffe wanted to see me, I couldn't exactly say no."

"Was he angry?"

"More resigned. He didn't even argue when I pointed out Chad was a disaster waiting to happen, and then he suggested both of us move. My bet is that the big boss isn't happy with him right now. Girls cost money, and now that the supply route's been disrupted, it's not as easy to get more."

"Ouch. Do you have to put it so bluntly?"

"Sorry."

Leandro did look genuinely chastened, and I reminded myself not to feel bad for snapping because he was part of the freaking problem. No, instead I had to focus on the issue at hand.

"But what if the new place is even worse?"

"How can it possibly be worse than here?"

I ticked off the points on my fingers. "Sadistic clients, unfriendly girls, brutal guards, a guy worse than Radcliffe in charge."

"You really don't want to leave?"

Leandro sounded incredulous, and rightly so. Who in her right mind would want to stick around and wait for a psycho to attack her? The thought terrified me too, especially without Leandro here to protect me. What if Grandma didn't manage to arrange a rescue?

"Do you know if everyone escaped the fire at the warehouse?" I asked.

"Huh?"

"The fire? The raid? Did they find any bodies afterwards? Did anyone get put in prison?"

"What's that got to do with anything?"

"I'm just curious. Do you know?"

Leandro shook his head and sighed as if he didn't

understand women in general and me in particular, but he answered anyway.

"It wasn't only you girls being kept in the warehouse. I never understood the exact arrangements, but the big boss rented space from some people my uncle knew. That's how I ended up with the job. They needed a man to keep watch over the women, and he recommended me. I swear I didn't know you were all getting kidnapped at first."

"We were locked in cells and accompanied to the freaking bathroom."

"They said that was so you didn't wander off into other parts of the warehouse." He pinched the bridge of his nose, a habit it seemed. "They were storing drugs there."

Why didn't that surprise me? Drugs and human trafficking—the perfect combination.

"So the raid—it was for the drugs?"

"Yes."

"And did they arrest the drug people? Did anyone get hurt in the fire? I heard a girl screaming."

"From what I've heard, they found two people dead. Some guy carried the other girl out, and the cops arrested him, but then he took a woman hostage and escaped from the police precinct."

Was that Rafael? He'd gone to get the girl, but would he really take a hostage? My brother wasn't a monster; I had to believe that. But I also had to hope he was free because otherwise, I was screwed. Who else could Grandma send to help? Vicente? The idea of a sixty-something sicario taking on Radcliffe's guards made a bubble of hysterical laughter escape.

"What's so funny?"

"Nothing." Oops. "What happened to the guy? Did they catch him again?"

"He's still on the loose, and Radcliffe's twitchy in case the Mafia blame the raid on us."

"The Mafia?"

"That's who was running the drug operation."

"And your uncle? He knows them?"

Oh, hell. Was there anyone not involved in this mess? All we needed were a few gang members and a terrorist or two and we could complete our bad-guy bingo card. But Leandro's news also made it sound more likely than not that my brother was still out there, even if he was a felon, which meant he'd be looking for me as soon as Grandma got my message to him. I couldn't leave.

"My uncle has nothing to do with the current situation."

"Fine. Let's forget I was kidnapped and ignore the fact that the Mafia are seriously scary men—I've seen *The Godfather*—and discuss the problem at hand. Is there any way you can convince Radcliffe to let me stay? Won't he be short of girls here? I mean, he lost Kelsie too."

"I just told you the Mafia are sniffing around, and now you want to sit back and wait for them?"

"Well, I..."

"I thought you'd be happy."

"*Happy*?"

"Wrong word. Relieved."

And any normal girl in my situation would have been exactly that. Relieved. There simply was no rational explanation for why I'd want to stay in the pink palace and face the wrath of Chad and a possible Mafia invasion when I had the opportunity to go somewhere safer with Leandro. Other than the truth, of course. But did I trust Leandro enough to let him into my secret?

He'd tried to set me free once, and despite his job, he'd been kind. What was the worst that could happen? Leandro would go running to Radcliffe and I'd get killed. Okay, that was a pretty big downside. Or perhaps they'd just move me anyway? And the other girls because they'd have to assume my brother would call the cops like a regular person.

And what about Izzy? Well, we had a lead now. There had to be a connection between this place and wherever she went, and somehow, we'd find it.

Leandro was still staring expectantly, waiting for an explanation.

"My brother will come here to find me," I whispered. "If I move, I'll be imprisoned for longer."

"Your brother? How the hell would he know to look for you here?"

Uh-oh. Leandro didn't look at all happy.

"Because I messaged him. Tonight. The client left his phone lying around. Well, I messaged my grandma, and she'll tell my brother, and—"

"Keep your voice down—these walls are thin. Your *grandma*?"

"It's a long story."

"Fuck."

Leandro began pacing the tiny space, tugging at his dark hair. I'd never seen him stressed like that before. One of his shoes squeaked a little. *Squeak click, squeak click, squeak click.*

"Your brother's in Colombia?" he asked.

"No, he's in the USA. He was at the warehouse, but

we got separated when he went back in to save the girl."

"*He* was the guy who escaped from police custody?"

"Probably."

A string of curses flew from Leandro's lips, and he paused his steps, visibly trying to compose himself. His fists formed tight balls, and he leaned against the closet until his head met the wood with a hollow *thud*. This wasn't going well.

"You can still leave tomorrow," I told him in what I hoped was a reassuring tone. "In fact, it's better that you do because I doubt my brother's gonna be in a good mood when he gets here."

And while I didn't care one iota for the other men, I hated the thought of Leandro getting hurt.

"No, I can't. If they don't have an extra girl, they don't need an extra guard. Either both of us leave or neither of us do. And we're leaving, Catalina. I need to keep this job."

"Can't you get a new job instead? Something legitimate?"

"It's not that simple."

"Sure it is. You're smart, you're mostly nice, and even if you don't have qualifications, there are people who'd employ you. I understand the money might not be so good, but it's perfectly possible to live on a budget. We did it for years in Colombia, and—"

"You don't understand. I need *this* job."

"Why?"

Now Leandro pushed away from the closet and put one knee on the bed, leaning over to whisper harshly in my ear.

"Because I'm a fucking FBI agent working undercover, that's why."

CHAPTER 32 - CORA

LEANDRO SOUNDED ANGRY, but when he sat on the bed again, shoulders slumped, his posture spoke of defeat. Meanwhile, my brain was still trying to catch up.

"You're an FBI agent?"

"That message to your brother might just have blown our entire operation."

Joder. Leandro was undercover? Suddenly, a lot of his behaviour made sense. The way he never touched me or any of the other girls. The attempt to get rid of me at the warehouse. His general caginess about the past. But one great big thing made no sense at all.

"Wait. You work for a law enforcement agency, and you and your colleagues stand by and watch while women get raped and murdered?"

"That isn't my choice," he said through gritted teeth. "I'm as trapped in this nightmare as you are."

"Somehow I doubt that. You can just walk out."

"But I can't. Even if we arrest Radcliffe and everyone else in this place, there are others like it and we don't yet know where they are. If you and I go tomorrow, we can find one more."

"Why can't you simply arrest Radcliffe and interrogate him?"

"Because the last time we tried that, the guy killed

himself rather than talk to us. His computer was encrypted, and the moment we tried to get into it, we tripped a switch and all the data got permanently wiped." He sighed. "Like you said, it's a long story, and I wish I'd never taken this fucking job."

"I'm kind of glad you did."

"Watching you get abused every night is tearing me apart." His lopsided smile flickered back for a second. "In case you haven't noticed, I like you a little more than I should. I wanted to rip Chad's head off earlier, but that wouldn't have gone down too well with my boss. My real boss."

Leandro liked me? "I'm not sure what to say to that."

"You don't have to say anything. In here, I'm the asshole who stands by while bad shit happens to you, and if we met anywhere else, you'd be way out of my league anyway." Another sigh. "But here we are, and now we've got a big problem to solve."

Yes, we did. Fully processing Leandro's confession would have to wait.

"When I got into this, I thought I had my eyes open, but this is worse than I ever imagined it would be. Not just the men forcing themselves on me night after night, but having to live with myself afterwards."

"What do you mean, worse than you thought it would be?"

"I got kidnapped on purpose."

His gaze snapped to mine, incredulous.

"Yeah, yeah, I know it sounds crazy. But the same man who sold me also took my best friend first, and I followed so we could find her and get her back."

"'We'? You and your brother?"

"Yes. I wore a tracking bracelet, but then the plan fell apart at the warehouse and I lost it. So he's out there, trying to find me, and I want to go home, but I also want to find Izzy, and if I don't, then everything I've been through will have been utterly pointless."

"Izzy? Isabella?"

"Yes."

"She was at the warehouse."

"And she came here—Hallie told me—but I don't know where she went after that. How did she look when you saw her?"

"Fragile. Quiet. She wasn't holding up as well as you."

"Of course she was quiet. You put drugs in our water."

"Drugs? No, we didn't."

"Not in the bottles? They did on the boat. The first time I drank it, I almost passed out, so I started drinking from the tap in the bathroom, and in the warehouse, I drank from the toilet cistern."

"I'm sorry." He gripped my hand so tightly it was almost painful, but I squeezed back anyway because his stricken expression made my heart stutter. "I'm so, so sorry. At first, I tried to block out what was happening to the girls, but then you came along, and all the lies I'd told myself didn't work anymore. After Kelsie died, I spoke to the agent in charge and begged him to act because this job has gone beyond fucked-up, but he won't until we can bring down the guy at the top. If I walk out, everything I've done so far is wasted. And if my cover gets blown, then not only is my life at stake, but the guy who recommended me for the position's in grave danger too."

"Your uncle?"

"He's not really my uncle. He's undercover in the Mafia."

"So what you're saying is that we're screwed."

"In a nutshell? Yeah."

"Who's the man at the top?"

"Shit. This is supposed to be classified."

"Surely I've earned the right to know? And besides, who am I going to tell?"

Leandro shifted so he was lying alongside me, not touching anything apart from my hand, but close enough that he could lower his voice to almost a whisper.

"Nobody knows his real name, but we call him The Banker. Think of him as the Goldman Sachs of money laundering. The crème de la crème. He takes the proceeds of crime and cleans it, hides it, and invests it in return for a cut."

"How do we fit in? The girls?"

"A reward for his associates. Most of your clients have been bankers, investment managers, realtors— they all help with the process. And we think he dabbles himself as a sick sort of hobby."

"You mean he could have been here and we didn't even know?"

"Yeah. We've only got a couple of old photos of him, and we think he's changed a lot since then. Most likely plastic surgery. Truth is, everyone thought he was dead for years."

"How did you find out he was alive?"

"Pure dumb luck. A phone intercept on an unrelated case. The guy's a mathematical genius, he knows the world's financial markets inside out, and the money he moves around helps to finance crime and terrorism on every continent. A task force of thirty agents has been working on this around the clock for two years, and so far, I'm the only one who's managed to get inside. I'm sorry I got mad at you, but now do you see why I was so upset?"

"And I'm sorry I messed up your case, but I get raped five nights out of seven. Now do you see why I texted my grandma?"

A long, heavy silence fell in the tiny gap between us.

Yes, I understood now that there was a serious problem, but the so-called task force had let this abuse continue for two years. *Two years.*

After what seemed like forever, Leandro spoke.

"I'll speak to Radcliffe in the morning. See if there's any way you can stay. Maybe there'll be some way I can go to the other house later on."

"Why has it taken so long? Finding The Banker, I mean?"

"Honestly? Because the Special Agent in Charge is a self-centred prick. He doesn't trust anyone, probably because he's a backstabbing asshole himself, so he vetoes anything risky. And by risky, I mean anything that might jeopardise his promotion."

"Like what?"

"I've worked for Radcliffe for seven months now, mostly at the warehouse but sometimes here. First, I wanted to try and turn Hallie, because I bet she's learned a lot since she came, but Childs said no way."

"Childs?"

"The SAC."

"If you thought it would work, couldn't you have gone ahead and done it anyway?"

Leandro scrubbed his hands through his hair. "Six months ago, I thought I'd be a career agent, and I was scared of getting a disciplinary. Childs doesn't take too kindly to people going rogue."

"And now?"

"Now, I just want to find this fucker, then get a job delivering pizza. I hoped going to this new place would be a breakthrough. Radcliffe's got to have records on his computer, but he's paranoid about security and I haven't been able to get near it. The next head honcho might be different."

"What if we went to the new place? Would you take risks or play it safe?"

"You'll go?"

"Answer the question."

"I'd take calculated risks, but not stupid ones."

"I want Izzy back, I want all the other girls set free, and I want The Banker's cocktail wiener impaled on an ice pick."

"The last part might be tricky."

"I'll settle for a bamboo skewer."

"Remind me never to get on your bad side."

Could I really do it? Forego rescue for weeks and possibly months of hell at the mercy of an unknown overlord with only an FBI agent I barely knew to keep me safe? I felt sick at the prospect, but then I thought of Izzy and what might be happening to her and knew I had little choice.

"We'd have to send another message to my brother. Maybe he could help?"

"Yes, we need to send him a message, but he's on the run from the police after his stunt at the precinct. He tried to stab a consultant psychologist in the neck with a fountain pen. If he accidentally leads the cops to us, that could jeopardise everything like it did at the warehouse. Your brother needs to lie low until this is over, then get his ass back to Colombia somehow."

"Can't he just explain that he was only trying to help?"

"One of the guys they found dead in the warehouse? He didn't die in the fire. Someone cut his throat, and your brother had the murder weapon in his pocket."

"But he wouldn't..." I started before realising that he *would*. New Rafe, the man I'd met right before we began this crazy crusade, wasn't the brother I'd grown up with. New Rafe could kill a man, and New Grandma probably gave him the damn knife.

"If he's innocent, we can clear his name later," Leandro said gently. "But if we're going to do this, we can't afford complications."

"Okay, so I'll tell him to back off." *Mierda.* I was going to do this, wasn't I? "Leandro, I'm scared."

"Leander."

"Huh?"

"Leander. My real name's Leander, not Leandro. Leander Arden."

I held out a hand. "Corazon da Silva."

Rather than shaking my hand, he brought it to his lips in an oddly sweet gesture.

"Corazon... That's a pretty name." I got a shy smile too. "My friends call me Lee, but nobody in here does."

"Everyone calls me Cora." There was a beat of awkward silence, and I cleared my throat. "So, now that I know your secrets and you know mine, what happens next?"

"We need to get some sleep."

"Can we message my brother first?"

"There's no signal down here, and Radcliffe told me to stay in the basement with you. When I went to the kitchen to get your ice, he was roaming the hallways."

"What about in the morning?"

Even Rafe couldn't act instantaneously. Waiting for a few hours wouldn't change things.

"As soon as we get a clear moment." Leandro—Leander—cupped my cheek in one hand. "Get some rest, Cora. We'll need our strength tomorrow."

"I need to use the bathroom first. Do you have a spare toothbrush?"

"In my toiletry kit—help yourself."

I only took five minutes to clean up, but when I got back into the bedroom, Leandro had fallen asleep on the bed, his mouth slightly open and eyelids twitching as he dreamed. I didn't want to wake him. My first thought was to sleep on the floor myself, but after a moment's consideration, I crawled up the bed and lay next to him. Why? Because no matter how unhealthy it may have been, I kind of liked him too.

CHAPTER 33 - BLACK

"RED, READY?" BLACK asked over the radio, using Nate's code name.

The team wore casual clothes—sportswear and jeans—but now they pulled masks down over their faces.

"Ready."

"Valkyrie, ready?"

"*Pronto*," Emmy replied, speaking Italian because they planned to blame today's escapade on the Mafia.

While the initial investigation had progressed slowly then stalled, when Corazon sent her message, things moved fast. By two o'clock in the morning, they had a list of sixteen potential properties to check. Emmy had taken the target house, jogging past a little after daybreak with Rafael's dog in tow. At that point, they'd gotten their second lucky break—the black SUV spotted driving away from the warehouse was parked outside the double garage, complete with the Orlando plate.

They say disasters happen in threes, but it seemed Lady Luck had adopted that tradition too. Their third break came when Justicia paused outside the house opposite to take a shit, and Emmy's camera recorded a station wagon turning into the driveway. The feed came through in real time to their mobile command centre.

Although compact, the customised panel van was fitted out with surveillance equipment, seats, and enough weapons to start—and finish—a small war, and from the outside, badged up with the logo of a non-existent furniture delivery company. They'd parked half a mile down the road, and their driver, Cruz, was in the front, dressed in civvies and pretending to nap.

And Alaric, never a morning person, had miraculously dragged himself out of bed and joined the team in the back, as if there wasn't enough testosterone in there already.

He choked out a laugh as he watched the footage. "Fuck me, it's shift change."

"What the hell are you talking about?" Black asked.

Alaric pointed at the driver's head. "I recognise that guy. He's FBI. And it's five to six, which means they've got the six a.m. to two p.m. shift."

"Surveillance?"

"Well, he can't afford that mansion on the pittance the Bureau pays."

So the FBI was watching the house. Why? And, more importantly, did they know a kidnap victim was being held there?

Those were both questions that could be answered later. Right now, their priority was to get inside and get Cora out in case the gang decided to move her again. The message she'd sent was short, urgent, and undoubtedly written by someone under pressure. At least she'd kept a cool head. Da Silva genetics at work?

Emmy climbed back into the van ten minutes later, barely having broken a sweat. Rafael petted his dog for a moment, and then Justicia curled up under his seat as the team convened in the back. With space at a premium, Emmy sat on Black's lap. Alaric jokingly offered up his lap to Ana, and she gave him a glare that would have stopped a lesser man's heart.

"What's next?" he asked.

Since he knew the area better than anyone, they'd brought him along to assist with the logistics, but he'd stay in the van. Alaric could hold his own in a fight, but his specialty was destroying people with information, not bullets. Black checked his weapons again. Yes, all present and correct.

"Next, we send in Rosie."

"Rosie? You've got another girl that I haven't met yet?"

"Rosie's a remote-controlled cockroach," Emmy explained. "Nate flies her."

"A cockroach?"

"You'd be perfect for each other," Black muttered.

By eight o'clock, they'd peered in every window of the hideous pink mansion and done a recon of the visible security. A guard in a hut by the gate. Cameras on every corner, although there were gaps in the motion arcs if you knew where to look for them. The house had bars on some of the windows too, although they seemed to be in place to keep people in rather than out. The women. They'd spotted five in the third-floor bedrooms, although worryingly, none of them were Cora. The second-floor bedrooms, more ornate and without the bars, were all empty, and downstairs, guards appeared from a basement as the house gradually came to life. Seven of them, and one had a black eye and a split lip. The only other person in the house was an older woman who looked like a housekeeper or maid.

At a quarter past eight, a grey-haired man, in his mid-fifties at a guess, arrived in a top-of-the-range Mercedes and walked into the house carrying two bags —a gym kit and a laptop. The boss, judging by the way he ordered the guards around. He appeared particularly unimpressed with the black-eyed asshole.

"Where's Cora?" Rafael asked, voicing the question on everyone's mind.

"I don't know, but I guarantee somebody in that house does."

The setup screamed high-class brothel, and the bars on the windows said *none* of the girls were there voluntarily, not just Cora. Black feared some sort of altercation had taken place last night after Cora sent her message—the injured guard backed that up—and Cora had been hurt. They needed to find her, and they had no time to waste.

"I vote we go in today rather than waiting for dawn tomorrow."

Dawn was always a good time to break into places— people were still half-asleep, but there was enough light that you didn't trip over the furniture.

Emmy shrugged. "You know I always like a challenge. We'll come along the beach and over the back wall?"

"Yes. Three couples strolling along by the sea won't arouse much suspicion." And a ten-foot wall was nothing to Team Blackwood, even with spikes on top. "When we get to the house, Nate and Carmen will stick together, you can team up with Ana, and I'll go with Rafael."

Carmen had arrived yesterday, a flying visit on her way back from Mexico, and when the possibility of some action came up, she'd stuck around to help. Given the choice, Black would have preferred to pair up with his wife or Nate, his usual partners in crime, but Ana didn't play nicely with anyone except Emmy, and Black wanted to assess his nephew's performance. Or rather, stop him if he tried to do anything stupid. Ideally, he'd have left Rafael back at their beachside base, but Black recognised a lot of himself in the younger man, and no way would he have stayed put if *his* sister's life were at stake. A quiet chat with his mother had confirmed that suspicion. So, like it or not, Rafael was on the team.

Black crouched beside his nephew amongst neatly trimmed shrubbery behind the ugliest house ever built, and considering the gothic monstrosity Black had inherited from his US parents, that was saying something. Pink. The whole damn mansion was pink.

But they had their plan, and now they were ready to head inside. After running through the sequence of events in his head one last time, Black gave the command.

"Go."

All the doors were secured by electronic RFID locks. Usually in that scenario, they'd simply follow one or two of the occupants and get close enough to clone their pass cards, but with so little time, they'd been forced to use alternative tactics.

Nate and Carmen went first, waiting until the housekeeper came outside then immobilising her and slipping in through the open utility room door. As soon as they announced their success, Emmy and Ana swung themselves up onto a second-floor balcony and used a glass cutter to carve an assassin-sized hole in one of the bedroom windows. And Black? He'd drawn what should have been the short straw—the back door—but he didn't even bother trying to bypass the RFID lock. He'd brought one of Nate's toys, a miniaturised thermic lance, and that baby would cut through anything from steel to concrete. A PVC door? They were inside in twenty seconds.

Before they went in, Rosie had spotted the girls being led from the third-floor bedrooms down to a room at the back where food was set out on a table. Four of the guards stuck with them while the rest disappeared into the bowels of the house. Nate had reluctantly passed control of his toy cockroach over to Alaric to keep them updated on any other movements, and now their new sidekick spoke up.

"Black, one coming in your direction."

Black gestured to Rafael. *Be my guest.*

As the guard passed the alcove where they were hiding, Rafael glided out silently and fell into step behind him. One hand over the mouth, firm pressure on the carotid artery, and the guard crumpled to the floor seconds later. Nice work. The guy didn't know what hit him. Black jabbed him in the neck with a syringe full of Ketamine before he woke up—that would keep him quiet for ten minutes, and then they'd decide what to do with him.

"One guard down."

And Black quickly liberated his pass card.

"Two down," Emmy announced.

"Three," said Nate.

That left four guards, Mr. Two-Bags, and the girls.

So far, this had all gone smoothly. Worryingly smoothly. Call Black superstitious, but Mr. Murphy, of Murphy's Law fame, rode along on every job no matter how well it was planned, and he always put in an appearance sooner or later.

"I'm missing a guard and a girl from the breakfast room," Alaric said.

A woman screamed from the other end of the house. Yeah, that was more like it.

CHAPTER 34 - BLACK

"DAMMIT," NATE MUTTERED over the radio as the sounds of the woman's scream died away. "I'll handle this."

Half a minute passed.

"Four guards down. My ears are ringing, and the bitch with him tried to bite me."

Thundering footsteps echoed along the tiled hallway as the remaining three assholes ran out of the breakfast room to see what the problem was, and Black's grip on his Taser tightened. Why the non-lethal weapons? Two reasons. Firstly, this operation had been planned in a hurry, and they didn't know for sure who in the house was a bad guy. Or girl. Being ninety percent sure wasn't good enough, and Black didn't like collateral damage. Secondly, they needed the men around to talk to. If the results weren't pleasing, they could always shoot them later.

Black ducked into a room on one side of the hallway, and Rafael mirrored him opposite. Seconds later, two guards hurried past, and each got a Taser to the back for their trouble. Synchronised shooting.

"Two more down."

An angry roar from upstairs got everyone's attention, and Rafael took three steps in that direction before Black pulled him back and shook his head. Too eager. Emmy and Ana were perfectly capable of dealing with the problem, and the two men had their last target to find. Black pointed in the opposite direction, and Rafael paused for a second then followed.

"Dime, you and Red look after the women."

Dime was Carmen, named for her ability to hit a coin from fifteen hundred yards with her sniper rifle.

"On our way."

Ah, target acquired. Black and Rafael found the grey-haired man in the study, frantically typing commands into a laptop. But as Black aimed a gun in his direction—a proper one this time—he tapped one final key, looked up, and smiled.

A nervous smile, but there was no mistaking the sentiment. Why was the prick so pleased?

"Hands in the air."

The man's hands rose, shaking.

Black had spent many years practising his Italian accent, along with French, Arabic, German... The list went on. After the fourth or fifth language, learning new ones got progressively easier. In case the cameras dotted around the house were also wired for sound, posing as a Sicilian seemed sensible, and he'd brought a special gun along too—a .22 calibre pistol he'd liberated from a Mafia soldier a couple of years ago and hung onto just in case it came in useful someday. Well, today was that day.

"Turn off that laptop. Take the damn battery out," he told Rafael, then focused on the older man. "Tell me about the girls from the warehouse. Where are they? All of them, not just the few you have here."

"I-I-I don't know what you're talking about."

"*Non dire cazzate.*" Don't talk bullshit. "The car

outside left our warehouse with four of your soldiers and a girl in it right after they burned the place so they could escape. So, I'll ask again; where are the girls?"

"Why do you care?"

"Because you destroyed our business, and now you owe us."

"I'm j-j-just an employee."

"Then take us to your boss."

"H-h-he isn't here."

"Where do we find him?"

"I don't know. He only ever calls me."

"What's his number?"

Rafael pushed a paper and pen towards the man, but instead of reaching for it, he clutched at his chest. A strange gurgling sound bubbled from his throat, his mouth dropped open as his face twisted in pain, and he keeled sideways off the chair.

Black and Rafael looked at each other. Well, shit.

"A heart attack?" Rafael asked.

"I'm not sure."

Could the man be faking? Black passed his gun to his nephew and knelt beside the man's prone body, feeling for a pulse. Nothing, and he wasn't breathing either.

Fuck.

"We have a slight technical problem," he muttered into the radio.

"Tell me you didn't shoot the target by accident," Nate said.

"Didn't have to. I just asked a simple question and he died all by himself."

Emmy burst out laughing.

"It's not fucking funny."

"I know, but...yeah, it is."

That bloody woman. More than once, Black had wondered why he married her, but deep down inside, in a part of himself he pretended didn't exist, he loved that warped sense of humour along with every other part of her.

"Okay, plan B. We need to interrogate the guards and the women."

Emmy, Ana, and Carmen would tackle the difficult part—talking to the girls. Over the years, Black had got better at deciphering the female psyche, but crying still freaked him out and the number of times women said one thing and meant the complete opposite confused the hell out of him. He'd far rather deal with seven overgrown gorillas in suits.

"Battle of the sexes," Emmy said. "Let's go."

Half an hour later, they'd ascertained from the prisoners that after getting into a fight last night with the dumpy asshole sporting the black eye, Corazon had departed before sunrise with another of the guards, heading for an unknown destination. Getting the gorillas to talk hadn't been a problem since they were all cowards at heart. Yes, the mansion was operating as some sort of brothel, and yes, the fuckers knew the girls were being held against their will. But they barely had one functioning brain cell between them, and none of them managed to shed much light on the logistics of the operation.

Now they lay on the floor in a neat row, hands and feet bound with rope rather than Blackwood's usual flex cuffs as Black considered what to do with them.

Before he made a decision, Emmy appeared from the hallway, leaning against the doorjamb in what a casual observer might mistake for a relaxed stance. But she was pissed. Black saw it in her eyes. She surveyed the room, her gaze pausing for a moment on the light fixture he'd smashed to destroy the hidden camera.

"How's it going?"

"These guys don't know much."

"Then you don't need them anymore?"

Black looked back at Rafael, who shrugged and shook his head. Nate had disappeared to hunt for security camera recordings.

"No, we don't need them."

Without another word, Emmy removed Black's silenced .22 from its holster with one gloved hand and fired two rounds into each man's head, pausing to reload after the fifth. She saved the dumpy guy for last and shot two into his crotch first. He died with his mouth open in a silent scream.

Emmy placed the gun on a nearby piano and smiled.

"We can go now."

"What was that all about?"

"These motherfucking spunk-maggots have been abusing the girls for months. Most of them can't remember a day going past when they didn't get raped."

"And the one on the end?"

"He used to choke them too."

Rafael's breath hitched. "What about Cora?"

Emmy blew out a breath. "There's one girl in particular who knows more than the rest, and mentally, she's tough as fuck. Hallie. I spoke to her separately, and she reckons at least two of the girls are suffering from Stockholm syndrome. It seems Cora talked to her too. They made your sister go with clients, but Hallie reckons only one of the guards touched her and there was something odd going on between the two of them."

"What do you mean, odd?"

"Cora slept in his room at night, but she told Hallie he never touched her. Hallie thought that was weird, but Cora was happy with the arrangement because she wanted to stay away from Chad." Emmy waved at the fucker whose dick she'd destroyed. "The freak had a creepy obsession with her."

"Does Hallie know where Cora went?"

"Nope, just that Cora and Leandro, the other guard, weren't here when she got brought down for breakfast this morning. But apparently girls getting moved isn't unusual."

"So we've got nothing?" Rafael asked.

Black shook his head. "We still need to interrogate the man whose phone she used last night, and we have a laptop to examine."

"Two laptops," Nate said from the doorway, holding up a computer. "This one runs the security system."

"And we've saved five girls from a whole world of hurt. But it's time to go."

They filed out of the room, and Black pulled the door closed behind them. It locked automatically. In the lounge, Emmy briefed the girls to stay where they were for an hour, then leave and call the cops. A simple enough task, but one Hallie couldn't deal with, it seemed, because she ran along the hallway after them as they headed for the door.

"Please take me with you."

After the morning's events, Black could feel the tension crackling through Emmy, but she still mustered up a smile for the blonde.

"You'll be fine, I promise. Just wait with the others."

"But I don't have anywhere to go."

"Your family?"

She shook her head.

"I'm sure the police will find somewhere for you to stay when you explain what happened."

"I may have a tiny problem with the police."

"What kind of a problem?"

"An outstanding warrant."

"What for?"

Hallie chewed her lip for a moment, then eyed up the guns they were carrying. "Uh, murder? But I swear I was framed."

"We're gonna need a little more information than that."

"It's kind of a long story."

And one they didn't have time to listen to while standing in a house where Black's wife had just executed seven men. *Murder?* Hallie didn't look like a murderer, but if there was one lesson Black had learned in life, it was that appearances could be deceptive. Still, Hallie had to be desperate if she'd risk going with a group of mystery marauders rather than waiting for the authorities to arrive. Perhaps she was telling the truth? Emmy had spent the most time with her, so he decided to delegate.

"Valkyrie, make a decision."

"Ah, fuck it. Come with us and tell the story later," Emmy said to Hallie. "We're leaving now."

As they passed the study, Black paused to flick a coin onto the old man's back. In Mafia-speak, that meant the attack was the settlement of a debt and would serve to muddy the waters further.

Then they were outside, stuffing their masks into their pockets before they scaled the wall between the garden and the beach. They'd tossed a thick blanket over the spikes to avoid impaling themselves. Rafael hoisted Hallie up to Black, who lowered her to Nate on the other side, and when her feet touched the sand, she sucked in a lungful of sea air.

"Ohmigosh. I haven't been outside in over a year. Freedom smells like salt water and flowers."

Freedom? Maybe. She'd seen their faces now, so if this story she had to tell wasn't fan-fucking-tastic, she'd signed her own death warrant. Meanwhile, Black's radio crackled, and Alaric spoke.

"I realise the timing sucks, but Marisol just got another message from Cora."

CHAPTER 35 - CORA

"WHERE ARE WE?" I whispered to Leandro as we walked towards our new and hopefully temporary home.

What was it with rich people and houses? They had · so much money, yet they couldn't buy taste? The place looked as if a blind toddler had gone crazy with Lego bricks, boxes stuck together at strange angles and accented in a sickly duck-egg blue. The colour matched the enormous wrought-iron gates that had closed silently behind us after we drove onto the property.

"North Carolina," Leandro muttered.

Why was I still calling him Leandro in my head? For the simple reason that I didn't want to screw up and call him Leander in front of someone. We'd got this far, and making a mistake like that would be a disaster.

A man in jeans strode out the front door to meet us. Was this Radcliffe's equivalent? He was younger, around thirty-five, and he wore his dark hair slicked back in a ponytail.

"Thanks, Carl. Why don't you go park the car around the back?" He nodded at the man who'd driven us, more of a pig than an ape since his flabby belly pressed up against the steering wheel and he only spoke in grunts. "So, you must be our newbies? Welcome to the party pad. I'm Nevin, the manager here."

"The party pad? You make it sound fun, like I'm not going to be raped every night."

He screwed up his mouth. "Rape... That's such a harsh word. And a comparatively modern concept. Back in the days when women understood their role in life, it didn't exist."

"Their role in life?"

"To serve men, of course. Modern society's gone quite mad with all this equality nonsense."

Was Nevin delusional?

"Why the hell should I serve a man?"

"Because you're inferior." He patted me on the hand, and I snatched it away. "Now, now, I don't mean to insult you—I'm merely stating a simple fact. It's all down to genes. If you've got a Y chromosome, you're stronger and smarter than somebody with two X's. It's only in the last century or two that people have started fighting against nature. Against evolution."

Coming from a man with little chicken legs, the claim that he was genetically superior only made me laugh. I swallowed the giggle, and it turned into a snort that became a cough.

"Are you sick?" Nevin asked. "We're big on hygiene here. There's hand sanitiser in each room, and everyone's expected to use it."

"Not sick, just a little..." Incredulous? Gobsmacked? Amazed that anyone could be so arrogant and so stupid? "Apprehensive."

"Don't worry; we're all friends here. Once you accept your place, you'll find you relax more and enjoy the atmosphere. Think about it... No need to worry about earning money or fending for yourself out in the big wide world." He patted my hand again. Seriously, he was gonna lose fingers if that continued. "And for a woman, you've done well in the genetic lottery. We use the ugly ones as maids."

Oh my freaking goodness. Was this a prank?

"Is he kidding?" I asked Leandro as Nevin turned on his heel and marched towards the house, beckoning us to follow.

"I don't think so."

"He's a lunatic."

"Agreed. But hey, apparently as a man, I'm genetically blessed, so it's all good."

"Shut up."

Since our respective confessions last night, dealing with Leandro had become a hundred times easier. I understood his motivations, he understood mine, and we could work together rather than at cross purposes. And, most importantly, I wasn't alone anymore. Radcliffe had woken us up before dawn, handing Leandro a bundle of my clothes and telling us to be out front in fifteen minutes. Leandro had grabbed a two-minute shower in the way only boys can, then left me in the bathroom to finish getting ready.

And when he walked out with his towel around his waist, I might have snuck a glance now I knew he wasn't a complete asshole, and I liked what I saw a little too much. Wrong. All wrong. I shouldn't be feeling this way, not right now when I was about to walk into hell, part III. I could just picture Nevin with a pointy tail and horns.

The ride to North Carolina had been a brief respite —well, a twelve-hour respite according to Leandro's watch. We'd stopped for gas twice and food three times, mainly because Carl the driver ate like a hog as well as looking like one. Before our first stop, Leandro had slipped me his phone, and I'd tucked it into my bra because Radcliffe had given me another stupid dress to wear. A dress and high-heeled freaking pumps. In the car, I kicked the shoes off and sat barefoot. I'd jumped as Leandro rested his hand on my thigh, and it took me a moment to realise he wasn't stroking my leg, rather he was tracing the PIN for his phone onto my skin. Seven-nine-seven-three. I committed it to memory, and when he and Carl followed me to the bathroom and hovered outside the grubby stall, I locked myself inside and sent a message to my brother.

That wasn't just a massive relief because it would give Rafael peace of mind, but also because it showed Leandro trusted me. And in return, I had to trust him, although the thought of walking into the so-called party pad made my heart sink to the toes of my ugly pink shoes.

The Florida house had a ghastly fountain in the middle of the driveway, but the North Carolina house went one better with a miniature waterfall in the atrium. A shiny gold crocodile lurked in the pool below, and I added crimes against taste to the list of Nevin's transgressions.

"Would you like something to eat or drink before I show you to your rooms?" he asked, pausing by a vase of hot-pink orchids.

"We ate on the way," Leandro said.

"Thank you," I mouthed at him.

There was an element of wanting to get the worst over with. Would my room have a bed? Or a leopard-print futon with twenty-five throw pillows and a cashmere blanket?

"Both of your rooms are on the third floor. We don't believe in segregation here at the party pad, so guards and girls are mixed together like one big family."

He may not have believed in segregation, but the women-are-second-class-citizens theme continued upstairs, meaning Leandro's room was twice as big as mine. And while I had a bed, it looked child sized, as did the tiny armchair by the window. Did Nevin realise how tall I was? And yes, the windows had bars on, not only mine, but Leandro's too.

"Carl will bring your things in from the car, but you won't need most of your clothes, Catalina. I've seen what Radcliffe sends with the girls, and it tends to be a little conservative for our tastes. But never fear—we'll provide you with new outfits." He flung open the closet door. "See?"

Yes, I did see.

"That's, uh, a lot of leather."

"Our clients here prefer that look. If anything doesn't fit, just let Lupita know. She's our housekeeper, but she's excellent with a needle and thread. Do you have any particular dietary requirements? Vegetarian? Vegan? Lactose intolerant?"

"None of that."

Leandro shook his head too.

"Good, good." Nevin patted his stomach. "I can't eat wheat myself. It makes me bloat. Now, let me show you our party room."

Party room? It was a freaking dungeon. Now I knew why Leandro's quarters were upstairs in this house—Nevin needed the basement for his sick games. A stage dominated one end, complete with a dance pole and a strange padded bench with shackles at each end. Whips and chains lined the walls, and I dreaded to think what the metal rack on the ceiling was for. *Joder*. Just when I'd almost written Nevin off as a weirdo with odd tastes in clothing and decor, he revealed his true self. A depraved miscreant. A monster. A Bond villain on acid.

Beside me, Leandro stiffened, having realised my fate right after I did.

"Do the girls work in here every evening?" he asked.

"Yes, but don't worry; you'll be able to use them after hours along with the rest of the team. We're all night owls."

Nevin's perverted playground made Radcliffe's domain look like summer camp in comparison.

"Look, here are some of your colleagues," he said, pointing at the door. "I'll introduce you."

Three girls filed in, and I snapped my head around to stare at them. Two blondes and one brunette, none of them Izzy, each wearing impossibly high heels and clad from head to toe in black leather. And they looked utterly miserable.

"Mercedes, Julieta, Ainsley, come and meet Catalina. She'll be joining us tonight."

"Welcome to the fun factory," the shortest of the three said—the brunette. "I'm Mercedes, but call me Mercy."

"Not in front of clients," Nevin warned. "Mercedes sounds so much classier, don't you think?"

Behind him, Mercy rolled her eyes, but I could hardly disagree in front of my new boss.

"I guess."

A quiet set of chimes sounded from Nevin's pocket, and when he checked his phone screen, his fake cheer turned serious.

"I need to make a call. Mercedes, would you finish showing our newbies around?"

"Yes, Nevin."

"Catalina, feel free to wander in the house during the day, but when clients are here, you should be dressed appropriately and ready for action downstairs. We have security on all the external doors and windows. Leandro, you're welcome to come and go, of course, but you'll need to buzz me first because I'm the only person with a pass card."

"What if there's a fire?"

"We have a sprinkler system." Oh, that was comforting. "You'll have to excuse me. There seems to be some sort of problem. Most unusual."

Once he'd gone, I turned to Mercy. She'd come from Colombia too, judging by her accent. Another of Roscoe's victims?

"Give it to me straight—how bad is it?"

She steered me away from Leandro. "Where did you come from? Radcliffe? Duxworth?"

"Radcliffe. Who's Duxworth?"

"The Kentucky guy. Okay, on a scale of one to ten, Radcliffe's place is a three and this is an eleven. I hope you're a good actress."

"Why?"

"Nevin and his cronies like to see us cry and beg and scream. Don't be fooled by his nice-guy act. As soon as darkness falls, he turns into one sick puppy."

Oh, hell.

Mercy showed me the kitchen, where all the food was prepared without knives—yes, we were back to the finger buffet—then the gym, the lounge, and the dining room. In the late afternoon, the atmosphere was less oppressive than that of the Florida house, but it seemed things would change as the moon rose.

Which would be any moment now.

"You should go and change," Mercy said. "Nevin likes us to be ready and waiting when the first client arrives, and he's due in just over half an hour."

"You're allowed watches?"

"We weren't at first, but Nevin got sick of us being late."

"How long have you been here?"

"Seventeen months. I was at Duxworth's before that."

"Have you tried getting out?"

She paled visibly. "Once. But the guards caught me, and you don't want to know what Nevin did with the cattle prod."

No, I really didn't. Bile rose in my throat. How could I possibly eat dinner after this?

"I'm so sorry that happened to you."

A tear rolled down her cheek. Mercy had seemed so tough, so confident at first, but now I saw the chinks in her armour.

"Just do what they say. It hurts less that way. And you're beautiful, so you might be one of the lucky ones."

"What do you mean, the lucky ones?"

"Some girls get sold into private ownership."

"Ownership? Like the freaking slave trade? But I thought the US abolished that in 1865?"

Yes, I'd been that one kid who listened in history class.

Mercy shrugged. "I guess nobody told Nevin. But anything's better than staying here forever."

That was debatable. "What about the guards? Are they cruel too?"

"They're animals, but Nevin gets angry if they leave marks, so they have to be careful." She glanced at the fancy grandfather clock in the hallway—another modern abomination—and her shoulders dropped. "Come on. We need to get ready." Another tear followed the path of the first. "And don't forget to smile."

CHAPTER 36 - CORA

"NEVIN'S AN ANIMAL," Leandro told me.

Two minutes ago, he'd muttered at me to act scared then hauled me into his room. After the evening I'd just had, there wasn't any need for the acting part.

"I already know that."

The clients at Radcliffe's had mostly been ageing bankers and investment managers who thrust away until their Viagra wore off. Here at Nevin's, they were younger and meaner.

"Shit."

Leandro looked as if he didn't know whether to give me a hug or a wide berth, so I walked past and flopped onto his bed.

"Tell me there aren't any cameras in here."

"No, it's the same as Radcliffe's. Cameras in the hallways and your room. Nevin warned me to bring girls in here if I want to get adventurous."

And Mercy told me Nevin himself liked it when the girls struggled. Whatever he did to me, I vowed to lie as still as a corpse so he wouldn't get his kicks.

"The only adventure I want is removing Nevin's testicles with a melon baller."

Leandro sat next to me. "How bad was it?"

"Everything hurts."

"Fuck. I'm so, so sorry. We shouldn't have come. I

should've smuggled you out somehow and left the case to the rest of the damn team."

"But what about the other girls? What about Izzy? Mercy told me they sell girls into private ownership like freaking pets. What if that happened to her?"

"They what?"

"Exactly. Look, I'll carry on doing what I need to do. But you need to get your evidence and find Izzy. Quickly."

Leandro sighed. "I know. But we might have a bigger problem."

"How? How can we possibly have a bigger problem than Nevin?"

"After we left this morning, a team of hitmen arrived at Radcliffe's and killed everyone except the girls and the guard on the front gate. We had agents in the house opposite, and they never saw a fucking thing."

My chest seized. "A *team* of hitmen?"

"Yes, a team. Who does your brother work with?"

"No way. That wasn't him." I reacted on instinct, but then I paused to think. My brother *was* a freaking hitman. He'd undoubtedly have killed Radcliffe if he got his hands on him, but he'd never been to the United States, nor had he mentioned working with anyone but Vicente and Grandma. "He doesn't know anyone in America, and he works alone. What happened to the girls? Are they okay?"

"Mostly. Hallie's missing. Tasha's been sedated, and the others won't say much. So far, evidence suggests it could have been a mob hit."

"Retaliation for what happened at the warehouse? You broke our toys, so we'll destroy yours?"

"Possibly. Forensics is still processing the scene. But Nevin's understandably twitchy, and he's reassigned two of the guards to perimeter security."

"That's good, right? Because that means there's less of them in here."

"Yes, it's good for us." But Leandro didn't look at all happy.

"What's wrong?"

"Radcliffe's computer's missing. I sure hope whoever killed him doesn't find out about this place and pay us a visit because I'm a dead man if they do. And what if they take you the way they took Hallie? There's no sign of her."

Every time I thought this nightmare couldn't get any worse, it did. Hallie had been so nice to me. Why had someone taken her and not the others? What if she got hurt? Or... Or... No, I had to block Florida from my mind and focus on the task at hand. Thoughts of Hallie's fate made it difficult to breathe, but I couldn't afford to lose sight of my goal: finding Izzy.

Oh, who was I kidding? Now I needed to look for Hallie too, because I'd never sleep while she was still missing. This was never going to end, was it?

"We need to solve the case and get out of here. Can the FBI help to keep a lookout for the hitmen?"

Leandro grimaced. "I kind of cut my boss off earlier. He seemed insistent on me continuing with the softly-softly approach again, but he wanted to send a surveillance team, and that isn't going to work. Nevin's keeping a close eye on movements in the neighbourhood."

Leandro had left the compound earlier to give SAC Childs an update and work out the lie of the land, and

I'd never felt so miserable as when I watched him walk away.

"What do you mean, you cut him off?"

"I literally hung up on him."

"Can't he track the phone?"

"He could if I left it on. My phone's been off since we got here."

"So we're on our own?"

"We're on our own."

A scary thought, but Leandro's colleagues hadn't exactly proven competent so far, had they?

"Did my brother send a message?"

"Nothing when I checked."

My turn to sigh. Where the hell had Rafe ended up?

"In that case, I vote we get some rest. I'm exhausted, and we'll need our wits about us tomorrow. Can I stay in here?"

"Too damn right you're staying in here. I don't trust any of the men in this house. I'll take the floor."

A sweet gesture, but we only had one quilt, and asking for more bedding in this place would ring alarm bells. Nevin was no Radcliffe, that was for sure. The old man had made a terrible career choice, but he wasn't out-and-out cruel, not like his North Carolina counterpart.

"Just share the bed. We're both adults."

"Are you sure?"

"I wouldn't have offered otherwise."

And right now, sleep was more important than my feelings.

Nevin had a thing for leather, I soon discovered.

"Calfskin," he'd told me earlier this evening. "Nothing but the best for my girls."

Pointing out that I wasn't his girl would not only have been a waste of time since his views on women dated back to the prehistoric times, it would also have made him unnecessarily angry. Mercy had warned me about his volatile temper, so I kept my mouth shut and took the shiny black bra and panties he offered.

Now I wanted to cover myself up as Leandro escorted me back to my room, because I looked ridiculous. It was nearly midnight. A month ago, I'd have been curled up on the sofa with a mug of hot chocolate and a good book, unwinding before bed, but now I found myself thinking, absurdly, that tonight hadn't been that bad. Yes, I'd still been mauled by a stranger, but I didn't have fresh bruises, so that was good, right?

Wrong.

All wrong, Corazon.

I was starting to normalise this, and that was a bad thing.

Leandro didn't ask how I was, and I was grateful for that. Talking about the details was the last thing I felt like doing. I just wanted to sleep, but it seemed I wouldn't get my wish when Leandro grabbed my wrist and pulled me into a side room.

"Hey, come here."

"What are you doing?"

"This is Nevin's office. It's usually locked, and I want to take a look at his laptop."

"What about cameras?"

"Not in here. Nevin likes his privacy."

The discomfort with my outfit was quickly forgotten. "What can I do?"

"Listen for anyone coming."

Sweat popped out on the back of my neck as I stood by the door. After everything I'd been through this evening, this was the most stressful part. Not only because of the risk, but also because it was out of my control.

"How long will this take?" I whispered.

"Going as fast as I can."

A minute passed. Two, although they felt like hours. Then I heard the soft *click* of footsteps on the tile outside, and worse, they sounded like the brogues Nevin wore rather than the rubber-soled shoes the guards favoured.

"Someone's coming."

"Almost done."

"Hurry up!"

Those were the longest moments of my life. And by the time Leandro shoved the chair back, we were trapped. There wasn't enough time to get out and around the corner before our visitor came down the corridor.

Think, Cora. Think!

"Kiss me."

"Huh?"

No time to explain. I yanked Leandro forward, and thankfully, he got the message and pressed his lips to mine.

"Get the hell off!"

A shadow darkened the doorway as I tried to push Leandro away, but his arms tightened around me. Good. He'd understood my plan.

"You know this is gonna happen."

Nevin clapped slowly as he approached. "Feisty, I like that. But why the hell are you in my office?"

Leandro looked around as if seeing the room for the first time. "Are we? The door was open, and I didn't realise it was off limits."

"Well, it is." He jerked his thumb towards the hallway. "Get out."

I started to follow Leandro, but Nevin caught my arm. "Not you." Now he smiled. "You can stay. I like it when girls struggle."

Oh *mierda*.

Nevin kicked the door closed, and I could have cried. On the plus side, Leandro hadn't been caught, but at what price? The vile little man pushed me towards his desk, closed the laptop, and pushed assorted papers and pens to one side.

"Bend over."

"You're a cockroach."

"No, sweetheart, I'm a snake."

He forced me down across the shiny wooden surface, and I yelped when his hand landed on my ass. *Don't give him what he wants, Cora.* I willed myself to stay still as he picked up a ruler. How did the girl in *Fifty Shades* ever find this sexy? Being spanked was about as much fun as swallowing barbed wire while rolling on a bed of hot coals. If it hadn't been for Leandro, I'd have been praying for the hit squad to turn up. As it was, I prayed for a miracle. Something, anything that would prevent me from being violated for the second time that day.

And someone up there delivered.

It was Nevin's turn to yelp as water cascaded from

the ceiling, and he abandoned me in favour of shoving his laptop into a drawer as the torrent continued. A high-pitched alarm sounded too, and I sent a silent thank you to whoever installed the sprinkler system.

"What the hell...?" he started.

"Is there a fire? We should evacuate."

"No, you're coming with me while I find out what's going on."

Bedraggled men and women dashed back and forth as Nevin strong-armed me into the hallway, and one of the apes rounded up the girls and herded us into the lounge. Mercy sat on a wet sofa, hugging herself in a leather basque. I joined her.

"What's happening?" I asked. "Is there really a fire?"

"I smelled smoke upstairs."

She began shivering, and I called out to the nearest guard.

"Can we get some blankets?"

"We're busy here."

"Well, we're getting hypothermia."

Another minute passed before the sprinklers shut off, and by then, everything was soaked. I squashed beside Mercy and wrapped an arm around her. Something flaked off her back, and I peered at it.

"It's candle wax," she mumbled. "One of the clients has a fetish for it."

Then I spotted the red marks on her wrists.

"He tied you up?"

She nodded. "It wasn't the first time. Greg and that new guy cut me loose. He seems kinder than the rest. The new guy, I mean."

Yeah, he was, which meant I'd have to remind him

to act like more of a dick so he didn't blow his cover.

"He came from Radcliffe's. I guess he hasn't been fully indoctrinated in the ways of Nevin yet."

Mercy hugged her knees to her chest and shrank further back into the cushions.

"It's only a matter of time."

CHAPTER 37 - BLACK

BLACK STARED UP at the words on the screen. Four sentences of neat text, but the implications were huge.

Everything's changed. Don't come and get me. I've found someone to work with, and we're on our way to somewhere new to look for Izzy and a banker. Will call when I can. C.

After the raid on the Naples house, they'd retired to their temporary base of operations to plan their next move in the search for Corazon, starting with unravelling her latest message. Which made no fucking sense. Had she been forced to write it?

Rafael stood beside Black, mirroring his stance. "Who the hell is Cora working with?"

"Who's Cora?" Hallie asked.

Shit. She wasn't supposed to be in here. They'd put her in the front of the van with Cruz for the trip back, crouched in the footwell until they cleared town, but now she'd wandered into the room behind them.

"Diamond, why don't you take Hallie and find her some proper clothes?"

"If you want to get rid of me, just say so."

"I want to get rid of you."

"Well, aren't you a sweetheart? You realise I could help, right? I'm totally on your side here."

"This is a private investigation."

"Are Cora and Catalina the same person? Because she's got to be working with Leandro."

Rafael gave her a tight non-smile. "Yes, but *who* is Leandro?"

An excellent question, and it was Alaric who came up with the answer moments later when Nate began scrolling through the security camera files they'd retrieved from the house.

"That son of a bitch."

Nate paused the tape as Corazon appeared in a hallway beside a dark-haired man an inch or so shorter than her. This must be their guy.

"Who? Leandro?"

"Possibly, but I meant Merrick Childs." Alaric jabbed a finger at the screen. "That man's an FBI agent, or at least he was."

"You know him?"

"Not personally, but I saw him around the Florida field office once or twice, and I've got a good memory for faces."

"What's his name? Presumably not Leandro?"

"I don't know. He joined right before I left. But leave it with me, and I'll make a few calls."

So Cora had hooked up with an FBI agent? Interesting. Nate played more of the footage, and as the pair walked, the gap between them was two inches at most. At one point, Leandro said something and Corazon leaned in closer. Too close. Had she hooked up, or had she *hooked up*?

Rafael didn't seem to register the connection, and that was a good thing. The younger man was more emotionally involved than Black, and he needed to keep his anger under control. Difficult given the circumstances.

"The FBI had a man in the house?" Rafael asked. "They knew what was happening in that place and they didn't stop it?"

"We don't know the full story yet."

"I don't need to. They should never have left the women there."

Black didn't disagree. "Let's concentrate on gathering information. Corazon mentioned looking for a banker, so it's clear the FBI think he's still alive. Who is he and, more importantly, *where* is he? I suspect at this moment, Corazon knows more than us, and whatever she's found out is bad enough that she's given up her freedom to carry on looking for the man."

"And Isabella."

"And Isabella. But if that was her only goal, she wouldn't have mentioned the banker in her message, and I suspect she wouldn't have been quite so willing to head to a new location. Which is where, Nate? Can you track the phone?"

"It's turned off now. The message was sent from Georgia. Mack carried on tracking the signal through South Carolina, but it disappeared around Myrtle Beach."

"Looks like we're heading north. Our first priority is finding Corazon, but I also want to find out everything there is to know about The Banker since he's wrapped up in all this."

"Easier said than done," Alaric said. "My source said Task Force Atlantis has been operating for two years, and if they've been looking for The Banker the whole time, he's not gonna be an easy man to find."

"Better get started then, hadn't we?" Black turned

to Hallie. "Did anyone at the house ever mention a banker?"

"Not *a* banker. Lots of the clients were bankers. And investment managers. And attorneys. They all liked to brag about the size of their wallets."

"So maybe our target is a client, and it's unlikely he's in Florida because the FBI agent didn't find him there."

"Have you got a photo? Then I can tell you if I saw him or not."

"We don't have a photo. What we need are some concrete facts, because this is all speculation. And I'm also curious to hear this story of yours."

Black took a better look at the girl. Hallie was pretty but too thin, she'd bleached her hair to within an inch of its life, and her jaded hazel eyes said that in her early twenties, she'd already had enough of life. Black had seen that look before in Dan, his second in command in Blackwood's investigations division. Emmy had brought Dan home as a stray one day, and although they'd both driven him crazy with their antics for a few long months, now he couldn't imagine life without her. So while his natural inclination was to shove Hallie out the door and keep her well away until this case was over, he hesitated.

And Hallie wrapped her arms around her skinny frame then sank onto a chair.

"The truth is, I have no idea what happened. I went out to a club, then woke up in a stranger's bed with a dead body lying beside me."

"Male? Female?"

"An old guy with a bullet hole in his head. And I was holding the gun."

"Your gun?"

"No! I'd never seen it before in my life. I don't even know how to shoot."

"And the man—had you seen him before?"

Hallie shook her head. "Uh-uh, and he was at least fifty. No way would I have been interested if he'd hit on me."

"So what did you do?"

"I heard sirens, so I got the hell out of there. Except I realised later I didn't have my purse."

"You left it in the house? Apartment?"

"House. I wasn't thinking straight, okay? Someone drugged me, I'm sure of it. But at least I remembered to wipe my prints off the gun."

"If this is true, then why did somebody frame *you*?"

"Truthfully, I have no idea. I was working sixty hours a week as a waitress in a shitty diner. I didn't have time to make enemies."

"What about the customers?"

"I made sure to be real nice to everyone, even the assholes." She shrugged. "Better tips that way. All I know is that I planned to go out to a club that night to unwind, and my whole life fell apart."

It wasn't the first time Black had heard a story like that. Dan herself had investigated a similar case, and despite the cops' conviction otherwise, the initial suspect had turned out to be innocent. That made him more inclined to give Hallie the benefit of the doubt, but he needed to hear the rest of her tale first.

Meanwhile, Hallie gulped in air as she tried to control her emotions, and Black made a conscious effort not to frown, a difficult task when he wanted answers, not fucking tears. Thankfully, his wife chose that moment to appear with two mugs of coffee, and the distraction allowed Hallie to pull herself together.

"Are you okay?" Emmy asked.

"I'm not sure how to feel. I thought I'd be stuck in that place forever, and now I'm out of there, but I have to face the future, and I'm not sure which is worse."

"What happened after you left the murder scene?" Black asked. "You mentioned a warrant?"

"The cops found my driver's licence and pulled me in for questioning. I had to admit I'd been there, but I said that when I left, the guy was still alive. And they started asking me all these questions about who he was and how I met him, but I didn't have any clue so I just ended up sounding even more guilty. My first attorney was useless and the cops wouldn't listen to anything I said, so I tried to find out what happened myself, but I ran out of time and money."

"That still doesn't explain how you ended up where you did."

"At Radcliffe's? Because I was stupid and desperate. I needed four hundred dollars to get a sample of my hair lab-tested so I could prove I'd been drugged, but I didn't have four hundred dollars, so I answered an ad for waitstaff. I was so freaking happy when I passed the interview, and the guy seemed totally legit. But then he offered me a ride, and I woke up in Florida."

"He drugged you?"

"You think I fell asleep by myself? I swear, I'm never accepting a drink from a stranger again." She glanced down at the mug in her hands. "Why am I even holding this coffee?"

"You have to admit that story sounds farfetched."

"Couldn't make it up, right? Yeah, that's what the

cops said too, about the first part."

"So you say you investigated the case yourself? What happened?"

"I visited the bar I was in and got ahold of video footage of me dancing with a completely different guy, only I never found out who he was. But the man I supposedly killed was a rich real-estate developer, and his wife was real pissed with me."

"Where's this tape now?"

"On a flash drive in my new attorney's office." Hallie crinkled her nose. "He's not a great attorney, but he was cheap, and he let me use his phone and his copy machine."

Sometimes, just sometimes, the most unbelievable stories turned out to be true, and Black's curiosity had been aroused. When he was a kid, his US mother complained he asked too many questions, but then he'd made a career out of doing precisely that.

Except this week, he had other priorities.

"We'll look into your case, but right now, our primary goals are to find Corazon and this banker. Everything else takes a back seat. If you want our help, you need to keep out of the way and let us get on with our jobs for a few weeks first."

"You won't tell the cops I'm here?"

"No, Hallie, we won't. Is Hallie your real name?"

"Sort of." She held out a hand. For all her brashness, she couldn't hide the way it trembled. "Halina Chastain."

Black shook her hand, then turned back to business.

"You heard the man," Emmy said. "Why don't you get some rest while we work?"

Black glanced over his shoulder, and Hallie backed away. Good move, Halina Chastain. He'd deal with her later.

Alaric actually whistled as he walked through the front door that evening, and Black wanted to punch him for being so cheerful, especially when he checked out Emmy's ass.

"You'd better have good news."

"That's what you're paying me for."

Yes, and handsomely at that. Since Alaric went freelance, he'd charged the big bucks for his information, although Black had no idea what he did with the money. He certainly didn't spend it on haircuts.

"Well?"

"Where's everyone else? In the dining room?"

Yes, and it was fucking crowded now. Carmen had flown back to Virginia to relieve two other friends, Tia and Eli, of babysitting duties, but that still left Nate, Cruz, Emmy, Ana, Sofia, Rafael, Vicente, and Marisol. At least Dores and Hallie were making themselves useful in the kitchen, and Black had to admit the weird Colombian food the older woman dished up tasted quite good.

"They're waiting."

"I need a coffee first."

For fuck's sake. "Hallie?"

She appeared almost instantly. "Yes?"

"Do me a favour and make coffee."

Alaric smiled at her. "One sugar and plenty of

cream for me, lovely. Did you do something to your hair?"

"Just washed it." She beamed back at him. "Coffee's coming right up."

"You're too fucking slick," Black muttered at Alaric's back.

"And you're a cantankerous asshole."

"Did someone give you a thesaurus for Christmas?"

"Yeah, your wife. Now I know six words for dickhead, ten for thief, and eight for traitor."

Alaric couldn't have found out what happened. No way. He was on a fishing expedition, and Black willed his expression to stay neutral.

"Good. The chances are, we'll need all of them during this investigation." He gestured towards the double doors of the dining room. "After you."

Finally, Alaric settled into a seat and began his update, and yeah, Black grudgingly had to admit the man had been busy.

"Leandro's real name is Leander Arden. Thirty years old, and he's been with the Bureau for seven and a half years, specialising in financial crimes. He's a computer whizz who was brought onto Task Force Atlantis to unravel the tapestry of overseas transactions, but they decided he had a face for undercover work and he ended up infiltrating a string of sex clubs operated by The Banker instead."

"He's running these places?" Emmy asked. "Not just visiting?"

"Apparently so. He's always been notoriously secretive, and nobody's seen him for years. The current theory is that he fled to South America after faking his own death and underwent extensive plastic surgery."

"So nobody knows what he looks like now?"

"They didn't have much of an idea in the first place," Nate said. "I've only found one photo, and it's blurry."

"How blurry?" Black asked.

Nate put the picture up on the screen, and yeah, it was bad. The snap had been taken on a yacht, and the photographer had been focusing on something else, namely a shapely brunette in a bikini. Black leaned forward for a closer look at the guy, but it didn't help much.

"Can we clean it up?"

"Mack's working on that at the moment."

Then something else in the picture caught Black's eye. An out-of-focus figure in the background behind the brunette.

"Sofia, is that you?"

She tilted her head to one side, squinting. "I thought the boat looked kind of familiar."

"And? What were you doing on it?"

"Drinking a Mai Tai, by the looks of it."

"Fia..."

"Okay, okay... That must have been years ago. I still had my navel piercing. Uh, let me think... Are there any more pictures of the yacht?"

"No."

"Shit. Hmm. If it's the party I'm thinking of, I snuck on board behind some TV star and his entourage." She got up and stepped closer. "Yes, it's all coming back now. That guy..." She pointed at a muscle-bound man standing near her. "He fell overboard, I'm sure of it. And I couldn't jump in to help him because my necklace had a camera in it, and I wasn't sure whether it was waterproof."

"A camera? So *you* have pictures?"

"No, the CIA has pictures. The yacht belonged to a Russian, and they wanted to know who he was associating with."

"Do you still have a contact there?"

"I'll call him."

Sofia slipped out of the room, leaving Alaric to take the floor again.

"If we can get decent pictures, we're one step ahead of the task force. They've been scratching around for months with few results, and rumour says Merrick Childs is getting desperate. Probably why he turned a blind eye to the abuse going on in that house. Oh, and he's also furious, but the good news is that he thinks this morning's raid was carried out by the Mafia, so everyone's treading very carefully while they try to unravel the crime scene."

They'd spend a long time doing that. Team Blackwood all had alibis. Black had met with his attorney for an early breakfast while Emmy had undergone a gruelling session with her personal trainer.

"Good. While they're pissing into the wind with that, we've got a clear run at Arden and The Banker. Have they ever put a name to him?"

"Not even a hint of one. The guy hides behind offshore investments and back-room deals. Did we get anything from Radcliffe's laptop?"

Nate grimaced. "Nothing. Not only did he delete the files, he also wiped the entire hard drive. Mack's trying to piece it back together, but it doesn't look hopeful."

Black hated to end the day on a bad note, but apart

from shutting down the Florida brothel, there hadn't been much good news. Corazon, Isabella, and The Banker were still in the wind. Alaric was still sleeping in the spare room. And after this morning's escapade, Emmy's demons were bound to make an appearance, so Black wouldn't get any sleep tonight.

As he brushed his teeth, he heard her on the balcony, speaking softly into the phone in Spanish, and he hoped it was good news.

"How's Eduardo?" he asked once she'd hung up.

"Small improvements. He responds to pain, sometimes he mumbles stuff, and he's opened his eyes a few times."

"Does he recognise anyone?"

"Not yet."

That old man had better pull through. After all, he'd been the one who'd started this.

"Have you thought about how we broach the subject of Rafael with the Garcias yet?"

"Nope. I was kind of hoping you'd come up with a brainwave."

"Sorry. But once he gives us the name of his client, we'll have a bargaining chip."

Emmy flopped onto the bed and stared out the window. "I'm still pissed he hasn't told me yet."

"What would you do if he did? Go running off to Colombia?"

Silence.

"Well?"

"I suppose I would. You're so similar, do you know that? Both stubborn assholes."

"Yes, I know." Black lay down beside his wife and wrapped her up in his arms, as was his custom. Both to keep himself safe and because he loved her more than life itself. "Get some sleep, Diamond."

CHAPTER 38 - CORA

NEVER IN MY life did I think I'd enjoy cleaning, but dealing with the aftermath of the sprinkler incident sure beat working on my back. Nevin had been furious, of course, especially when he had to start cancelling clients.

"What the hell happened?" he demanded. "Did the system malfunction?"

"Looks as if a candle fell over in one of the rooms upstairs," an ape said. "At least the whole place didn't burn down."

"How? How did a candle 'fall over'?" He used air quotes around the words, and his pinky ring flashed in the moonlight streaming through the window.

"One of the clients got rough with Mercedes, so it probably happened in the struggle," Greg said. "We didn't notice because we were too busy cutting her free."

"And checking she was still breathing," Leandro added.

There wasn't a lot Nevin could say to that, so he just paced the dungeon, his slimy little hands balled at his sides.

"Nobody gets any time off until this mess is cleared up. And candles are banned. Banned!"

The electronic door locks malfunctioned from all

the water, which meant the guards had to resort to keys to lock us into our rooms that night. Greg took me upstairs, but when we walked past Leandro, he winked, and I knew exactly what he'd done. He'd saved me again.

That night was the first in over a week I'd spent apart from him, shivering in darkness under a soggy quilt. Yesterday, I'd woken in his arms again, my head resting on his chest. Talk about awkward. At least I hadn't drooled, and neither of us said anything as we wriggled back to our respective sides of the bed.

But now I was alone again, and I came to the worrying realisation that I really didn't like it.

Logically, I understood that Leandro couldn't fetch me, not when playtime was banned. If the cameras were still working, it would look suspicious as hell. But that didn't stop me from jerking my head towards the door at every sound, every squeak or shuffle from the hallway. Where was he? What was he doing?

I barely slept a wink, and when an ape unlocked my door in the morning, I yawned before I even sat up.

"Why haven't you showered?"

"Is the electricity on again yet?"

"No, but you have water."

"What about light? My bathroom doesn't have a window."

He scowled at me. "Hurry up and get ready. We've got this whole fucking house to clean, and Nevin's pissed."

The guard made no move to close the door, and I wasn't about to strip off in front of him, so I just rolled out of bed in my damp pyjamas, stepped over the puddle of last night's leather underwear, and reported for duty.

Mierda, the place was a mess. The sprinklers had only run for two minutes, maybe three, but they'd left pools of water everywhere, and the house already smelled of damp. The lounge and the dining room were bright with all their windows, but gloom veiled every other area and I dreaded venturing into the basement.

Nevin held a clipboard as he stood in a sunbeam. "Greg went out this morning and bought mops and buckets for everyone—thank you, Greg—and we've got three hours to mop up the water before the electrician arrives. Once he's checked the power, we can bring in dehumidifiers and get this place dried out." He clapped his hands. "Go. Go!"

I trailed Mercy through to the kitchen, followed by one of the apes, just in case we decided to make a break for it through a double-glazed window or a locked door.

"Are you okay?" I asked in a low voice. "After last night?"

"I wish the whole damn house had burned down."

"Never give up hope."

"That's easy for you to say. Did you know they have cameras in our rooms? I tried to kill myself once, but they saw me and now we're not allowed kimonos anymore."

"Someone will find us. They can't hide us away forever."

"You think? It's been three damn years and I'm still here. Nobody's even looking for me."

Three years? *Joder*. "What about your family?"

"What family? None of us has any. That's who they target. Girls who nobody will miss."

Well, Roscoe had made a colossal mistake with

Izzy, hadn't he?

The shadow of our designated ape loomed over us. "Enough talking. We don't pay you to chat."

"You don't pay us at all."

He just laughed.

By late evening, the electricity had been restored, and industrial dehumidifiers hummed in the rooms downstairs. I was still wearing my pyjamas, and every limb ached from mopping and squeezing and moving furniture around.

But my heart jumped a little when Leandro came to escort me back to my room. I'd hardly seen him all day, and at first, I feared he was avoiding me on purpose. Then I realised that of course he was avoiding me on purpose, because if Nevin realised I was Leandro's friend rather than his fuck-doll, he might suspect last night's candle issue wasn't the accident it had initially appeared to be.

"Thank you," I whispered as we left the lounge.

"I wasn't gonna leave you with that psycho."

We stopped talking as another pair of guards walked past with girls in tow. What I wouldn't give to be able to have a proper conversation again... I waited for their footsteps to recede before I spoke, nervous about the request I was going to make.

"Can I stay with you tonight?"

"No."

I froze. Yes, I'd been scared to ask, but I'd never truly thought Leandro would turn me down.

"Just walk," he hissed, and I jumped at his tone.

"Sorry."

"Shit. I'm the one who's sorry. I didn't mean to upset you. But the electronic locks are still out right now. Nevin's got a guy coming in tomorrow to fix them, which gives me tonight to get into his study. I can pick normal locks, and I watched him put his laptop into his desk drawer earlier."

"What about the password?"

"I used a back door in the software to load a keylogger onto it last night before...you know. I didn't get a chance to tell you."

"So you have the password?"

"Yes."

"What if he catches you?"

"I have to take the chance. It may be the only one we have."

"But—"

"You know I'm right."

I did, dammit. I just wished there was another way. Something less risky, because if Nevin saw Leandro in his study again, he'd get madder than Chad.

We reached my bedroom door, and Leandro pressed the length of his body against mine. I knew it was only for the cameras, but a flash of heat still tore through me.

"Leander," I whispered. "If only we'd met under different circumstances."

"Under different circumstances, you'd be the beautiful girl on the far side of the club dancing with her friends and wondering why the weirdo by the bar wouldn't stop staring at her."

"You should just invite her to dinner."

"I'd be too nervous."

"She's not gonna say no."

He smiled that tilted smile I liked so much. "I'll take that under advisement."

I wanted him to kiss me. No, I wanted to kiss him, but I couldn't because if anyone was watching on the cameras, that would look strange as hell. But he didn't go for my lips. No, his fingers crept under my waistband, and before I could gasp in shock, I realised he'd tucked an object in there. Something small. His phone.

"If you don't see me by the morning, it means I've fucked up. Call your brother and tell him to get you out of here. Do you remember the PIN number?"

"Yes, but don't go." I tried to grab his wrist, but he stepped to the side and unlocked my door. "We'll think of another way."

"But none of them will be quick, and I can't stand by and watch men hurt you night after night."

"That's my decision."

"No, honeybee, it's my decision."

"Honeybee?"

He'd given me a nickname? That was...cute. I kinda liked it.

"You're sweet as sugar but you've got a sting in your tail. Just make sure you use it on Nevin."

Leandro gave me a gentle push backwards, and I stepped reluctantly into my room. We'd spent most of our time clearing up downstairs, so everything on the third floor was still cold and damp, and we didn't have the Florida heat to help dry things out.

"I'll see you tomorrow." I choked out the words because they didn't come easy.

He didn't answer, just gave me a tight smile—no

humour, only tension—and closed my door. The lock tumbled, and I was on my own again. The question was, for how long?

CHAPTER 39 - CORA

I STILL DIDN'T have a watch, but the *thump, thump, thump* of my heart counted down the moments until dawn. *Come on, Leandro. Where are you?*

How long did it take to break into a computer? What was on it? At first, my nerves were tinged with optimism. By tomorrow, we could have the information we needed and begin plotting our escape. And Izzy's, because I had to believe that there was some record of where she'd gone.

But as the seconds ticked by, then the minutes, then the hours, I began to lose hope. At one point, I thought I heard voices coming from downstairs, but I didn't dare to press my ear to the door in case I got caught. Leandro had said the electronic locks weren't working, but he hadn't mentioned a thing about the cameras.

Should I call Rafe? The phone grew sweaty in my palm. If Leandro had got caught and I left it too late, his life would be at risk. But if I called too early, Rafe might come barging in and ruin everything. The difficulty was, I didn't know either man well enough to predict an outcome. No, not even my brother. As a child, patience had never been his strong suit, and I suspected he hadn't improved with age. Leandro? I trusted his intentions, but could he get out of a sticky situation if one arose?

I wasn't sure, but I did know I couldn't bear to lose him. Not just because he was my biggest ally in this hellhole, but also because every moment I snatched with him, I wanted to last an hour. He thought I was out of his league? No, he was out of mine.

The sun began to rise. An orange glow spread over the horizon, followed by yellow. Dammit, where was Leandro? Even if he'd been delayed with the computer, he'd have let me know, surely? Because he wouldn't want me calling my brother unless it was absolutely necessary.

Yellow turned to white. The black sky turned blue. And still I heard nothing—not a squeak, not a whisper.

Time was up. I had to call Rafe.

I burrowed under the quilt and turned the phone on. A full battery and two bars of signal—not perfect, but a good start. I realised my hands were shaking as I dialled. How did people like Leandro work undercover for a living? I was a wreck.

My grandma answered. "*Hola?*"

"It's Cora. Is Rafe okay? I need to speak to him. Do you have a number?"

"He's right here. Are *you* okay?"

My whole chest seized. "What do you mean, he's there? In Medellín?"

If Rafe had gone back to Colombia, then how the hell would he rescue us?

"No, America. We're all in America. Hold on a moment, and I'll put you on speaker."

Grandma had come to America? What about Vicente? And Dores? The line crackled, and I almost cried with relief when I heard my brother's voice for the first time in weeks.

"Cora? Are you all right?"

"Yes." Not in the slightest, but I was still breathing while Leandro might not be. "But a friend of mine's probably in trouble, and I don't know what to do."

"Leander Arden?"

"You know about him?"

What? How?

"He's an FBI agent. What happened?"

Where did I start? "I'm not sure how much time I've got to talk. The guards might come."

"Just give me the basics."

Another male voice spoke in the background, an American, not Vicente.

"Who's there with you?" I asked.

"There's no time to explain everything now. Just know that we're on our way."

"I think we're in North Carolina."

"We've got the exact location from your phone. Tell me what we're walking into."

"Eight girls, eight guards, plus the housekeeper and a *bastardo pequeño* named Nevin."

"Eight and eight. Are you including yourself and Leander in that?"

"Yes."

"What about Isabella?"

"She's not here. The place is a hideous space-age mansion, and she's not here."

"I'm looking at a satellite picture right now."

"And it's got a huge basement. A dungeon. But you need to be careful because it's not only you and the FBI after these people. The Mafia went to the last place we stayed at and killed all the men, and...and..." I choked on my words. "They took my friend Hallie as well."

"Hallie's fine. She's in Florida with Dores and Vicente and Grandma."

"You found her?" A corner of the crushing weight lifted from my chest, then it slammed back down full force when I realised what that meant. "That was you at the house? Not the Mafia?"

"Yes."

"You killed all those men?"

"Not personally, but I'm gonna buy a drink for the person who did. What did you expect us to do, Corazon? I saw the tapes of them making you walk into those bedrooms."

I may not have been able to see my brother, but there was no mistaking the anger in his voice. No doubt when he and whoever he worked with got to this place, the guards and Nevin would be facing the same fate, and do you know what? After my initial shock, I couldn't get upset over that. They'd subjected Mercy and the others to years of abuse, and they deserved everything coming to them.

"Just don't hurt Leander when you come here."

"We won't. Tell me more about the house."

"It's got the same electronic locking system as the pink palace in Florida, but it's broken at the moment, so they're using keys. Everywhere's damp because there was a tiny fire and the sprinklers came on, and be careful not to trip over the cables from the dehumidifiers. The layout's different—the client space is mostly in the dungeon, with a few rooms on the first floor, and Nevin's office too. That's where Leander went last night, and he hasn't come back. What if he's hurt? Or worse? One of the guards killed a girl in Florida."

"The blonde? We saw them carrying her out on tape."

A sob burst out of me. "Her name was Kelsie."

"We can discuss her later, but right now, I'm more worried about you. Tell me about the entrances? Exits? Cameras?"

I opened my mouth to speak, but before I got any words out, I heard footsteps in the hallway outside.

"Someone's here," I hissed. "I have to go."

"Stay strong, and I'll see you later."

All night, I'd been hoping for a visitor, but I'd given up hope of it being Leandro. If it *was* him, I could call Rafe back and beg him to hold off, but I knew in my heart it wouldn't be. Something had gone terribly, terribly wrong.

The ape didn't knock, just opened the door and marched right in.

"Time to get up."

"Is it breakfast already? Isn't it kind of early?"

Stay calm, Cora. He doesn't know what you've done. Unless they'd beaten the information out of Leandro, of course, in which case I was screwed in an even worse way than usual. How long would Rafe take to get here? Four hours? Five? And then he'd have to work out how to get in, and...

"The boss wants to talk to you."

"What about?"

"I think you know."

"He's going to complain about the mop yesterday? Because I didn't break it on purpose. The thing wasn't designed for doing an entire house."

"Just get your ass out of bed."

Fuck, fuck, fuck. I shoved the phone under my

pillow and got to my feet as slowly as possible. Every second counted. What had Nevin done to Leandro? And what did he plan to do to me?

CHAPTER 40 - BLACK

BLACK THREW THE rented Porsche Cayenne into a curve, taking a perverse pleasure at his wife's sharp intake of breath. There, see how she liked it. Rafael sat behind Emmy with Ana beside him. They were the advance team, speeding towards yet another mansion, this one near Wilmington. The van was somewhere behind them, but since time was of the essence, Black wanted to go on ahead and get some of the groundwork done so they could go in as soon as the others arrived.

Satellite photos had shown that this new house was more isolated than the last, set amongst trees rather than beside the beach. No doubt that made it easier for the sick fuckers to hide what they were doing, but it also gave Team Blackwood an advantage. Plus it sounded as if the men in the house might be distracted —by Leander, Cora, the fire, the sprinklers, and the inevitable mess that came with all that. Hopefully, they hadn't gotten much rest, which would also play into Blackwood's hands. Black's merry band of men and women had taken it in turns to sleep on the journey, and they'd been in this situation often enough to quash any nerves.

If he'd had the choice, Black would have brought Nate with him and left Rafael in the van with Cruz, Sofia, and Alaric, but one look at his nephew and Black understood that would never happen. He'd rather have had Carmen on the team than Sofia too, because Carmen was far more predictable. Yes, Sofia was a good shot and sneaky as hell, but there was a good reason Emmy had roped Fia and not Carmen into her crackpot scheme to kidnap Rafael.

"Twenty minutes out," Emmy muttered.

Twenty minutes, and Black could feel his trigger finger twitching.

"We want to leave everyone alive this time, especially Nevin. If anyone can lead us to The Banker, it's him. And we need to get every fucking laptop before they pull the same trick as Radcliffe."

"Dying of a heart attack?"

Black cut his eyes sideways at Emmy.

"Look on the bright side—we saved a bullet."

"I don't care about the laptops," Rafael said. "Only Corazon."

"And Isabella? If she's not at the house, the laptops might lead us to her. You need to see the bigger picture."

Rafael fell silent, and Black knew work was needed there. Rafael might be good with a gun, but he was used to working simple jobs—one target, in and out—not the multifaceted cases that Blackwood took on, where one thread led to a whole tangled web of secrets and lies that needed to be unravelled.

"Just keep your head," Black warned.

An hour later, Black crawled forward on his stomach. Rafael was twenty yards away in the trees, barely visible, and Black hadn't seen Emmy or Ana since they melted into the woods a quarter mile away. The car was parked in a rest area, but since Emmy had replaced the registration plate with a borrowed one before they left Florida, Black wasn't too bothered about it being spotted.

If all went according to plan, they'd be calling the FBI themselves before the end of the day, anyway. That promised to be a fun conversation. He couldn't imagine Merrick Childs would thank them for their efforts in breaking up The Banker's little funhouse, but Black was looking forward to the job. He'd always preferred being out in the field over sitting behind a desk. That was why he'd joined the Navy, then become a SEAL, then accepted a dangerous job with the CIA before he started Blackwood with Nate. Cheating death gave him a rush like no other.

Little seemed to be stirring in the house, although it was difficult to see every room since the architect had obviously been on crack when he designed the place. Rosie was temporarily unavailable, having been attacked by a hawk on a test flight yesterday, and some fucker had placed palm trees in oversized metal planters in strategic positions around the outside of the building. By accident or on purpose? At least the pots gave them cover.

The occasional guard walked past a window, but Black saw no sign of the girls. As in the Florida house, bars turned the upstairs rooms into jail cells.

Nate's voice came over the radio. "Approaching from the south."

Good. They'd discussed strategy as Cruz drove, and Nate would go in the front door with Sofia. Black and

Rafael would take the side door while Emmy went through the back with Ana.

There was no need for the thermic lance this time. Thanks to Cora's information, they went armed with lock picks and got the doors open in under a minute. Rafael stacked up behind Black.

"Ready?" Black asked.

His nephew nodded.

Inside the house, they both paused for a second, listening. Low voices from the left. Then a female shriek from the right. Shit.

Rafael started forward with Black close behind. Perhaps not the most sensible approach, but fuck it. Black enjoyed a challenge.

"Deal with the guards," he told the others. "We're going for Cora."

A guard stepped out of a doorway ahead, but he was still fumbling for his gun when Rafael chopped his vagus nerve with the side of his hand, and the asshole crumpled to the floor. Black followed up with flex cuffs on his wrists and ankles, and they moved on.

"One down."

"Two down," Emmy said. "The twat still had his safety on. It's almost as if they've spent too much time mistreating women and not enough time training."

Sofia giggled. "Three down. And you're so right."

Three down, five to go, and six people on his team. Black liked those odds until he and Rafael found three of the fuckheads in the same damn room. The two guards lurched into action, and while it took only seconds to subdue them, those seconds gave the third man time to drag Corazon in front of him and press a knife to her neck. And the laptop on the desk beside him whirred alarmingly. Was it already wiping itself?

"Drop the guns!" the man shrieked.

Was this Nevin? He sounded like Bradley's evil twin. Looked like him too. What self-respecting bad guy wore gold cowboy boots?

"That's not gonna happen."

Rafael shifted to the right, and Nevin took a step back, angling Corazon so neither of them could get a good shot. The point of the knife was worryingly close to her carotid artery, and there wasn't much she could do to help with her hands cuffed behind her back. Blood trickled from her nose, one of her eyes was bruised, and her clothes hung in tatters. Nevin was a dead man walking.

"I'll kill her."

"And then we'll kill you. If you let her go, we can discuss this like adults."

Emmy's voice came through Black's earpiece. "Four down, and the housekeeper's sobbing in the kitchen."

"Five and six down," he said. "But we've got an issue with seven."

"Okay. Oh, hey—Ana just found eight." *Crunch.* "Ouch. I felt that."

"Search the house."

"Who are you talking to?" Nevin demanded.

"Satan. I'm reserving you a room. If you don't want to check in, I suggest you put the knife down."

"You'll kill me anyway."

True. "How about if I promise to make it quick?"

"If you want her to live, you'll back into the hallway and let me leave."

Okay, because then they could shoot him as he walked past.

"And put the guns on the floor first."

Maybe not.

"You've got nowhere to go. Your guards are asleep on the job, and we've disabled your vehicles."

Nate heard Black's comment over the radio. "On it. I'll shoot out the tyres."

"I'll stick this knife right into her neck. I swear!"

"How about we negotiate? I'm not interested in you; I want your boss. The Banker. Tell me what you know about him, and you have my word I'll let you walk out of here."

As far as the front gate, then Emmy or Ana could put a bullet through his brain. What? Black was a habitual liar. He'd already admitted that, hadn't he?

His hope had been to scare Nevin into talking, but at the mention of The Banker's name, the man's hands started shaking. A scarlet trickle ran down Cora's neck, and Black realised Nevin was more scared of his boss than of Black himself. A new kind of fear showed in the man's eyes. He'd rather die than spill the beans, which meant the rules had changed again. Black needed to kill the fucker and shut down that laptop before everything got erased.

But how?

Little caught Black by surprise, but when Nevin's head exploded, that was...unexpected. Sofia stepped through the shattered remains of the tempered glass she'd just destroyed and looked down at the bloody mess.

"You forgot the window, you stupid jizz-nozzle."

Black leapt for the laptop, leaving Rafael and Sofia to take care of Cora. But it was too late. *Wipe complete* flashed on the screen, along with a skull and crossbones. He pulled out the battery anyway, but it looked horribly like a repeat of the Radcliffe situation.

"Fuck."

"What is it?" Nate asked.

"Another fried laptop."

"We've got a bigger problem in the basement," Emmy warned. "Don't bring Corazon down here."

Which meant the problem was Leander Arden. "On my way."

Sofia's platinum necklace incorporated a hidden handcuff key, and she'd already released Corazon. Rafael held his sister in his arms, and although Black was desperate to meet his niece, he knew that had to wait. Sofia was on hand to offer assistance, and probably better equipped to do so given the circumstances.

Black jogged through the house, past the writhing body of one guard who he silenced with a swift kick to the balls, until he found the stairs to the basement. Cora had been right when she described it as a dungeon. BDSM toys lined the walls, and at the far end, Emmy and Ana stood over a body tied to a padded bench. Even in the dim light, it was obvious the man had been badly beaten. His mottled skin matched the blood-red walls and the dark purple carpet.

"Is he alive?"

Emmy looked up. "Breathing, but barely."

"Unconscious?"

"Drifting in and out. Where's Fia? He needs drugs."

He needed more than fucking drugs. Yeah, it was probably time to call the emergency services and Special Agent Childs. He could assist with clearing up the mess since he'd helped to create it by ignoring the systematic abuse of at least fifteen young women for months. Black would also have to call in a favour or two to make the small matter of Rafael's escape from custody go away, but why bother banking them if he didn't cash a few in occasionally?

He patched through to the control room in Virginia, where Mack had been listening to the raid.

"We need an ambulance dispatched to this location. Also state police and the FBI."

"On their way."

"Nate, can you check that laptop before they arrive?"

"Doing that right now. It's fucked."

"Check the desk for backups."

"Already did. Nada. But we've got seven women locked in rooms upstairs." A pause. "Make that six. One of them seems to have escaped."

"For fuck's sake, go after her."

"Sofia's already doing that. Hey, now they're wrestling on the lawn. People would pay good money to watch this."

"Just get her back in the damn house."

Black walked closer to the scene at the far end of the room, blocking out the chatter on the radio. So, this was Leander Arden? He barely even looked human. Angry welts covered his chest, and snot mixed with blood bubbled from his nose. Both arms had been stretched above his head and tied to the bench, but one was at a strange angle. A dislocated shoulder? All of Blackwood's people carried basic first aid kits on jobs like this, but it was difficult to know where to start. How much damage had been done on the inside?

The sound of sobbing came over the radio. Corazon,

or the other woman?

"Any update on Leander?" Rafael asked.

"Not good. Emmy's right. Keep Corazon away."

Sofia appeared moments later with her top ripped down the middle and grass stains on her face.

"Did you have fun?" Black asked.

"Don't you dare say anything."

The girls began cutting Leander free, sawing carefully through the ropes around his wrists and ankles. Sofia gave him something to ease the pain, but none of them were stupid enough to try moving him. Since the enemy had been neutralised, they could leave that to the professionals when they arrived with a spinal board.

While they waited for the cavalry, Black made a quick search of the house for anything useful, but like Radcliffe's, the place was clean. Usually, a place this size would be a treasure trove of evidence and papers— terrorists in particular were fond of writing things down—but the most he found was a handful of receipts for electrical goods and work to the house, and a grocery list. A quick chat with the guards revealed nothing of note either. Whoever The Banker was, his fetish for privacy had been well implemented.

"I've copied Nevin's phone," Nate said as the first sirens sounded in the distance. "Time for Rafael to make himself scarce."

"And Ana," Black said. She always liked to keep a low profile.

"You go to the hospital with Emmy, and I'll stay here with Sofia."

"Are you sure?"

A world of shit was about to be unleashed in this

house, and Black hated to dump that in his friend's lap, even though he and Fia were more than capable of dealing with it.

"We're sure," Fia said. "Even if Corazon doesn't know who you are yet, she should still have family with her."

Family. According to the monitor in his wristwatch, Black's pulse had stayed under one-twenty all the way through the raid, but now it sped up as an unfamiliar sensation of nervousness flickered through him. What would Corazon say when she found out he was her uncle? And how would she cope when she realised the man she so obviously cared for had been badly injured?

CHAPTER 41 - CORA

I LOST TRACK of time as I held onto my brother. The man who'd come with him vanished, replaced by a second who looked equally tough but slightly shorter and not quite so cold. Other strangers moved back and forth, talking quietly, but my ears still rang from the gunshot that had made me jump out of my skin.

"Are you hurt?" Rafe asked. "Is any of this blood yours?"

Blood? I pressed my fingers against my neck, to the spot where Nevin had jammed the knife in, but instead of the tiny trickle I'd imagined, my whole hand came away red and sticky. As my brain caught up with my racing heart, I realised it wasn't my blood but Nevin's, and I puked up the contents of my guts before I could stop myself. Then I kicked him in the balls. Yes, I realised he was dead—half of his head was missing— but it still felt good.

Shouting came from outside, and the dark-haired girl who'd just jumped out the window came back into view with her arms wrapped around a struggling Mercy.

"It's okay," I shouted. "She's here to help us."

At least, I thought she was since she came with my brother.

Mercy stilled long enough for the woman to lift her

back inside, and her eyes widened when she saw Nevin. Then she kicked him in the testicles too. The man standing with my brother rolled his eyes.

"I think we get the message, ladies."

"Who are these people?" Mercy asked me.

"Uh, I'm not totally sure." I pointed at Rafe. "But this is my brother."

"He shot Nevin?"

"No, I think it was..." I turned towards the dark-haired girl, only to find she'd vanished. My thoughts were jerky, disjointed, but as more awareness filtered back in, I suddenly realised who else was missing. "Where's Leandro? Nevin did something to him, and... and...I need to find him."

I tried to run out of the room, but Rafe pulled me back again.

"Stay here."

"But—"

"He's downstairs. People are with him."

"Is he...? Is he...?"

Tears welled up, and I fought against them. Leandro couldn't be dead. He *couldn't* be. He'd been alive half an hour ago, because when I'd denied everything and hypothesised that Radcliffe might also have been an FBI snitch, Nevin had sent one of his henchmen to ask Leandro if that was true.

"He's alive," the other man said. "But I'll be honest —it's not good. Rafael, you need to get out of here before the cops arrive."

"Why?" I asked. Then I realised. "So it *was* you who kidnapped a policewoman?"

The other guy laughed. He actually laughed.

"It's not funny."

"Oh, but it is. Your brother tried to hold my friend's wife hostage, and he ended up duct-taped to a weight bench."

"Is this true?" I asked.

Rafe scowled. "You were right. It wasn't fucking funny."

"We'll discuss this later," the guy said. "Get out of here, and take Ana with you."

"Who's Ana?"

"Later."

Rafe pointed Mercy and me to a still-damp sofa, and we sat together as the house became an official crime scene. Cops, EMTs, and even a fire truck turned up. Although there were people everywhere, most of them were unfamiliar, and I'd never felt so alone.

"What do you think's gonna happen?" Mercy whispered. "Will they arrest us?"

"I have no idea, but we haven't done anything wrong. We didn't abduct ourselves from Colombia, did we? How did you get out of your room?"

"Picked the lock with a couple of bobby pins. That's how I escaped the first time too, but then they brought in those electronic cards."

A commotion in the hallway made me swivel towards the door as a team of medics shuffled past, carrying a body on a stretcher. A cop walked behind, holding up a bag of fluids for the IV line running into the man's arm, and I realised who it was. *Leander*.

I scrambled to my feet. Not because I wanted to see his broken body, but because I couldn't stay away.

"*Ay, dios mio.*" The words slipped out at the same time as my tears.

A blanket covered Leander's torso, and if it was half

as bad as his face, I was glad I couldn't see it. His lip was split open, his nose was unmistakably broken, and everything just looked...wonky. Asymmetrical. What other damage lurked beneath the swelling?

"Hey, hey. You shouldn't be here," a blonde woman said.

"I'm not leaving him. He's my..." What was Leander to me? My saviour. My confidant. The man I wanted to eat dinner with and wake up next to in the morning. The man who treated me as though I meant something and sent hot flashes through me even in the most awkward of circumstances. "He's my friend."

The blonde sighed. "Fine. Ride with us to the hospital, but you'll have to promise to keep out of the way."

A policeman stopped beside us. "These ladies can't go anywhere. They're witnesses."

"Uh..."

Before I could form a sentence, the blonde took over. "Witnesses who need medical attention. Do you want to be held responsible if they suffer complications?"

I clutched at my stomach. "Nevin kicked me. I keep getting this shooting pain."

In reality, I was okay apart from a handful of bruises. When Nevin began his interrogation, I'd played innocent and said I didn't have a clue that Leander was an FBI agent, and Nevin seemed unsure whether to force a confession out of me or keep me nice and tidy for clients. Rafael had arrived faster than I ever dreamed he would, although it was still too late for Leander.

Mercy joined in with the charade. "It hurts when I

breathe."

"See?" the blonde said. "You've got seven incapacitated guards, six more girls, and one dead body to deal with, so I suggest you go and do that." When he didn't move, she made a flicking motion with her wrist. "Off you trot."

"And who are *you*?"

"Somebody you'll regret annoying. If you want more details, you'll have to talk to your boss."

She sounded so sure, so confident, and so *British*. The officer backed away slowly, clearly unhappy but unsure what to do about it. The blonde just ignored him. Asshole: dismissed.

"Hi, I'm Emmy. You're Corazon, right?"

"Yes."

Emmy lowered her voice. "Okay, here's the deal. The cops have got a bunch of questions about the mess we just made, and we don't particularly want to answer them. We can make all the questions go away, but it's gonna take a few phone calls. So in the meantime, don't speak to anyone."

Leander was almost at the door now, and I didn't want to get left behind. "Okay, I'll keep my mouth shut."

"I won't talk either," Mercy said.

"This isn't a bloody field trip," Emmy told her. "You need to stay here."

The last of the confidence Mercy wore as a mask faded away, and her lip quivered. Leaving her on her own would be cruel.

"She's coming. I need some moral support, okay?"

Emmy rolled her eyes. "Fine. Who is she, anyway?"

"Mercedes. Mercy."

"She's from Colombia too?"

"Yes."

Outside, we watched as the EMTs loaded Leander into a waiting ambulance. He still hadn't talked or even moved, and I felt more scared then than at any other point since I left Colombia.

"Do you think he'll be okay?" I asked Emmy.

Her hesitation told me everything I needed to know. "We'll ensure he gets the best medical care available."

"Don't cry," Mercy said, wiping away my tears with a sleeve. "He must be a fighter if he's survived this far."

He was. But would it be enough?

The man who'd talked to Nevin opened the back door of a black SUV and ushered Mercy and me inside. Up close, I realised how huge he was—the same height as my brother, but bulkier. Usually, I felt big and awkward beside men, not dainty and pretty like so many other girls, but I felt almost small beside him.

"This is Black," Emmy said. "My husband."

Well, married life sure must be interesting for them.

Black spent most of the trip on the phone in the passenger seat, talking softly, while I gripped Mercy's hand. Not just because of the Leander situation, but also because Emmy drove like a lunatic. Amazingly, we beat the ambulance to the hospital, and a doctor came out to meet Black right after we abandoned the car at the entrance.

"Joseph Chen. I head up the emergency room here. Colin Beech called to warn me you were coming."

"Dr. Beech works at our local hospital in Virginia," Emmy whispered.

"Good," Black said. "Then you'll understand that the patient who's about to arrive gets the best care you can offer, no matter what the cost. We'd also like his room kept clear of anyone but our people, and this lady..." He pointed at me. "Wants to stay with him."

"Absolutely." Dr. Chen bobbed his head. "We can do that. Let me show you inside."

Leander arrived two minutes later, and the EMTs transferred him from stretcher to bed with practised efficiency. The doctors' voices stayed quiet, calm, but there was no mistaking the underlying urgency in their tones.

I buried my face in Mercy's shoulder when they unwrapped Leander. His body was purple. Freaking purple. Words like *broken ribs*, *fractured cheekbone*, *elevated heart rate*, and *internal bleeding* drifted across, but it wasn't until someone mentioned a scan that he moved, coughing and choking as two nurses tried to hold him still.

"Is he trying to speak?" one of them asked.

I couldn't help it; I pushed my way through. "It's okay. They're trying to help you."

His eyes were swollen shut, but his lips moved. "No... No scan."

"Is he claustrophobic?" a doctor asked.

"I don't think so. Leander, the scan will help."

I longed to offer some comfort, but I couldn't squeeze his hand or give him a hug or even kiss him without causing more pain. I traced my thumb along his palm, and he hooked one finger around it.

"No scan. I... I..." He began coughing again.

"Is there any water? Can someone get him water?"

A beaker with a straw appeared, and I helped

Leander to take a sip. Swallowing made him wince in pain, but he kept drinking despite that. Finally, he spoke again.

"I swallowed the evidence. A flash drive. No scan."

Black stepped forward. "Did I hear that right? You swallowed a flash drive with evidence on it?"

Leander nodded then groaned. "Files from the laptop."

Emmy gave a low whistle from behind me. "Holy shit."

So a scan would damage the flash drive? My first instinct was to insist Leander have the scan if he needed it, but what if the files could tell us where Izzy was?

"Mercy, was there ever a girl called Isabella at Nevin's place?"

"How did you know? She left last month."

"Do you know where she went?"

Mercy shook her head. "Girls disappeared all the time, but Nevin never told us what happened to them. One evening Isabella was there, and the next morning, she'd gone."

Black understood my dilemma. "A magnetic field will damage the flash drive, so we can't use an MRI scan. But a CAT scan will be fine, as will ultrasound and regular X-rays. Can you make do with those?"

Dr. Chen nodded. "That should be enough. We're concerned about his spleen. It feels enlarged."

"What about the flash drive?" I asked. "How do we get that out?"

"It should pass through in a few days."

Oh. Yuck. Leander groaned again.

"You need to move back now," Dr. Chen said. "Let

us look after him."

I did as he said and retreated to the corner with Mercy. A nurse brought us chairs, and I chewed so much skin off my bottom lip that it started bleeding as the doctors performed a barrage of tests, conferred amongst themselves, then wheeled Leander into the operating theatre for emergency surgery to fix his ruptured spleen.

"You really like him, don't you?" Emmy asked as we waited.

"Is that crazy? My feelings are all over the place right now."

"Sometimes you just know."

"He hated it in there. Having to stand there and do nothing while the clients and the other guards..." I screwed my eyes shut because I didn't want to discuss the details. "He said he was quitting his job when it was over."

"From what I've heard, his boss is a dick."

"He said that too. This is all such a mess, isn't it? Did my brother tell you the whole story?"

"Pretty much. We'll find Isabella, don't worry."

"How did you meet Rafe?"

"That's an even longer story, but it's not mine to tell. We'll talk about that later. Do you want anything to eat or drink? I'll get someone to bring you both fresh clothes."

I still had my freaking pyjamas on, and Mercy was in sportswear. Funny how low my appearance came on my list of priorities when I realised there were more important things to worry about. But I was getting cold, and I shivered involuntarily.

"Thank you."

Relying on the kindness of strangers was also a foreign concept. In Colombia, my tiny family had spent years fending for ourselves through one crisis after another. In America, everyone from Hallie to Mercy to Emmy to Leander had helped us, and it was oddly comforting to have people on our side.

Two hours passed, and I was dozing through exhaustion alongside Mercy when a brunette who looked a year or so younger than me appeared with a bulging suitcase and hugged Emmy. I snuck a quick glance at her, then pretended to be asleep because the last thing I wanted to do was speak to another visitor today. Not while Leander was still in surgery.

But I felt her eyes on me, assessing.

"Wow. I see the resemblance."

"Shh. She doesn't know yet."

The resemblance to who? Rafael? What didn't I know?

"Oops. Bradley's freaking out because the builders installed the wrong handrails in one of the bathrooms, so I got Brett to bring me in the helicopter. How much of this stuff do you want here? I brought four changes of clothes each for the three of you. Most of the outfits for the other two girls are stretchy, so they should fit."

"Leave it all. Did someone organise a hotel?"

"We've booked a block of six rooms nearby. Do we need more? I've already left clothes for everyone else there."

"Me and Black. Nate. Rafael. Fia. Corazon. Mercy, maybe. That's six. Cruz and Alaric are on their way back to Florida, and Ana'll fly to Riverley with you."

"Ana? Great."

"She's not that bad."

"What about the other girls?"

"The police have taken responsibility for them."

"And the Colombian people in Florida?"

"I haven't discussed it with Black yet, but we'll probably take them directly to Virginia."

"Okay. I'd better head back and help. Bradley says he needs another assistant, by the way."

"He *is* the assistant." Emmy paused. "But everything's been so busy lately, I guess I can see his point. We should look for someone else."

"I'll tell him. When are you coming back?"

"Not sure. A day or two? I'll call you later."

Clothing rustled as they hugged again, and I was careful to keep my eyes closed. Who were all those people? This adventure threatened to overwhelm me. Feigning sleep was definitely the best option. If only I could do that forever, life would be so much simpler.

At least until Leander came back, still unconscious as a pair of orderlies wheeled his bed into place. A heart monitor beeped steadily at his side, and I took comfort in the fact that he'd made it this far.

"The spleen repair went well," Dr. Chen told us. "And we've popped his shoulder back into place. Your boyfriend's also got a fractured cheekbone, three cracked ribs, and a broken finger. Amazing there wasn't more damage when you look at the state of him."

Joder. If Nevin hadn't been dead, I'd have killed him myself and taken pleasure in it. And I didn't bother to correct the doctor about his assumption regarding our relationship status. Leander might not have been my boyfriend, but I kind of hoped he wanted the job when he woke up.

"What do we do now?" I asked.

"Now, we wait."

CHAPTER 42 - CORA

"I CAN'T BELIEVE you're still here."

Those were Leander's first words when he woke earlier this morning, and I'd just stared at him.

"Shouldn't that be my line?"

"Or have I died and gone to heaven?" He lifted his head an inch and looked at all the tubes sprouting from his body. "Nope. I'd be better dressed in heaven."

"Try something less cheesy."

Leander tried to laugh, but his face quickly screwed up in pain. The doctors said he was on the road to recovery, but he'd only mumbled when he opened his eyes last night, then he slept for eight hours straight. Me? I'd dozed for two or three uncomfortable hours in the chair beside his bed, and now I leaned forward in my seat and took his hand.

"Just rest, okay. I'm not going anywhere. And I guess I should call you Lee now?"

That earned me a weak smile. "Definitely."

Before Lee could close his eyes, Black stepped forward with a few questions, and Lee's answers made me realise how selflessly he'd acted. He'd been willing to give up his own life for Izzy, a girl he'd never even met. That was the moment I realised I loved him, and the feeling hit me so hard I barely heard the rest of the conversation.

I loved Lee.

Now what the hell did I do? We hardly knew each other. Our only kiss had happened under duress. We lived on different continents, not to mention the small matter of him being sworn to uphold the law while my brother killed people for a living. But I loved him. Even if we had no future together, I loved him.

And I was confused as hell. Watching him rest for another hour did nothing to help.

"Cora?"

"Huh?"

My brother looked down at me, one eyebrow raised. "Are you okay?"

"Uh, totally fine. Did you say something?"

"I said, I have to go with Black. Emmy's staying." He glared at Lee. "Don't say anything to him or anyone else from the FBI."

When the door clicked closed behind Rafael and Black, Lee slumped back against the pillow and groaned.

"Your brother hates me."

Yes, unfortunately it seemed that way. "Rafael doesn't like many people."

Emmy pushed off the far wall where she'd been standing for the past forty minutes. Rafe had given me his watch, and now I couldn't stop looking at it.

"Don't take it personally," she said to Lee. "He's not keen on me either."

"But my actions hurt his sister."

"Well, I imprisoned him in my friend's basement and poured vodka into his bullet wound."

My mouth dropped open. "You did *what*?"

"He tried to kill my stepfather. It was justified.

Look, the point I'm trying to make is that a whole bunch of very different people have been slammed together to work on this job, and some of us have conflicting motivations. Yes, there was animosity between me and your brother to start with, but we've called a truce because we share common goals. Leander, you share those goals too. You proved it with your actions yesterday."

"Freeing the girls and catching The Banker? Yes."

"Too bad your boss doesn't think the same way."

"Ex-boss. I'll write my resignation letter as soon as I can hold a pen."

"You can probably tell him in person. He's been terrorising the receptionist for the last half hour. The doctor told him you were still unconscious."

"The doctor's willing to lie like that?"

"He is when you've just donated fifty thousand dollars towards a new teenage eating disorder clinic. Dr. Chen's sister suffers from anorexia, so it's a cause close to his heart."

"You think he can pretend for a few more days? Then I might feel well enough to sneak out the fire exit."

"And go where?" I asked. "Don't you live in Florida?"

"Near Miami." Lee closed his eyes, looking frailer by the second. "On second thought, dying's a good option right now."

"You don't seem to hold a very high opinion of Merrick Childs," Emmy said.

"When I first got picked for his task force, I was so damn happy. I saw all the hurt The Banker facilitated, and I thought I could make a real difference in the world, but Childs is only in it for himself. He wants to be director of the FBI one day, and he needs a big-name case."

"He won't get it."

"Does he know about the flash drive?"

"What flash drive?"

Lee squeezed my hand, weakly, but it was a start.

"Thank goodness. You're from Blackwood Security too?"

Emmy nodded. Lee and Black must have discussed that when I zoned out earlier.

"I'm not a wealthy man, but I have some savings. Could I hire you to look for Corazon's friend? With whatever's on that flash drive, you might be able to find her."

"We're already looking for her, and we don't need your money."

"Why?"

"Why what?"

"Why are you already looking for her? Don't you people usually charge the big bucks?"

"We also do some pro bono work." Emmy sighed. "Okay, our involvement is a fairly epic tale. We started off working one case and ended up in the middle of this mess instead. All will become clear later, but first, we have to get you out of here."

"I was only kidding about the fire exit. My gut feels like it's been hit by a semi."

"Dr. Chen will be here soon to check you over, then we plan to transport you to Richmond. We've got a bed waiting for you in the hospital there."

The way Emmy spoke, Lee didn't get much say in the matter.

"Why Richmond?" I asked.

"Like I said, we'll explain later. Just trust me, okay?"

Did I trust her? I trusted my brother, and he seemed to be on board with Blackwood's plans, plus I didn't want to be around when Lee's boss arrived because I'd probably get arrested for assault.

"Can I come to Richmond too?"

Emmy smiled. "Our housekeeper's already got a room waiting for you."

CHAPTER 43 - BLACK

"WHAT DO WE have?" Black asked.

Mercy had offered to bunk in with Corazon, which gave them a spare hotel room to use as a temporary command post. Nate had set up a trio of laptops on the desk and rigged up a projector to turn one white wall into a giant link chart, although there was precious little on it so far.

"We don't have a whole lot," Nate said. "The contents of Nevin's phone. No surprises that most of the contacts are unregistered and half of their devices are turned off. Security videos from both houses. I copied the contents of the hard drive Nevin's surveillance system used before the FBI arrived and confiscated it."

"So we can trace the clients, but the FBI will be doing the same thing. And they already know who the clients at Radcliffe's were because the fuckers were watching the place."

"Yup. There has to be a link to The Banker somewhere."

"On that memory stick."

"What are the chances of recovering the data after it's been through a colon?"

They hadn't yet discussed who would do the physical processing, but Black was quite sure it wouldn't be him. That job gave a whole new meaning to the phrase "getting your hands dirty."

"It's doubtful the memory stick itself will function, but we should be able to transfer the chip to a new shell. Agatha's testing the process as we speak."

Ah, Agatha. The new girl. Well, everybody had to start somewhere.

"That could take days," Rafael said. "What if The Banker runs again?"

"At the moment, it's unlikely he knows Arden stole the data. That gives us a day or two."

"Couldn't we give Arden laxatives? Get it out faster?"

"Do you want to explain to your sister why her boyfriend, who's currently recovering from major surgery, is shitting his guts out on the toilet?"

"Boyfriend? Corazon's judgement is impaired right now."

"Because of her choice in men?"

"You don't agree?"

No, Black didn't. He'd been in the hospital when Arden woke up after surgery early this morning, and he'd seen the way the man looked at Corazon. And when Black asked why he'd swallowed the flash drive, Arden had struggled to drag his eyes away from her to answer.

"The data was almost copied when I heard movement outside," he'd said. "I had the choice of finishing what I started or getting the hell out of there, but I realised if I left, Corazon might never find her friend. Since I'd given Cora a phone, I knew help was coming, and I figured someone would find the memory stick during my autopsy."

Yeah, he'd basically sacrificed himself to save Isabella, so Black had to give the man kudos for that. And thanks to Alaric, Black understood what an utter asshole Merrick Childs was. No doubt he'd ordered Arden to stand by while the girls got abused, putting the man in an impossible position.

Rafael tended to judge people on instinct, but in Black's view, those instincts still needed honing. His nephew was young and malleable. By his age, Black had already spent six years in the Navy and two with the CIA, which had done wonders for his evaluation skills. Rafael had been trained to shoot straight and dodge bullets, but finesse and social skills had passed him by.

Fia skipped in, still worryingly happy. Black wanted to suggest she start taking her meds again, but he also didn't want to end up dead.

"Happy Christmas."

She tossed him something small and black, and he caught it before realising it was a flash drive.

"Tell me this isn't…"

"From Leander's ass? No. It's the photos from that party. My contact just delivered them."

"The Banker?"

"Let's take a look, shall we?"

Most of Fia's pictures homed in on two men—her targets, but not Blackwood's. But they did find a couple of photos of The Banker, and both were clearer than the FBI's. Which put them one step ahead. Why did that matter so much? Because Black had plans for the man who'd put his niece through hell, and they didn't involve arrest followed by a long, drawn-out trial.

Nate projected the pictures on the wall, twice life-size, and Black took a better look. The Banker was slim with fine features, almost dainty. Blue eyes. Nondescript. The kind of man you walked past in the street without a second glance. The only thing of note was the tattoo under his left pectoral—a mathematical formula. Black snapped a picture and sent it to Lara, the girlfriend of a colleague and a lady who knew far more about math than he ever would.

Black: Any idea what this means?

The answer came back seconds later.

Lara: It's basic trigonometry, and it's also a mathematical joke. tan c over sin c = sec c = sexy.

What kind of asshole had that tattooed on his chest?

Someone knocked softly on the door, and Black checked through the peephole. Mercy, carrying a tray of drinks from the coffee place next door. She'd offered to run errands, even though she was clearly nervous about leaving the hotel, so Black had sent her somewhere easy as a way of getting her to take that first step back into the world.

"Four black coffees. Rafael's has sugar."

The boy needed to ease up on the junk food if he wanted to go to the next level, although Emmy still snuck shit into her diet whenever possible.

"Thanks. You feeling okay?"

Mercy bobbed her head. "I thought going out would be worse than it was. Uh, why do you have a picture of Dirk on the screen?"

"You know him?"

"I don't *know* him exactly, but he was one of Nevin's clients." She pointed at the tattoo. "But this must be an old picture because he had that removed a year ago. He said he got it for a bet when he was at college, but I never understood what it meant."

Could this be the missing piece of the puzzle?

"You're sure it's the same man?"

"I think so. His chin's different—he has a dimple now—and his nose is straighter, but apart from that, it's Dirk. I'm sure he's a cosmetic surgery addict. If you're up close, you can see the scars behind his ears."

"Nate, is there a Dirk in Nevin's contacts?"

"Two seconds... Yes. There is."

"Is the phone turned on?"

"It is at the moment. Located fifteen miles from here, a little way inland. Looks like a housing development. Do you think that's him?"

"Only one way to find out, isn't there?"

Records showed one occupant living at the spacious detached home near Wrightsville Beach, and that occupant was a woman named Dinah Weaver. She'd bought the place seven years ago, just before The Banker supposedly died in the fire. An exit strategy?

"Do you think she's been hiding him all this time?" Rafael asked.

"Possibly," Black said. "But who is she? A relative? A lover? Someone he's paid a fuck-ton of money to? Nate, do we know how old she is?"

"Fifty-two, according to the DMV."

Weaver's driver's licence appeared on the wall. She wore her light brown hair short with bangs falling over her forehead, and her glasses might have been fashionable in the nineties, but she'd only learned to drive eight years ago. Brown eyes. Straight nose.

Cheeks that looked puffy like a hamster and out of proportion with the rest of her face, and a mole beside her nose. Plus a dimple in her chin.

Hmm...

Mack had back doors into the networks of more corporations than Black wanted to know about, and before long, they knew Dinah Weaver paid her utility bills on time, ordered sushi twice a week, enjoyed cable TV, and recently installed a new home gym. Oh, and she bought a lot of wigs.

"Can you put one of the pictures Sofia took of The Banker up next to the one of Weaver?"

Nate complied, and Black stared at the two. Weaver's eyes were brown instead of blue, and she had fuller lips, but apart from the cheeks and the dimple, the underlying facial structure was the same. Strip away the hair and the glasses and the mole, and they already knew Dirk had changed his chin...

"It's the same person."

"You think? Her face is a different shape. Fatter."

"All she'd have to do is stuff something into her mouth. Silicone pads, probably. Dermal filler for the lips. Coloured contacts. Look at the distance between the pupils, the proportions of the eyes to the nose to the mouth. Things it would be difficult for him to change."

Mercy tentatively stepped forward. The girl was a contradiction—when she felt threatened, she put on a confident front, but that was all it was: a front. Underneath, she was as broken and vulnerable as they came. Whatever happened after this, Black knew they wouldn't simply be packing Mercy off back to Colombia. She needed support, and they'd give it to her.

"I also think it's Dirk," she said. "He had fatter lips when I first met him, like hers."

No wonder the FBI hadn't found The Banker. They'd been looking for a man with balls, not a coward who abused women as a hobby while living as one himself.

But Blackwood had found the fucker. Now they just needed to work out what to do with him.

With Rosie back to full working order after a hasty wing repair, Nate hunkered down in the back of the Porsche to take a look at Dinah Weaver's house and its grounds while Sofia jogged around the neighbourhood with Emmy. Mercy had traded places with Black's wife at the hospital so Cora wasn't alone, and two men from Blackwood's executive protection division had driven down from Raleigh to stand guard outside Leander's room.

And when Rosie's feed popped up on the monitor in the hotel room, it became immediately obvious they had a problem.

One, two, three suitcases stood in a row by the front door, and in an upstairs bedroom, The Banker paced while he spoke on the phone, wearing a knee-length floral shift dress and high-heeled pumps. He actually had quite a good figure, but he'd need to shave his stubble before he left the house.

"Mack, can you find out who he's speaking to?"

"Give me two minutes…"

The asshole was getting ready to run, that much was clear. But where to? He finished his call, then opened a safe built into his bedroom wall. A thick white envelope, stacks of cash, a laptop—it all went into a briefcase. Nate flew Rosie around the rest of the windows, and the house wasn't much of a home. If Black were a betting man, which let's face it, he was, he'd put a thousand bucks on The Banker having another similar bolthole lined up after this one. Once he left, they might never find him.

"He called Prestige Limousines in Wilmington," Mack said. "Call lasted six minutes and twelve seconds."

If he wasn't taking a car of his own, that suggested he was going to fly somewhere, but they had no idea what name he'd be using. Which meant the most efficient strategy would be to stop him from reaching · the airport.

Black didn't hesitate, just picked up his phone and dialled. "Ortiz, this is Charles Black. I need to speak to the smaller of the two women in Leander Arden's room."

The bodyguard from Raleigh put him through right away.

"*Hola?*"

"Mercy, we may have found our man, but I need to know how he spoke. Did Dirk have an accent?"

"Did you ever see the movie *American Psycho*?"

"He sounded like Patrick Bateman?"

"No, he behaved like Bateman, but he spoke more like Evelyn."

"Bateman's fiancée? He spoke like a woman?"

"*Sí*, his voice was sort of high pitched."

Well, that certainly made things easier. Who should he use for the next part? Emmy was too British, Mack too southern, Ana too Russian, and Dan too New York. Black's next call was to Sofia.

"Our target's just called a limo company. I need you to find out where he's going and when he's leaving, and delay the car."

"We're going to intercept him?"

"That's the plan."

"Send me the number."

"On its way. According to Mercy, he sounds like Evelyn in *American Psycho*."

"He talks like a girl? I bet that didn't cause him any issues growing up whatsoever."

Weaver's issues ran far deeper than a feminine voice. Black may have understood his career choice—understood it, but not condoned it—because greed clouded the judgement of many men. The Banker wouldn't be the first to succumb to the lure of money. But the women? Weaver was sick to his rotten fucking core.

Why did he feel the need to lock them up like that? Like animals? Black didn't know, but he'd take pleasure in asking that very question later.

But first, they had to catch the man, and they were so fucking close Black could taste his fetid blood. He paced the soulless hotel room in a manner reminiscent of The Banker himself, minus the pumps, of course, until Sofia called back five minutes later.

"The car was due to pick Dinah up at three thirty this afternoon. I've moved the booking to tomorrow, and now Dylan at the limo company thinks I'm an idiot who doesn't know what day it is."

"They'll think you're even more of an idiot tomorrow when their driver turns up and you're not there."

"Thanks. That makes me feel so much better."

Two hours. They had two hours. Time to call Mr. Fix-it.

"Bradley, I don't care what strings you have to pull, but I need a town car at the hotel within an hour. No driver, but I need a chauffeur's hat."

"Is this for some undercover thing?"

"Yes."

"OMG! This is so exciting!"

"Just find me a car, Bradley."

He did, because irritating though Bradley may sometimes be, he was also a genius when it came to organising the shit out of things. The Mercedes S-Class even had an entertainment system and a fully stocked minibar. Black tried the peaked cap on in front of the mirror and practised slouching just as Emmy and Sofia walked in.

"Hi, honey. We're home."

"Just in time. You both need to change into something that'll hide your guns."

Rafael watched silently from his spot beside the window. He'd wanted to be involved with the capture, but Black had vetoed that idea. Not only was Rafael operating in an unfamiliar country and wanted for murder, he was also angry, even more so now he'd found out what The Banker had done to his sister.

Black was angry too, but he'd long since learned how to lock the heat away and channel his emotions into cold fury. Rafael was still full of fire, and today, Black needed a cool head alongside him. Two, even— Emmy and Sofia.

Weaver barely gave him a second glance when he

pulled up outside the soon-to-be-abandoned house and beeped the horn. The front door opened almost immediately and Dinah emerged, freshly shaved and wearing immaculate make-up.

"Let me take those bags, ma'am," Black said.

"Thank you. I'll keep the small one with me."

Important, was it? They'd find out soon enough. Black squeezed the three cases into the trunk, slammed the lid, and took his place behind the wheel. In the back, Weaver sat stiffly, fiddling with his phone.

"There was a smash on Route 74 earlier, but it's clear now. Don't worry, I'll get you to your destination in plenty of time. Are you flying for business or pleasure?"

"Business."

"Must be nice to see the world. Going somewhere hot?"

"I'm paying you to drive, not have a conversation."

That was okay. They could talk later. Black paused for the stop sign at the end of the road, and with impeccable timing, Emmy and Sofia materialised, one each side of the car, and slid into the back with Weaver.

The fucker hardly had time to breathe—let alone speak—before Sofia jabbed the needle into his neck, and Black allowed himself a rare smile as he set the satnav for Richmond. One more task checked off the list, and they'd make it home in time for dinner.

CHAPTER 44 - CORA

EMMY LEFT THE hospital in the morning, and Mercy came to keep me company while Lee slept. Slept and healed. His bruises were already starting to turn from angry red and purple to blackish brown, although they still looked just as painful.

That same pain was reflected in Mercy's eyes.

"I can't believe it's over," she whispered.

"It isn't. Not until we find Izzy."

"I'm so sorry. I meant—"

"It's okay, I know what you meant." I wrapped an arm around her shoulders. All the confidence Mercy first showed in the house had vanished, leaving behind a scared young woman. "And we're close to the end. I'm sure we are. Have you..." I nearly asked whether she'd spoken to her family, but then I remembered she didn't have any. "Have you thought about what you're going to do now?"

"I don't even know how I'll get back to Colombia."

"We'll help. Me, my brother, Leander, all the other people involved in this. You're not alone."

Mercy's eyes glistened with tears, and when she tried to blink them back, they cascaded down her cheeks.

"Hey, it's okay. I mean it. We're here for you."

"I get that it sounds crazy, and I know Nevin was a

freak, but being in that house was the first time I'd ever fitted in. I hated the men, but the girls... It was almost like having friends."

"What about when you were growing up?"

Silence.

"Mercy? I won't judge; I promise."

How could I with my dysfunctional family?

"When I was six, my mama killed her boyfriend and went to prison. The other kids were horrible afterwards, especially when I ate to make myself feel better. Then in high school, the boys made jokes about me squashing them to death, so I just stopped going."

"Who brought you up?"

"I lived in an orphanage in Bogotá. The people who ran it were nice, but so busy, and..." She gulped back more sobs. "I just wanted to be normal, you know?"

"But you changed. How did you get to Medellín?"

"Once I hit eighteen, I got emancipated from the welfare system, so I moved to Medellín for a fresh start. I lost weight quite quickly when I couldn't afford food."

Lee held out a hand as far as he could. "Hey, sweetheart, don't cry. We'll all do whatever it takes to get you back on your feet."

"I don't even know where to start. Since I wasn't there to pay rent, the landlord will have emptied my apartment."

"My family has an apartment in Medellín. It's only small, but you can borrow the sofa until we work out a better solution."

Or maybe she could take my bed, because my heart was begging to stay near Lee. He'd said he liked me, but how much? Enough that he'd want me to stick around in the United States for a while to see if we had a future together?

I wasn't sure how to broach that subject, but I didn't get a chance to because Dr. Chen came back to check Lee over.

"How do you feel?" he asked.

"Weirdly happy."

"Did the nurse adjust your painkillers?"

Lee flicked his gaze in my direction. "I think that's part of it. Somebody mentioned a possibility of me being moved to Richmond?"

"When you're ready. You had laparoscopic surgery on your spleen, but the incision was tiny, so the recovery time isn't as long as it could be. In fact, I bet your ribs hurt more."

"Right."

"Your vitals are as they should be, and if there aren't any setbacks, you should be able to travel tomorrow. I take it you don't want me to mention your improvement to the gentleman haranguing the staff in reception?"

"I'd appreciate if you didn't."

"My lips are sealed."

Our plane took off for a private airfield near Richmond just before nine o'clock the next morning. Rafael had materialised in Lee's hospital room two hours previously, along with a man I recognised from Nevin's place.

"Cora, this is Nate Wood. We've been working together." Another person from Blackwood? "Are you ready to go?"

"Go where? To Virginia?"

"Yes."

"Merrick Childs is getting twitchy," Nate said. "He's on his way through here as we speak."

Dr. Chen himself accompanied us to the airport. A fully equipped air ambulance waited on the tarmac, and as we boarded, it felt like the beginning of a new chapter. I had no idea what awaited me in Virginia, or even why Rafael wanted to go there rather than back to Colombia, but as long as I was with Lee, I bit back any difficult questions. At the moment, I was a passenger in my own life, hanging on by my fingertips until the ride slowed down.

Rafe's confidence held my nerves together as the plane roared along the runway, and he flashed a smile as the wheels lifted off the ground. What did Virginia have in store for us?

"I want to stay here with Leander."

I'd stayed overnight with him at the hospital in North Carolina. Why was it such a problem in Richmond?

"Cora, we need to talk."

I froze at Rafe's tone. He always sounded serious, but now he sounded *intense*.

"Why? What's wrong?"

"Nothing's wrong. It's just...big."

Lee squeezed my hand, ignoring Rafe's glower, and because Rafe needed to lighten up and also because I wanted to, I leaned down to press a kiss to the corner of Lee's lips.

"I'll come back first thing tomorrow morning."

"Not going anywhere, bee."

Rafe hadn't been kidding about *big*. When we pulled up outside Riverley Hall, I thought we'd arrived on a movie set. The massive building looked like an English stately home, complete with stone columns flanking the front door and hideous gargoyles staring down from the roofline.

"Is this a freaking house?"

"Yes."

"Whose house?" I asked, but I didn't wait for an answer because Grandma appeared in the doorway. I nearly tripped over my feet in my haste to get to her. Words escaped me, so I just hugged her as tight as I could, burying my face in her hair the way I had my whole life whenever I needed comfort.

"What are you doing here?" I mumbled.

A nose pressed against my leg, damp even through my jeans, and I found Justie, Rafe's dog, staring up at me. Then I looked around properly and saw Dores and Vicente too. And Hallie. I wanted to hug them all, but I didn't have enough arms.

"Why is *everybody* here? The dog?"

"We have news, Cora," Grandma said.

"What news? Did you find Izzy?"

"Not yet. No, this is about family."

What *about* family? They were all here.

Ohmigosh. "Are you sick? Tell me you're not sick."

"No, I'm not sick. This is good news." She turned me around so I was facing Black. "Meet your Uncle Mathias."

"Huh?" I looked from Black to Rafael, and now I saw what Grandma did. The way they stood. The same stoic expression. The identical freaking eyes. How could I have missed it? This must have been what Emmy was talking about to that brunette at the hospital.

Still, I struggled to believe the truth. "Are you serious? One of the twins is alive?"

Grandma just smiled.

My screech would probably have woken the dead, and when I ran at Black, it was like hitting a wall. He hugged me back, and I didn't ever want to let go in case he disappeared. My family had kept me anchored for my entire life, and now I had more of it.

"How did you find out?"

"Let's discuss that over dinner," Black said. "It'll be served soon."

"What about Emilio? Do you know where Emilio is?"

He nodded, and his eyes told me the news wasn't good. "I'm sorry. He died three years ago." Black focused on Grandma, and a small smile flickered at the corners of his lips. "But I do have one more piece of news. Marisol, you have another grandson. Emilio's girlfriend was pregnant when he died."

Now it was her turn to gape like a fish. At least I wasn't the only one.

"A grandson?"

"His name's Hisashi, and he lives in Boston with his mother. I spoke to her this morning, and she'll come to visit as soon as we've cleared up the case."

An uncle and a cousin. I'd doubled my family in just a few minutes. I wanted to squeal with joy, but then I spotted Mercy standing to the side, trying to smile through her tears. I moved in her direction, but Emmy got there first.

"Do you have family in Colombia?"

She shook her head.

"Well, now you have family in Virginia. We may not be related on paper, but love can bond people tighter than blood ever can. You're not on your own, honey."

Joder. I loved my new family.

CHAPTER 45 - BLACK

THE SUN ROSE above the balcony outside Black's bedroom at Riverley. Home, sweet home. And today, it was sweeter than ever. He had his mother, his niece, and his nephew under the same roof and Emmy sleeping peacefully in his arms, her blonde hair spread over his chest.

Black's phone buzzed on the nightstand. Six thirty, and Alaric was already awake.

McLain: Childs is pissed. Where have you stashed Arden?

Well, good. Childs was an asshole.

Black: Richmond. Currently waiting for him to shit out the evidence.

McLain: Did you make some sort of typo there?

Black: No typo. BTW, we also have The Banker so you can stop looking.

The phone rang, but Black diverted Alaric to voicemail as Emmy stirred. He had plans for the next half hour, and they didn't involve talking to his wife's ex-boyfriend. After that, he'd scheduled a seven a.m. chat with The Banker, and then he'd promised Corazon he'd go with her to pick Leander up from the hospital.

"Who was that?" Emmy mumbled.

"Doesn't matter."

"What time is it?"

"Time for you to eat breakfast."

His words took a moment to filter through, and then she smiled.

"I'm so fucking hungry."

At the hospital, Leander sheepishly held out a plastic baggie containing a slim silver flash drive. So many hopes rested on such a tiny device.

"I rinsed it a bit, but I didn't want to scrub it."

"That's probably for the best."

At least the bag was sealed.

Black had hoped that if the data couldn't be recovered, they'd be able to force Isabella's whereabouts out of The Banker, but after this morning's session, he wasn't sure the man knew. He may have been a financial genius, but he had a low pain threshold, and Nevin had apparently dealt with that side of the business.

Black didn't tell Cora that, of course. Not when she looked so happy to be bringing Leander back to Riverley to recuperate. No, he'd pass the flash drive to Nate and hope they could get enough information to find Isabella.

Cora had ridden in the front of the Cayenne on the trip to the hospital, but now she sat in the back with Leander, holding hands across the empty seat in the middle. Young love. And it was love—you'd have to be blind to miss it. Unlike Rafael, Black was happy for the pair of them. Better to find the right person early on than spend the rest of your life searching, or worse, do what he'd done and waste years waiting to make a move. Years spent waking up alone when he should have had Emmy beside him.

"I need to go to the office after I drop you off, but just ask Bradley if you need anything. Or Mrs. Fairfax, our housekeeper. And keep an eye on Mercy. Hallie's tough, but Mercy isn't."

"I will," Cora said. "Thank you for letting them stay."

Black only owned Riverley Hall because John and Audrey Black had stolen him as a baby. While he'd led a life of privilege in Virginia, his real family had suffered tragedy after tragedy. Sharing his home with Corazon and her friends was the least he could do.

People accused Black of being a machine, a cyborg, and at one time he'd lived up to that reputation. But the events surrounding Emilio's death had taught him what it was like to be human, and now he *felt*.

Pain, anger, hurt, love, happiness—he never wanted to stop feeling.

"We can't all go."

Agatha, Mack's new assistant, had worked a miracle with the flash drive. Twenty-four hours after Leander's bowel had done its thing, they had data, data everywhere, but for the moment, they were only interested in one line on Nevin's "sales" spreadsheet. Isabella had been purchased—fuck, Black hated that description when it related to a human being—by an attorney from Chesapeake. Simeon Michaels had been the first man in his firm to make partner before the age of forty, and today, he'd be the first to die before the age of forty too.

The only problem was that assassins were lining up to do the job. Even Marisol had offered to put a bullet through Michaels's frontal lobe if someone could just give her a hand with the steps at the front of his McMansion. Black gave his head a little shake. His mother was a sicaria—he still struggled to believe that, but he had to admit it was appropriate.

"Maybe we could draw straws," Sofia suggested.

"Or use a random number generator," Nate said.

Black shook his head. "I'm going." There were benefits to being the boss. He rarely enjoyed killing, but on occasion, it did leave him with a deep sense of satisfaction. "Rafael's coming with me because he's a familiar face for Isabella."

"But—" Emmy started.

"Diamond, you've already killed seven people on this job. I'd go so far as to say you've exceeded your quota."

"Dammit."

"But how about you and Sofia watch Michaels at work? We need to know when he's coming home."

Not anytime soon, it turned out. The attorney had a basic security system—hardly surprising since a monitoring service might have noticed the girl locked up in his house. No cameras either. Black bypassed the alarm in minutes, then he and Rafael slipped inside just before six o'clock. According to Emmy, Michaels was still in his office. She and Sofia had a perfect view of his desk from the café opposite, which also served great coffee and eight different kinds of muffin, apparently. Great. His wife would come home wired on sugar and caffeine, and he wouldn't get any sleep.

Hmm... Actually, that could have its advantages.

Black searched the first floor while Rafael took the second, but the still air told them the upper levels were empty. The basement with two bolts on the outside of the door? That was more interesting.

"Ready?" Black murmured.

Rafael nodded his agreement, and Black swung the door open.

Well, well, well. Somebody had been taking decorating tips from Nevin. The dimly lit basement was a homage to the dungeon at the glass eyesore, except this room had one major difference. The defeated-looking woman curled up under a blanket on a padded bench at the far end. She blinked a few times when she saw them approach, then screamed when she realised neither of them was Michaels.

Rafael quickly holstered his gun and ran across the room.

"Izzy, it's okay."

"Rafe?"

The blanket slid away as she sat up, and she quickly pulled it around herself again. The fucker had left her naked. Rafael scooped her into his arms, blanket and all, and carried her towards the stairs.

"Emmy, is Michaels still in his office?" Black asked.

"Yup. Now he's on the phone."

"In that case, I'll drive a car right up to the house. Tell me if the situation changes."

They'd brought a blue Ford Explorer and a maroon Honda. Nothing flashy, nondescript vehicles that wouldn't turn heads in this neighbourhood. Black fetched the SUV. Bradley had worried Isabella might not be in good shape when they found her and packed a bag with clothes, drinks, and a blanket into the trunk. The men turned their backs while Isabella wriggled into a shapeless kaftan thing that was perfect for the occasion, then Rafael wrapped the fresh blanket around her and tucked her feet into a pair of furry boots.

"Where are you taking me?" she asked, her first words since she left the basement.

"A friend's house. Your mama's waiting there for you."

"Mama's in America?"

"And Cora, and Marisol."

"Wait! Shouldn't we call the police? I think I got drugged in Colombia, then I was in two houses, then the man who lives here locked me up and...and..."

Isabella began trembling, and Rafael hugged her close. "Shh. We know what happened, and we'll handle everything. Just focus on getting back to your mama. She's not far away."

"I'll see her today?"

"In less than two hours. Do you want something to drink?"

She nodded, and Black passed her an energy drink. The poor girl was shell-shocked, but hopefully she'd feel better once she joined the other survivors. Tomorrow, they could start to consider what professional help might be needed to get the girls through this.

Rafael climbed behind the wheel for the journey back to Riverley. "Good luck."

Luck?

Today, Black didn't need luck. Not when he had training, practice, and anger on his side.

You'd think any man with a woman locked up in his basement might hurry home after work to, you know, feed her, but Simeon Michaels proved what an utter cunt he was by heading out to a bar with his law firm buddies and hitting on the waitress. He was also one of the most inept criminals Black had ever come across. Firstly, he didn't realise Isabella had disappeared, and secondly, he didn't notice as Black tracked him through his house.

Then his phone rang.

"Hey, baby. Sorry I missed your call earlier. There's a big case at work, and I spent the evening taking a deposition."

Michaels had a girlfriend?

"Sure, lilac sounds great for the bridesmaids' dresses." A pause. "I thought we'd agreed on the Maldives for the honeymoon?"

Bridesmaids? Honeymoon? This asshole was engaged? *He kept a sex slave in his basement.* Michaels held the phone in the crook of his neck as he poured himself a generous glass of Scotch.

"Yeah, baby, an over-the-water bungalow sounds great. Show me the brochure tomorrow evening and we'll talk about it." He listened for a moment, then hung up. "Women," he muttered.

Killing this guy wouldn't be murder. It would be a public fucking service. Black followed him upstairs and waited in the hallway while he stripped for the shower. This was getting boring now. How did the guy pass the bar exam when he only had half a dozen functioning brain cells?

Michaels wasn't a big man, five feet seven with the muscle tone of a desk jockey. Black simply picked him up and slammed his head down on the edge of the ceramic shower tray. His skull made a satisfying *crunch*, like crumpling a Coke can. Blood trickled across the linoleum, and Black rubbed his gloved hands together.

Another task completed.

Bradley motioned Merrick Childs into the conference room at Riverley, and the FBI agent looked down his nose at him. Prick.

"Can I offer you coffee? Tea? Water?" Bradley lowered his voice. "Pliers to take that stick out of your ass?"

"Is the coffee filtered?"

Bradley put his hands on his hips. "Does this look like the sort of place that serves instant?"

Black stepped in before their visitor got a lecture on coffee blends. "Bradley, just bring a jug of Colombian roast." He sized Childs up. "You look like a skim milk and stevia man."

"How do you know that?"

"I do my research."

And Black's research told him that real men didn't put skim milk and stevia in their coffee. Usually, he arranged meetings like this one at the office, but he'd invited Childs to his home today because there something innately satisfying about holding a meeting to discuss The Banker in a conference room five feet above the man himself. They'd stashed their prisoner in a soundproof holding cell in Riverley's basement, and there he'd stay until he outlived his usefulness.

"Why did you ask me to come here today?" Childs asked.

"I want to make a deal."

"You mean, you'll turn over the evidence you stole and tell me the whereabouts of the special agent you corrupted, and I won't charge you with impeding an investigation?"

"Not exactly. Blackwood may have come across some data from an unnamed source, namely the location of a number of trafficking victims, some in private dwellings and a number in two properties run as—for want of a better word—brothels. We'd like your task force to liberate these young women and ensure they receive appropriate care."

"That's not our job."

"Well, it is now," Black snapped. "Unless you want the world to find out that your agents stood by while seven young women were raped repeatedly at a house in Florida. Stood by on your orders."

"What do you know about the house in Florida? And where's Special Agent Arden?"

"Leander Arden asked me to give you this." Black slid a cream-coloured envelope across the table. "It's his resignation letter. And as for the Florida house, I've spoken with two of the former occupants, and we know you used the house opposite for surveillance. You could have rescued those girls, but you chose to turn a blind eye to the abuse instead."

"The task force I head has nothing to do with trafficking. It was formed to catch one specific individual, so you're barking up the wrong tree."

"The Banker? My sources tell me he's abroad, so whatever your task force thinks it's doing, it's wasting its time."

"What sources?"

Good. Childs had lost a little of his bluster. Bradley picked that moment to come back with coffee, and Black waited patiently while Childs fixed his drink. The man tried to hide the way his hands trembled, but he didn't do a great job of it.

"I prefer to hold those cards close to my chest, although it's clear I've spoken to Mr. Arden. But I will tell you this. Unless you find some way to salvage what you've been doing for the past year, your career is fucked."

"How dare you speak to me like that?"

"Simple. I just open my mouth and the words come out. Do you want our data or not? I should mention the files also include the details of Nevin's clients. The Banker's associates. I'm sure you could find plenty of crimes to pin on them too."

Black held up a flash drive—not the one that had been through Leander, although it had been tempting to use it. Childs made a grab for the device, but Black moved his hand away.

"Not so fast. There are conditions."

"What conditions?"

"One, you excavate the garden at the Florida house and give the girl buried there a proper funeral. Yes, I'm well aware that your inaction resulted in her death. She had a name: Kelsie. Did you know that?"

Childs stayed silent.

"Two, you ensure that all the women receive proper

psychiatric help, plus assistance in rebuilding their lives."

"How the hell am I supposed to do that?"

"You're a resourceful man. I'm sure you'll find a way. Oh, and I expect weekly progress reports."

"Is that it?" Childs stood halfway up.

"Almost."

Ah, the look of a defeated man. Childs slumped into his chair, and Black took a second to savour the moment. Then he got back to business.

"A member of our surveillance team ran into a slight problem at a warehouse in Fort Lauderdale. I'm sure you're aware of the situation. It involved *your* surveillance team almost letting a girl burn to death. She's awake now. Did you know *that*?"

Childs shook his head like a sulky teenager.

"You should send flowers. Anyhow, there was a small issue at the police precinct afterwards. The cops breached procedure in numerous areas..." Black ticked off the points on his fingers. "Unclear reading of his Miranda rights. No offer of legal advice. Errors in the chain of evidence. For various reasons, we need to keep his involvement quiet, so I need you to tell the cops he was your guy."

"Are you crazy? He kidnapped a woman."

"No, he walked out of the precinct with my wife. And don't even get me started on all the fuck-ups the cops made in that incident. Just tell them it was a security exercise and they failed."

"What about the knife he was carrying? The murder weapon?"

"He saw it on the floor, thought it might be evidence, and figured he'd better pick it up before the place burned. Perhaps you should take a look at the Mafia? After all, you'll be needing something new to do in a few weeks." Black smiled, and Childs shrank back another inch. A broken man, and one who'd never advance further up the ladder at the FBI. "Now I'm done."

CHAPTER 46 - CORA

"WHAT IS THIS place?" Izzy asked.

Last night when Rafael brought her back to Riverley, Izzy had barely said a word, just cried along with everyone else. Dores's initial elation that her daughter was back from the dead had quickly turned into devastation when she realised what Izzy had been through. Up until Izzy's return, Grandma had kept Dores sheltered from the details, but now there was no hiding what had happened to both of us. Izzy had regressed from the confident, sometimes brattish girl I'd grown up with to the child who'd withdrawn into herself for years after Valento was destroyed.

Dores blamed herself for not doing more after Izzy disappeared—as we all did—and when Blackwood's doctor came, she had to sedate Dores rather than her daughter. Izzy huddled in my bed all night, silent, and only as the sun rose did she start asking questions.

"Where am I? I don't even know where I am."

"This place? The Riverley estate. It belongs to..." Deep breath. "It belongs to my uncle."

"Your uncle? What uncle?"

I told Izzy the story. The whole horrible, crazy, beautiful story of what had happened after she disappeared, and every word stirred up emotions, both mine and hers—some good and some bad.

If she'd never met Roscoe, Rafael would have kept his distance from us, and Grandma would have carried on making bandeja paisa and skulking around with Vicente while Dores worked at the hospital until she retired. And me? I'd be teaching English in Medellín today, happy, but also incomplete. I'd have avoided the humiliation of having to submit to so many different men, but I'd never have met Lee or the rest of my family.

I still felt sick when I thought of those men on top of me, of having to lie there and take it in pursuit of my goal, but knowing what I knew now, would I do it again? In a heartbeat.

Because I'd won. I'd fucking won.

I had a new goal too. Somehow, I had to help the other girls to put their lives back together, starting with Izzy, Hallie, and Mercy, then moving on to the thousands of other women who found themselves in similar situations every year. For so long, I'd drifted in life, but now I had a purpose.

A soft knock at the door made Izzy jump, and I padded across the room to see who it was.

Emmy. With coffee.

"Hey. How are you both?"

"Izzy's...frail."

"And you?"

"Drained, but okay."

"Leander's up. You'll probably want to keep an eye to make sure he doesn't do anything stupid."

At the mere mention of his name, warmth spread through my chest. "I'll take care of him. Do you think we could get some clothes for Izzy?"

"Bradley's downstairs with a garment rail,

champing at the bit. Is she up to his shenanigans?"

I'd only met Bradley briefly, and although he could be over-exuberant, his heart was in the right place. Izzy would love him.

"Send him in."

How should I describe life at Riverley? The place was an odd mix of house and hotel with the facilities of a country club and an atmosphere that changed from all-business during the day to party-like in the evening.

Twenty-four hours after Izzy's return, I curled up on a sofa beside Lee with a plate of food balanced on my lap and an almost-empty glass of wine in my hand. I was just contemplating whether to get up for a refill or live with a dry mouth because I was really, really comfortable when Black appeared with a bottle of white in his hand.

"Top-up?"

"Yes, please."

He filled my glass, then took a seat on the coffee table in front of us. "Busy day. How are you both doing?"

My smiles came easily these days. "Good. We're doing good."

Black tapped his head. "How about up here? We've got a lady coming in to talk with Isabella and Mercy tomorrow—would it help you to have a session? Either of you?"

"You mean a therapist?"

"Yes. She's a good listener."

My time in the two houses of horrors haunted my

dreams and stopped me from sleeping, but the prospect of discussing my innermost thoughts and feelings with somebody I didn't know left me cold.

"I'm not sure I could talk to a stranger."

Black nodded. "I can understand that. Leander?"

He directed his answer at me rather than my uncle. "We can talk to each other, okay, bee? Don't bottle things up."

"Okay."

"Does that mean you don't want an appointment either?" Black asked.

Lee shook his head too. "Never did trust shrinks."

"Let me know if you change your mind."

"I'll be all right. I'm just a little worried about safety. Not here, but when we have to leave." His arm rested across my shoulders, and now it tightened. "The Banker has deep pockets, and he's also got connections to dangerous people."

"You don't need to worry about The Banker anymore."

My turn to stiffen.

"You found him? What happened? Is he in jail?"

Black barked out a laugh. Silly me. No, of course The Banker wasn't in jail.

"Never mind."

"Thank you," Lee said. "Thank you for everything. You didn't have to help us in the way you did, and I probably wouldn't be here if you hadn't stepped in."

"We always help family. Just pay it forward."

"I intend to."

I shoved myself off the sofa and flung my arms around Black. "Thank you from me too."

He hesitated a second, then hugged me back.

"Stay here for as long as you want."

"Really? Both of us?"

He nodded. "We've got a lot of lost time to make up."

Midnight had come and gone when we finally went to bed. Bradley settled Izzy into her own room along the hallway from mine, next to Dores, which left Lee to walk me upstairs. I suggested taking the elevator, but he insisted he wasn't that much of an invalid, even though he was basically still purple. Emmy's earlier words about stopping him from doing anything stupid suddenly became more prescient.

"Do you think Black was serious about us staying for a while?" he asked. "I mean, this place is something else."

"I'm pretty sure he was. But are you happy here? What about your home? Your family?"

"My apartment's on a month-to-month lease, and I hardly spent any time there, anyway. Plus I don't have a job now. Saving on rent for a few months would be good." Lee leaned closer and kissed my hair. "But my number one priority is being close to you while you recover enough to go back to Medellín."

I'd barely thought about Colombia since I arrived at Riverley. Perhaps I should have felt guilty for that, but Medellín had never quite become home. Valento was home, and everyone from Valento was here.

"Medellín. Right. What about your family?"

"My dad left when I was two. We see each other a couple of times a year, but..." He shrugged. "He was never much of a father. Mom had a midlife crisis and moved to Cabo with a guy fifteen years younger. He's a dick. I figure she'll come back eventually, but right now, she's too busy partying."

"Do you have any siblings?"

"A sister, Daria. She took a study trip to Italy when she was twenty-one, and she's still there."

"So I'm stuck with you then?"

"Yeah, bee. You're stuck with me."

I only meant to give him a quick peck on the cheek, not a full-on snog, but he tangled the fingers of his good hand in my hair and pulled me closer.

"What about your lip?" I asked. "Doesn't it hurt?"

"Not enough to stop me from kissing you."

My heart pounded as Lee took the first step towards erasing the bad memories of the last few weeks. He kissed like a magician—the world around us disappeared, and flames licked their way through my insides until Emmy walked past, laughing.

"Get a room, guys."

"Shit." Lee buried his face in my hair then winced when he remembered his sore cheek. "You taste so sweet."

"Can I stay with you tonight? I know we can't do anything, but..."

"Are you sure you're ready for that?"

"I like waking up next to you." I gave him a sheepish smile. "I promise I won't molest you in my sleep."

"Give me a couple of weeks to heal, and you can molest me as much as you want."

"Is that a yes?"

Lee reached behind himself and pushed the door open, then took both of my hands in his.

"Corazon da Silva, I'll never be able to say no to you."

CHAPTER 47 - BLACK

LOOSE ENDS. BLACK hated loose ends, and right now, there were still too many of them.

One less since a businessman named Theodore Symonds had gotten his Viagra confused with a counterfeit Fentanyl pill and breathed his last in the ER, but even so, work was piling up at Blackwood and Black had only been to the gym once so far this week. It was time to unravel all those nasty little threads that were left so everyone could get on with their lives.

He poured himself a coffee and sat at the kitchen counter with his tablet to make a list. He liked lists. Lists led to order.

Hallie's arrest warrant.

Having spent a few days with the girl, Black had come to the conclusion that either she was worthy of an Oscar or she'd been framed for murder, and he knew which option he was going with. But who had framed her and why?

Roscoe.

He'd last popped up in Italy, but he couldn't hide forever. The man had kicked this whole case off with his greed, and after Black had thanked him, he'd take great pleasure in watching the fucker's slow death.

The Banker.

That damned oxygen thief was still breathing in the

basement. How long should they keep him alive?

Who hired Rafael to kill Eduardo?

Rafael had made Emmy a promise, and Black would make sure he kept it. He was about to summon his nephew when the subject of item number one walked in with Corazon.

"Hallie, we need to talk."

Her smile faded, but Black beckoned her over anyway. It was for her own good.

"Is everything okay?" Corazon asked.

"Hallie has a small problem we need to solve." Black tried for a comforting expression. Did that work? He was used to intimidating people, not reassuring them. "Everything will be fine."

"Can I help?"

"You can help Bradley. He's decided the sun loungers by the pool need replacing."

"But—"

"Don't worry; everything's under control here."

Corazon didn't seem convinced, but she backed slowly out of the kitchen, leaving a nervous Hallie behind. Hallie looked healthier now—still too thin, but she'd lost the gauntness present when they first met in Florida.

"I guess I figured if I didn't think about this, it would all go away," she said.

"It *will* go away, but we have to make it. Passivity is rarely the answer. Now, tell me what we've got. You mentioned a videotape?"

"Yes, and I still have the hair sample. It's with my attorney too."

"Where's your attorney?"

"Kentucky."

"We'll send someone from our local office to pick everything up. For now, I want you to give me a detailed account of everything you remember."

Which wasn't a huge amount more than Hallie had told him in Florida. She'd gone out dancing with one of her colleagues, the other girl had met a guy, and Hallie had woken up in bed with a corpse. An online search confirmed the basics. The victim, a fifty-one-year-old property developer named Damien Dewer, had no history of infidelity according to his wife. At the time of his murder, he was supposed to be in a business meeting.

Statistically, around forty-five percent of murders were committed by friends, family, or acquaintances, and only ten percent by total strangers. The victim's inner circle was always a good place to begin an investigation, starting with the spouse.

Annabeth Dewer, Damien's wife, looked to be one of those high-maintenance women who preferred spending money to earning it. What did she have to gain from her husband's death? Were they having problems in their marriage? Life insurance? Then there were the Dewers' three adult children—two sons and a daughter. Any squabbles there?

Black spent the morning creating a link chart with Hallie. Back when he started Blackwood with Nate, he'd been the lead investigator on every case. He rarely got involved at this level of detail anymore, and in some ways, he missed it. Working with Hallie reminded him of his days training Dan. They both asked a thousand questions, both thought things through methodically and recorded everything carefully.

Black was even more impressed when the courier

arrived from Lexington in the early evening. Not only had Hallie taken a hair sample from herself, she'd also had two people witness her removing the strands and sign statements to say so, then sealed the whole lot in an envelope with her attorney's dated signature on the flap. The video came with a statement from the owner of the bar saying he'd given it to her. Meticulous. Hallie was smart.

"Can you get the hair sample tested?" she asked. "I don't know yet how I'll earn the money to pay back the cost, but I promise I will."

Black had a good idea, but he just nodded. "I'll make the arrangements. Let's have a look at this tape."

Thirty seconds in, and Black couldn't decide whether to laugh or pick up the phone to the police chief in Lexington and give him an earful. No, the asshole deserved more than a lecture. His inaction on Hallie's case had led to at least two more deaths.

"What?" Hallie asked. "Why are you smiling?"

"Because this is the easiest case I'll ever solve."

"What do you mean?"

Black pointed at the man standing with Hallie in the centre of the TV screen. "He did it."

"Well, I figured he was involved, but how do we prove it? Or find him?"

"His name is Ricky Carter, and he's dead. You didn't have TV at Radcliffe's?"

"Only Netflix."

"Then you missed the trial of the century. Carter pulled a remarkably similar trick on somebody else, only that time, he got caught. By us."

Hallie's hands flew to her mouth. "Ohmigosh. I can't... Until now, I always thought there was a tiny chance that I *had* done something, that I just couldn't remember... Are you sure it's him?"

"Positive. I'll call my attorney and get him involved, but with the video and the hair sample, it should only be a formality."

It all made sense now. Dewer's occupation—he'd been Carter's competition. The business meeting in his calendar. A young woman used as collateral damage. Hallie had been Carter's practice run, and if the Lexington police had investigated properly, they could have prevented a world of heartache.

But sometimes things happened for a reason. If Carter's killing spree had been stopped prematurely, Dan wouldn't have met her boyfriend or her son. Black's attorney had also met his soon-to-be wife through the case.

And while everything The Banker had done made Black incandescent with anger, and he hated the fact that Eduardo Garcia was still minimally conscious, he'd never have found his family if those events had never happened. Balance. The world was about balance. The good and the bad.

And today, Hallie's happiness was part of the good.

"Are you sure they'll clear me?" she asked. "I mean, they could say we colluded or something."

"They won't."

Black braced as she flung her arms around him. Hugs were usually restricted to Emmy, Dan, and occasionally Fia, but now it looked as though he'd have to add Corazon and Hallie to that list.

"Thank you. I'll be able to get on with my life, and... and... I don't even know what I'm gonna do."

"How would you like to work for Blackwood?"

She loosened her arms enough to look up at him. "What?"

"An entry-level position in investigations. The job's yours if you want it."

Hallie's work on her own case had been basic but thorough. She understood how to research. With training, she'd make a useful addition to the team.

Emmy appeared in the doorway. "Is there something I should know about?"

"I'm going to work at Blackwood!" Hallie squealed.

Emmy looked to Black and raised an eyebrow.

"We have another Carter victim."

Black pointed at the screen, still frozen on the picture of Hallie and Carter in the bar.

"Fuck. Will this ever end?"

"Who knows?" The man had left a trail of dead bodies and chaos in his wake before he finally got caught. "But Dan has a new sidekick to break in."

"So does Bradley. He's got Isabella picking out fabric swatches for new curtains in the lounge. I'm not sure whether to be thrilled she's stopped crying or handcuff the pair of them to the door handle."

"If Isabella's happy, I don't care about damn drapes."

"Fair enough. Are you coming for dinner?"

Black turned Hallie around so she faced the door. "Yes, we are."

After dinner, Black sat on the leather couch in his study beside Emmy, idly swirling his Scotch around in its glass. The twenty-four-year-old Bruichladdich came from a small island off the Scottish coast, a Christmas gift from Nate last year. The Scotch, not the island. Black already owned an island. Emmy had stuck with wine, although Black had a feeling she'd need something stronger after this.

"So," he said to Rafael, seated in an armchair opposite. "You owe Emmy some information."

"I do."

Emmy tensed, knowing what was coming. Who did she have to kill?

Black was more concerned with the logistics of the job. Last time Blackwood had gone after a murderer in Colombia, it had taken weeks of planning and a small army. How difficult would things be this time?

"Who hired you to kill Eduardo Garcia?"

"Floriana Garcia."

"His *wife*?"

Emmy sounded as incredulous as Black felt.

For all his musings about Annabeth Dewer earlier, Floriana had been one person Black didn't suspect. She'd stayed with Eduardo at Riverley, for fuck's sake, and she'd always seemed devoted to her husband and stepsons, and Eduardo to her. Yes, she was his sixth wife so he didn't exactly have a great track record, but Emmy had met a couple of the others and expressed her hopes that he'd finally found the right match. Seemed she'd been wrong. Boy, she'd hate that.

Rafael shrugged. "*Sí.*"

"Why? Why would she do that?"

"I didn't ask that question. When I found out who the target was, I simply accepted the job. As I said before, I don't like drug lords."

"Wait a minute. How did she even hire you?"

It was a fair question. She'd always been a quiet woman, happy to stay in Eduardo's shadow, and you didn't hire a sicario like Mercurio by looking for recommendations on the internet.

"Floriana Gonzalez grew up in Medellín. In Comuna 13. She knew the right people to contact."

Well, shit. One more thread had unravelled, and now they were tangled in yarn. What next? Emmy could hardly just shoot the woman, and Black would rather grate his own skin off than have that conversation with Sebastien and Marco Garcia. Thank fuck they had a guard in Eduardo's hospital room; otherwise, the woman might have been tempted to finish her dear husband off by now.

"What's the status of the contract?" Black asked. "Does she expect you to finish? Or is she likely to hire someone else?"

"She cancelled the contract right after I screwed up."

"Shit. You realise it was her who shot you?"

No, by the look of him, Rafael didn't. "Fuck. The bitch hired me then tried to kill me?"

"She's got balls, all right."

Emmy merely sighed. "Looks like we need to make a trip to Colombia in the near future."

Rafael picked up the Scotch and poured himself a generous measure. "Yes. It looks like we do."

Emmy grabbed the bottle from him and poured half the contents down her throat. "I'll go pack my stuff."

Black had been about to give her a lecture on knee-jerk reactions and why they weren't a great idea when his phone buzzed with a message.

Mack: Roscoe Ward just bought a ticket to Bogotá.

He flies from Sicily the day after tomorrow.

How satisfying it was when the puzzle pieces slotted into place. Black needed to get his bags packed too.

CHAPTER 48 - CORA

"CORA, I'M NOT sure I can do a long-distance relationship."

Two weeks had passed since our first night together at Riverley. Lee and I had been curled up together on the sofa in the bedroom all afternoon, him reading a novel and me thumbing through a magazine, and now he decided to drop that bombshell?

I thought things had been going okay considering the circumstances. We spent almost all of our time together, his bruises were barely noticeable, and although I was still terrified of hurting him, we'd got as far as second base. And this morning we'd taken a shower together, purely because he couldn't reach to wash his back, you understand.

Yes, there had been setbacks too. The day before yesterday, we'd gone on our first proper date—nothing flashy, just Mexican food at a local restaurant—and I'd had a funny moment when an older couple sat at the next table. A sort of sweaty, dizzy moment where my heart raced out of control and I couldn't think or speak or breathe. A panic attack. Okay, it was a panic attack. The man had worn the exact same cologne as Alan, the pig of a man who'd been my first "client" at the pink palace, and I'd freaked.

Lee had got me out of there, tossing down a handful

of bills onto the table as he half carried me to the door. And in the car, I'd cried. Not like a waterfall or anything, but enough that Lee hugged me tightly and apologised on behalf of all mankind.

So I understood why he might be reluctant to stay involved with me, but that didn't make his words hurt any less.

"But—"

He placed a finger over my lips. "Please, hear me out."

"Okay."

"I've been thinking. Hell, I've done nothing but think. I realise we've only just met, and the circumstances are far from ideal, but I can't stand the thought of not seeing you for months. I've done some research, and it should be possible for me to get a migrant visa for Colombia."

"You want to move to Colombia?"

He didn't want to leave me? A huge knot of tension unravelled itself in my stomach.

"Uh, yes? You don't sound too happy about that."

"Only because I want to stay here."

"In America?"

"In Virginia. Grandma wants to be near her son. I see it in her eyes. And Black's whole life is here, so she'd never ask him to move to Colombia. And I think my brother wants to work at Blackwood. I know staying won't be easy for me, and the visa application process is long and it might not work out, but I want to try because I can't bear to be apart from my family or from you."

Lee hugged me as tightly as he could with his bad ribs, then kissed me with plenty of tongue and I almost forgot what we were talking about. At least until he cupped my face in his hands and gave me a hesitant little smile.

"Cora. Honeybee. The visa thing... Do you think it would help if we got married?"

My legs almost gave way. Was he...? Did he just...?

"Lee, was that a proposal?"

"The worst one ever, but yes. Too soon?"

I didn't know what to say, so I kissed him again instead. Of course it was too soon, but life could get snatched away from us in an instant—I knew that all too well. And when I thought of waking up next to Lee every morning with his ring on my finger, my happiness bubbled over and leaked out through my fucking eyes.

"Bee, what's wrong?"

"Nothing. Everything's so right I'm scared it'll turn into a disaster."

"Uh, is that a yes or a no?"

"A yes. A huge, big yes."

And my teary acceptance wasn't the only thing that was huge and big. As our kisses grew more heated, Lee's cock swelled and pressed into my belly, and I didn't want to wait any longer. Black was right. I needed to focus on the future, on the good in life. I pushed the bad memories further into the recesses of my mind then shoved Lee onto the bed.

"Shit! Sorry. Did that hurt?"

"With that look on your face, I don't care about the pain."

"What look?"

He wrinkled his nose.

"Tell me. What look?"

"Overachieving porn star meets sex-starved vampire."

"Oh my…"

I wasn't sure whether to slap him or gasp, so I settled for a fit of giggles.

"I'm *not* a porn-star vampire."

"You can eat me alive anytime, babe."

Where did I start? I was trying to decide when his expression turned serious.

"Cora, are you sure about this?"

"Yes. I'm not letting a bunch of assholes ruin the rest of my life. Of *our* lives." I lay down beside Lee and nestled close. "I won't lie. I'll probably freak out at some point, and I'll want the most boring sex imaginable for a few months, but I want it with you."

"I always knew you were a secret romantic."

"Shut up!"

I kissed him to emphasise my point, then sighed into his mouth when his hands began to roam all over me. I repaid the favour, careful to avoid his ribs and the scar on his abdomen and his sore cheek. There would be plenty of time for exploration later. We had our whole future to spend together, so invalid sex would do for now.

"This is a bit awkward," he said. "My good finger's broken, so I'll have to try this left-handed."

Well, it turned out Lee was ambidextrous, and his tongue worked just fine too. I bit my lip to stop myself from screaming as he sent me over the edge, then wriggled back around on jellied limbs to face him again.

Lee was the perfect mix of hard and soft. He had muscles, but not too many, the sweetest lips, the gentlest hands, and a gloriously solid cock nestled between his thighs. Then there was his kind heart offset by gritty determination and a clever mind.

"I love you," I whispered.

"I love you too, honeybee."

"How are we gonna do this? Should I go on top?"

"I think you'll have to."

Every nightstand at Riverley resembled a low-budget sex shop, and I selected a condom from the top drawer. Ribbed for extra pleasure. My mind would probably explode, but I didn't care. Lee would help me to pick up the pieces afterwards.

He held my hands as I lowered myself onto him, and I gave myself a moment to adjust. Why rush? Lee was my *freaking fiancé*. I'd get to do all of this and more every single day. And when I did start to move, it was more than the simple race to get each other off that I'd experienced in the past. This was a meeting of minds as well as bodies, and when we both came—me first, then Lee with a heaving shudder—the connection only intensified.

Whatever crazy mix of desperation and emotions had thrown us together, it was where we were meant to be. I'd officially lost myself to this man.

There was only one problem. We had to tell my brother.

"I vote we get it over with," I told Lee.

"Or maybe we could just elope?"

"Rafael would hunt us down, and there's no way he wouldn't find us."

"Yeah, I know. Wishful thinking, I guess."

After the sex, we'd snuggled for an hour, talking and laughing and planning our future. At one point, it all felt too good to be true.

"Tell me this is real."

Lee feathered kisses up my jaw before he answered. "We've walked through hell and come out the other side. We've earned our happiness, bee."

Logically, I knew he was right, but hell felt like a warm-up as we walked out of the bedroom to face my family. I'd rehearsed what to say—keep it to the basics, don't let my brother spoil my good mood—but every single thought flew out of my head when we walked around the corner and found my grandma kissing Vicente.

What the actual heck? She was on her feet next to her wheelchair, her arms around his neck, and I didn't know where to look. Beside me, Lee froze too, and we'd only managed to take half a step backwards when she opened her eyes and caught us staring.

Then she giggled. She actually freaking giggled.

"Don't run away, Cora," she said. Vicente turned too, holding Grandma up with an arm around her waist. "It's time you found out."

"How long...? I mean, has this been going on for a while?"

"About two decades."

Holy shit. Grandma had a secret boyfriend?

"Does Rafael know?"

"I don't think so. Sometimes, that boy's blind to the things he doesn't want to see."

"Are you going to tell him?"

"We plan to do that tonight. No more family

secrets."

Oh, thank goodness. That took some of the heat off us. We could slip our news in afterwards then run. A few of my nerves dissipated, and I managed to smile.

"I'm so happy for you. For both of you."

"As we are for you." She took a deep breath, her dreamy look disappeared, and her steely gaze came back. "Well, we'd better go and face the music."

Vicente lowered her into her wheelchair and made sure she was comfortable. Seeing them together, I realised I should have spotted their connection long before, but perhaps I'd been guilty of wearing the same blinkers as my brother. Now I shared a certain empathy. We all squashed into the elevator, and Vicente gave Grandma's hand a reassuring squeeze. Time to face the music indeed.

Grandma laughed and chatted through dinner, which was more than I accomplished. How did she do it? Put on a mask and hide her feelings like that? Black succeeded at the feat as well, as did Rafael when he chose to. Luckily, with a full table, nobody noticed when I just stayed quiet and ate Mrs. Fairfax's pot roast.

The news that Alan had been mauled to within an inch of his life by an ostrich distracted me momentarily, and I joined in Emmy's toast to all things avian, but three mouthfuls later, I was back to worrying again. When did Grandma plan to make her announcement? Or had she chickened out? Vicente topped up Rafael's wine glass to the brim, and I realised their delay was tactical. They'd been playing this game a lot longer than I had.

We'd got through a mountain of profiteroles, which

were undoubtedly delicious but tasted of sawdust to me, before she cleared her throat.

"I think it's time we had a family discussion."

Black went from relaxed to alert in the blink of an eye. "What is it? Is everything okay?"

"It's more than okay. So much has happened, most of it good, but that's left many of us with some big decisions to make."

"How big?"

"As wide as the Caribbean Sea."

"I'm signing the papers on an apartment in Medellín tomorrow."

"You might not need to."

"What are you talking about?"

"Vicente and I would like to spend some time here if we can. We've been tucking money away over the last few years, and it's time to enjoy our retirement."

"How much time?"

"That depends on everyone else's plans, but a good amount. We've got alternate passports, so travel back and forth between here and Colombia shouldn't be a problem. We'll just have to be careful with visas."

"I've made contacts over the years. Don't worry about visas. But you keep saying 'we.' Is there something I should know?"

"Even after a tragedy, it's possible to fall in love again, Mathias."

My brother's eyes widened, but Black only smiled.

"Then I'll offer my congratulations. I should also mention that I've offered Rafael a job at Blackwood. He's hesitated over accepting because he was worried about leaving you alone."

"Rafael, is this true?"

Finally, Rafe relaxed his frown. "Yes. I'd like to move here permanently. Having an almost legitimate job would be a novelty, but I could learn a lot from Black."

"I want to stay too," I blurted. Everyone stared at me, and I gripped Lee's hand for support. "I'm going to marry Leander. We can get jobs and rent an apartment together."

Rafe's frown came back. "Corazon, you met the guy a month ago."

"I know. But I... I... I just *know*, okay? And it'll be easier for me to get a visa."

"You're marrying him for a fucking green card?"

Support came from an unlikely corner. "I married Black for a green card," Emmy said. "Don't knock it until you've tried it."

"Technically there was also some encouragement from Nate and a considerable amount of alcohol involved, Diamond."

"Yeah, yeah, but it was the visa discussion that started the ball rolling."

Black held up his ring finger. "Fifteen years and counting. Sometimes I want to kill her, but on the whole, it was a good move."

Emmy nodded her agreement. "Absolutely. I can't deny that I've considered suffocating him in his sleep on occasion, but he looks good on my arm at parties."

"Wait until you fall in love, buddy. It's like getting hit by a truck, except you can't even jump out of the way."

My brother barked out a laugh. "Entanglements are easy to resist."

"That's what I thought when I was your age."

"Did you seriously just say that?" Emmy asked. "You sound like an old man. Next thing we know, you'll be sitting there with your pipe and slippers telling us what happened 'back in my day...'"

"Refer to my earlier comment about wanting to kill my wife."

She elbowed him in the side. "He loves me really."

"Enough arguing," Grandma said. "We should be celebrating. Dores and Isabella also want to stay. Can you help with that?"

"I'll make the arrangements."

"What about me?" Mercy asked. "Do I have to go back to Colombia alone? I don't even have a passport."

Black shook his head. "No, you don't have to go back to Colombia alone. It seems we have some plans to make. Accommodation to sort out, a wedding to arrange..."

A squeal came from behind us, and I turned to see Bradley gripping the doorjamb so hard his knuckles were white.

"Did somebody say wedding?"

A collective groan went up from around the table, and Emmy spoke first.

"Yes, but we'll have plenty to keep you busy without playing wedding planner."

"You said I could have an assistant."

"Who you'll have to train and supervise."

"I'm excellent at multitasking. Who's getting married?"

I tentatively raised a hand. Bradley scared me a bit with all his enthusiasm.

"Oh, you'll make a stunning bride. I'm thinking a cream strapless dress and dusky pink roses."

"Bradley, she doesn't even have a ring yet."

He gasped, and his hands flew to his cheeks. "No ring? Do you want classic or quirky? I know some excellent designers, and—"

"Bradley! Stop talking and go hire yourself an assistant."

"Okay, okay." He turned to Isabella. "Are you looking for a job?"

Izzy stared back at him, wide-eyed. "Me?"

"You're excellent with colour, and wouldn't you just love to pick out flowers?"

Oh, go on, Izzy. She'd signed up for nursing school because she thought she should, not because she wanted to. At heart, she was an artist. She loved to create.

"I'm not sure..."

"How about a temporary arrangement to start with?" Emmy suggested. "See how you get on?"

Finally, Izzy smiled. "I think I'd like that."

"Amazeballs." Bradley put his hands on his hips. "Now we can discuss the wedding. Have you thought of a theme? How about something tropical?"

"Uh..."

"Bradley, we're eating dinner," Emmy said. "Either get a plate and join us, or sod off and order wedding brochures or whatever it is you do."

He backed away, and I heard him muttering to himself down the hallway. What had I been let in for? One thing was for sure—I wouldn't be having anything pink in my wedding. Just thinking of the colour left me nauseous. And if anyone dared to suggest a finger-food buffet...

"Don't worry," Emmy said. "He can act over-the-top, but as long as you rein him in from time to time, he really is good at organising things. And we also need to sort out where everyone's going to live. Black and I have been talking too, and we may have a solution. Originally, we were assuming you'd want holiday homes, but it'll work if you want to stay permanently too."

Black took over. "We value our privacy, and every time a parcel of land comes up for sale nearby, we buy it so nobody else can. We own a dozen or so properties bordering the Riverley estate, and they're all sitting empty. Most of them need renovation, but you can take your pick. Or we have empty apartments in Richmond if you'd prefer." He reached over to take Grandma's hand. "Having you around... I'd like that very much."

My uncle was offering us a house? An actual freaking house? This day officially went down in history as the best of my life. Renovations would be fun with Lee. Anything would be fun with Lee.

"Best day of my life," he whispered, echoing my thoughts.

Even my brother didn't look totally pissed off. A truly memorable day indeed.

The sun shone the next morning as we piled into SUVs and drove into the countryside. Black wasn't kidding about the number of properties they owned—everything from a dilapidated cabin that needed to be torn down to a neat ranch house on a small plot to a farm with half a dozen outbuildings. They surrounded the Riverley estate, a sort of no man's land between the

Blacks and the outside world. Only two plots were occupied—one by a friend of Emmy's, his girlfriend, and their baby daughter, and another by Ana and her family.

"Can we truly have any of these?" I asked Black.

"Yes, but Marisol gets the first choice. Don't worry about the state of them. Bradley will arrange all the repairs."

Or in Grandma's case, a complete rebuild. Her eyes lit up when she saw a tumbledown cottage with a view over a small lake.

"I always wanted to live by the water again, but I'm not sure the cottage is suitable for a wheelchair."

"Then we'll build you a place that is. It won't take long."

"You don't need to do that."

"No, but I want to. I've got more money than I can ever spend and years of us being apart to make up for. A new house is only a small part of what I'd like to give you."

"Could we build an annex for Dores and Isabella?"

"We can build anything you want."

Grandma pretended she wasn't crying, but she totally was. Vicente passed her a handkerchief when he thought no one was looking.

Rafael chose a sprawling house with a separate barn. A project, he said. A lifetime's work, more like. He'd confessed that he'd spent most of his time in Medellín living with Vicente while they trained together, so having his own space would be new for him too.

And I was looking forward to having him around. Rafe smiled more now.

Hallie and Mercy decided to start off by sharing an apartment in town. Neither was ready for the isolation of the Riverley estate, but I relished the thought of living among the trees and wildlife again, albeit in a cooler climate than Valento. At least there would be fewer bugs.

"Which place do you prefer?" Lee asked.

"The house next to Grandma's."

A solid two-storey brick-built home with big rooms and good light. And eighties decor, but we could change that. Most importantly, it was near the people I loved, and it wasn't stucco like the pink palace or glass like Nevin's party pad. One of the places Black had shown us, I couldn't even step over the threshold because the hallway had a tiled floor that reminded me of Radcliffe's.

"How about you?" I asked Lee.

"It doesn't matter, because we're having the one you like."

"But—"

"I love you, and I've already got everything I want. We'll take the brick house."

"Are you sure?"

"Yeah. It was in my top three, anyway." He leaned closer to kiss my hair. "Plus it's got plenty of space for a family."

"You want a family?"

"It's on my wish list. Do you?"

"One day."

Right now, I already had more family than I'd ever dreamed of. And soon I'd have a husband too.

CHAPTER 49 - CORA

"IS EVERYONE READY to go?" Emmy asked.

She'd been pushing for a trip to Colombia for over a week now, and I didn't quite understand the urgency. Yes, I wanted to chop Roscoe's dick off and beat him to death with the soggy end, but I was so happy in Virginia. Why upset that balance?

Ten of us would be making the journey. Lee had offered to provide some much-needed moral support, . Rafael and Vicente needed to pack up their belongings as well as Grandma's, and when Mercy and Izzy heard we'd be confronting Roscoe, they insisted on joining us. Black was coming too, of course, and Sofia tagged along with Ana for a vacation. Or so they claimed.

Ana scared the crap out of me. I'd met her last week when she appeared beside Emmy at dinner, and although she'd been polite, every vibe she gave out said *touch me and die.*

Hmm... Perhaps I should introduce her to Roscoe?

"I'm ready," I said.

Lee slipped his arm around me. "Are you sure you want to do this?"

"No, but I might as well get it over with. Thank you for coming with us."

He pressed a soft kiss to my cheek. "For better or for worse, right?"

Freaking heck! I was engaged, and I still could hardly believe it, even though I had a diamond ring that reminded me every time it caught the light. A simple, half-carat solitaire on a platinum band, nothing too flashy, even though Bradley had tried to convince me I wanted a rock the size of a golf ball.

"Definitely for better."

I'd left Colombia as a prisoner on a grotty boat, but now I flew back on a private jet. The bigger of the two Emmy and Black owned, apparently, and I pinched myself as we climbed on board. Judging by Izzy's and Mercy's expressions, they felt the same way as I did.

Sofia sat opposite me on the flight, and every so often, she gave me a reassuring smile. Two days ago, I'd sat down and talked to her, really talked, and she'd confessed that she used to run honeytrap stings for the government, sleeping with men to get access to secrets and evidence they couldn't obtain by any other means.

"Didn't it make you feel icky?" I asked.

"Honestly? Yes. But every time I did it, I was laughing inside. They fucked me, but I fucked them over, and not only that, I got paid a hell of a lot of money in the process."

"If you had the choice, would you change anything about the way you've lived your life?"

"Only my childhood, but that was out of my control. My adult years? There've been ups, and there've been downs, but I'm in a good place now. No, I wouldn't change anything."

That was how I felt. In a nutshell, as Lee would say.

Yes, I was still overcome with nausea every time I let my mind stray back to what I'd done in those bedrooms, and vivid nightmares woke me every other night. But when I compared what I had before I flew to Barranquilla with what I had now, the price was worth paying. I'd never forgive those men—*never*—but I wouldn't hate myself for what I'd done.

In a strange way, I was proud of my achievements.

And as the jet descended over Medellín, I was kind of looking forward to fucking Roscoe over.

"Shh!" Izzy said, but I couldn't help giggling.

This was like waiting for a surprise party, except we were in Roscoe's apartment and I was pretty sure he was going to die at the end of the evening. A girlie night, Emmy called it, and Black had grudgingly agreed to us going it alone. Ana had picked the lock and let us in earlier, and now we hid nervously behind the door in the kitchen while we waited for Roscoe to get home. Sofia and Emmy had offered to fetch him, or, as Emmy put it, "Rowr. We're gonna act like cougars."

"I can't decide whether to kick him in the teeth or set his nuts on fire," Mercy said.

"No fire," Ana said. "Not unless we dismantle the smoke alarm first."

Surely she was kidding? Uh, she didn't look as though she was kidding.

"What about—"

"Quiet. They're on their way up the stairs."

The front door crashed open and hit the wall, followed by laughter. I peeped into the living room and saw Roscoe between Emmy and Sofia, laughing as Sofia rubbed a hand over his chest. A gloved hand. But Roscoe looked as if he'd been drinking, so he didn't realise what was wrong with that picture, and two seconds later, he had a needle sticking out of his left biceps. Sofia pushed the plunger on the syringe all the way in.

"What the...?"

"We invited some friends over. Hope that's okay."

"Huh? This is my fucking apartment."

"Oh, I know, but since you don't seem to place much importance on personal boundaries, we figured you wouldn't mind."

"I don't unner...unnerstand."

His words slurred a little as Emmy and Sofia lowered him onto the sofa and beckoned in our direction. Alcohol? Or was whatever they'd given him starting to take effect?

"Come on out," Emmy said. "Roscoe's dying to hear what you've been up to. You've got about five minutes."

I'd remember the look of shock on his face until my last day on earth, which would be a lot further into the future than Roscoe's.

"Hi. Do you remember us?"

He tried to struggle, but Emmy and Sofia held him down, one on each side. Ana wrapped an arm around his neck for good measure.

"Mercedes, Isabella, and... Well, you knew me as Catalina, but that's not really my name." Oh, this was fun. "I'm a friend of Izzy's, and when I realised she was still alive, I went through you to get to her."

"The police found a hand wearing my ring," Izzy said. "Whose hand was it?"

"Some girl... I don't know."

Izzy picked up a lamp and walloped him between the legs. His eyes bulged and watered a bit, but he still shook his head.

"I swear I don't know."

Emmy took the lamp away and carefully replaced it on the side table. "Try not to break anything, yeah?"

Okay, I wouldn't break anything, but I had brought Roscoe a small gift. Concentrated wasabi paste, all the way from Japan. Akari, Hisashi's mother and my new aunt, had got her brother to send it by express courier.

"Open wide."

Ana forced Roscoe's lips apart, and I squirted a generous amount into his mouth.

"Enjoy."

Lee said I was sweet like honey, but to Roscoe, I was sweet like the wasabi he'd fed me on our first so-called date. Now he coughed and spluttered but in slow motion.

"What did you inject him with?" I asked Sofia.

"Curare. I cultivate the vines myself. Mercy, do you have anything to say? He won't be with us for much longer."

She crouched down, and Ana shifted her grip to hold open Roscoe's drooping eyelids.

"I hope you rot in hell."

Emmy turned businesslike. "Right, I think we're done here. Girls, do me a favour and wait over by the front door. Don't take your gloves off."

They'd done this before, that much was obvious. Emmy scrawled out a note and set it by the body, and Sofia stuck the needle back in Roscoe's arm and pressed his fingertips onto it while Ana headed into the kitchen. I heard a sharp intake of breath followed by the *clink* of ice in a glass, and she came back with a tumbler full of clear liquid. Aguardiente?

"He might have lied about the hand," she said as she set the glass onto the table beside Roscoe. "The other one's next to his ice cube tray, the head's resting on a tub of ice cream, and there's a foot and what looks like a part of her ribcage in with the frozen vegetables."

Freaking hell. And he'd suggested I come over to his apartment for dinner? What would he have done if I'd accepted? Made sure to only use fresh ingredients?

"Fuck." Emmy picked up the pen again, so matter of fact. "Hold on. I need to add an addendum to this note."

"Won't they analyse the handwriting?" I asked.

"Honey, there's a dead girl in his freezer. Nobody's gonna care whether he killed himself or not. Trust me."

With Roscoe out of the picture, we could finally relax and enjoy a few days in Medellín. Black had just bought a wheelchair-accessible penthouse in Poblado, and Izzy and I needed to divide everything in our old apartment into three groups. Things we wanted to move to Black's new apartment, which was to be a holiday home for all of us, things we wanted to take back with us to Virginia, and things to throw away.

But first, I needed to call Esther. She'd been the only person who believed in me at the start of this nightmare, and I needed to thank her for everything she'd done. And Juan, my old boss. He'd been good to me, and I felt guilty for leaving with barely a word.

"Esther?"

"Cora? Is that really you? I've been so freaking worried."

"Yes, it's really me."

"What happened? You stopped answering your phone, and I didn't know whether to try and find you or call the police, and then Roscoe vanished too. Juan didn't know where you were either, just that you took two weeks of vacation, so I told him your grandma died in case he tried to fire you."

Oh, Esther. "It's a long and crazy story." Of which she'd get the edited version. "Do you want to meet for dinner?"

"Our place?"

"Okay. Can I bring my fiancé?"

People in Cali probably heard her screech, and it was a miracle my eardrums didn't burst.

"You got engaged?"

"All part of the long and crazy story."

"Wow. I mean, of course you can bring him. Seven o'clock?"

"Perfect."

On the other side of the room, Emmy's phone rang, and she put down the box she was carrying to answer.

"It's me." Her eyes widened. "Holy fuck. Are you kidding? He's properly awake?"

Who was she talking about? For a moment, I panicked in case it was Roscoe, but he'd definitely been dead. Sofia checked his pulse before we left the apartment.

"We'll be there by..." She glanced at her watch. "Three o'clock. Can you pick us up at the airport?"

What airport? What had happened?

"Is everything okay?" I asked as soon as she hung up.

"Better than okay. I need to get to Cali. Black, get

your ass out here." She gave me a quick hug. "Stay safe, okay? Look after Mercy and Isabella. Black! Hurry up!"

CHAPTER 50 - EMMY

FOR DAYS, EMMY had been putting off the trip to Cali. Cleaning an apartment was more fun than explaining to Seb and Marco that their stepmother tried to kill their father, because where did she start with that? Even scrubbing the toilet was preferable.

But with the news that Eduardo had woken up, everything changed. Now she wanted to get to Cali as soon as possible.

She rummaged around in her purse, pulled out a handful of notes—probably about a million pesos because money was crazy in Colombia—and thrust it towards the cab driver.

"Here's a bonus if you can get us to the airport in forty-five minutes."

The journey usually took an hour, so that wasn't totally unreasonable, right? Emmy could do it easily if she was driving. Half an hour on a motorbike. A kid zipped by on a moped, and for a moment, she considered... No. Black would be super pissed if she stole that. And Eduardo was probably having all sorts of tests and stuff right now, so they might not be allowed to see him for ages anyway.

"Diamond, Eduardo might not be the same man you remember."

"I know that. But don't rain on my sunshine. This

has to be a good thing, okay?"

"Don't rain on your sunshine? Did you get that from Bradley?"

Maybe. "So what if I did?"

Black chuckled, and Emmy couldn't even be mad. *Eduardo was awake.*

One of Seb's regular drivers met them on the tarmac in Cali, and it didn't take long for them to get to the hospital. Floriana was sitting outside Eduardo's room, the little bitch, and Emmy wanted to strangle the woman with her bare hands. But that would come later. For now, in public, she'd play nice so the hospital staff didn't get upset.

Seb and Marco hugged her, kissed Fia on both cheeks, then took a pace backwards when Ana smiled at them. Why were people always so nervous around her? She really wasn't a bad person most of the time.

"How is he?"

"We don't know yet," Seb said. "He opened his eyes and mumbled a few words, then the doctors kicked us out. But Sierra just went in there, so we'll get an update soon."

"Who's Sierra?"

"The nurse Marco likes."

Marco turned pink. "Be quiet."

"See?"

Yes, Emmy did. And Marco didn't usually act coy about his conquests, which meant he *really* liked her. But today, Emmy was more interested in Eduardo's condition than his son's love life. The closed door didn't even have a window, and when she pressed her ear against the wood, all she could hear was the low hum of voices, no actual words. Being patient sucked.

"Is it my imagination, or does Floriana look nervous?" she whispered to Ana.

"She does. But if she knew that we knew, she wouldn't be here."

When Sierra appeared, Emmy had to admit she was beautiful. And sweet. And totally gaga over Marco. Her face lit up when he gestured her to come closer, and even though she was talking to a group of people, she couldn't take her eyes off him.

"Mr. Garcia's responding to commands. There's a little confusion on occasion, but overall, he's better oriented than the doctors expected."

"Can we see him?"

"I'm sure you'll be able to, but one at a time."

Shit. The guard had been moved out of the room to make space for all the medical staff. Floriana had better not try to stick a pillow over Eduardo's face because then Emmy would have to throw her out the damn window. Of course, the bitch got the first go with Eduardo—the perks of being married. Never mind that she'd tried to bloody kill him.

Emmy so desperately wanted to tell Seb and Marco that the woman they'd just hugged wasn't the person they thought she was, but the hospital wasn't the right place. As long as Eduardo stayed safe, exposing Floriana could wait until later. She came out with tears rolling down her cheeks and sat on a chair alone, but Emmy ignored her. The woman deserved her pain. The two boys each spent fifteen minutes with their father, and finally, it came to Emmy's turn.

Black squeezed her hand as she hesitated in front of the door. She understood Eduardo wouldn't be the fit, tanned, exuberant man she was used to, but how bad would it be?

The answer? Both awful and not as bad as she'd feared.

Eduardo had better colour than the last time she'd seen him, but he looked exhausted and he'd lost more muscle tone. At least his eyes were bright.

She squeezed his hand. "I won't stay long."

"I know why you're here."

"To see you."

He shook his head, a tiny movement, but still a clear one. "No. To kill Floriana. Am I right?"

Fuck. "How did you find out?"

"Then I *am* right."

"Yes, but I meant how did you find out she did it?"

"I've been able to hear for weeks. She apologised at least ten times a day, every time that stupid guard went to take a leak."

"*Mierda.*"

"My thoughts also, angel. I woke up days ago, but I've been lying here like a corpse because I don't know what to do."

"What do you mean?"

"Floriana's nearly twenty years younger than me. Her ex-husband abused her, and when I had the *bastardo* shot, she was left with nothing. No home, no money. Did I ever tell you how we met?"

"No, you never did."

"She didn't know who I was, and she offered herself to me on the street for ten thousand pesos. Ten thousand pesos!" Whoa. Less than four dollars. "I gave her the money, then took her to dinner." A small smile played across Eduardo's lips. "Until I met Floriana, I never thought I'd get married again."

"Well, perhaps you shouldn't have."

"Perhaps. But Floriana and I, we are the same. And you, Emerson. We all do what's necessary in order to survive."

"I've never tried to kill my husband."

"You've never had a need to. I was stupid. Floriana looks quiet on the outside, but fire runs through her veins and she's a fighter. She thought I was going to get rid of her, and she panicked."

"Why would she have thought that?"

"I kept secrets. Shut her out rather than talking to her. Also, she knows I shot my fifth wife."

Shitting hell. "I really didn't want to hear that."

"That *puta* cheated on me with one of my guards. I shot him too."

"Do you know what TMI means?"

"Too Much Information. Floriana taught me that, but I didn't give her *enough* information. She thought I was planning her funeral, when in fact, I was buying her a beach house."

"You've talked to her about it?"

"Before my sons came in."

"And? Do they know all this?"

"Those boys can be so hot-headed. I thought I'd talk to you instead."

Emmy wasn't sure whether to feel honoured or groan out loud. Why her? She'd gone out of her way to cultivate a prickly personality rather than one that encouraged people to overshare.

"I should've stayed in Virginia."

Eduardo acted as though she hadn't spoken. "Florrie thinks she deserves to die. She's sitting out in the hallway, waiting for you."

"She kind of does deserve to die."

"I understand that, logically. But I'm fifty-eight years old, and I don't want to be alone. I'd miss her. And when Seb told her about the beach house, she realised what she'd done and cancelled the contract she took out on me. We've talked, and we understand each other much better now. No more secrets."

Good grief. "So you want me to let her live?"

"Sometimes, people deserve a second chance."

Eduardo was crazy, but then, Emmy already knew that. She'd abide by his wishes. "Fine. But if I hear so much as a whisper that she's planning another stupid stunt like this, I'll put a bullet through her head before she can fucking blink."

Eduardo squeezed Emmy's hand with surprising strength. "I wouldn't expect anything less of you, angel. I appreciate this is awkward."

Yeah. And speaking of awkward... "We also have another teensy problem."

"Sí?"

"The sicario Floriana hired turned out to be Black's long-lost nephew. Don't you dare laugh. I'm still trying to get my head around it myself."

Eduardo did laugh. Then he coughed, so Emmy poured him a glass of water and held the straw while he drank.

"You see how this is tricky? I promised Seb and Marco I'd hunt him down, and I did. I even tortured him a bit before I realised the connection, but I can't exactly kill him now. And he's gonna work for Blackwood. They're all bound to meet eventually, and I really don't want a gunfight."

The Garcias were family. They couldn't hide from

each other forever. Unless Rafael took a leaf out of The Banker's book and tried a little plastic sur—

No, that was ridiculous.

"I'll talk to the boys. They will understand it was just business."

"And Floriana shot Rafael."

Eduardo rolled his eyes to the ceiling. "*Joder*. She's too smart, trying to get rid of the evidence."

"Smart, but not such a good shot. She only winged him."

"What are the chances of him letting that go?"

"Well, he seems to have forgiven me for pouring vodka in the bullet wound."

"You'll talk to him?"

"I'll talk to him."

"*Gracias, ángel*." He held his arms out for a hug. "I thank God every day for bringing you to me."

"I love you too, old man, but you need to learn to communicate better. And stop marrying psychos."

"Maybe when I get out of here, we could take a trip to the beach house? The whole family?"

Yup, the dude was a fucking lunatic. "Just concentrate on breathing, okay?"

CHAPTER 51 - CORA

"IS THIS A joke?" I asked. "The whole reason you went to Colombia and found Rafael is because a drug lord decided to surprise his wife with a new house?"

Emmy looked as if she was desperately trying to keep a straight face. "That's about it, yeah."

"And he's honestly forgiven her for trying to have him killed?"

"He's gone soft in his old age."

Soft? Insane, more like. But had Eduardo Garcia really ever been sane in the first place?

We'd flown back to Virginia yesterday, everyone far more relaxed than on the trip out. Then, I'd been questioning the wisdom of getting Mercy and Izzy involved in Roscoe's death, but in the end, it had turned out to be a bonding experience. A shared exorcism of our demons.

Yes, we still had our bad times. I leaned on Lee for support. Mercy cried herself to sleep at night, and Izzy rarely slept at all. No, Izzy sought solace in music. I heard the quiet strains of Black's grand piano in the early hours most mornings, and it wasn't him who was playing it. And Hallie? Hallie drowned out her thoughts with gunfire, her new hobby, an hour on the range every morning, and I pitied any man who looked at her funny again.

But above all, we were survivors, sisters, our bond forged by a shared hatred of pink walls and black leather and men who preyed on people they saw as weaker than themselves.

We'd won, and we'd carry on fighting for what we believed in.

Much like Emmy and her team. She was more relaxed on the trip home too, and now that she and Black had sat me down and explained the situation with Eduardo, I understood why.

"What did Rafael say? Does he know?"

"He's written off the gunshot wound as an occupational hazard."

Huh. An occupational hazard. Floriana Garcia shot him and he brushed it off, yet he still held the entire time in the Florida house against Lee and eyed him up suspiciously at every possible opportunity.

"What?" Emmy asked.

"Rafael forgave Floriana, but he hates Leander, and Leander hasn't even done anything to him."

"Ah, but Floriana isn't doing the nasty with his little sister."

My mouth dropped open. I couldn't believe she'd just said that, not in front of my uncle. But Black only laughed.

"Rafael will come around," he said. "When I first met Nate, we acted the same way towards each other. He thought I was a stuck-up jerk, and I thought he was a judgemental asshole. Then our commanding officer shoved us off a boat and we bonded by almost drowning. I have a yacht available. It might help."

"We're not drowning anyone."

"Then they'll just have to grow on each other. But

Rafael's overprotectiveness wasn't the main reason we wanted to talk to you. We have a proposal."

"A proposal? What kind of proposal?"

"We've seen the way you've tried to help the other girls, and we're hoping you might be interested in expanding that assistance."

"Of course, but how?"

"As well as Blackwood Security, we run an offshoot, a charitable foundation set up to fund causes we're passionate about. Helping homeless teenagers and providing interim accommodation for women escaping domestic violence are two of our projects, but now we'd like to assist victims of people trafficking too."

"I'd love to be involved."

They looked at each other, then Emmy took over.

"Until now, we've mainly funded the foundation from our own pockets, plus the occasional fundraising event. But we've recently come across a new source of money we'd like to somehow...integrate."

"What do you mean?"

"The Banker had several billion dollars sitting in offshore accounts, which we've now liberated. Obviously, we can't dump it into the foundation in one go, but over time, we could filter the funds in alongside other donations."

"You stole The Banker's money?"

"It's not like he needs it anymore. Since it's all the proceeds of crime, directly or indirectly, it seems right to use it to help others. Just keeping it would be wrong, and if we turn it over to the government, they'll probably use it to buy new office furniture for Congress or something."

Theft didn't usually sit well with me, but Emmy

made good points. Billions of dollars? That could help so many people.

"What would I need to do?"

"We'd like you to head up The Blackwood Foundation, with some assistance, obviously. Meet people who need help, decide on projects to fund, and act as an advocate for people whose voices aren't strong enough alone. Find a way to use bad money for good."

They were offering me a purpose in life. A goal. Society failed so many people, and now that I'd been thrust into this unexpected role, I could use my position to offer other people the support that I'd come to rely on.

"I'll do it. Perhaps Mercy could help me?"

Emmy smiled, and that was the warmest I'd ever seen her. "Great idea. You'll need to hire an accounts assistant, plus someone to give you a hand with the admin. You'd run it almost as a business, just without the aim of making a profit."

"I've never run a business before."

"Don't worry; we'll guide you. It's easy enough to hire in corporate expertise, but what you need for a venture like this is heart. You'll do a good job. We both know it."

"I think I might cry again."

Emmy held out a box of tissues. "Go right ahead. But hurry up, because we've got work to do."

I sniffed a bit but managed to hold back the tears. "Speaking of work, is there any news on The Banker's other houses? And the girls who got sold?"

"The houses have been located. One in Kentucky, one near Chicago, and another in New York. But Merrick Childs is insisting on doing things by the book, which is somewhat ironic considering how many rules he broke before."

"The girls are still in there? That's...that's..."

Horrific. Disgusting. Unfair. All of those words weren't enough.

"We've given him a deadline. Two weeks to make his move or we're going in ourselves, but we'll have to avoid leaving a pile of dead bodies like we did in Florida. Unfortunately."

"But two weeks is fourteen more days of hell."

"They need to gather enough evidence to get convictions, otherwise the fuckers could walk." Emmy gave my hand a squeeze. "I get that it's hard to stand by and do nothing, but if we went through three more places the way we did in Florida and North Carolina, too many questions would get asked. And the FBI can't sit on their hands, not this time. They'll act."

"And we can help the girls with the foundation's new money?"

"You've got two weeks to work out the best way to do that."

When she put it like that, two weeks didn't seem very long at all. "Where do I start? I mean, I was an English teacher. I've never done anything with finance or charity or organising. Grandma used to give me a list to buy the freaking groceries."

"I'm sure Leander would be happy to help. Did you know he has a degree in accountancy?"

"He does?"

"That was why he got seconded to a money-laundering investigation in the first place."

Gradually, all the broken pieces were slotting together, and I finally had a future to look forward to. I pulled Emmy into a hug before I realised what I was doing.

"Thank you. I'm so sorry about the horrible things that happened these past few months, but I'm glad to be here."

"*Everyone's* glad you're here. I'll get Georgia to call you about the foundation—she'll be one of your new neighbours, and she helps us out with the books at the moment. You can meet up for coffee."

Emmy grinned over her shoulder as she headed for the door, and I stared at her retreating back. I had a new job, a new family, and soon I'd be getting married. Freaking hell. My heart did a little skip, but this time, it was out of joy. Not everything in my life was perfect yet, but things were definitely heading in the right direction.

CHAPTER 52 - EMMY

EMMY FELT LIKE whistling as she sauntered along the hallway after the meeting with Corazon. Which would have been stupid because people only did that shit in movies, plus she couldn't hold a tune to save her life.

Only one loose end left. The Banker was still alive, but Mack had all the information she needed to move his money, so he didn't need to stay that way for much longer. The rebuild of the lake house was progressing nicely and would serve a dual purpose—give Marisol, Vicente, Dores, and Isabella somewhere to live, plus provide a nice, deep hole to toss a body into once the foundations were dug. Far easier to keep The Banker alive until that point than kill him now and have to deal with the smell of a decomposing corpse.

Plus Black seemed fond of spending time with him, and Emmy had to concede that the way The Banker's past had shaped his future was fascinating to study. His mother had been a prostitute, much like Emmy's, and Black theorised it was her penchant for entertaining men in the room next door to her son's that had planted the seeds of his deep-rooted issues with women. Locking them up gave him power, and punishing them through sex was a way of getting back at the bitch who'd screwed up his childhood.

Keeping him at Riverley was kind of like having a pet that lived in the basement. A grumpy little troll. Speaking of pets, at least Bob and Stewart had turned up back in their tank at the office. Emmy still didn't know who'd taken them or where they'd been, but if she ever found out...

That train of thought was interrupted when her phone rang. Alaric calling. Although their romance was long since over, she'd secretly missed him in his self-imposed exile. Of all the men she'd dated, he'd been the most similar to her in terms of character. They'd shared the same impetuous streak, the same willingness to take risks, and the same inability to face up to their problems. Oh, and Alaric was a dirty fucker.

It had taken Emmy almost dying to bring Alaric into the light again, and they'd gradually been increasing their contact, although Black may not have been entirely aware of just how often they spoke. Why stir up his jealous streak over a relationship that was purely platonic?

Especially since Black had been a little more easy-going around Mr. McLain lately. Barely disguised hostility had turned into grudging tolerance, and Emmy had hopes that the two men could have a decent professional relationship in the future. Because she intended to keep throwing work in Alaric's direction. Guilt still weighed heavy over what happened seven and a half years ago, and even though she was as innocent as Alaric in the whole mess—she knew damn well he hadn't done what he was accused of—the fact that they'd never got to the bottom of the mystery bugged the hell out of her.

And truthfully? It was kind of nice having him

around again.

"Hey."

"How was Colombia?"

"Productive. Are you back in Florida?"

"No, I'm in Italy."

"Business or pleasure?"

"Business, baby. It's all about the business now."

"So this isn't a social call?"

"No, Cinders, it isn't." Her old nickname. Black had called her Diamond ever since they met on the streets of London, and Alaric harked back to her rags-to-riches past. "You owe me a favour, and it's time for me to collect. I need you in England in three days."

"What for?"

"Maybe nothing. Maybe everything."

Alaric's tone said what his words didn't. Excitement with a hint of nervousness could mean only one thing. He had a lead on Emerald, and he was looking for closure.

Uh-oh.

Black was gonna be so thrilled about this. But Alaric was right—Emmy owed him, and she always paid up. Even though she hadn't had a proper day off in months and tiredness had crept into her bones like a malevolent spirit, she'd pay up.

"England, three days." Fuck. "I'll be there."

What's next?

The Blackwood Security series will continue in The Girl with the Emerald Ring.

After a nasty divorce, Bethany Stafford-Lyons is forced to transform herself from a high-society housewife into one of London's worker bees. Using a last connection to her previous life, she lands a job at Pemberton Fine Arts, a world-renowned gallery and restoration studio. With her art degree, it should have been the perfect role, but she soon finds interning for Hugo Pemberton is a challenge in more ways than one.

Eight years ago, Alaric McLain got fired from the FBI after an undercover operation ended in disaster. Still missing? One masterpiece, ten million dollars in cash and diamonds, and his once-glowing reputation. When he retreated overseas to lick his wounds, he made a vow—he'd find The Girl with the Emerald Ring if it was the last thing he did.

The trail leads to Chelsea, where assisted by his ex-girlfriend and a seventeen-year-old brat he wants to handcuff to a railroad track, Alaric's soon embroiled in a game of cat and mouse with a talented team of thieves. Let the fun begin...

For more details: www.elise-noble.com/emerald

My next book will be Lead, the sixth book in the Blackwood Elements series, releasing in 2019.

Imogen Blair's best friends are both engaged, and their joy makes her realise what's missing from her own life. Or rather, who. With her future happiness at stake, Imogen comes up with a plan to land the guy of her dreams, pastry chef Jean-Luc Fortier. But you know what they say about the course of true love? It never runs smooth.

With Malachi Banks—special-ops commando turned reluctant sidekick—strong-armed into helping her, Imogen's determined to win her man. But will the prize be worth it?

For more details: www.elise-noble.com/lead

.

If you enjoyed Quicksilver, please consider leaving a review.

For an author, every review is incredibly important. Not only do they make us feel warm and fuzzy inside, readers consider them when making their decision whether or not to buy a book. Even a line saying you enjoyed the book or what your favourite part was helps a lot.

WANT TO STALK ME?

For updates on my new releases, giveaways, and other random stuff, you can sign up for my newsletter on my website:
www.elise-noble.com

Facebook:
www.facebook.com/EliseNobleAuthor

Twitter: @EliseANoble

Instagram: @elise_noble

I also have a group on Facebook for my fans to hang out. They love the characters from my Blackwood and Trouble books almost as much as I do, and they're the first to find out about my new stories as well as throwing in their own ideas that sometimes make it into print!

And if you'd like to read my books for FREE, you can also find details of how to join my review team.

Would you like to join Team Blackwood?

www.elise-noble.com/team-blackwood

END OF BOOK STUFF

I bought a plant! This week, I looked around my workspace and realised that my desk essentials consisted of chocolate, hand cream, coffee, Percy Pigs, iPads, and gin. One of my Team Blackwood crew told me I needed greenery (thanks Jody), so I did, and now it's gently breathing oxygen over me. I feel healthier already, and it's far better than pretending I want to go to the gym :)

Anyhow, I should probably say something about writing.... Oh, I waited for the longest time for this book. Ever since I wrote the Colombian part of Forever Black, I wanted to know what happened to Black's family, and while I always planned for him to have a niece and nephew alive, his mother came out of nowhere. Marisol's a tenacious old bird, and she elbowed her way into the story despite my best efforts.

As with Ultraviolet, there's a bit of geekery at the heart of Quicksilver. Genetics has always fascinated me, how we're basically coded out of atoms to become these thinking, moving beings. Whether you believe in God, science, or witchcraft, there's something magical there. And nature versus nurture—what's the balance? Emmy and Black were both born to be assassins, but they still needed a kick along the way—Black from the military and Emmy from our favourite dark lord.

There's more genetics coming up in my next Electi book too, with Nicole determined to find out what gave them their supernatural powers. I love the whole research thing—I was the kid at school who read textbooks for fun.

But back to Blackwood... Like the directors of every good company, Black et al have to think about succession planning. Nobody lives forever, something the da Silva family are all too aware of. In Rafe, Black's got a new sidekick to train. But what about Emmy? Well, I have plans for her, but you'll have to read the next book to find out. That'll be Alaric's story, and when I was just writing for fun (did you know I drafted the first seven Blackwood novels—badly—before I let anyone read Pitch Black?), my goal was to think up a happily ever after for each of her exes, plus a story for James because I like him. But I've had so much support from my reader group (Team Blackwood—I love you guys! *blubs*) that there'll be at least two more books in the Blackwood Security series after that.

What about Emmy and Black? So many people have asked to see more of them that I've written them an extra story. Stolen Hearts is a mystery/thriller, and if people like it, I'll write more books in that series. When I stop crying into my gin over the editing, I'll get around to publishing it. But Lead's up next—Imogen and Malachi's story, complete with a hot rickshaw rider, a trip to Fort Lauderdale, and Emmy's terrible attempts at drawing.

See you in Florida!
Elise

OTHER BOOKS BY ELISE NOBLE

The Blackwood Security Series
Black is my Heart (Emmy & Sofia prequel)
For the Love of Animals (Nate & Carmen prequel)
Pitch Black
Into the Black
Forever Black
Gold Rush
Gray is my Heart
Neon (novella)
Out of the Blue
Ultraviolet
Red Alert
White Hot
The Scarlet Affair
Quicksilver
The Girl with the Emerald Ring (TBA)

The Blackwood Elements Series
Oxygen
Lithium
Carbon
Rhodium
Platinum
Lead (2019)
Copper (2019)

Nickel (TBA)

The Blackwood UK Series
Joker in the Pack
Cherry on Top (novella)
Roses are Dead
Shallow Graves
Indigo Rain (2019)

Blackwood Casefiles
Stolen Hearts (2019)

Blackstone House
Hard Lines (TBA)

The Electi Series
Cursed
Spooked
Possessed (2019)
Demented (TBA)

The Trouble Series
Trouble in Paradise
Nothing but Trouble
24 Hours of Trouble

Standalone
Life
Twisted (short stories)
A Very Happy Christmas (novella)

Printed in Great Britain
by Amazon